THE
ORCHARDIST

A Novel

AMANDA COPLIN

WEIDENFELD & NICOLSON

LONDON

First published in Great Britain in 2012
by Weidenfeld & Nicolson
An imprint of the Orion Publishing Group
Orion House, 5 Upper St Martin's Lane, London WC2H 9EA

An Hachette UK Company

1 3 5 7 9 10 8 6 4 2

A CIP catalogue record for this book is available
from the British Library

978 0 297 86790 6 (cased)
978 0 297 86791 3 (trade paperback)

The Orion Publishing Group's policy is to use papers that are natural,
renewable and recyclable products and made from wood grown in sustainable
forests. The logging and manufacturing processes are expected to
conform to the environmental regulations of the country of origin.

www.orionbooks.co.uk

THE
ORCHARDIST

Amanda Coplin was born in 1981 in Wenatchee, Washington, a town famous for its orchards. She holds an MFA in Creative Writing from the University of Minnesota and now lives in Minneapolis. *The Orchardist* is her first novel.

TO MY FAMILY

AND IN MEMORY OF MY GRANDFATHER

DWAYNE EUGENE SANDERS

1936–1994

The roses you gave me kept me awake
with the sound of their petals falling.

—JACK GILBERT

I

H IS FACE WAS as pitted as the moon. He was tall, broad-shouldered, and thick without being stocky, though one could see how he would pass into stockiness; he had already taken on the barrel-chested sturdiness of an old man. His ears were elephantine, a feature most commented on when he was younger, when the ears stuck out from his head; but now they had darkened like the rest of his sun-exposed flesh and lay against his skull more than at any other time in his life, and were tough, the flesh granular like the rind of some fruit. He was clean-shaven, large-pored; his skin was oily. In some lights his flesh was gray; others, tallow; others, red. His lips were the same color as his face, had given way to the overall visage, had begun to disappear. His nose was large, bulbous. His eyes were cornflower blue. His eyelashes nothing to speak of now, but when he was young they were thick-black, and his cheeks bloomed, and his lips were as pure and sculpted as a cherub's. These things together made the women compulsively kiss him, lean down on their way to do other chores, collapse him to their breasts. All his mother's sisters he could no longer remember, from Arkansas, who were but shadows of shadows now in his consciousness. Oh my lovely, they would say. Oh my sweet lamb.

His arms were sun-darkened and flecked with old scars. He combed his hair over his head, a dark, sparse wing kept in place with pine-scented pomade.

He regarded the world—objects right in front of his face—as if from a great distance. For when he moved on the earth he also moved in other realms. In certain seasons, in certain shades, memories alighted on him like sharp-taloned birds: a head turning in the foliage, lantern light flaring in a room. And there were other constant preoccupations he likewise

half acknowledged, in which his attention was nevertheless steeped at all
times: present and past projects in the orchard; desires he had had as a
young man, worries, fears, of which he remembered only the husks; trees
he had hoped to plant; experiments with grafting and irrigation; jam recipes; cellar temperatures; chemical combinations for poisoning or at least
discouraging a range of pests—deer and rabbits and rodents and grubs,
a universe of insects; how to draw bees. Important was the weather, and
patterns of certain years, the likelihood of repetition meteorologically
speaking, what that would mean for the landscape; the wisdom of the
almanacs, the words of other men, other orchardists, the unimportant
but mostly the important words. He thought of where he would go hunting next fall. Considered constantly the state of his land, his property, his
buildings, his animal. And mostly he thought of the weather that week,
the temperature, and existence of, or potential for, rainfall; recent ca-
lamities and how he was responding to them; the position of the season;
his position in the rigid scaffolding of chores—what he would have to do
that day, that afternoon and evening, how he would prepare for the next
morning's work; when were the men coming, and would he be ready for
them? But he would be ready for them, he always was, he was nothing
if not prepared. He considered those times in life when he had uttered
words to a person—Caroline Middey or Clee, or his mother, or a stranger
who had long forgotten him—he wished he had never uttered, or had uttered differently, or he thought of the times he remained silent when he
should have spoken as little as a single word. He tried to recollect every
word he had ever spoken to his sister, tried to detect his own meanness
or thoughtlessness, his own insensitivity to certain inflections she might
have employed. How long ago it was now. At times he fretted about forgetting her, though in fact—he did not like to admit this—he had already
forgotten much.

Now, at his back, the shrouded bushels of apples and apricots rustled
in the wagon bed, the wagon creaking forward beneath the weight; the
old, old familiar rhythm in accordance with these leagues of thought.
Dazzled and suspended by the sun. The mountains—cold—at his back. It
was June; the road was already dusty. His frame slightly hunkered down,
the floppy calfskin hat shielding his brow, under which was a scowl

holding no animosity. The large hands, swollen knuckles, loosely holding the reins.

From the wheatfields he entered the town, and drew down the
main street. Quiet. It was Sunday. The nearer church, he thought—
the Methodist was on the other side of town—had yet to release its
congregation. He hitched up outside the feed and supply store, watered
the mule. While he was setting up the fruit stand—tugging forward each
burlap-covered bushel in the back of the wagon and unveiling them and
unloading them—a woman rounded the corner and gained the platform,
approached him. Half her face was mottled and pink, as if burned, her
mouth an angry pucker. She held defensively to her breast a burlap
sack and bent and inspected the uptilted bushel of Arkansas Blacks. She
reached for an apple but did not touch it; glanced dubiously at a bushel of
paler apples he presently uncovered. What're those?

He glanced down. Greenings. Rhode Island Greenings.

When he spoke, his voice was low and sounded unused; he cleared
his throat. The woman waited, considered the apples. All right. I'll take
a few of those. From the folds of her skirt she brought out a dull green
change purse. How much?

He told her. She pinched out the correct change and handed it to him.

As he filled the sack with fruit, the woman turned and gazed behind
her. Said:

Look what the cat drug in. Those two looking over here like that, you
aren't careful, they'll come rob you. Hooligan-looking. She sniffed.

After a moment he looked where she nodded. Down the street, under
the awning of the hardware store, two girls—raggedy, smudge-faced—
stood conspiratorially, half turned toward each other. When they saw
Talmadge and the woman observing them, they turned their backs to
them. He handed the burlap sack to the woman, the bottom heavy and
misshapen with fruit.

The woman hesitated, still looking at the girls, then turned and nodded shortly to him, stepped off the platform, moved down the street.

From the wagon he retrieved his wooden folding chair and sat down
next to the bushels. Wind gusted and threw sand onto the platform, and
then it was quiet. Rain was coming; maybe that evening, or early the next

day. The girls moved; stood now with their shoulders pressed together, looking into the window of the dry goods store. A gust of wind blew their dresses flat against their calves, but they remained motionless. He pulled his cap low. What did two girls mean to him? He dozed. Woke to someone addressing him:

That you, Talmadge? Those girls just robbed you.

He righted his cap. A slack-mouthed boy stood gaping at him.

I saw them do it, said the boy. I watched them do it. You give me a nickel, I'll run them down and get your apples back for you.

The girls had gotten farther than Talmadge would have expected. They made a grunting sound between them, in their effort at speed. Apples dropped from their swooped-up dresses and they crouched or bent awkwardly to retrieve them. The awkwardness was due, he saw, to their grotesquely swollen bellies. He had not realized before that they were pregnant. The nearer one—smaller, pouting, her hair a great hive around her face—looked over her shoulder and cried out, let go the hem of her dress, lurched forward through the heavy thud of apples. The other girl swung her head around. She was taller, had black eyes, the hard startle of a hawk. Her hair in a thick braid over her shoulder. She grabbed the other girl's wrist and yanked her along and they went down the empty road like that, panting, one crying, at a hobble-trot. He stopped and watched them go. The boy, at his side, looked wildly back and forth between Talmadge and the ragged duo. I can get them, I can catch them, Talmadge, he said. Wildly back and forth.

Talmadge, the boy repeated.

Talmadge watched the girls retreat.

HE AND HIS mother and sister had come into the valley in the summer of 1857, when he was nine years old. They had come from the north-central portion of the Oregon Territory, where his father had worked the silver mines. When the mines collapsed, their mother did not even wait for the body of their father to be dredged up with the rest, but gathered their few belongings and set off with Talmadge and his sister at once. They traveled north and then west, west and then north.

They walked, mostly, and rode in wagons when they came along. They crossed the Wallowas and the Blue Mountains, and then came across great baked plains, what looked to be a desert. And then when they reached the Columbia they took a steamboat upriver to its confluence with another river, where the steamboat did not go farther. They would have to walk, said the steamboat operator, uncertain; if they were thinking of going across the mountain pass, to the coast, they would have to find someone—a trapper, an Indian—to guide them. And still Talmadge's mother was undeterred. From the confluence of the river they walked four days toward mountains that did not seem to get any closer. The elevation climbed; the Cascades rose before them like gods. It was May; it snowed. Talmadge's sister, Elsbeth, who was a year younger than him, was cold; she was hungry. Talmadge rubbed her hands in his own and told her stories of the food they would eat when they set up house: cornbread and bacon gravy, turnip greens, stewed apples. Their mother said nothing to these stories. Why did she lead them north and then west, west and then north, as if drawing toward a destination already envisioned?

They had heard that many, many miles away, but not so many as before they started, on the other side of the mountains, was the ocean. Constant rain. Greenness. Maybe that's where they were going, thought Talmadge. Sometimes—but how could he think this? how could a child think this of his mother?—he thought she was leading them to their deaths. Their mother was considered odd by the other women at the mining camp; he knew this, he knew how they talked about her. But there was nothing really wrong with her, he thought (forgetting the judgment of a moment before); it was just that she wanted different things than those women did. That was what set them and his mother apart. Where some women wanted mere privacy, she yearned for complete solitude that verged on the violent; solitude that forced you constantly back upon yourself, even when you did not want it anymore. But she wanted it nonetheless. From the time she was a small girl, she wanted to be alone. The sound of other people's voices grated on her: to travel to town, to interact with others who were not Talmadge or Talmadge's father or sister, was torture to her: it subtracted days from her life. And so they walked: to find a place that would absorb and annihilate her, a place to be her home, and the home for her children. A place to show her children: and you belong to the earth, and the earth is hard.

They climbed through cold-embittered forest and sought respite in bright meadows thick with wildflowers and insect thrumming. Maybe, thought Talmadge, they had already died, and this was heaven. It was easy, at moments, to believe. They came to a mining camp where five men sat inside an open hut, shivering, malnourished, warming their hands around a fire. It was lightly raining outside. When Talmadge and his mother and sister came and stood before them, the men looked at them as if they were ghosts. Their mother asked the men if they had any food to spare. The men just stared at her. They stared at the children. Where are you going? said one of the men finally. You shouldn't be here. The men had some beans that they shared with them, ate them straight out of the can. And then—Talmadge would always remember this—a man took out a banjo and began to play, and eventually, to sing. His teeth were crooked and stained, as were his mustache and his beard. His eyes were light blue and watery. He sang songs about a place that sounded familiar to Talmadge: Tennessee. It was where his own father was from.

Talmadge thought later that the man was crying. But why was he crying? He missed his home, said Talmadge's mother.

The men told them that there was a post ten miles up the creek where they could trade for supplies. It was a good time to travel, since it was summer, but in the winter it would be impassable. Talmadge and his mother and sister set off from the miners and reached the trading post later that day. And then they kept walking. What are you doing? the people said. Turn around. You have young children. There were two days of rain, and cold. His sister developed a hacking cough. And then they came through dense forest, and stood on the rim of a valley illuminated as if it was the end or the beginning of the world. A valley of yellow grass. Still but for a ribbon of water moving at the bottom of it. His sister, beside him, caught her breath; and on the other side of him he could feel his mother's silent, reluctant satisfaction.

They walked into the valley.

On a plateau stretching back from the creek was a filthy miner's shack, and two diseased Gravenstein apple trees. On the opposite side of the creek was the outlying field, bordered on its far edges by forest. To the east was a dark maw of a canyon. Three weeks later they discovered, a mile away into the canyon and through more forest, along a portion of the upper creek, a cabin. And here, as well as down below, was a miner's sluice box situated along a shallow portion of the creek. One of the first chores Talmadge's mother assigned herself was to dismantle the sluice box and take this, as well as other tools she found pertaining to that trade, and bury them in the forest. I've had enough of mining for one lifetime, she said.

For a year he and his mother and sister tended the ailing Gravensteins and also planted vegetables from seeds his mother had sewn into the linings of their winter clothes. The summer of the next year they sold fruit to the miners at Peshastin Creek, and traded for supplies at the post in Icicle.

Late that first summer and then again in the spring, a band of native men came out of the forest with a herd of over two hundred horses. The men did not try to speak to Talmadge or his mother or sister; and neither did Talmadge or his mother or sister attempt to speak to the men. They remained in the field for three days.

When the men arrived again the following summer, Talmadge's mother went down to the field where they camped and offered them fruit and vegetables, loaves of potato bread. The men accepted her gifts; and when they returned, four weeks later, they offered her a deer they had killed, strapped to the back of a horse.

They were horse wranglers—mostly Nez Perce at that time, but later there were also men from other tribes: Palouse, Yakama, Cayuse, Walla Walla, Umatilla. They hunted horses in the ranges to the southeast—the Blue Mountains, the Wallowas, the Steens, the Sawtooths—and trained them and sold them at auctions abroad. They had been stopping over in the valley for the last decade or so to feed and rest the horses, and to avoid the lawmen who scouted the countryside searching for rogue bands such as theirs.

On their trips south, after selling the horses at auction—when the men came into the orchard with their herd largely diminished, and many of them sporting handsome leather vests and saddlebags—they brought gifts for Talmadge and his sister: candy, or bits of milk glass in the shapes of animals. They let Talmadge and his sister explore their packs, and took them on easy rides around the field, the children sitting before the men in the saddles.

These trips south the men would stay just overnight, and would be gone by the time Talmadge woke in the morning. The ash of their firepits not yet cold, and the general odor of horses and tobacco hung in the air for hours afterward, provoking in the young Talmadge a particular mel-ancholy, and emptiness.

Among the men there were sometimes boy children—sometimes two or three, but rarely more. Some of these children appeared only once; they came for a season and then were not seen again. The only child con-stant from the beginning was the nephew of the Nez Perce leader, a boy known to Talmadge and Elsbeth as Clee; he had another, private name used only among the men. He was dark-skinned, muscular, tall, with a wide, pensive forehead and a large, careful, expressive mouth, although he was not known to smile often, or make exaggerated facial expressions. Even as a child he was quietly, fiercely attentive. His hair came down to almost his elbows; at times it was fixed in two braids, with hair crowding his eyes.

But there was from the beginning something distinctly different about Clee. He did not speak. It was not just that he was shy, or particularly wary of Talmadge and his sister, or chose not to speak to white people; he did not speak at all, even to the men he rode with. He was not deaf, for he heard the noises Talmadge and his sister heard, turned his head, physically reacted when they did. He had the habit of cocking his head, slightly, to speakers who addressed him. But no words issued from him, ever.

What's wrong with him? Elsbeth asked their mother once. Their mother, who was washing dishes at the time, crouching creekside, shrugged. There might be something wrong with his vocal cords, she said. Or—maybe he just doesn't want to talk.

But why?

Their mother shrugged again. I don't know, child, she said.

There was no exact moment Talmadge could recall when he and Elsbeth became friends with Clee; but when the men came into the field with the horses, Talmadge and Elsbeth sought Clee out, and in the privacy of the outer forest, or in the canyon, they would show him treasures they had acquired—rocks, candy, bits of animal hide—and also show him places, nooks and crannies, weird sunbathed basins of grass deep within a bramble hedge, they had discovered. And likewise Clee showed them objects he had accumulated that year from auctions—small toys and carvings, folded illustrations, carnival and sideshow posters, even swatches of fabric—velvet, satin, chamois—they rubbed between their fingers, against their lips and cheeks. It did not seem to matter, then, that Clee could not—or did not—speak. There was no deficit in their relationship, no lack.

Talmadge and Elsbeth's mother died of a respiratory disease in the spring of 1860. Two years later they harvested two acres of apples and one acre of apricots, and with the money they earned from selling the fruit they razed the miner's shack and built a two-room cabin. He was fifteen years old, and Elsbeth was fourteen. The next spring they planted three plum trees around the side of the cabin, and the first apple trees inside the canyon mouth.

In the fall of 1864 Talmadge contracted smallpox and nearly died. The sickness left him badly scarred on his face, chest, and arms, and partially deaf in his right ear. In the spring of the next year the canyon flooded, and they lost many apple trees. That summer, in 1865, Elsbeth went into the forest beyond the field to collect herbs and did not return. He enlisted the help of the miners at the Peshastin camp, and when they did not find her, he asked the men who came through with the horses if they would help him search. Clee found her bonnet, and another, her picking basket. That was all they ever found.

Elsbeth Colleen Talmadge. She had black hair like him, like their mother, and a large bulbous nose. That nose will be the end of her, murmured his mother's sisters. A deformity (but it was not that, only an exaggerated feature) one wore inside one's clothes was one thing, but on a face—they pitied her. Talmadge's mother did not comment; she did not talk about such things as a girl's looks, because she did not think they were important. Her daughter was simple, but sturdy-bodied, largefooted. She would do well on a homestead. She had Talmadge, also, to guide and help her. It was Talmadge who was the brains of any operation the two of them—he and Elsbeth—undertook. Always thinking, always planning. A new way to plant, to harvest. Ideas for irrigation. Even at that age. This is what we will do, he would announce, quietly, seriously. What do you think? He always included her: every project he engineered that succeeded, he credited her as well, naturally. Once or twice, very rarely, she had her own opinion about how to do things—or a variation of his own idea—and if it was a poor idea, he corrected it, silently, in the doing. But she was not stupid—brain-addled—no matter what people said. He loved her, he loved her deliberation and her decisiveness in certain small domestic activities, her gentleness with animals; her heavy, serious inwardness. She was able to cross-stitch elaborate scenes without the aid of a model or picture—scenes that bewildered him, and her too, if he asked her about them. Where did such images come from? Groves, large lakes, lions, angels. And yet it was true she had trouble, at times, constructing sentences to speak into the air, the air that seemed to get thinner when she was speaking to someone who was not Talmadge or their mother, on the verge of tears. He protected her, he placed himself between her and the world. She did not have to go to town and interact with the people; he would do that, though he was shy, too.

And though she trusted him—had always seemed to trust him—and did not seem to begrudge him, or withdraw from him, she must have had aspirations that she did not tell him about, that she kept to herself. He remembered one day, as she entered a room, he suddenly seemed to recognize her—her physical being came into stark relief for him—but he did not know why. And then he realized: it was because she wore a new frock. It was not a new dress, but an apron. Sky blue and not like the other gray one she usually wore. What's that? he said. Where did you get that? This was after their mother died, when, very rarely, his tone became careless. She touched the cloth but did not look down at it. I made it, she said. I got the fabric from—but he did not remember where now. He said, because he was suddenly angry, You can't be spending money on things we haven't discussed. We're supposed to be saving up for— but again he could not recall what he had said. Some project or another. The whole time she did not move her head. Her eyes—an opaque light blue, the same color as his—did not alter, but her mouth hardened. A barely perceptible change. The fingers of her left hand hanging at her side twitched—a reflex, maybe, of the hurt or anger that did not show on her face. And all at once he was no longer angry. Moments passed in silence. When he was angry it was not serious, and it came out in little sideways bursts like this. He was quickly ashamed afterward. Now he said quietly, not looking at her: Your frock is nice. And: I can see you did a nice job with the—but he had no vocabulary for what she had done—the tailoring—and so gestured generally instead. She responded a moment later with a slight nod of her head. And then they broke out of the scene and continued as if it had never happened.

He came around always to that frock, as if the key to her disappearance lay there. Why that frock? It was new, the material—the color—was strange, even fetching. It was not like the clothes she usually wore. Later he would think of it as a traveling outfit—a start to a traveling outfit. She was preparing already to go—

Or perhaps it was on sale, in the bin with other cheap scraps at the general store, and she had bought it impulsively—not out of any vanity, or with any motivation attached to it, but because it was a bargain. That was something that she would do, he could imagine her doing something like that.

But, finally, what the apron meant—if it meant anything at all—he would never know.

The night after Clee came out of the forest with a piece of fabric—Elsbeth's bonnet—clutched in his fist, he and Talmadge sat together on the darkened porch, and Clee wanted, though he was unable to do so, to communicate to Talmadge the events of his life. About how he was related to many of the men by blood, but did not have any immediate family. His father and two of his brothers had died in wars in the 1850s. His own mother had taken care of the remaining siblings—and how many of them were there? how many brothers and sisters had he had, once?—and even though the others told him that he was too young to remember his mother or what had happened to her, he remembered: the tepee walls shuddering as if from a great wind, his mother, who squatted across from him—she was attempting to light a fire—ceasing her movements, gazing at him, her eyes wide, listening. And then the animal skins ruptured and Clee could see the sky beyond the man's head, and a hairy arm grabbed Clee's mother around her waist. Clee's mother was sucked out of the tepee, into the sky. She disappeared all at once, in the blink of an eye. And although this was one act of violence among many in their village that day, dozens killed, and tepees and storehouses set afire, he remembered a kind of peace afterward: just the sky and the animal skins flapping.

He had made sounds, the others said, when he was a baby. But after the raid he was speechless. His voice had been carried away; it had pledged allegiance to his mother, or to some other element of that day;

and without those elements restored to that place, his voice also remained outside it, outside himself.

After the main village was destroyed, his other brothers—the ones who had remained after the others had left—simply disappeared forever. He did not even know how many sisters he had had. When he found Elsbeth's bonnet, his own family had been gone for over half his life.

The other men thought Elsbeth had run away, or the forest had claimed her. It was not so very strange. But Clee searched with a certain quiet resolve uncommon for someone his age. He tried, with his skills, to track her, but she could not be tracked. Maybe at one time she could have been, but no longer. He circled and recircled where he had found the bonnet. When the men set up camp, far away from where she had disappeared, he nevertheless scouted a wide perimeter, watching out. The other men regarded him warily but did not interrupt him, did not mock him, understanding, in a way, his sickness. He never stopped looking for Elsbeth—not really—but he forgot what she looked like. There was something about the color of her eyes, and the shape of her nose. But the rest of her, for him, had faded. He would know her when he saw her, he thought, to comfort and encourage himself.

Out of this brief obsession Clee and Talmadge's relationship solidified. When the men passed through with the horses, Talmadge and Clee sat on the porch in the evening, looking out over the land and with a view of the field below where the other men camped, their fires like distant stars. Clee and Talmadge smoked tobacco, and Talmadge did not speak much. Sometimes one or both of them would come away from the evening— and who was the first to move? had they slept?—with the impression that leagues had been discussed between them. Talmadge knew little of Clee's past, and Clee had forgotten Talmadge's sister's shape, her face, but the young men appeared regularly in each other's dreams, where it was as if their chests were unstoppered, and they walked together and sometimes turned and faced each other directly, and spoke volumes.

By the time Talmadge was forty years old the orchards had grown to almost twenty-five acres. It was an expansion of what he had originally

planned with his mother, and then his sister. On the hill above the creek
was the cabin and three acres of apricot trees, and around the side of the
cabin, surrounding the shed, a half acre of plum trees. In the field across
the creek, before the canyon mouth, nearly a quarter mile away, were
nine acres of apples; and inside were twelve acres.

The men helped him groom and harvest the orchards in season, and
he in turn lied to the authorities who infrequently came through asking
about the men and their business. Horse stealing, emphasized the authorities; but Talmadge feigned supreme innocence. What the men did
or did not do within the realm of legality was not his concern: he provided a place for them to stay, and they in turn helped with the chores,
the scale of which would overwhelm him otherwise. When the bulk of
the fruit became too much for him to manage at harvesttime, he sent a
portion with the men, who sold it at auctions and fairs, and he split the
profit with them.

The land claim was officially one hundred and sixty acres under the
Homestead Act of 1862; he purchased the land as soon as he was able, on
his eighteenth birthday. Over the years he bought the lots around it as
well so that he owned over four hundred acres of land. He left this other
land uncultivated, was satisfied to keep it as forest.

He did not articulate it as such, but he thought of the land as holding
his sister—her living form, or her remains. He would keep it for her,
then, untouched. All that space would conjure her, if not her physical
form, then an apparition: she might visit him in dreams, and tell him
what had gone wrong, why she had left him. Where did she exist if not on
the earth—was there such a place?—and did he want to know about it, if
it existed? What was a place if not earthbound? His mind balked. He was
giving her earth, to feed her in that place that was without it. An endless
gift, a gesture that seemed right: and it need never be reciprocated, for
it was a gift to himself as well, to be surrounded by land, by silence, and
always—but how could this be, after so much time?—by the hope that
she might step out of the trees, a woman now, but strangely the same,
and reclaim her position in that place.

THREE DAYS AFTER he saw the girls in town, he was braced aloft in an apricot tree on the homestead and saw them come out of the upper forest. He quit the shears and watched them. It was morning. They paused at the treeline and then came down through the pasture, their dark hair like flags riding the grass. At the edge of the yard they hesitated, discussing between themselves—what?—glancing repeatedly at the cabin, the outlying land.

He climbed out of the tree, the shears clamped in his armpit. When he walked out of the orchard, the taller girl—the one with the braid over her shoulder—turned to him, and froze. The other girl—her hair also dark, but fuzzy, tangled, unkempt—had been chattering to the other, but ceased abruptly when she saw him approaching. Both stood watching him, their eyes swarming the shears. He halted twenty yards from them.

You-all lost? he called. They looked away at the trees. The shorter one—younger one, he decided—held her mouth open and panted slightly. Their faces were filthy. Even from where he stood, he saw their arms discolored with dirt.

He crossed the yard and went into the cabin. He laid the shears on the table and took his time stoking the ashes in the woodstove. When he went outside again, they had come closer, but feinted back when he came out onto the porch. He took the buckets near the door and went down to the creek and gathered water. Returning to the cabin, mounting the rise in the orchard, he saw that the lawn was empty. Then he saw them; he tried not to fix them directly, where they lay now in the border between the lawn and the outer grass, peering out, thinking themselves hidden.

In the cabin he rebuilt the fire, and made thick cakes out of meal and creek water, and fried them over the stove. Lost himself in the task.

When he came to, he thought: Why was he making so many? And then he reminded himself: the girls had come to eat with him. He set the cakes on the table along with an uncapped jar of milk. He hesitated. Finally he left the cabin, shears in hand, and walked to the apple orchard, a deeper section up the creek, leaving them to themselves.

Late afternoon, when he returned to the cabin, there was no sign of them. The food had been eaten. The plates were clean. They had even eaten the crud on the griddletop, the charred remains of the mealcakes. The bowl on the table was empty of fruit. He stood for a moment, then checked the cold pantry. They had taken his eggs and milk. Backing out, he checked the cupboard by the stove. They had taken his cornmeal, and salt. He waited a moment, then went out onto the porch and looked across the lawn, at the trees. They were not there any longer, he thought; they had gone. He looked at the trees. Dusk settled within the branches, touched the ground.

Inside, he took off his boots, and slept.

THE FOLLOWING DAY at dawn he hitched the wagon to the mule and loaded a small supply of apples and apricots. Before stepping into the wagon, he carefully counted his money. He fit the soiled bills into his leather wallet and gazed at the trees sharpening in the blue light.

Before he reached town the sun was high and rinsing the standing wheatfields, quiet but for their resplendent shushing. The heat warmed his face but was not oppressive, and blew a clean scent down the road. A few white wisps of cloud in the sky posed silently.

He tied the wagon outside the feed and supply store and watered the mule, walked down the platform to the café. Inside, he sat at the counter and ordered fried eggs and coffee. The girl who took his order was maybe thirteen years old. He studied her from under his hat brim as she wiped down the counter, carried a stack of dirty dishes to the kitchen. He guessed the girls he had seen were about the same age. When she came back out, she set his eggs in front of him. Refilled his mug quickly. He watched her awhile longer, until she looked at him pointedly, unsmiling, and he looked away.

A little while later she came to pour him more coffee and said, My daddy's got something to say to you. She withdrew and disappeared into the kitchen. A moment later the proprietor, Weems, came out from the back.

I told you, Pa, said the girl, and floated past them down the counter.

Weems came to sit down next to Talmadge, looked after the girl. Only after a moment did he seem to recognize her.

My youngest, he said. Been working here a week and thinks she owns the place. He smiled faintly, scratched his chin. That's all my girls working here now—and the boys, all but the youngest, working next door.

Talmadge nodded absently—he was not really interested in the other man's family dynamics—and drank his coffee.

Weems half turned toward Talmadge, regarded him. I told her you only come Thursday to Sunday—

Well, said Talmadge. Need supplies.

Weems motioned for coffee, and peered past Talmadge to the lot in front of the café. The day glaring now. You bring the wagon? You planning on doing some business?

That's what I come about.

Weems nodded distractedly. With Sykes?

With Sykes. Or you.

Weems squinted outside again. But you're just in here a few days ago. You got something new? He frowned. You still got some of those Northern Spies?

Talmadge shook his head. Naw, he said. Just more of the same. And some 'cots.

Well, I don't know, said Weems after a pause. I just don't know. Couldn't give you money no way.

Talmadge nodded again, absently. What about trade?

Show me what you got, and we'll talk. I'd like to see those 'cots.

On the way out the door, Weems said, Lord, I almost forgot. I had Jinny out there keeping an eye out for you, and I almost forgot. Somebody's looking for you.

Talmadge frowned at the ground. Outside was a breath of hot air. Who's that? he said.

Don't know. Said he's from up Okanogan way. Hunting some girls.

Talmadge looked up. Some girls?

I think so. He come into town a few days ago asking around about his girls, run off or something, and Willie Angell said there were some girls matched his description who'd run off with some of your apples not just last week.

Talmadge hesitated beside the wagon. He tugged his hat brim while Weems pulled a bushel of apricots toward him for inspection.

Is that so? said Weems. Some wild girls steal your fruit?

Talmadge tugged his brim. Naw, he said. He could feel himself making a face of disgust. Nobody run off with anything.

You saw them, though? Those girls?

Talmadge didn't answer. He flicked his eyes over the man's back. Weems had leaned over to study the fruit. You going to take these 'cots or what?

All right, all right, said Weems, smiling now. He pulled the bushel forward in the wagon and hauled it up onto his shoulder and trudged with it back into the café.

Talmadge waited a moment, looking up the empty street. In the distance the range rose above the wheat, the principal ridges snowcapped even now. He looked at the dark mass of mountains, the wheat undulating below, and then followed Weems inside.

He stopped at Caroline Middey's on the way out of town. She had made venison stew. They brought the bowls to the front porch and sat and ate and looked out at the wheatfields before the house. He told her about the girls. If she was surprised to hear such a thing, she did not show it. She continued eating and narrowed her eyes a little and was silent for a long time after he had spoken. Finally she said, When was this? And he said: Two days ago. And again she was silent.

He had known her since he was a boy. As a young woman of twenty she had apprenticed with the town's original herbalist, and it was they whom Talmadge and Elsbeth approached when their mother was ill. Caroline Middey had traveled to the homestead to visit the cramped and foul-smelling miner's shack where Talmadge's mother lay under the heavy quilt, Talmadge's coat wrapped around her feet. Pale as a fish. She's going to die, said Caroline Middey to the children, who stood away in a spindly grove of apple trees. Even then, Caroline Middey was unflinching in her diagnoses. Do you understand? she said to the children. She told Talmadge and Elsbeth what to do to ease their mother's suffering, and then what to do afterward with her body. Elsbeth cried, but Talmadge had listened and tried to remember everything Caroline Middey was saying. Caroline Middey too was dry-eyed. Even then she did not pander to children. Who has a childhood, she often said, in these parts? When one was born, death was right there waiting for you, right there in the room. And she would know this because as well as being the herbalist she was also the town's midwife. You'd better learn to recognize his—Death's—face right away, she said.

Caroline Middey had not come to the orchard when he contracted smallpox because she did not want to be infected, and she was annoyed and angry with Elsbeth for coming into town for help when she could be carrying the sickness with her. But Caroline Middey had given her a satchel of herbs and instructions and sent the girl away again. Told her not to come to town again, not even if Talmadge died. She was to stay in the orchard for a month by herself if he was to get worse or die. Caroline Middey herself stayed in her house with a quarantine sign posted in the outlying field to wait and see if she became ill. She did not, and neither, miraculously, did Elsbeth.

The year after his sister disappeared, Talmadge cut his hand badly on a fishhook and sought Caroline Middey for help when it became infected. She made him a tincture and properly bandaged his hand. He stayed that afternoon on her porch and ate supper with her, and then, since it was too late to drive back home, he stayed in the spare room with the herbs hanging from the rafters.

Caroline Middey's house was small and compact, located on the edge of town, the mountains looming in the distance. It was very quiet, with a great field out in front of it, and beyond the strip of dirt road, the river. There was a front porch, very small, room enough for two wicker chairs and a low table between them. Inside was a small parlor with a high window, and at the back the kitchen. There were two bedrooms, one very small that belonged to her, and the other, which was rectangular, and dominated by a large window. Here dried herbs hung from the ceiling; it was where the invalid or sick person stayed, or guests. The room was aired often; there was little in it to absorb personality. The window was almost always open, the bed stripped of linen except when it was being used. The kitchen was small and close, like the galley of a ship, pots and pans hanging from nails on the wall, the sticking drawers clattering with cutlery, all of it mismatched. She could strive for perfection only in certain, few things; beyond that, it was important only to be tidy. And she was that. From the kitchen you stepped through a narrow hallway and then from there into the back garden. This garden was larger than the whole house and was rife with vegetables and herbs and flowers. It was here where she spent most of her time, in her large straw hat and gloves, with the wide gray apron covering her front, the apron strings doubled around her ample waist.

After his first visit as a young man Talmadge stopped frequently on his way out of town to see her, brought her fruit. They would eat a meal on the porch or indoors, depending on the season. If he stayed so long that he would not be able to make it back to the orchard by nightfall, he would sleep in the room with the drying herbs. In the morning he would wake and there would be coffee for him. She would be outdoors working in the garden, and he would leave without saying good-bye. At one time people thought they were courting, but that was never the case. Talmadge was stuck in grief he only partially acknowledged. It was not from his mother's death, from which he would have healed, more or less, eventually; but the festering issue was Elsbeth's disappearance, which his mind could not accept, could not swallow; and so he suffered always and abstractedly, and would never, as far as Caroline Middey was concerned, be cured. Besides this, Caroline Middey felt herself too old for Talmadge, romantically speaking, and was totally uninterested in his sex. When he was twenty-two years old and contracted a venereal disease from a prostitute at a fair in Malaga, Caroline Middey prescribed medicine for him and also recommended a woman in town he should see if he was interested in further business of that sort. She had spoken of the whole affair matter-of-factly, and it was this, finally, that saved their friendship. He had thought he could never approach her again after she saw what was wrong with him. He would never have approached her in the first place if he had not thought that he was dying.

But that was many years ago now. He saw the prostitute she had recommended a few times over the years, and then she, the prostitute, moved away and he saw another woman for a while, but not for many years now. He and Caroline Middey, after the initial conversation, did not discuss such things. He did not know much of her private life, except that at one time she had had an apprentice, a young Cayuse girl, who had died of scarlet fever when she was seventeen. The girl was the only person as far as Talmadge knew who Caroline Middey had ever lived with, besides the old herbalist when she was younger. There was an ambrotype of the Cayuse girl set in a floral wreath on a shelf above the table in the kitchen. A beautiful girl with twin braids, wearing an intricately beaded shirt. Talmadge asked about the girl once, and Caroline Middey had said the girl's Christian name was Diana. And then Caroline Middey had moved quickly out the back door to the garden. It was only then that Talmadge understood she was overcome and did not wish to speak about the girl. And so they never did.

You watch yourself, said Caroline Middey, now, on the porch. You don't know what these girls are mixed up in.

It could be their father, thought Talmadge. It could be they ran away from home—

Oh, I doubt that, said Caroline Middey, although he had not spoken. Her gaze did not change. Her face was heavily lined, her cheeks sagged. She sat hunched in the chair, glowering.

He said, after a long silence: Don't have to worry about it, anyway. They've cleared out.

They'll be back, said Caroline Middey, glancing at him now. You fed them, didn't you? They'll be back.

The next morning he made coffee and ate a bit of biscuit and bacon he'd saved from the night before. It was early yet, and cool, and he decided to chop wood.

Sometimes, in the morning, it was necessary to strain himself physically in order to clear his mind—and also his body, his body was not immune—of dreams. The acidic aftertaste of some dreams.

There were long periods where he did not think of Elsbeth at all. Time had intervened, after all, so that grief had not killed him. At times he could imagine her fate matter-of-factly, he could distance himself from it: he had had a sister who had disappeared into the woods, and no one knew what had become of her. It had all happened so long ago; he had continued with his life, accepted her absence. This is what he told himself; and it was partly true. But other times even his flesh was sensitive to the air, and what could have befallen her—and what she had suffered—tortured him. The litany of possibilities always hung about him, and during periods of weakness he turned to it, scrolled through it; amended some possibilities, added others.

She might have run away. She might have run away to a place she had heard about, imagined. (Had he, after all, known her mind as intimately as he thought he did?) And she hadn't told him because she didn't want to hurt him. She didn't want to be in the orchard anymore. Would he have accepted that? She might have accepted the help of a stranger, only to be taken advantage of. Robbed of the small amount of money she would have taken with her. Or maybe she was delivered, eventually, to a city, where she suffered the poverty unique to cities. Maybe she was in Seattle. In Spokane. Canada. San Francisco. Maybe she was somebody's wife. Maybe she was a mother. Perhaps her children had died—of disease, of catastrophe—or it was the death of her husband she had suffered. Maybe her husband was alive, but unkind. Maybe she was hungry. What did she think of when she tasted an apple, now? An apricot? It did not occur to him that if she was alive, she might be happy. For if she were, then she would not have excluded him for so long. It was too cruel. *Talmadge, I had to go, you would not have understood then, but I hope you understand now, and will come see me—*

Or maybe that day she had no intention of leaving him at all, and was actually hunting in the forest for herbs when a person came upon her and struck her, a heavy object to the back of the skull—practiced, sure—and then took up her body, carried it away. Talmadge did not like to dwell on the possibility that Elsbeth had been taken away, strapped to the back of a horse, to serve a dark purpose he would not even permit himself fully to imagine. How was a mind to sustain such speculation? But sometimes— some mornings, upon waking—he had a deep, calm, seemingly bottomless capacity for imagining it. The horror. What had happened to her, and what had he done? He had searched for her, but was he careful enough? Had he searched long enough? Called her name loudly enough? (But he had gone hoarse, calling her name: her name, the shape of it in his mouth, ached—he could not say her name now without a pulse of sick regret, and actual physical pain at the back of his throat, and in his mouth.) Thinking of her in such a situation, other terrible scenarios became more palatable: she had fallen into a hole; was attacked by a bear, a cougar. Murdered quickly by some natural force, and not by the hand of a stranger.

He walked with the ax past the apricot orchard and down the slope, crossed the creek, traversed the field. (Maybe she had joined a circus.) Long cuts of evergreen lay stacked near the forest edge. (Or, obeying some impulse hitherto unknown to him, entered a religious group; it was a nun, or a friend of the church, who had gently abducted her.) He spent the morning cutting an entire half tree into sections and then stood sweating and looked over the broken length. (Maybe she had left a note that had been upset by the wind, and drifted and floated into some crack or crevice that he had yet to discover.) He left his work and walked back across the field to the creek. (But there was no note; she did not know how to read or write.) As he knelt and splashed water in his face, an image of the deer that had recently gotten into the apricot orchard entered his mind. He drank from the creek and then stood, the blood pounding in his ears, and returned to the edge of the forest where the broken tree lay. He placed each round block upon a stump and proceeded to strike the block for kindling. (Would he ever know what had happened to her?) The sound of the creek was muffled by the line of gargantuan trees at his back. (Was it a matter of patience that kept him from discovery? Or was it goodness? Had some force—God?—kept the knowledge from him, because he was not good enough?) The crack of the ax splitting wood echoed and roamed the sky.

In the afternoon he investigated the fence along the far side of the apricot orchard. The barbed wire was mangled in one section near the back that he could not see from the porch. He walked the avenues and inspected the trees. Limbs were broken where he imagined the deer reared up on their hindquarters to get at the fruit. The damage was not great, but he would have to be more careful. Some men shot deer that ravaged crops, but he was not one of them. It was vulgar, he thought, to shoot a deer in the orchard.

One badly damaged tree at the end of the row was a sapling he had planted the previous spring. He crouched down and touched the limbs.

In the shed next to the barn he kept a collection of apple, plum, and apricot saplings. They grew incrementally in clay pots. Summer afternoons he set up a table under the eave of the cabin and worked on the saplings. He manipulated their shapes to networks he envisioned, performing multiple surgeries upon the tiny twiglike limbs. Youth had provided the advantage of better sight, much needed when he had begun the craft and relied upon sight as well as coordination; but now, though sight was not gone, it was impaired, and for several years he had depended solely upon the feel and texture of the limbs between his fingers. The myriad operations and surgical implements were second nature to him now, each practice fluid and exact.

When the saplings were ready, he planted them at the end of the orchard rows. He kept constant watch over them, building wooden latticework to support them during their precarious adolescence. Some of his experiments failed, were destroyed by weather or circumstance. Others, however, flourished.

In the shed he surveyed the apricot saplings and decided upon one and took hold of the clay pot in which it was secured and carried it outside, across the grass to the orchard. He knelt and studied the broken limb and compared it to those on the healthy sapling. Finally he chose a limb on the new sapling and cut into the bark with his pocketknife. Likewise he cut two inches above the ragged limb, and fit the appendages together so they joined at complementary angles. He had chosen and cut well and was pleased. He returned to the shed and retrieved a jar of wax and twine and set to work setting a wax cast for the new limb.

He sat in the grass bent over his work like a large child. The dread of last night's dreams had all but evaporated. The two girls watched him from the edge of the field. They did not speak to each other but sat in the heat motionless. One girl clawed the ground with her fingers and brought a fistful of dirt to her mouth and ate it.

He did not see them that day. But the next day he stood in the midsection of an apple tree and saw them come meandering down the orchard rows. He continued cutting with the shears in the high branches and watched them indirectly. They stopped down the row from him and sat in the grass. The smaller one ran her hand up and down the stalks of grass and then desisted, turned her head as if hearing a call. When he climbed down from the tree they sat up straight and held still but did not look at him. He pretended not to notice them—they seemed to prefer it that way—and momentarily considered walking around the row to avoid passing them, but walked toward them instead. They stiffened. He approached them, passed. He walked out of the orchard and they followed him across the field and through the creek, up the hill and to the shed, where he replaced the shears. When he came back out they were standing, hesitant, at the edge of the plum orchard. As he approached them, the smaller one stepped back, but the other—braid over her shoulder, sleepy-looking now—remained.

In the cabin he set to frying trout he had caught that morning. As he turned from the stove, he glanced out the door and saw that the taller one had crept forward across the grass. The smaller one stood at the edge of the lawn and looked over her shoulder as if gauging escape.

Fish, tomatoes, eggs and onions, fried bread. His face flushed. He worked with possession. When he was finished, the cabin was hot and pungent with the odor of fried fish and onions.

The long-haired one hung back from the porch. Dusk had fallen across the grass, and the other girl stood now a shadow on the edge of the lawn. He set the two plates of food on the porch. Then he turned and walked back into the cabin.

He sat at the table with a plate of fish in front of him. A minute later he got up from his chair, blew out the lantern perched on the stove mantel, walked to the door, and looked out. The girls knelt in the grass and ate with their heads together, silently.

One hundred dollars apiece, the poster said, for the capture of two girls called Jane and Della. To be returned to James Michaelson of Okanogan, Washington.

He stood looking at the poster nailed to the wall outside the feed and supply store and thought of the notice he had drawn up those years ago, the notary at the bank saying, How do you spell that—Elsbeth? And Talmadge looked up at him raw-eyed—he was seventeen years old, and his sister had disappeared into the forest for going on three days now—and the notary sighed and wagged his pen and bent and wrote: To those persons with information regarding the whereabouts of Miss Elsbeth Talmadge, please contact William Talmadge—What's your address, son? Again the blank stare. How do you expect them to get ahold of you? Talmadge shook his head, lifted his arm, and gesticulated west, toward the mountains. The notary said, almost angrily, How about if they leave word at the P.O.? How's that? Talmadge nodded, and the notary wrote the rest of the notice and looked up and said, There. Talmadge said, There's a reward. The notary eyed him ruefully. How much? he said. Talmadge said, A hundred dollars. The notary sat back in his chair. Son, do you even have a hundred dollars? Talmadge hesitated. He didn't see what the problem was. If Elsbeth returned, the money wouldn't matter. If they had to pay a hundred dollars, then they would pay a hundred dollars.

Talmadge unpinned the poster from the wall and stood looking at it and then folded it and put it in his pocket.

The next evening the girls sat at the edge of the lawn. He turned from the window to the pantry, regarded his supplies. Took a bag of cornmeal and set to making cakes and fried apples. Turning in the kitchen, he glanced out the window and noticed a girl moving slowly across the grass toward the porch. He stopped working and watched her. It was the older one again, he thought, the one with the braid. She clasped a plate to her breast. The oil spat in the pan behind him and the room warmed with the odor of cornbread. She stopped at the edge of the porch. He wiped his hands on his pants and went to the door. She held the plate tightly to her chest and stood outside the sphere of light the lantern cast. He stepped out onto the porch. She looked past him into the cabin, as if the food and the odor of the food was a body she had expected to greet her. Finally she looked at his chest and then stepped forward, held out the plate. He took it from her and went inside and heaped food on it. When he returned, she was walking back to him across the grass with another plate. The other girl stood alone on the edge of the grass, watching. He held out the plate of food to the girl, and after a moment she took it. He took the other plate inside, filled it.

When he returned to the porch, the girl lifted her face from the plate. Her cheeks were filled with food and her eyes watered. It's hot, he said. She blinked rapidly. For some reason she would not take the other plate from him, and so he set it on the porch and returned inside the cabin.

From the window he watched her retreat across the grass, pausing to lower her face into the food. The other girl met her and seized the heaping plate. They sunk to their knees in the grass and ate as they had before.

Oh, I wouldn't do that, said Caroline Middey.

She and Talmadge sat on her front porch again, this time eating brisket and steamed carrots and greens in broth. Talmadge wiped his mouth with a blue-checked napkin. He should not have spoken. But he could not help himself. Even if her response was not what he wanted to hear, he needed her advice. He had told her, once they had begun the meal, that he was going to visit Michaelson on the Okanogan.

If you were able to catch them, said Caroline Middey suddenly, reverting to an earlier conversation about the girls, I could have a look at them. I could have a look at them, and see what kind of shape they're in. Could you do that?

He thought for a moment. But why was he considering it?

No, he said. After a moment: You can come out there and see if they'll come to you. You're a woman; it might be different. But there is to be no—*catching*—

She said nothing to this, was thinking.

You go up there and see this fellow, she said, nodding. All right. But you best bring a gun. She brought a forkful of brisket and put it into her mouth, chewed.

He was still. He had already thought of that. The rifle was in the wagon, underneath a canvas bag in the back. But he did not want to tell her he had already thought of this, because he did not want her to think that he too expected to find an adversary. He was disgusted that that had been his first reaction. He said, without inflection: I brought it. But I won't need it.

Caroline Middey raised her eyebrows. Again she stabbed a forkful of meat.

Never know what you might need, she said, and brought the meat to her mouth, ate it.

It was not a negligible distance he would have to travel—seventy miles, more or less, as the crow flies—and he considered how he would do it. Finally he chose to leave his mule with Caroline Middey, who then drove him in her wagon to Wenatchee. He boarded a steamboat heading north, into the highlands. It was a Tuesday, just before dawn; not many people boarded with him.

Up the Columbia, the water splashing steadily against the hull; past Orondo and Entiat, the orchards along the benches materializing in the dawn. Chelan Falls, where morning broke. The sun glinting on the water. He crossed to the other side of the boat, looked out over the country. East of there was the place he hunted in the fall: a place of long flat fields and sweeping rock quarries, weak, haunted sunlight. The animals moving suddenly in that landscape—strong, beautiful, unexpected forms.

He arrived in Okanogan late afternoon. He found a place to eat, and then a boardinghouse, where, despite the hour—the sun had not yet set—he fell immediately asleep.

The next morning he inquired at the general store where he could find James Michaelson. The storekeeper, an elderly man with whom Talmadge had just had a pleasant conversation about the weather and the season, set his jaw. Looked past Talmadge, out the window. Said, after a moment, stiffly: We aren't party to any of that. When Talmadge said, What do you mean? the man turned his head farther away and said he didn't know any James Michaelson. And was that it, he said, or did Talmadge have any other business at the store?

Talmadge received more or less the same answer at the feed and supply store. And then he questioned an ironmonger working in an open stall at the end of the street, who regarded him briefly before telling him the Michaelson outfit was north of there, on the Salmon Creek just beyond

Ruby City. You get to Conconully, said the man, you've gone too far. He fixed Talmadge in one long compassionless stare before bending again to his work.

Talmadge rode a mule out of Okanogan—Are you sure you don't want a horse? You want a horse, don't you? the man at the stables had asked, incredulous. No, a mule suits me fine, said Talmadge—and into the hot, dull country of the Okanogan highlands. His saddlebag packed with sandwiches and water, his rifle slung across his back.

An hour outside Okanogan he entered a town where the buildings were ramshackle and squat and looked as if they had weathered a thousand storms but would not survive another. Was this Ruby City? Or had he somehow ridden past that place and come too far north, to Conconully? He didn't think he had ridden far enough to have reached Conconully. A dog ambled around the corner of a building and halted when it saw Talmadge and the mule, and backed up a little ways and began to snarl. Talmadge slowed the mule, leaned forward and touched the mule's neck. A child came around the side of the building the way the dog had come and drew close to the dog and squatted down and put his arms around the dog's neck. The dog struggled and whined as the child spoke into its ear. The dog gave one long creaking moan and then remained still as the child stood and gazed at Talmadge. He was a gaunt boy, with brown eyes that seemed too large for his skull.

Morning, said Talmadge. He straightened up in the saddle. The mule sidestepped, chewed the bit, stomped. Talmadge said: I'm looking for the Michaelson place.

The boy stared at him. It seemed he would not move at all, but then he turned slightly and lifted his arm and pointed to a stand of evergreens in the distance.

Talmadge peered at where the boy pointed. He thanked him and was about to leave when he noticed the boy still staring at him, as if he had something to say.

Talmadge waited.

The boy came forward. The dog rocked on its tailbone and scratched frantically behind its ear. The boy stopped next to the mule and stood looking up at Talmadge until Talmadge said, What?

The boy said: Usually they give me something for it.

Talmadge gazed at him for a moment and then reached into his pocket and pinched out a penny and leaned down and put it into the boy's outstretched palm. The boy glanced at the penny and then turned and walked back to the corner from which he had appeared. The dog followed him.

Talmadge waited, looking in the direction the boy had gone. There was no other sound, no movement in the town. He looked at the trees—the evergreens—the boy had indicated. He knew enough to turn around and go home. But still he hesitated. Eventually, he urged the mule forward.

As soon as he entered the clearing from the trees, a boy separated from a gambrel-roofed barn in the distance and drew toward him. As he neared, Talmadge saw that this boy was lean, pale, and red-haired, and walked with his elbows held slightly out. Talmadge saw the strong jaw and hardness around the eyes. He was about fifteen years old, Talmadge guessed.

Your mule, mister.

Talmadge sat the mule a moment, taking in the land and the situation of the house and barn. The house was maybe fifty yards away. No smoke came from the chimney. The barn was farther away, set back in the expansive field. One portion of the barn was charred and had collapsed in on itself. Swallows flew intermittently in and out of the collapsed portion.

Talmadge got down off the mule.

Somebody tried to burn it down, said the boy. A couple of good-for-nothing girls.

What?

The barn.

Talmadge handed him the reins. He adjusted the strap that held the rifle—hooded in canvas—on his back. I'm here for Michaelson.

The boy nodded toward the house. Hey, he said, when Talmadge turned away.

Talmadge turned back to him.

Your gun, said the boy.

Talmadge again touched the strap across his chest, reflexively. But he did not remove it from his body.

The boy finally raised his eyebrows. Suit yourself, he said. But he won't like it.

The house was a blend of pulpwood and spruce timber and was poorly built. The porch groaned nauseously beneath him. Two lanterns hung on hooks on either side of the door, the glass oily with soot. The door was open but screened. He could see inside the house, into a room like a parlor and then beyond that into another room, the kitchen, maybe, with a window of smudged light. He hesitated and then rapped twice on the doorframe. From the bowels of the house there was movement, and Talmadge drew himself up and listened. There was someone clearing his throat and muffled steps and then a man appeared behind the screen. He was tall—a whole head taller than Talmadge, who was just over six feet— with a large head, dun-colored pate, a wide mouth, large, stone-colored, heavy-lidded eyes. Talmadge was struck with the possibility that the man was blind: he aimed his stare, heavy, over Talmadge's shoulder. And he moved very slowly: shuffled. But then he met Talmadge's eyes, and there was recognition there. The man could see him. Talmadge looked at him and then looked away. Gripped—again, reflexively—the leather strap at his shoulder. The man watched Talmadge without blinking—but he had taken in the rifle, Talmadge felt—and opened the screen door while si-multaneously rolling up the cuffs of his worn white shirt. Come in, he said. An uninterested murmur.

Talmadge stepped inside.

The screen door thwapped shut.

The man absently splayed his hand to indicate the wealth of seating— several sofas covered in crushed velvet, musty smelling, and three chairs in the same velvet in different colors—emerald, ruby, mustard. Have a seat, said the man, and scratched the back of his head—again the unin-terested tone—and sat down on the edge of the emerald chair. Talmadge sat opposite him, lifting the rifle over his head and laying it across his lap. Michaelson leaned forward and opened a cigar box on the low table and lifted his eyes in Talmadge's general direction—an offering—but

Talmadge raised his hand to decline. The man took a cigar for himself and lit it and took one puff and remained sitting still in his chair. He stared at the floor—worn, scratched pine boards—and seemed to fade into a stupor; he pressed his lips together as if recalling a former agitation.

And then he seemed to come out from whatever spell he was under.

No one offered to relieve you of your weaponry, I see, he said.

Talmadge didn't answer. Was the man sick? he thought. Had Talmadge just woken him from a nap? And another thing that was bothering Talmadge: he could not locate the man's age. He had sensed, when the man first appeared behind the screen, that he was in his forties—a muscular, hard, but graceful body, and a wide but also lean, weary face. As he smoked, he seemed to age: was he near Talmadge's age? Beyond it? Talmadge was dismayed that he could not tell. The man seemed a chameleon.

Doing some hunting? Michaelson said, without inflection.

Talmadge hesitated. Yes. He cleared his throat. I've been south of here but—thought I'd see what's north. Good hunting here, I've heard—

While Talmadge was speaking, Michaelson's eyes had traveled, bored, to the corner of the room. When Talmadge fell silent, Michaelson turned his head to him but did not meet his eyes. Lifted his eyebrows. The girls are sleeping, he said. You'll have to wait. Unless, he said, you want me to wake someone up. His gaze traveled to the opposite corner of the room. You understand, he said.

Talmadge understood he was referring to money. By this time he understood much. He listened to the sounds of the house, aware now that it was filled with girls. He thought of the two girls in the orchard and looked up to see Michaelson watching him now hard, frowning. Talmadge couldn't decide if it was Talmadge—his person or visage—of which Michaelson disapproved, or if he was thinking of something else and had just let his gaze rest there, on Talmadge's chest. There was a faint wheezing as Michaelson puffed on his cigar.

Where are you from?

He, Talmadge, must be very careful now, he thought. He looked to the window.

Oregon.

Michaelson smoked and continued to look at his chest. His frown increased by a degree.

Long way from home. You a mining inspector? He smoked. Or a bounty hunter? They send you to hunt me? You going to shoot me?

There was a silence as Talmadge, baffled, decided how to answer.

He stood. I have to be going.

Michaelson did not look up at him.

I was looking for another Michaelson, said Talmadge. Looks like I got the wrong place, here.

Michaelson brought the cigar up to his lips. I'm the only Michaelson around here, and everybody knows it.

The floorboards whined softly. Talmadge turned to see a child in the doorway between parlor and kitchen. She was small, maybe nine years old, with limp black hair and black eyes. A child's pouting mouth, stained red. She rubbed her eyes. She was wearing a man's cotton undershirt and nothing else. Pa, she said. A gentle croak.

He lifted his chin in assent, and the girl trod lightly to him, climbed onto his knee. He put one arm around her waist—casually—and with the other brought the cigar again to his lips. Scowled at the floor. And then he leaned forward and crushed the cigar on a saucer on the nearest table and cleared his throat. Again he addressed the corner of the room: Two dollars, he said. For twenty minutes. He paused. This is Mary Elizabeth.

Talmadge looked away. I have to be going, he said.

I'll clean her up, put her dress on. It won't take long. If she's up the others will be up, he said again, more to himself than to Talmadge. With the heel of one hand he rubbed his eye and stretched his legs. The girl slid off him, scampered away through the doorway from which she had come. You can have your pick, said Michaelson. What do you like?

But Talmadge had stepped outside onto the porch and down into the stunning light. He walked quickly across the clearing, his eyes on the mule standing in the stippled shade beside the barn. It took him a long time to reach his destination. His foolishness overwhelmed him. The boy scrambled up from where he had been sitting with his back against the barn wall and hurried to unfasten the reins from the post. That was fast, he said to Talmadge, grinning.

In Okanogan he stopped again at the general store. The old man working behind the counter, recognizing him, stuck out his jaw.

That man Michaelson, said Talmadge. What's he about?

The man looked askance at him. He had picked up a rag, had begun wiping the counter.

You went up there, didn't you? he said after a minute. You know what he's about.

Something wrong with him? said Talmadge. He sick?

The man snorted. Glanced at Talmadge, to see if he was serious. When he saw Talmadge's question was in earnest, he said: He's hibernating now, I suppose.

Hibernating?

The man snorted again. The man is a fiend. Goes through rages more than any person I've encountered in my life. Ups and downs. Some mental sickness, I suppose. And then he's into that stuff—that opium. When he's in the stuff you don't hear from him for a while. But then he comes to town and wreaks all kind of trouble. Don't know why they don't permanently jail him. His newest thing, the man said, as if suddenly remembering it, is chasing girls—I think it's two—who ran off from the place earlier this year. He's frothing at the mouth to find them. I hope they're long gone by now, said the man, looking out the window to the street. Hate to know what he'd do if he found them. Man's not in his right mind.

Didn't seem to be frothing when I saw him, said Talmadge, after a silence.

That's because he's hibernating, said the man. Any time he has that stuff—that opium—he stays up there and eats it. Or whatever he does. Smokes it, I don't know. Waits for one of his men to bring him more. Woe the man who comes empty-handed. He'll eat it until he runs out of money. Harmless as a puppy until then, I suppose. Though I don't know. The man is a menace. The man glanced at Talmadge again. Why'd you go up there? he said. If you pardon my asking. You don't seem the type.

Talmadge considered carefully how to answer.

I thought it was a different kind of place, he said.

WHEN HE ARRIVED back at the orchard, a day and a half later, the two plates were stacked neatly on the porch. He made eggs. He left the steaming plates on the porch steps and walked past the girls, who had crossed the grass toward him, down to the creek and washed his face. Had the girls come by steamboat? he wondered. Or, as he increasingly believed, had they come by foot, through hard country and forest?

The girls had finished eating by the time he passed the cabin again and the plates were stacked as before. They sat at the mouth of the apricot orchard, waiting.

He spent the morning deciding what to do. The image of Michaelson at times rising to harass him. Early afternoon he loaded down the mule with supplies and led him out of the barn and across the grass. Crossed the creek. A moment later he heard the splashing of their crossing behind him. He walked slowly so they would not fall too far behind. He led the mule into the outer apple orchard, into the canyon. Up the short incline where the path veered away into a band of aspen. The ground was hardened ash and clay and covered with a dull confetti of mulch. He slowed, gauging their stride, and kept on.

For their beds he filled burlap bags with leaves. He had three quilts besides his own, which he packed. He brought a lantern, and thought as he led the mule up the hill: What if they were unfamiliar with lanterns and burned down the cabin in the middle of the night? He thought he should try to explain the mechanics of the lantern but could not imagine such a conversation. Sun winked through the trees. He anticipated the small rent in the forest to the right and soon found it and waited to make sure they saw him, then stepped off the road and guided the mule up the embankment. He heard them struggle behind him, and hesitated. The mule looked over his shoulder.

He came to the small clearing, the narrow, clattering creek. Beyond the creek the cabin stood backed by two massive overhanging evergreens. The cabin and trees sat on a small rise overlooking the valley on the opposite side. He crossed the creek and walked around the side of the cabin to view the orchards below. There was his own cabin, the elbow of creek.

The girls sat on the opposite creek bank and watched him. The mule entered the water and moved over to them and they arranged their postures to accommodate his grazing.

The cabin was one room, dank and cold but solidly built. (Too wet up here, their mother had said, when they first discovered it. They chose to settle below, in the valley, even though early on it meant huddling in the miner's shack, which, for its closeness, was as dry as a bone.) The cabin's single window—large, paneless—overlooked the valley. He swept away most of the leaves with his boot and then constructed their beds and draped the quilts atop them.

Outside the cabin he hailed the mule and unstrapped his fishing rod, and hiked along the creek for a half mile to the pool. The girls followed him and sat on the rock outcropping jutting two dozen feet out into the water. He scouted the ground and found pale larvae on the underside of a log and then baited the hook and cast into the water. In an hour he caught three fish.

At the upper cabin he started a fire. The girls crossed the creek and resumed their previous positions. They watched as he gutted the fish and threw the entrails into the water. By the time he cooked the fish, it was late afternoon. He set the plates of fish on the porch, and from the saddle-bags he removed apples and apricots and biscuits wrapped several times in a cloth and set these on the porch as well. He went around the side of the cabin where the mule had gone to warm his rump in the sun and gathered the reins and led the mule across the creek. As he passed the girls they gathered their legs close to them and looked in opposite directions. He continued down the slope and listened for their footsteps but did not hear them.

When he made his own supper, it was dusk. He ate cornbread, an apple. He did not light a lantern. The flesh of the apple shone moon-white, and he ate it and chucked the core into the orchard. He sat on the darkened porch and rolled a cigarette, a ceremony he saved for Clee but for this one time, and he did not bother to question the impulse. He sat smoking. After a while he saw, like twin phantoms, the girls creep down the avenue between apple orchard and canyon. They momentarily disappeared and then came out of the canyon mouth. Crossed the field, disappeared again, and then alighted at the edge of the apricot orchard, settled into the grass. Awaited, with their peculiar and indifferent curiosity, what he would do next.

D ELLA WAS HAPPY.

    She and Jane were submerged to their necks in the pool beyond the upper cabin where the man had made them a place to stay but where they did not stay. A mile or so down the hillside the man worked in the orchard, or he was done for the day, he was washing himself in the creek, the same creek that fed the pool in which the girls now swam, and that flowed out and down the hillside through the forest, to where it clattered below the apricot orchard. When hunger struck one of the girls, they immediately swam to the rock abutment from which they had lowered themselves into the water a half hour before; but, finding they could not pull themselves up again because of their weight, they swam to the shallows and slogged, fully clothed, up onto the rocks. Panting. Dizzy. Clutching each other for support, both giddy with hunger, they made their way through the heaven-reaching evergreens, found the path that led down to the orchard.

    The air along the path was warm and shrilling with insects. Out of the water, despite their cumbersome bellies, they felt light.

    The path lowered down into the far orchard; and since it was inside a canyon, it was darker and quieter and was at that moment full of cold hush. In almost total silence the bats darted through the tall grass. One grazed Della's knee; she slapped at it.

    It was two months since Della and Jane had left the place where Michaelson was, and their experiences with people had been few and far between. They roamed the forests mostly, after they escaped, and when they came upon a homestead, or came into a town, they sized people up in terms of what could be extracted from them. It was the easiest way to get by. Jane was especially good at it. She was able to determine who would give them money, shelter, food, or other things. Some people weren't willing to give anything, some were persuaded to give one or maybe two of those things, and a few—these were very, very few—would give you whatever you wanted. It was important that none of these people want anything in return.

They sat now in the long grass between the apricot orchard and yard. The man had begun to cook supper and had left the cabin door open, an invitation they did not take him up on. Not yet. And preferably, not ever. Living with Michaelson had taught them both that you could read nothing definitive in a man's face, even if he appeared kind. Kind could turn on its head instantly; could throttle you, or hit you across the face with the back of a hand.

The odor coming from the cabin was of frying mealcakes, and bacon. Della fell back in the grass, a fake swoon, and then after a moment, when the joke failed to garner any reaction from Jane, sat up again, continued to wait.

And then finally he came out onto the porch and set the plates on the top step. He stood and looked out over the grass for them. If he saw them, he did not show it. He went back into the cabin.

It was Jane who fetched the plates. Della stood on the edge of the yard, in case they needed to run. When Jane reached her, they sat down in the grass and lowered their faces to the food, breathing in the odor of it at the same time as they ate, so that they choked, gasped, slurped. Jane folded an entire mealcake into rough quarters and stuffed it into her mouth, her eyes bulging with the effort to chew it.

The man brought his meal out onto the porch and ate quietly with the plate on his lap. The lantern was turned up in the cabin behind him and illuminated the room at his back.

Afterward Della, stuffed and sated with food, again waited in the grass while Jane returned the plates to the porch, and took the quilts that had been placed for them on the top step. He had made beds for them in the upper cabin—nothing much, just sacks filled with leaves, to give their backs some relief—but they preferred to sleep outdoors. Sleeping indoors, where the trees and moonlight cast violent shadows on the walls, was unnatural. When one slept indoors, there was always the possibility that danger lurked just outside the door, the window, was waiting for them. When one slept outdoors, on the other hand, danger was confused, passed them over. At Michaelson's they had slept together with the other girls in the basement. You could tell nothing of the life of the house from the basement, which was more like a large cellar. It smelled of roots, and urine. Someone perpetually crying, bodies turning over and grumbling, sighing, whispering, all day long. For that was when they slept: in the daytime. The darkness complete, liquid black. Della could not see her hand in front of her face. And so she and Jane, if they had a choice, would not sleep indoors—in a man's house—ever again.

They chose a different spot to sleep each night, usually in the long grass under a fruit tree, and bedded down. One quilt under them and one over them. They slept with arms entwined, as they had in Michaelson's basement, and were often immediately asleep. Della might wake and see the sky through the branches, choked with stars, and squeeze Jane's hand, only to have Jane keep breathing heavily, anchored in a private depth.

We're still here, Della would whisper in the morning, to Jane; and Jane would respond: We're still here. It was a game of theirs, a ritual; and like many of their games and rituals, Della could not remember how it had begun.

They entered the cabin repeatedly while the man was not there, and were touched each time, irremediably and despite themselves—they did not discuss this—by the domestic warmth. If such a house existed, why could it not be theirs alone? The boards creaked and sang beneath their weight. The plate-glass windows, recently washed, were streaked, admitted soapy light. The pine countertops fairly gleamed. A black cast-iron stove stood kingly against the back wall. The range had a stone top; a bucket with ashes sat on a shelf beneath it. On the back burner sat a scuffed navy blue kettle. Above it, on the top shelf of a doorless cupboard lined with newspaper, sat a white coffeepot, and dishes. Between the range and the stove was a low-slung hamper stocked with wood. On the opposite side of the stove was a white porcelain basin and a pitcher of water, and above it, a dented oval mirrorglass hanging from the wall by a wire. On a tin tray sat a black comb and container of pomade. An almanac calendar from the year 1865 hung beside the mirrorglass. A small walnut table, more rectangular than square, and two chairs were situated before the woodstove, filling the area between kitchen and sitting room. In the sitting room a horsehair love seat stood against the wall, and beside it, in the corner, a horsehair chair, the seat tattered and lumpy. Near the chair was a shelf of old almanacs, newspapers, magazines. Before the love seat was a rug of hooked fabric scraps, rose and green and purple; and in the opposite corner, a steamer trunk and a rocking chair so old and delicate it seemed to have sprouted from the room itself. This was where the sun came and lay, and the rocker, which was mahogany, was wrung of color. The odor of the room was baked fruit, beeswax, pine, and old newspapers.

There was an apricot tree in the orchard that was perfect for stepping up into. Once one of the girls did this, a curved branch invited another step up, and a branch above that dipped slightly in the middle, inviting a hand to grip it for leverage. Once one girl had situated herself on the second tier of branches, the other was able to climb up as well, and situate herself on a level slightly lower. The branches had formed to the girls' slightly reclining positions, to the arches of their feet. Their strange girth. They climbed up there until the wood became soft under their palms and feet. From here they could watch whatever was happening below in the field; and if they climbed higher into the tree, which they had done, they could locate the man wherever he was working. They were camouflaged—or they thought they were—and suspended, safe from danger on the ground.

There was a type of heat and light that was direct and overhead and bleached the orchard of color. The orchard at noon on the hottest days. And then there were mornings when the air was blue and soft, and the leaves of the trees looked like velvet.

There were times when the girls knew where the man was in the orchard, and times they did not. These times they trod slowly and carefully, not that they thought he would harm them—not really—but it had become a kind of game. You might turn the corner into an orchard row and find him there, walking toward you or away, or maybe you saw his legs, his trunk, obscured in leaves.

Della, distracted for a moment in the heat of the day—the sun hung high, and sweat trickled down the back of her skull—turned the corner and almost ran into him. She stepped back and held very still, did not look up at him. Said, lightly, before she stepped around him: Afternoon.

He had become for them not a threat, though he was not devoid of threat—why had he taken them in, why did he stand for them to roam the place without demanding anything from them?—and this threat entertained them more than the fact that they were curious about him. They were not interested at that point in the history or emotional life of men they encountered. This was not a rule they had set up for themselves, but rather a consequence of their experience. It was only important to know—to sense, but also to recall—if the man before them would fly into a rage, would lunge at them; was capable of swift and unremitting violence. And yet Della found herself those hot days roaming the avenues, struck by a sharp and intermittent desire to see this new man's—this orchardist's—face. She was dissatisfied with seeing the front of his overall pockets, his denim legs in trees, his large burnished hands hanging at his sides. Through glances she had caught various features— his nose, the set of his shoulders, the striking color of his eyes. But he had one of those complicated faces that one had to consider at length to understand how emotion lay on it, to understand it at all. It was like a landscape: that wide and complicated, many-layered expanse. She wanted to study his face: because it was different in an important way, but she did not know, exactly, how.

While Jane napped in the grass a little distance off, Della sat three trees away from where the man worked. She put a long piece of grass between her lips and mouthed it. He came down out of the tree a few minutes later. Approaching her—she stared straight ahead, careful not to look at him—he wiped his hands on his thighs, and then bent low and picked a honeysuckle. Straightened up, studied it. Plucked the purple needlelike petal, put it between his teeth. Finally she glanced at him. Honeysuckle, he said, his voice low and disinterested. You take the petals like this— she glanced at him again, and he bared his teeth to show her how to put the needle between her front teeth—and suck on it. See? There's a little honey in there. A little sweet. What the bees like. He unceremoniously spat out the petal and turned and walked in the other direction, whistling now, down the row.

It was usually Jane's job to fetch the plates of food from the porch— she was the brave one, she was the one who would sound the alarm if there was danger, and Della must start running first—but one morning Jane would not be easily roused. She batted away Della's hands when Della prodded her shoulder—I'm hungry!—and so Della crept to the edge of the lawn, crouched, waited for the man. He had again left the door open, and again the odor of the hot food wafted out. She shifted in the grass, impatient. She had grown very large—increased size, even, in the last two days, she could feel it—and rocked on her haunches, lost balance as his form passed the doorway. He had not even come outside yet, but she lumbered up onto her feet, dizzy, panting like a dog, and headed across the grass. When he came outside, she was standing at the bottom of the porch steps, her chin lifted but her gaze askance, her elbows held out in the attitude of accepting the food. Well, hello, he said. And then, when she didn't answer, didn't change position: Here you are. But she would not take the plate from him; he had to set it on the porch before she would accept it.

While Jane slept again, this time in the afternoon, Della waited two trees away from the man working. She chewed honeysuckle, sweated though she was in the shade. Was remembering how Michaelson would come out of his room, stark naked, and chase them—all the girls, set loose like a bunch of stags, or does—in the upper part of the house, and whoever was caught was either let go—a boundless relief—or taken to his room to love him, or maybe whipped. Or both. You could not tell what he would do. The girls rushed through the rooms, shrieking with excitement and fear.

Here, said the man suddenly, coming down the ladder, and she startled. She pretended not to pay attention, but she listened, and glanced at what he was talking about when she couldn't help herself: You hold the apricot like this. (The apricot small and glowing in his palm.) For apples it's different, but this is how you hold an apricot. You see the little bit of the stem there? That's the scion. You have to be careful there. You damage that and you damage that part of the tree, the limb where it grows, it won't be able to produce any more. Then, looking down the avenue: That's probably all you need to know, for now, if you want to help. And then he turned and walked down the row again. Whistling and then singing in a slightly wavering baritone. A hymn? She thought she might know it. But she didn't know where from.

Jane disapproved of the communication between Della and the man, though she said nothing to Della about her behavior. Perhaps Jane didn't know about it, but that seemed unlikely, since Jane knew everything. She had not told Della she should not talk to the man. Jane did not think, probably, that Della was growing sympathetic toward him, because to her, to both of them—they did not have to state this—this was an impossibility. Men were, by definition, untrustworthy. They were to be sized up, to determine what they, the men, might want from Jane and Della, and likewise, what Jane and Della might get from the men, if they had anything that the girls wanted or needed. The men were there to trade with, and to perhaps fear; but not to like for the sake of themselves. And, this also went without saying, they were definitely not there to be loved.

Those weeks—was it months?—in the summer orchard, Jane and Della roved, and crouched in the grass, and slept, and ignored or pretended to ignore the man, and ate ravenously, like animals, when they were fed. It was unclear how long they would stay.

Oddly, though their bellies were full to bursting and it was apparent they would soon give birth, there was no urgency to the days. They slept late, cast off the quilts from their sweating bodies, rolled over or crawled on hands and knees to find shade, and slept another hour or so on their sides, their mouths hanging open. One day faded into the next, and one was much like the other. There was little change. Perhaps time had stopped; perhaps it had never existed. It was unclear, even, what was happening. Did they want to stay, or would they leave? The days transpired in a dreamlike haze, made so by the incredible heat and the long hours of light. Grasshoppers shrilling their one-note song. The meaning of the day, if it had any, was to track, however abstractedly, the movement of the man, for what purpose it was unclear. Immediately the purpose was food; and more distantly, there was a feeling, a notion originating inside the deepest parts of their brains, that he might be needed for other purposes, mainly having to do with what was happening to their bodies: the arrival of their children.

Their children were from God. Jane had seen them in a vision—it was when she was with Michaelson, and he had given her the seed paste to try, as he sometimes did—and she had fallen asleep and dreamed that their children, hers and Della's, grew inside them, and when they were born— they were also angels—they would carry Jane and Della on their backs, away from Michaelson's place, to safety. Jane described their moonward journey. That was in the beginning.

And then Jane's interpretation of the dream changed. It wasn't the children who carried Jane and Della out of that place, but the other way around. Of course babies weren't angels, of course they could not fly. Jane bided her time. But they would escape by spring: Jane promised.

They rose one morning in the orchard and it was humid, and cool, and the sky overhead was dark gray. They woke with the quilt pulled up to their chins; they had not kicked it off in the night. They rose when the first raindrops hit their faces. They did not discuss what they were doing but crossed the yard and hesitated only briefly before going up onto the porch. Jane's brow furrowed. The door was open. There were two birchwood chairs on the porch, but when Della went to sit in one, Jane grunted and motioned that they should not sit there. The man, when he came to stand in the doorway, found them sitting with their backs to him, legs dangling off the side of the porch. Della turned to look over her shoulder at him, but Jane told her in a low voice to turn around.

That morning the two of them ate on the porch while the rain poured down a foot from their knees, and behind them, inside the cabin, the man sat in the chair in the corner, drinking coffee—Della could smell it—and reading a newspaper.

Jane had thought that if there was ever a moment that presented itself
for him to forget his manners and take advantage of them, then that moment on the porch, in the rainstorm, was it. But he did not even sit outside with them. He waited indoors until the rain stopped, and then a few
minutes later, the sun showing palely through the breaking clouds, he
passed by them and walked across the grass and into the orchard.

Two days later, as he crouched creekside washing dishes, Jane passed
close to him on his right side, entering the creek to cross it, and Della
came a moment later on the other side, slightly behind her sister. Absently, as if he were a rock or another solid object she was using as a
crutch in her forward progress, Della placed her hand on his shoulder,
and then, a moment later, removed it. The man kept still until after they
had passed. They crossed the field at a slow pace, heading for the canyon.
They did not look back.

There was a cache in the outer orchard, near a bend in the path, where
Jane stored various objects: rope, twine, shears. A wooden sawhorse that
had been difficult to move from the shed without the man noticing. Della
did not ask at first what Jane was doing.

In case, said Jane, when Della finally asked her. In case he comes. By
he Della knew—the hair rising on the back of her arms and neck—Jane
meant Michaelson. He won't come here, said Della, meaning: He doesn't
belong here. Jane nodded, absently. Just in case, she said again. We have
to be ready—

The girls spent most of their time in the apricot orchard, or in the
plum orchard around the side of the cabin, where it was coolest in the
heat of the day, but they had also become familiar with the outer field, its
shaded borders along the forest treeline. They had wandered enough into
the canyon, and along the path up to the cabin that was meant as their
own. They had spent hours submerged to their chins in the upper pool,
except for lately, when they had grown too large to do so. They would
not have the strength now to pull themselves up out of the water.

All of this—the land, the trees, the weather, the water—they considered the man's domain. Nothing happened in these parts that he was not aware of and over which he did not have power. If he did not have the power to prevent certain things—this they almost believed—then at least he had the knowledge necessary to protect himself, or the strength to endure it.

They found, in the closet of one of the two small bedrooms—the bedroom that was not his—a box with a pair of girls' boots in it, and a dress, and what looked to be a gown for a baby. And a baby's small booties. The girls sat on the floor and exchanged these items wordlessly between them, piecing together the man's past, trying to create a story out of it that would make sense, that would draw him more clearly in their minds.

Had he bought these clothes for them—Jane and Della—and the baby's clothing as well, for the children to which they would soon give birth? They did not believe he had done this, but said it only to practice, to begin, a line of speculation. The clothes were old, threadbare. Motheaten. Another possibility, of course, was that the clothes belonged to another girl, a girl who had been there before them. They took turns holding up the dress before them and did not look at each other. Did not wish to believe that it was so. For the girl who wore those clothes no longer existed, they were sure of that. You do not save the clothes of a person who has simply gone away.

They laid the girl's dress on the dining room table. They discussed where to put the other items—the girl's boots among the man's own in his closet, the laces of the baby booties tied and hanging from the same nail as the picture calendar—but in the end the dress laid out on the table was enough, they thought, to let him know they had seen his secret.

It was just before dusk when he arrived home again. He had been to town. The girls were situated in their apricot tree, facing the cabin this time instead of looking out over the field. They wanted to see his reaction. He led the mule and wagon to the barn and then he was there a long time. It was full dusk when he crossed the grass to the cabin. There was a flare in the window as he lit the lantern.

The door of the cabin stood open and they waited for the activity and the odor that accompanied the preparation of their evening meal. It did not come.

Jane scratched her calf in the tree. They were both very hungry, and disappointed about the food. But it was worth it. Now he knew they were paying attention.

A ND THEN THERE was a strange movement from deep inside Della, a sort of turning.

It was morning. Jane, who had gone to vomit a little ways off, behind the outhouse beyond the shed, made her way back to Della now. The sight of Della in pain provoked Jane's own sickness, and thinking that Della was suffering too from nausea—she was not—Jane gathered Della's hair hanging over one shoulder and twisted it in her hand, and bent slightly, to support Della if she needed to retch. That movement—that gathering up of the hair in her fist, and leaning close—reminded Della of their mother, who did the same thing when they were sick as small children.

Earlier, before the sun rose—or maybe it was still night, because the stars were out—Della woke on her back with a terrible tightening in her belly. Lay breathing shallowly until the pain was too great and she attempted to roll onto her side, but could not. She kicked Jane until Jane rose and finally realized Della's trouble. Jane's face looming above hers, concerned.

What is it?

I don't know—

The pain, instead of increasing throughout the day, waned. By evening she felt better than she had for a long time, clearheaded, even a little giddy, her body loose and limber as if she had run a great race.

The woman, Caroline Middey, came into the orchard that afternoon. She and the man sat up on the porch now. The evening was not yet dark enough to warrant the lanterns.

Caroline Middey had come into the orchard once before. She had walked in the orchard alone while the man worked elsewhere, and tried to get the girls to come to her. She called to them, even if she could not see them. She sensed they were near. She stalked the orchard, walking slowly, holding her skirts up out of the grass.

You come to the cabin, she called, and let me have a look at you. Let me have a look at your babies. No one's going to hurt you, here, there's no need to be afraid—

They would not come to her, but she had anticipated this and finally pulled from her front skirt pockets wrapped pieces of toffee, and called: I have candy here, I have toffee, I've got—let's see—the hard kind you can suck, and I've got the soft kind, like a caramel, like a butter caramel. And at that Della broke out into a sweat—toffee!—and when she started forward, Jane grabbed her arm. They could see the woman from where they crouched in the grass. Finally Della broke free and came forward, came up quietly behind Caroline Middey so that the woman turned suddenly, and said, Oh! There you are—

The two girls would not go into the cabin to be examined, and so Caroline Middey made them lie on a table—an enormous twine spool set on its end—in the shade at the side of the cabin. It was where the man sometimes worked on his tree projects. Della lay now on her back, her dress up around her armpits, sucking a toffee and looking distractedly at the sky.

Men had been their most common tormentors, but there had been women too. Before Michaelson there was Louisa Glassley, "Miss Weeza," the director of the girls at the camp in Tacoma—the first place the girls were sent after their mother died—who laughingly said, when Jane at first complained about what was happening to them: You'll get used to it. That was the only woman in charge, but there were others, other older women at the camps who resented the younger girls and would spite them, hurt them, at every possibility. Jane, who was a favorite among the men, went to put on a pair of good boots for the evening entertainment, only to have her foot meet shit. She recoiled, and the women, who were waiting in the wings, peering around the doorway, screamed with laughter. Other times it was the casual beating that disguised itself as rough-housing, teasing, playful fighting. *Come on, love, you can do better than that! What do you do when he tries to—* And then more screaming laughter.

Della glanced several times into the older woman's face and saw large gray eyes, fine hair on her upper lip. A large flesh-colored mole on her cheek with a perfect brown hair coming out of it.

I have no doubt that is most likely the case, said Caroline Middey now, to the man, on the porch. Jane and Della lay in the shadows along the side of the cabin. Caroline Middey had brought them a small black kitten, and now the animal crouched on Della's chest, Della's fingers threaded over its spine. The kitten stared at her with china blue eyes.

Hush, said Jane, although Della was not conscious that she was making noise. She, Jane, was trying to hear what they were saying on the porch. Della was interested in the conversation only in theory. What absorbed her was the tiny creature on her chest, staring at her so intently. It had two white front paws. Wasn't that something? Like he stepped in milk! How did— Hush! said Jane, sharper now, and Della at once heard herself, the end of it, cut off, cooing to the kitten.

There was the sound of rustling in the leagues of the orchard, the wind in the moist leaves. Combing the long grass. The moon was revealed and obscured by the leaves above their heads. Inside of this soft noise certain words were carried around the side of the cabin, certain words spoken by Caroline Middey. The man said something, but it was a murmuring too low to understand. He went on for a long time, a considerable amount of time for him. At the end of it he cleared his throat, which they could hear distinctly. Caroline Middey said something, briefly, and then it was quiet. The wind had died down.

That's what I would do, anyway, said Caroline Middey.

Della knew that they were discussing her and Jane. Of course that was why the woman traveled all the way out there. To give them the kitten, yes, but also to confer with the man. He had been gone for three days earlier in the week. He had left food for them in the cold pantry, wrapped up, for them to eat when he was gone. He had stood on the lawn and called to them where they sat in the high grass that he was going on a trip, he had left food for them, they should feel free to eat that and whatever else they liked. He would be back in a few days.

The wind came again, and Jane shifted beside her. The cat startled, and Della brought the creature up into her neck and held it there. It struggled for a moment and then began to pant and purr at once.

Stop it, said Jane, watching her. You're hurting it. It can't breathe.

The adults continued talking. Della relaxed into half sleep. The cat had gone, escaped. Jane beside her was tired, but she held herself awake, listening. Della thought of the cat bounding away into the orchard—the action to her was comical—and, startling awake, laughed suddenly and loudly. The two voices on the porch ceased abruptly, and Jane clapped her hand on Della's mouth and leaned over her, breathing into her ear. Only when the voices resumed did Jane lean back, relax, resettle into the grass.

The cat, said Della after several minutes, waking again. Without understanding why, she had begun to cry.

We'll get it tomorrow, said Jane. Hush now. Go to sleep.

Della continued to cry until she discovered that the voices on the porch were conspiring with the moon and the stars through the trees, and the wind that covered it all, and those powers knew where the kitten moved in the orchard and would inform her, if she just went to sleep, of its location the first thing in the morning. All that was required of her was to sleep. And so she did. At once, suddenly, as if stepping off a cliff.

It was Jane who intuited when the elements—human and otherwise—shifted around them and were no longer amenable to their presence, and who determined when they should linger, and when they should flee. She had told Della months before their departure from Michaelson's that they were going to escape. How? Della had asked, but Jane had just shaken her head, as if to say that that was not the right time to speak of it. And it was a wonder she told Della at all, because the girl was known to leak things—information, stories, and rarely but horrifyingly, *feelings*—like a cracked kettle. But this information about their escape she kept quiet. Nothing came out of her during times with the other girls—during meals, or settling down to sleep—which was remarkable, for she was filled with the urge at times, she did not know why, to dazzle them, the other girls, with a story, or a joke—to make them appreciate her perhaps, or even envy her intelligence, her wealth of stories: her cleverness. But she thought about what Jane had said and knew this information was different; it could not be shared, no matter how much Della wanted to be liked. And she knew her sister would do it: plan their escape. It was as good as fact: she and Jane would escape from that place. When would it happen? Jane would let her know. She was waiting for the right time. Timing, according to Jane, was everything.

Caroline Middey left the orchard, promising to return at the week's end to check up on them. Two days later, when the man went to town, Jane and Della entered the cabin again and went through his things. Della did not know what they were looking for, but this looking through his things had a different feel to it; it was not like the other times when they entered the cabin out of boredom or simple curiosity, this had the feeling of a mission about it.

In an old cigar box atop the bureau in his bedroom—the box was full of odds and ends: old coins, buttons, pins, screws, bits of twine and colored thread—Jane found a folded piece of paper that had her and Della's names on it, and Michaelson's. She could not tell what it said other than that, but it was enough. They had to leave, said Jane, and Della nodded, absently. She was wondering if he'd left them any food in the cold pantry, even though he said he would be back by evening. She wondered also if he was bringing any sweets from town.

Jane packed some food in a burlap sack, and then they were in the woods, walking. Jane kept looking over her shoulder as if expecting the man to appear suddenly with the mule and wagon. Della wanted to laugh. It was like a game. Surely she and Jane would return by nightfall, because he would have cooked them something to eat. Surely they were not really going away! Jane was playing a game. But they kept walking, and by late afternoon Della was hot and dizzy and empty—alarmingly empty—and wanted to rest. Where was the creek? Where had the creek gone? Jane said she didn't know where the water was. They had forgotten to bring a container of water to drink from. Now they had to go back. But Jane seemed not to hear her when Della said this. I need to lie down, said Della, and then in a high, helpless voice: I'm going to be sick. And she went into a grove of trees—cedars—and fell immediately asleep. When she woke, her cheek was in the dirt and she was retching, and pushing, and something hot and wet was coming out of her buttocks. She tried to call for Jane, but she was too weak. She wept onto her folded arms.

And then she was asleep again, and when she woke it was the morning of another day and her arm was around Jane's neck and they were moving slowly through the trees. I'm sick, said Della. Yes, said Jane. Della turned and looked at her sister's face and saw that it was raw from crying.

She was immediately again asleep. When she woke she was not moving but lying on her back. The world was slowly spinning. There was a face of an Indian looming above her. She was very hot. She tried to say something to him—to ask for water—but her mouth wasn't working, it felt stuffed with a rag.

When she woke again she was in a room slightly familiar to her. But she could not place it. It was night, the windows were dark. There was Jane on a bed above her—Della for some reason was on the floor, on a mat—and Jane was stripped of clothing but for an undershirt, and she was crying.

It's happening, thought Della. It is all happening again.

And then Caroline Middey entered the room. It seemed she was coming to Della from far away. The old woman approached her and leaned over her and said, in a voice also muffled and far away: It's going to be all right, dear. The worst is almost over—

I N TOWN, AT market, Talmadge accepted samples of gooseberries, tufts
of bread. He did not leave immediately, as was his custom, but toured
the stalls. He bought an onion loaf, and a handful of aniseed to make into
a pudding a woman recommended. He bent over a scrap of paper, writing instructions given by different women, translated by his hand into
pictographs and bundles of sticks, undecipherable to all but him.

Potatoes, molasses, cheddar cheese. Cream, and a silver tin to store it in.

When he arrived at dusk the girls were not at the base of the apricot
tree or in the plum orchard, where they sometimes squatted in the grass,
watching him work. He waited on the porch, anticipating their forms
separating from the trees. The water, full and reckless in the creek, was
loud in his ears.

He hiked to the upper cabin, holding a lantern before him. In his
pockets were biscuits and bacon wrapped in thin cotton towels. Perhaps
one of them had given birth, he thought, but then he thought: No. For
some reason he thought he would intuit when one gave birth. And it was
not the right time for it yet.

He arrived and found the upper cabin empty. He stood in the en-
tranceway, looking at the leaf-filled sacks, the lantern light shuddering
on the fine-grained walls.

Two days later, in the afternoon, the men arrived with the horses.
Talmadge went down to speak to Clee, but Clee wasn't among them.
Talmadge questioned one of the men, who told him that Clee and the
wrangler—another one of the men, a Cayuse—had stopped to help some
travelers. A person who was sick. The man shrugged.

Talmadge returned to the porch and waited.

Clee and the wrangler arrived in the orchard at dusk. Talmadge went down into the field to meet them. Clee, atop one horse, held the younger girl, who appeared unconscious; atop the other horse, led by the wrangler, was the older girl, wide-awake and alert.

They stopped at the creek. Clee delivered the younger girl—dirt- and blood-smudged, half conscious—down to the wrangler. The wrangler was unnaturally small of stature, and the girl's form dwarfed him. The other girl would not be helped—she raised her arms and made a hissing sound when Talmadge held out his arm to her. She attempted to dismount by herself. As she struggled, sliding off the horse, he held up his arms to brace her but she turned, holding herself up by the pommel, and struck him in the face. He shied away, held his nose. Clee grabbed hold of her and dragged her from the horse. She howled in anguish. Talmadge spoke gruffly from beneath his hand to let her go, and Clee let her go. She leaped away from them and spun around, feinted back. Turned in wide arcs, kicking the dirt. Murmured some unintelligible, breathless story out the side of her mouth. She had the surprised look of wanting to run; but there was the girl unconscious over the wrangler's shoulder; there was that. Talmadge held his nose and then took his hand away and looked at it, wiped his hand on his thigh. He went to the wrangler and the man delivered the girl to him. Talmadge jumped a little to resettle the weight and started for the cabin. The men hesitated, not knowing if they should follow him or not.

The other girl, furious, bewildered, covered her face with her hands. A moment later she kicked the dirt, followed Talmadge to the cabin.

Inside the cabin he tried to enter his own bedroom with the unconscious girl but the other girl objected to this, she wailed high in the back of her throat as soon as he went into the room, she would not follow him. And so he entered the other room, which he had not set foot in for several months—he did not visit it except to air it out every three months or so—and laid the girl down on the bare mattress. It was dusty in the room, and cold. The other girl did not object, but stole into the room behind him. He thought he should take the girl's clothes off her, they were filthy.

But he could not imagine such an act, could not imagine going through with something like that, especially with the other one watching. He left them, went to the porch, and told Clee and the wrangler, who stood waiting on the grass, that someone would have to go fetch Caroline Middey. The wrangler said immediately that he would do it, and turned and started down the hill for a horse.

Talmadge and Clee exchanged glances; then Talmadge turned and reentered the cabin.

He removed his hat before stepping into the room. The older girl sat on the edge of the bed, clutched the other girl's wrist. Protective. She looked up at him as he came in, aimed her gaze over his shoulder.

After a few moments of silence, Talmadge cleared his throat and said: Caroline Middey's coming. She'll come right away; she'll know what to do.

The girl looked back at her sister on the bed, who, though apparently asleep, had an agonized expression on her face.

The older girl said quietly, still gazing at her sister: She'll be all right. Then: It's just happening, is all. There was a moment where it seemed she would continue—she had more to say—but then she let the moment pass, was silent.

He hesitated. We should get those clothes off her—

And then the girl looked at him. The quality of her gaze did not change—she still looked through him—and while her face appeared to relax, he recognized it as a hardness: her eyes became slightly hooded, her nostrils dilated. She gripped the mattress edge, as if to brace herself. Her voice when it came out of her was hard as steel.

You touch her, she said, and I'll kill you.

Clee, sitting in the birchwood chair, turned his head to look at Talmadge—a very slight raising of the eyebrows, an appraisal: What is happening? You know them?

I don't know them, said Talmadge, and sat down in the opposite chair. He took off his hat and then put it back on again. A gesture of frustration, weariness. It was early evening, but darkness had not drowned out all objects: the hides of the horses shifted below, and the sky, far above, was still pale. It was quiet—too quiet, Talmadge thought—in the cabin at his back. But the girl would not speak to him; she would not let him close to examine her sister; and so he decided to leave them alone for a time.

He accepted the pipe Clee lit for him now, and after pulling on it briefly, he told the story: how the girls had come into the orchard, and he had been watching out for them; how they were wanted by a man—their father, maybe, he didn't know, but a strange and violent criminal—who lived north of Ruby City, up on the Okanogan. The man had already been to town, looking for them. I thought I'd help them until they had their babies, Talmadge said—surprising himself, for this was the first time he had heard himself articulate such a plan—and then they can be on their way. If they want. It's not proper, he said after a silence, for a girl to give birth in the forest. Without a woman's help, he added.

Clee had brought out his pipe and sat smoking while Talmadge talked. After a minute he took a few brief pulls and then set the pipe on his knee to rest.

I wish she'd come, said Talmadge suddenly, and his voice seemed loud, and startled.

When Clee had found the younger girl, he thought she was dead. He brought the pipe to his mouth. He thought she was dead but she was not dead. Not dead on the ground when he leaned over her and put his hand into the sweltering crevice of her neck, to check for a pulse. The other girl speechless from fear and anger beside her. She was not dead then, and not dead sitting before Clee on the horse, the long ride back to the orchard. The men guiding the horses carefully across the landscape, as if the girls were made of glass. Not dead when the wrangler took her down from the horse; not dead when Talmadge took her next upon his shoulder. Through this all, she was vital, though crouched down near, and hovering over, death. Perhaps feeding on it to stay alive. There were people like that, he knew: they existed. This one was one bright nerve. Once, before he had taken her up on his horse, when she still lay in the hot wheat, she had opened her eyes and taken him in. The black eyes burning: and in them no insanity but the insanity to live: the pure animal will decked with human desire. This one was too fierce to die. The girl will not die in that room, he wanted to tell Talmadge now. He had read in her eyes, in the riddle of her face, that she would not die in that room. Although, he thought ruefully—taking the pipe from his mouth and knocking its bottom, gently, on his palm—he had assumed events according to such intuition before, and had been turned on his head. And remembering such slights, such crimes, a challenge was erected suddenly between him and the outside air, though he sensed the futility of such a challenge: the girl would die tonight, or she would not. Let the night do its work: he defied it to take her.

I wish she'd come, said Talmadge, again, of the old midwife, as if he had forgotten he had said it the first time; and Clee wanted to say: It does not matter when the woman comes. The night has made up its mind. It's we who are too slow, who move in the wake of events already decided for us, who refuse, who are too weak or too simple, or are perhaps, strictly, *unable* to understand—

Caroline Middey arrived after midnight. Talmadge stood at the pasture edge, holding a lantern aloft, watching for the horses he sensed, minutes before, were coming. The wrangler's horse materialized first out of the darkness—a suggestion of a form and then a form—and then another horse appeared in its wake. Atop this horse sat Caroline Middey. She wore a large straw hat and was wrapped in a blanket so she resembled some sort of doll. She wore a severe expression, and Talmadge thought, as he helped her down off the horse, that she was angry; but, firmly planted on the ground, looming and sharp-featured in the lantern light, she removed the blanket from around her shoulders and handed it to him, and untied the ribbon from under her chin, took off her hat, and grinned. I don't know the last time I took a ride like that, she said. And then she turned to unstrap her bag from the side of the horse. When she turned to him again, she was serious.

Where are they?

Inside.

They walked to the cabin, shadows bounding before them. Down in the field, the men had lit fires. The horses spread to the forest, shifting and reshifting under the moonlight.

Caroline Middey took this all in.

There was a young man waiting on the porch steps who took Caroline Middey's horse and led him to the barn.

Talmadge hesitated on the porch.

What is it? said Caroline Middey.

I ought to stay out here.

And why's that?

Again he hesitated. They don't like me.

Caroline Middey snorted. She looked at him now. For a moment it seemed she would argue with him, but she did not.

I'm going to need you, she said. You can stay out here, if you want, but don't go far. She hesitated again, as if she wanted to say something—but then she said nothing. Regarded him briefly one last time before going indoors.

He sat in the birchwood chair. Leaned forward with his elbows on his knees. His stomach was empty, lightly convulsed. His head ached. He could not remember the last time he had eaten.

Caroline Middey returned soon afterward, and he stood. How much time had passed? It might have been only a few minutes, it might have been an hour. Her gaze took a moment to realize him.

You didn't say both of them were laboring.

He started.

I didn't know it had anything to do with laboring, he said finally. Just the one was sick, I thought, just the one was having trouble.

Caroline Middey shook her head.

What, he said.

Both of them are laboring, she said. It's started, now. She frowned down at the lawn off the porch. Heat some water. I need something for my tools if it comes to that. And you got some towels?

He was silent, wondering at it all.

Talmadge.

Yes. A few. I got some quilts.

It'll ruin your quilts.

Don't matter.

I'm talking about some animal blankets or such as that.

I got some in the barn.

Get those. And get towels.

Later in the cabin he poured water from buckets into a pot on the stove and then opened the stove and stoked the fire within. The door to the bedroom where they lay was shut. There were at times brief mur-murings behind the door but for the most part it was silent. Was this how it all went, he thought, in quietness like this? He thought he would have to go gather more firewood from the barn, but when he went out onto the porch he saw a pile of kindling and logs had been stacked near the door.

He went and sat in the birchwood chair, downtilted his hat over his eyes.

When he woke—he had not realized he had slept—it was still night, black-dark and motionless. Caroline Middey sat before him on the porch steps, smoking a sweet-smelling cigarette. The lantern glowed still be-tween them. A rabbit at the mouth of the apricot orchard froze, its eyes catching in the lantern light, and then bounded away down the avenue of trees.

Talmadge cleared his throat. Are they—

Caroline Middey glanced over her shoulder at him. She turned for-ward again, flicked ash off the side of the porch.

They're all right for now, she said. Then, several minutes later, glanc-ing at him again: You still planning on looking out for them, after all this is finished?

Talmadge looked at the field below, the remaining fires winking in the dark. The horses, stirring slowly. Marauders. He said nothing at first.

I reckon I would help them if they needed it.

Caroline Middey frowned out at the darkness. They're going to need it, all right.

He said nothing.

After a while she crushed out her cigarette and said, Well— and stood. Placed her hand on his shoulder as she passed him, went indoors.

———

The morning was bright. Down in the field the horses grazed and the men picked fruit, their bodies appearing and disappearing among the foliage.

Talmadge waited on the porch for Caroline Middey. When she came through the doorway, she blinked rapidly in the light.

Well? he said.

She blinked. From within her skirts she pulled out a cigarette she had rolled earlier, put it between her lips, and lit it with a match from the same pocket. Moved slightly on the porch, as if disoriented. The older one will have hers tonight, she said. But the other one. She paused, glanced out across the grass. The other one's baby died. Or one of them. Yes, there were two. That's what I think. She hesitated. Yes, that's what I think. What I think happened is that she passed one some days ago, but there's still the rest that needs to come out. Either that, or she hasn't passed either baby at all. I asked her about it, asked her when she stopped feeling it. Poor thing doesn't know. Caroline Middey smoked and then smiled, but it wasn't meant to be a smile. Going to have to go through it anyway, bearing that thing out of her, whatever it is. But it ain't going to be no live baby, whatever it is. She smiled again the smile that wasn't a smile, and rubbed her eye with the heel of her hand and continued smoking. She looked out over the bright yellow field. Lord, she said.

Talmadge didn't know what to say. He too looked out over the field. What happened to it? he said finally.

I don't know. After a moment, she said: I could be wrong. But from her voice, Talmadge knew she was saying it for his sake.

Is she going to—die?

Caroline Middey looked at him quickly. Who, the girl?

Talmadge didn't say anything.

They ain't but little girls, both of them. But the body will do what it will, unless it just can't. She was going to say more but then she didn't. She smoked and looked out at the field. Lord, look at those horses, she said.

At dusk, the fires glowed at the edge of the field and the men stood around eating their supper in the firelight. At intervals there came from the cabin a strangled cry, not of the baby but of the mother before the baby, where she doesn't want to make sounds but cannot help herself. Talmadge sat waiting on the porch, his hat in his hands. The cries subsided, and then rose. Finally Caroline Middey came to the door and said his name.

He stood and went inside the cabin.

The bedroom was lit by a single lantern on the bedside table, turned high. The center of the room, in contrast with the outer darkness, was bright.

The older girl, sitting up in the bed, looked away when he entered the room.

The other girl lay on a pallet on the floor. Like her sister, she wore only an undershirt, and her body shone with sweat. Her stomach ballooned before her. She held her fists over her eyes, and shook: a fine, constant tremor.

The room bristled with heat, smelled of iron. He took off his hat.

In the intense light the skin around Caroline Middey's eyes was bruised-looking. She crouched beside the girl on the floor. To Talmadge she said: I don't know how much longer it'll be with that one—nodding to the girl on the bed—but this one I have to help quick. She stroked the girl's head. I think I might have to pump it out of her.

Talmadge was speechless.

I want you here if I need help. This here is Della. That's Jane.

Jane was watching him. When he looked at her, she turned her head carefully away.

You sit down there, said Caroline Middey, indicating the bed. In a few minutes I'll want her to start pushing, and you put your hands—there—on her legs to help her.

Talmadge went to the bed. When he sat down, Jane pressed her lips together. On the floor, Della began to moan.

Caroline Middey stood over Della now, had reached under her and was kneading her back. The older woman's face was reddening from exertion. She looked over to Jane. Lie back a little, she said. Just like I told you. Talmadge—make her lie on her back. Hold her down.

Talmadge hesitated. Lie back, he said.

The hair at Jane's temples was wet, and her eyes, for a moment, were pleading. He felt as if she was going to say something to him. And then all at once she bent to the side and gagged. He wanted to help her; but he knew better than to touch her before he had to. A moment later she lifted her body, wiped her mouth, and eased back against the headboard. Her eyes closed.

That's it, murmured Caroline Middey. Looking up: Move forward, Talmadge. Take her legs, there—

Jane let him touch her, for a moment. But then she placed her hands on his hands and removed them. Batted his hand away when he reached out again.

You have to take hold of her, Talmadge, said Caroline Middey. And then, raising her voice: You have to put your hands on her—

Jane pushed his hand away.

Jane! admonished Caroline Middey.

Jane opened her mouth and wailed—high, pleading—and directed her gaze over Talmadge's shoulder.

In an instant Caroline Middey stood and reached over the bed and took hold of the girl's shoulders and straightened her. You push! she said into the girl's face. Jane twisted within her grasp, and Caroline Middey shook her. To Talmadge, angrily: You hold her down, do as I say! This ain't going to take all night if I can help it. When Talmadge hesitated, she took hold of his hands and placed them on the girl's thighs. Hold there! She squeezed Talmadge's hands, which in turn squeezed the girl's thighs.

Jane pushed back against the wall, her eyes wide and helpless.

Now push! said Caroline Middey. Push up against the wall if you need to! Talmadge will hold you—

Jane bent to the side again, gagged.

All right, said Caroline Middey, crouching down. It's going to be all right, dear, she said to Della. You just do as I say and you'll be all right.

Every few minutes, Talmadge looked over to Caroline Middey and the girl on the pallet. Caroline Middey stood over her and massaged her stomach from above. The girl cried open-throated and low. It was a terrible sound. There were moments in the room when it was completely silent, and then it was raging with noise of the girls' separate pain. Jane half sat up, straining against the headboard. She pushed with her feet against

Talmadge's thighs, her toes curling with effort. She held his forearms. When necessary, he leaned back, away from her, to counter the force. She rocked in that position, and they bore against each other. When the head of the baby crowned Jane's vagina, the girl's hair was wet with sweat and the sheet beneath her was bright with red blood.

Mama, Della cried. Mama! The makeshift bed beneath her was black.

Hush! said Caroline Middey. Looking over to Jane: Push!

The girl pushed.

Caroline Middey looked over to the crowning head. She squinted. You're going to have to handle it, she said to Talmadge.

What, he said.

You're going to have to take hold of it gentlelike and help it out. Raising her voice to Jane: You push, girl! You hear?

Jane let go of his arms. When he released the girl's thighs his handprints lingered in her flesh before fading.

You put your hands in her and get it out! yelled Caroline Middey.

There was nothing else but for him to do it. He put his fingers inside the girl and told her to push the thing out. She gasped and gripped the sides of the bed—her knees wide open—and Caroline Middey echoed his demand: Push! His voice was low and quiet: Push! It was a purple and red mess. The girl struggled, and began to relax.

Talmadge! said Caroline Middey.

He disregarded hurting her for one graceless moment and put his hands inside her up to the wrists and she screamed and he dug in farther and felt the shoulders of the thing and he pulled on them not harshly but not gently either. God damn it, he said. God damn it. When the shoulders were out, the little beast turned its body toward its mother's thigh. The girl grabbed her knees and yanked them apart and in one shivering closed-mouthed cry pushed the body from her own.

There! called Caroline Middey. But her voice to Talmadge was far away.

That singular movement—a body falling from another body—confused him the moment it occurred. He did not know where he was. He dwelt upon the image of the body—tiny, hot, bloody—in his hands. What was it? Where did it come from? The room oriented itself around it. He cut the umbilicus with his pocketknife and brought the infant close, hooked his finger across its face and into its mouth for the mucus, brought it to his shoulder and slapped its bottom—how did he know to do this?—and the thing screamed in his ear. The room seemed to swell, to pulse; the elapsed time, the snug hours, blossomed grossly. The room had grown increasingly warm and thick with the odor of sickness and birth and it was into this world that Talmadge surfaced. He held the body close and felt that it belonged to the room as much as to the girl and at the same time that it belonged to nobody.

Caroline Middey said, Wash it off.

He stood and left the room.

Outside, it was night, but he made his way to the creek without difficulty.

Beside the water, he knelt and took a handkerchief from his pocket and plunged it beneath the riffle. He wrung out the handkerchief in his fist and situated the infant in the crook of his arm and dabbed at its face. It was a mewling thing, and small. He felt the name on his lips, the name of the thing he could not name, the name that would not come to him. He felt himself approaching it, stuttering over it, not making a sound. He dabbed at its face.

The moonlight on the creek danced and splintered on the surface of the water.

He returned to the cabin. He swaddled the body in a towel and stood before the fire. For a moment he hesitated as the confusion flared: Was it animal? He could not name it, the being or the feeling. It passed.

The baby was female.

DELLA STOOD FULLY dressed at the edge of the apricot orchard and looked down into the field. It was morning. She leaned on a walking stick. The horses had been there—when she lay in bed she could hear them through the open window—but now they were gone. Talmadge said that any day now, however, they would return, and she would be able to see them, if she wanted to.

She walked into the apricot orchard and when she saw Talmadge in the tree—his legs were visible, he was up on the ladder—she did not crouch down the row from him but went straight to the ladder and looked up. After a few moments he recognized her presence and looked down at her. His face was flushed and sweating, framed by branches. He was wearing the floppy calfskin hat. Are you hungry? he asked her, uneasy, and she didn't answer, but moved away from the ladder, continued down the row. What was she looking for?

Later, in the cabin, she sat on the edge of the bed and Caroline Middey showed her and Jane again how to feed the child. Della unbuttoned her dress to the waist and came out of her sleeves and so sat with her whole torso bared. It was easiest that way. Caroline Middey gave her the infant and showed her how to hold the child, how to brush the nipple against its mouth, how to situate the child once it started feeding.

But like the time before, the child would not take Della's nipple. They tried for several minutes and then Caroline Middey took the child and gave her back to Jane, whose nipple the infant greedily took into her mouth. Jane drew her face close to the infant's skull, her eyes wide.

It's early yet, said Caroline Middey. We'll keep trying. The little one has to learn she has two mothers.

And then Della leaned into Caroline Middey—her forehead pressed against the older woman's shoulder—while she took Della's breast in her hand and proceeded to milk it. The milk drained into a cup below. Della tried very hard not to, but she cried. The room was very quiet except for the sound of this weeping and the sound of the child feeding.

A T THE CAFÉ where Talmadge had gone again to sell fruit, Weems came up behind him as he sat eating at the counter, and placed a hand on his shoulder.

Talmadge craned his neck to look up at him.

Did that Michaelson fellow find you? said Weems. He was here a couple days ago, looking. And Weems's eyes, which had been merry—with nervousness, maybe, concern—became sober, almost sad. The townspeople who knew anything were keeping quiet, he said. But you know how that goes. He smiled again that sad, reticent smile. You might have some trouble on your hands. That man isn't in his right mind—

Talmadge asked Caroline Middey if he was doing the right thing, letting the girls stay with him, or if she thought he should find a better place for them. Caroline Middey had been thinking about it all, of course, but had just been waiting for him to ask her. She told him that he should at least apprise the sheriff of their situation, that it was possible they might all be in some danger.

He told her she was right. But he did not talk to the sheriff. What if there was some law of which he and Caroline Middey were ignorant, that judged the girls, and the baby, as Michaelson's property? It was preposterous, and immoral, but there were immoral laws out there, he knew. And what if he had broken a law in fostering the girls? What if, in contacting the authorities, he inadvertently made things worse? He sensed looming trouble, but could not verify its shape. He would wait and see; he would ask the Judge about it, maybe.

He knew that he should be careful, he should be clearheaded and strategic more than ever, but he felt, those first few weeks after the child's birth, as if he could not concentrate, as if he was living in a dream.

He was startled, now, coming up through the apricot orchard, to see the cabin vivid with moving forms; girl-shapes floating past the windows, the chimney perpetually exuding thick smoke. Caroline Middey beating rugs on the porch, her voice moving like a constant chord over the lawn, some objects absorbing, and others reflecting, her voice. Sounds moving over the planes of wood of the cabin and porch. And above and below all this was the sound of the child's cries, hovering in the trees, seeming to come from all directions at once. Was it a comfort? It was all new—the company, the sounds—but also he felt as if it had been going on for a long time. He was, he thought—and was shocked at this discovery—happy.

DELLA LAY BESIDE Jane, who was sleeping turned to the wall. The door of the room was open, and Talmadge and Caroline Middey sat out in the front room and talked. They had left the door of the cabin open out of sympathy toward the girls, since they—the girls—were not allowed to go outside the cabin after nightfall. They must stay indoors now, they must rest. With the door open, perhaps it was not so bad. An hour ago Caroline Middey had examined Della and applied ointment to the stitches. Della was to lie still and not move.

And what if the stitches tear? Della had asked her.

Well, it would be unpleasant, said Caroline Middey. There was a risk of infection, besides. And what was infection? Della had wanted to know, but had not asked.

Jane? whispered Della now, but Jane did not answer.

The night air came through the cabin door and crossed the threshold of the outer room and reached the bedroom where she lay, her face turned to it. She could see the darkness off the porch. The air was cool, with an edge of cold, even. She could hear but not see the trembling leaves.

Again there was the murmuring back and forth of the two adults, punctuated by one word or a string of words spoken louder than the others, or Talmadge clearing his throat. Spans of long silence. A sigh, a single sentence. Talmadge crossed the room to stoke the fire in the woodstove. There was the sound of the upset heat and embers and then the creak as the stove door was closed. Talmadge cleared his throat, returned to sit.

Della rose and put her feet over the side of the bed. There was a tightened feeling, a deep itch, where the stitches were, and she wanted to laugh and cry. She stood and went into the other room where they were, and they both stopped speaking and turned to her.

What is it, dear? said Caroline Middey.

Della stood near the table. She had come to get something. Had she been sleeping? Was this all a dream?

Della?

She went over to where they sat. Between them lay the sleeping child, stomach-down on a folded quilt. An ogreish-looking thing. Della was still amazed that it had come from the inside of Jane. No one had told them exactly how it would work. And yet Jane had known, somehow. They were blessed, said Jane; they were going to give birth to themselves. It would be themselves they gave birth to, only better. That was why she and Della must work so hard to protect them, their children. In protecting the children Jane and Della would also (Jane explained this over and over again) save themselves—

Della took up the child awkwardly and put her against her shoulder. The gentle snuffling, the warm weight. Hush, said Della, jostling her. Hush. Talmadge and Caroline Middey watched her silently. Warily. She turned and walked to the open door and stood looking out into the night and then turned, went to the woodstove. There was a slow and penetrating heat coming from it. With one hand she took the leather mitt and put it over the handle and opened the door.

What are you doing, dear, said Caroline Middey now, and both she and Talmadge rose. But they did not come forward, not yet.

What do you want? said Caroline Middey. We'll get it for you. Are you hungry? Are you cold?

Jane appeared in the doorway of the bedroom, her eyes small with sleep. She glanced at Della and then looked out the open door, into the night. After a moment she came forward and took the child from Della, who resisted her only momentarily, then shuffled back into the bedroom. Shut the door.

Della, her arms suddenly empty, stood and stared into the orange heat.

Caroline Middey came and closed the stove door. Her hand rested on Della's shoulder. They tried to talk to her a few minutes more, but then Caroline Middey gave her a mug with a little brandy in it and she drank it and Caroline Middey put her back to bed.

Don't close the door, murmured Della.

We won't.

No, I mean the other one, the other one. Keep it open.

All right, dear, we will. We'll keep it open. You go to sleep now.

Yes.

TALMADGE WALKED THE apricot orchard, slowly, looking at the trees, which appeared the epitome of health. The bright fruit. His hands, reaching up to feel the branches, surprised him. Had he always had hands like this, red and splotched? Was he really so old? The bark beneath his thumb was gray and ridged; he rubbed it several times before he took his hand away.

In the weeks following the child's birth, he felt a precarious weight in his stomach. Instead of feeling relieved, as he had expected to feel—the girls had given birth, and it was terrible, but it was over, and neither of them had perished—he felt as if he had forgotten something. It was Michaelson, of course. But Talmadge told himself that Michaelson would not find them; even if one of the townspeople did surrender the information of his whereabouts, the orchard was tucked far back into the foothills, hard to access if you did not understand the roads or the lay of the land. But nevertheless he could not avoid the feeling of deep unease; it would not leave him. He did not tell Caroline Middey about it, but suffered alone, thinking it would pass.

Two days after Caroline Middey left, he woke to his room full of light. The baby was crying. He sat up, confused. Della stood in the doorway of his bedroom. She had reached out her hands to brace herself within the doorframe, placed one bare foot on top of the other, and gazed at the corner of the bed.

Jane told me to come get it, she said, of the child, who lay beside him. It took him a moment to remember what she, the infant, was doing there. And then it came to him: she had fussed in the middle of the night, and neither girl had roused to tend her, and so he had brought her into his own bedroom, and fallen asleep as she cried. Still confused, Talmadge understood that Della would not cross over into the room to retrieve the baby. And so he lifted the child and delivered her to the waiting girl, who retreated with the child into the other bedroom. Slammed the door—carelessly—behind her.

In the outer room he opened the door of the woodstove and stoked the cold ashes. He could not believe the brightness of the day; he had overslept. Before he reached for the matchbox, he had a moment of disorientation. As he leaned to light the stove, he felt, suddenly, a wetness on his mouth, and reached up and touched his face. Blood. His nose was bleeding.

The door of the other bedroom opened and Della stood looking out at him. Expectantly, as if he had called her. Talmadge saw behind her to Jane in the bed, the infant nursing at her breast. Jane looked at him, frowning slightly. But it was also as if she did not see him: was deeply absorbed by some thought or memory, and his sudden presence—his trouble—was an irritation.

It's all right, said Talmadge, thinking they would be spooked by the blood. His voice shook (but why?). It's all right.

I sn't it market day? said Caroline Middey. She had come at the end of the week to tend to the girls, and that morning noticed Talmadge had not gone into the barn to see about the mule, had not prepared the wagon. She thought maybe she had gotten the day wrong.

But Talmadge, who had worked that morning in the far apple orchard, said he wasn't going to market.

Caroline Middey stared at him. He had not missed a market day for as long as she could remember.

Maybe next week, he said.

WHEN THREE MEN came out of the forest and into the upper pasture, Talmadge got down out of the limbs of the apricot tree in which he worked and went to meet them. He was not expecting anybody. Only when the men were almost in the yard did he recognize Michaelson. Or Michaelson's likeness, for this man had none of the sloth of the other whom Talmadge had met; but there was a certain gravity to this man's movements that still recalled the other. As the man steered his horse through the grass, Talmadge felt his stare upon him, a singular, contained attention aimed at his chest. Talmadge touched his hat as if to remove it but then changed his mind, pulled it lower on his brow. Righted it at the last moment so he could see properly.

All the men had rifles in their scabbards. The man on Michaelson's right was red-haired, sleepy-looking; the other was lean, mean-looking, with deep lines around his eyes and mouth. As Michaelson dismounted, the mean-looking man looked up toward the cabin. When he looked at Talmadge, the man fixed him in one long unintelligible stare before looking away.

Michaelson squinted at Talmadge, briefly, and in that moment Talmadge understood that Michaelson did not know who he was, did not remember him. Talmadge found this extraordinary. There was a moment when Michaelson seemed to consider the possibility of their acquaintance, but he dismissed it, quickly.

Where are my girls? he said. His voice shook with barely contained rage. They in town said you had my girls.

Talmadge wanted to turn and glance across the field, at the canyon mouth, where the girls had taken the baby earlier, to the far apple orchard. He willed that the girls had found a game that would occupy

them, that they would stay there for as long as it took to rid the orchard
of the men.

Michaelson was still staring at him. What was he, Michaelson, capable of? Talmadge again looked at the rifle in the scabbard.

Where are your manners? said the mean-looking man, suddenly, to
Talmadge, and Talmadge looked at him. You have any coffee? Let's take
a load off, boss, he said to Michaelson. I'm thirsty.

Go down and lie in that creek for all I care, said Michaelson, and spat
dramatically to the side. I'm not here for hospitality. Looking again at
Talmadge, his eyes bloodshot and unblinking and, Talmadge could not
help but note, desperate: Where are my girls?

Michaelson, who had seemed so heavy and withered and distracted
that day on the Okanogan, was now filled with nervous energy. He
seemed, suddenly—this entered Talmadge's mind at once—an ancient
adolescent. It was there in his fevered gaze, in his movements as he
shifted from one foot to the other. His zeal and worry.

Talmadge took off his hat, started toward the cabin. He heard the men
follow him: Michaelson on foot, and the other two still on their mounts.
When Talmadge entered the cabin, he heard the saddle creak of the others dismounting. The men, at least, did not follow him inside. He saw
into the girls' room. A pair of small boots by the bed. He put the kettle on
to boil. He went into his own bedroom and opened the closet door, took
his rifle from where it leaned in the corner.

That's not a good idea, said the mean-looking man, who had come in
behind him and stood now in the doorway of his bedroom. Talmadge,
after a moment, replaced the rifle in the closet. The man came close
behind him and made sure the gun was unloaded, and then closed the
closet door.

Talmadge went out and stood before the stove and waited for the
water to boil. Helpless. Every sound was exaggerated: the ticking of
the water in the pot, the shuffle of the men's boots on the wood floor.
The red-haired man had also entered the cabin and was reading the
spines of the almanacs on the shelf. The mean-looking man bent his
knees slightly, studied his image in the mirrorglass hanging on the wall.

Took up the pomade tin, opened it, sniffed. Made a face. Went over to Talmadge at the stove, clapped a hand on his shoulder. I like my coffee strong, he said. The red-haired man went into the girls' room, then came out a minute later. Was holding a pair of underpants. Talmadge felt his body empty of feeling. Talmadge heard the man say, outdoors, to Michaelson: They're not in there. Their stuff is, though. And then high-pitched, hysterical laughter.

Talmadge prepared the coffee, took the mugs out onto the porch.

Here. It was difficult to keep the bitterness from his voice.

The mean-looking man took a mug, and so did the red-haired man, who thanked Talmadge. But Michaelson stood on the lawn, looking out across the field. There were men working there, the haycatchers Talmadge had employed to cut the rest of the grass. They were four of the horsemen who had stayed behind after the rest of the men had gone.

Talmadge stood staring at Michaelson's back. He felt he could read the man's designs there between his shoulder blades. Again he thought: What was the man capable of?

I'm willing to buy them, said Talmadge suddenly. I'm willing to buy them from you, is what I'm saying.

Michaelson turned to him, surprised. Were you talking to me? he said. I know you weren't talking to me.

How much? said the mean-looking man, who was chewing something—a tiny seed?—in his back teeth. He leaned and spat.

Shut up, all of you, said Michaelson. Can't you see I'm trying to listen? And he turned back to the field. According to the posture of the other men, this behavior of Michaelson's—vacillating between bully and idiot—was not unusual. The men stood at different spots on the lawn, drinking coffee. The red-haired man wandered into the apricot orchard, and exited a minute later, eating an apricot.

At that moment two forms in pale dresses came out of the canyon, floating toward them out of the darker mouth.

God in heaven, said Michaelson. Hallelujah. Hallelujah. And then what sounded to Talmadge like the snapping of his jaws. The mean-looking man placed his coffee mug on the ground and went for his rifle, which was leaning up against the porch. Talmadge had not noticed it before. The mean-looking man addressed the red-haired man, who still ate the apricot: What are you doing? Cut that out.

The girls slowed in the middle of the field, stopped. The haycatchers worked around them. It was too far away for the girls to see Michaelson clearly; they must've seen his horses, and the men, who were also regarding them. One girl turned and retreated back to the canyon mouth, but the other remained a moment before coming forward.

Michaelson waved frantically. Can she see us? he said to no one in particular. His voice was high, like a child's. Should we go down there? Is she coming? The mean-looking man scratched the back of his head.

Talmadge moved down the slope, toward the creek. Foolishness for allowing this to happen. How would the girls ever forgive him?

Run, he called to the girl, waving his arms. Get back! Get away!

But the girl—she was halfway across the creek, holding her skirts up out of the water—stood still and watched him. It was as if he were speaking a different language.

Get away! Michaelson was shouting to him. Jane! Jane! Come here! He was laughing, boyishly. The sound sent a chill up Talmadge's spine. Look at you! Jane!

The girl moved past Talmadge and trudged up the hillside. Talmadge, weak with indecision, followed her. Michaelson met her; embraced her. She was like a rag doll in his arms. Jane, he said: part admonition, part sob. Talmadge remained standing several feet behind them, not understanding what was happening, what he should do.

After a minute Michaelson and the girl separated, and she walked through the yard and then up onto the porch, not looking at any of the men, and went into the cabin.

Talmadge stared at the grass of the lawn. Tried to make sense of the gestures, the correspondence that had passed between Michaelson and the girl, but failed. What was happening? Michaelson waited off the porch steps, was just shy of wringing his hands in happiness; the mean-looking man seemed more bored than ever, was looking off toward the plum trees; and the red-haired man was nowhere to be seen. And then

Talmadge saw him, bending creekside, picking up a river rock, inspecting it.

And then Jane came onto the porch, and down onto the lawn. Continued through the grass. Passed Michaelson and the mean-looking man, and Talmadge. Michaelson moved after her, surprised, but she held up her hand to him, and he halted.

I'll be right back—

Where—

I'll be back—and she was striding across the grass, down the hill. The red-haired man lifted a hand to her in greeting but she did not respond. They watched her cross the creek, traverse the field. Eventually she passed into the canyon.

The mean-looking man emitted a low, drowsy whistle. He pulled a cigarette out of his pocket, lit it. Smoked. Eventually he came to stand near Talmadge. Watched the canyon mouth.

That sister, he murmured. That's who she's gone to get, I suppose. I would just as soon leave without that one. But Jane—

Talmadge studied the canyon mouth.

Jane won't allow that. The man cleared his throat, and after a moment took out another cigarette.

Michaelson came to stand near the mean-looking man, a subservient, doglike expression on his face: questioning. Talmadge was surprised Michaelson didn't whimper.

Wait, said the mean-looking man to Michaelson. Then: I say we wait, don't you? Then, lowering his voice so only Talmadge could hear him: It's better to do things peaceable-like. Calm. Without the antics. Things go wrong when there are antics. People say they are just girls, how hard could tracking girls be? He smiled faintly. These people have not had the pleasure, he said, to be in our position—

After a minute the man turned to Talmadge, as if just remembering something.

And the children? Did they—

Talmadge did not take his eyes from the field.

Ah, said the man. After a moment, laughed. Began to say something.

Aren't no children, said Talmadge.

What?

I said there aren't no children—

The man smiled. Oh, I doubt that very much. I doubt that the children have perished. He paused. We'll see soon enough. A baby can't stay hidden, can it?

Talmadge looked at the canyon. It had been more than ten minutes since the girl had gone into the orchard. Maybe they were making an escape, he thought. And then the man said, as if reading his thoughts—

Shall we? He flicked the cigarette away from him. To Talmadge: Will you escort us? Or are we going by ourselves?

They walked across the creek, entered the field. Michaelson waved frantically to the haycatchers—but it was unclear whether it was a greeting or a warning. The haycatchers each in their turn glanced at the men; but Talmadge, in his increasing anxiety, did not know how to regard them. There were four of them: strong, capable men though not all of them young; dark-skinned and oily with sweat, naked to their waists. He caught the eye of one man, Clee's cousin—who was young, in his midtwenties, Talmadge guessed—who stared at him. For a moment the man's eyes were all Talmadge could see. The man did not pause in his work; but then he looked down, and Talmadge looked at the canyon looming ahead of them; and Talmadge willed his and the men's strides to lessen, to gain weight. He willed the feet of the girls to fly; he willed them to float through the air.

Once they entered the canyon mouth, Michaelson skipped ahead, like a demented child.

How far does this go? said the mean-looking man, nodding to the trees. And then, a minute later: You have a regular empire here—

Up ahead was a cry of pain—something between a howl and a moan. It was Michaelson.

Talmadge's heart thudded in him like an overlarge bird trying to overcome its cage. They turned the corner. Michaelson stood beside a towering oak, his head tilted far back, his mouth open. In the tree hung two bodies. One—Jane's—hung still; but Della danced in midair, her feet pedaling, her hands at her neck. Talmadge felt at once his body empty, and also felt that he was floating toward them.

Jesus Christ, said the mean-looking man, who stood next to Talmadge. To the red-haired man, who had gone ahead and gazed up at the girls almost dreamily: What are you doing? Cut them down!

The man stood at the tree's base, looking up. Michaelson shifted his weight from foot to foot, and cried up at the bodies.

How do I— The red-haired man had a soft voice; gestured toward the tree, at a loss.

The mean-looking man too stood at the base of the tree, but found no way to access the trunk, no foothold. He looked up.

Jane! he called. Jane! Damn it!

Talmadge had a scythe in his hand. There was a man beside him, Clee's cousin. He was saying something to Talmadge, but Talmadge didn't understand him. The man took the scythe back and climbed the tree—he shimmied up the trunk, grunting, with the scythe over his shoulder— and crawled out onto each limb and hacked at the ropes by which the girls hung. Della came falling first, and Talmadge half caught her—he had positioned himself under her. He collapsed under her weight, the wind knocked out of him. The sun in his eyes. She snuffled and gagged, grasped his shirtfront. It's all right, he said, holding her. It's all right.

Jane was farther up on the tree. When she came down, Michaelson held open his arms beneath her, but he shied at the last moment, covered his face with his hands. Jane fell before him in a heap.

Talmadge delivered Della to the haycatchers standing by, and went to Jane. Got to his knees. The mean-looking man had not moved, but watched the scene as if observing it from a great distance. Michaelson peeked from between his fingers. Talmadge bent over the body, breathing heavily. He put his ear to her mouth, listened. Waited for breath. There was none, not even a whisper. But for her sake he waited. He sat up finally, gripped her shoulders. He remembered the heat and moisture of the birthing room. The lantern light garish on the walls. Her struggle to give birth to the thing that had grown inside her. Her pain. Her grasping his arms from sheer necessity, because she wanted to live. She had, at that moment, accepted his help. But even then the situation was mean: she did not have a choice.

Her leg was splayed awkwardly to the side, and he situated it beneath her. Michaelson came forward now, was weeping.

Talmadge got to his feet.

Jane! called Della, feebly, hoarsely, from where she sat propped up against a tree.

The mean-looking man gazed at her as if he didn't recognize her. A calculating expression on his face.

That's enough, said Talmadge, though no one had spoken. Then, gruffly: Are you done here?

With great effort Michaelson took his hands from his face.

Talmadge did not know Michaelson was close until he was almost upon him.

Again Talmadge held a scythe. He must have reached for one, and one was handed to him. Michaelson reached out an arm as if to embrace him. His face ghastly white. Della, who had stood and leaned heavily against the tree, widened her eyes, and looked as if she would scream.

Talmadge raised the scythe.

The mean-looking man strode to Michaelson, punched him in the jaw. Michaelson staggered; the man struck him again. Michaelson bent in half, held his face. Was still.

The mean-looking man, breathing hard, held his fist to his heart, as if nursing it, looked away into the trees. Seemed to think, to blink; and then he appraised Talmadge. His voice shook:

A little while back there was talk of compensation.

Talmadge's heart beat quickly now: from confusion, but also relief. If there was talk of money, there was also talk of a solution; of the men going away. He lowered the scythe blade to the ground.

Yes, he said. I said that.

Yes, said the man, nodding. And—he looked at Della, and then away—we'll take money for her as well. If she interests you. Looking away at the trees again, he sighed deeply. I suppose I could take her back, there's always a use for her—although, honestly, I don't think he would want her. Not now. But the children, continued the man after a pause, his voice rising—I will take them off your hands, or you may pay for them, whatever you wish. How many of them are there? Where are they? No, never mind. He shook his head. I heard once that this one might have been carrying two—

Talmadge did not even begin to argue. Did not see the purpose of it. He leaned on the scythe blade, exhausted.

You'll have to come back to the house. I have some money there.

They moved in one large group back to the cabin: Talmadge still carrying the scythe; Michaelson mute and bent miserably, covering his face with his hands; Della limping, the haycatchers forming a loose ring around her. Jane's body was strapped onto the back of a horse. Everyone—including the haycatchers—waited in the yard while Talmadge went inside the cabin for the money. When he returned, the mean-looking man met him at the base of the porch steps, and Talmadge peeled the bills from a large roll. He paid for them all: Jane, the infant, Della, and Della's unborn children. Everyone watched: it was like a ceremony.

There, said Talmadge, and handed the man the final bill.

The man folded the money and put it in his breast pocket. His mouth puckered with grimness.

A pleasure, he said.

Talmadge hesitated. How do I know you'll stay away?

The man looked at him.

I mean, I don't want *him* coming back here anymore. Looking for them.

Michaelson glanced at Talmadge and the mean-looking man, but seemed uncomprehending that they were discussing him.

The mean-looking man smirked.

Him? He won't remember a goddamned thing.

He remembered before.

Well, I'll remind him then. How's that?

Talmadge didn't answer him. It would have to be fine. He would have to be satisfied; there was no other choice.

Jane was unstrapped from the horse, and Talmadge took her indoors, placed her on the bed she shared with Della. Covered her with the quilt up to her chin. Again he had the sensation—the memory—of her animation, her struggle of the birthing night. And now she lay unmoving. Unable to sense any temperature anymore, any texture on her flesh.

He covered his face with his hands and stood for a moment before he went outdoors.

Michaelson and the men mounted their horses and headed slowly toward the upper forest. Before they reached the treeline, Caroline Middey and her mule and wagon came out of the forest before the men entered it, and they passed each other. The mean-looking man tipped his hat to her, and Caroline Middey gave a small nod. When she reached the yard, she dismounted and asked Talmadge, who was waiting for her: Who was that?

Where is the child? cried Caroline Middey. Oh: where is the child?

Talmadge returned to the canyon alone. He heard the cries, faint but getting louder as he neared the upper cabin. Still he had to search for her. The girls had placed the child in a shallow basin behind the upper cabin and covered her with leaves and branches. How was it that she had kept there all the afternoon without crying? Or maybe it was that they could not hear her over the other racket. A blessing, he realized now. He crouched down and scooped her up, picked the debris off her, tucked her inside his jacket, near his armpit, his heart, for warmth; carried her down into the canyon and through the orchards, across the field—the haycatchers looking up from the treeline where they had prepared their supper—to the cabin.

Caroline Middey likewise inspected the child and washed her in a basin of warm water, wet-eyed and praising God, and then Talmadge left the cabin while Caroline Middey helped the girl nurse the child. He did not know how long he was gone; just walked up and down the aisles of the apricot orchard. Unseeing, fatigued. Numb. And then they all went to bed, although it was newly dark. Caroline Middey slept with Della in the girls' bedroom—Jane's body was cleaned and bound in the sapling shed, ready for burial the next day—and Talmadge took the baby into his bed. They had not yet named her, he thought, rousing from shallow sleep. He had asked the girl just the day before if she had chosen a name—to be without a name for too long was not good for the child, he thought—but Jane had turned her face away and had not answered him. It had offended her, somehow, his asking it.

When the infant cried in the night, he gave her his finger to suck. Her gentle noises and whimpers roused him all night from deepest sleep.

II

TALMADGE HAD LIVED forty years in the orchard without any exceptional event happening to him, barring inclement weather or some horticultural phenomenon. Nothing to speak of in the human realm, really. And then this happened. Death in the orchard. The infant's screams sounded different to him, now. He walked among the apricots at midday, squinting in the heat and light, disoriented, until Caroline Middey called him for dinner.

What do we call her? said Caroline Middey, of the infant who slept now atop a pillow beside her on the love seat. Caroline Middey was knitting. It was after supper. Della sat at the kitchen table, and Talmadge stood at the stove, heating water.

It had been two weeks since they had buried Jane up-mountain, on a plateau near a grove of pears he and his sister had planted after their mother's death, and which had since gone wild. The pear trees—there were four—from a distance reared against the sky; but up close they curled in a thick, woody bramble over a cliff edge. Standing beside the trees, one could look down on wheatfields, miles below, rolling to the horizon. Jane was buried under the only tree that was not a fruit tree on the plateau: an enormous prehistoric-looking cottonwood with small silver-green leaves that flashed constantly in the wind.

And the wind was alive the day they put Jane into the ground; it played over the plateau and made the sound of rain in the tree and in the long dry grass. And Talmadge was relieved: for the sound hid them all from each other, and Della in her grief. Her hair blowing over her face as she stood beside the grave, unmoving.

He said to her, now, of the child:

What do you think we should call her?

Della was motionless, as if she hadn't heard, but then she shrugged. Gazed to the far corner of the room. As if she didn't care at all what they were discussing.

We have to call her something, said Caroline Middey.

Talmadge wiped his hands on his thighs and went to the window, to the trunk beneath it. Got down on one knee, heaved open the lid. And how long it was since he had investigated there. Out of the trunk rushed a cidery smell.

Della had already explored the trunk with Jane, but despite herself, she looked at what Talmadge was doing now.

After searching for a moment he found a large Bible, and after looking at it he took it up, and went and sat at the table across from the girl. Della—again, despite herself—glanced at what he was doing. She was acutely aware of the onionskin pages whispering between his fingers. He took out a sheet of paper stuck within the middle pages. There were other markers—letters, notes, recipes—but this was the main one, the important one. He unfolded the paper and ran his palms over it, several times, to flatten it. On the sheet was drawn a family tree, the names in flourishing script. After a minute of looking, he placed his fingers on a tier of names.

My mother's sisters, he said, and cleared his throat. And he read off the names: Angelene, Theodora, Carol-Ann, Beverly, Sandrine, Louisa, Minna and Martha (twins), Susanna Ray, and the baby, Lorene Ada. Talmadge's own mother, Beatrice, was the second youngest.

Talmadge was silent, remembering.

Della said, stirring, The first one, I like the first one, I think that should be it—

Surprised, he touched the paper. Angelene?

Yes—

And they all looked at the child atop the pillow, with her crimped and glowing face, her miniature hand near her temple. They silently agreed it was too soon to judge if the name suited the creature, or vice versa, just yet. Time would tell—

Talmadge, though he did not show it, was pleased. His pleasure came from the fact that the child was named for a good woman—all his mother's sisters were good, he was sure of that, though he had never met this one, Angelene, or he could not remember her distinctly; his aunts, all of them, variations, in his mind, of his mother—but really the pleasure came from the sense that, thus naming her, he bound the child to the place, and to himself.

As for Della, she chose the name because it had excited some memory the moment she heard it. She could not remember her own mother's name, but that name—Angelene—was close to it. Angelene, Della murmured to herself that night before she went to sleep. Angelene. It was close. It wasn't exactly right, but it was close.

She thought Jane would be pleased.

At times, when they were eating supper, Talmadge felt the girl's eyes on him, and regarded her. They stared at each other, and then, after a moment, she slowly looked away. What did she think of him? he wondered. What kind of man did she think he was? He had raised the scythe toward Michaelson, but that was all. In the end he had not threatened Michaelson at all, but simply bought him off. He had let Michaelson get away. Did she think he was a coward? Or clever, for understanding that that was the best way to get rid of him?

The girl's mind, her thoughts, eluded him.

After Caroline Middey left for home that first time after Jane's death, he let Della do what she wanted, which was mainly to sit for long hours on the porch, and then to wander in the outlying fields, sleep in the waist-high grass. She wore the same dress, the same stockings, for days on end before he suggested, over supper, that she change them. You'll feel better, he said, embarrassed. He washed their clothes in the creek while she sat in the apricot tree, watching him. He made other suggestions: that she help pick the fruit coming in, that she hunt herbs in the forest. At times she obeyed, or at least with the fruit. He did not know that she was afraid of the forest, which was a realm Jane had navigated.

She was fairly good about tending to the child when she cried to be fed, but there were times when the child cried and Della did not appear.

Talmadge kept Angelene more or less with him at all times now, in a covered basket at the end of the orchard rows, or on the porch, if it rained. During one of her visits, Caroline Middey presented a long swath of fabric to be wrapped around the body, in the style of an Indian papoose, to strap the child to his back or front while he worked. For a long time the child thus accompanied Talmadge in the pouch as he walked the rows. He became used to her humid weight, her specific presence, on his chest.

Della increasingly slept outdoors despite the cold, and so the apple crate in which Angelene slept was moved from Della's room into Talmadge's own. Not near the window, where there was a draft, but between the bed and the closet, under an applique wall hanging his sister had stitched when he was a boy.

This first year passed in silence, weariness, troubled dreams, confusion. Despite this, Della was able to begin to recognize the landscape around her, and from several aspects and objects she drew, unconsciously, a sense of comfort and orientation. There were the areas in the long grass of the outer field and the nearer plum orchard where she slept, depending on the weather and the time of day, curled and dreaming. There were certain avenues between trees where she preferred to walk over others, because of some singularity in their design, or because of other conditions born out of circumstance—the grass was in shadow, it was in light; it was slightly warmer, colder, brighter, it smelled particularly earthy, dank, of honey—and there were avenues through which she passed in order, simply, to reach her destination. Each time she walked through the avenues it was as if she was also experiencing, on some other level, a dream that was as unique as the avenue itself; and each time she walked through it, she experienced the dream over and over again. These dreams were not distinct, they were not, exactly, known. Some of these avenues were the ones Talmadge frequented, others were not. The avenues needed someone to walk through them, however infrequently, and look at them. In this way she exhibited a superstitious streak—if she did not walk these avenues, if the avenues were not looked at, then *something would happen*— though if asked why she did this, she would deny any major feeling for the avenues; she was just walking in certain directions according to some vague desire.

But there were other, more concrete comforts she absorbed. The color of the grass, almost blue, at dusk. The good order of the toolshed, where she sometimes slept at night. The same order of the kitchen, when she stood there alone, after searching the cupboards for something sweet to eat. She admired in the man his order, even though she herself was outwardly slovenly. On a wall in the shed was various horse tack, bridles and lead ropes, spurs, blankets, a saddle on an old, carpeted rack. She drew to these objects; took the bridle from the wall, tested its weight along her arm.

The winter was quiet. Della huddled on her pallet in the toolshed, refusing to come indoors. Inside the cabin Talmadge read bits of old almanacs to the child between bouts of stoking the stove. On Christmas Day, Caroline Middey arrived, driving a sleigh. She laughed, her cheeks splotched red from the cold, as she dismounted. She hailed the girl, who peered at her from around the side of the barn, to help her bring in the presents. Inside, they sat drinking hot cider. The girl opened her gifts: a woolen dress, winter stockings, a new pair of boots. Also, a tin of shortbread, a sleeve of strawberry candy, and a hot chocolate mix. The girl was unimpressed by the clothes, but coveted the food. She was already thinking of the places she would hide it. She wanted to be shown immediately how to prepare the hot chocolate: and so Caroline Middey showed her. The girl attentive—wolfishly so—at her elbow, watching her every move.

As early as March Talmadge was working outdoors again, clearing the debris between the rows, checking for rot and early pest damage. He walked the avenues of the apricot orchard, the child strapped to his front, drawing the air—cold, with notes of deep thaw—into his lungs. The sun reflected off the planes and islands of snow in the field, which at that hour—still early—were dazzling. His breath vaporous before him. Della came out of the cabin and stood on the porch, a bit of dried oats at the corner of her mouth. When Talmadge saw her, he told her to go put on a sweater, it was too cold to be standing on the porch like that. She went back inside the cabin and, miraculously, did as she was told.

In the early spring he started to evaluate the apricot orchard to determine a pruning design and schedule, and also to note which trees needed to be repaired, destroyed, or replanted. Just to perform a proper evaluation took two weeks. He took notes in his fine, crimped hand in a notebook he kept in his front shirt pocket.

In April the true labor began. He rose before dawn and was at work in the trees as the sun rose. On a ladder, with his shears, maneuvering into the farthest reaches of the understories. At times whistling, at times muttering to himself. But mostly silent. Always working in that calm, deliberate way that made it impossible to imagine that he would ever complete the row, not to mention the entire orchard, in time. How could he afford to be so careful? It's that it was just possible, but barely. The design, the organization he achieved in the rows, in each tree, pleased him like nothing else. It was his passion, his whole life.

Della watched him warily the first spring, not understanding quite what it was he was doing.

Late April the horses arrived. Della climbed into an apricot tree on the upper creek bank and watched the men exercise and train the animals in the early morning, watched Clee and the wrangler separate certain horses—the wild ones—from the herd and attempt to dominate them.

Della asked Talmadge one evening: Where do they come from?

Who?

The horses.

From the auctions, he said, and then, thinking she meant something else: And the mountains.

But she was unsatisfied. No, she said, I mean: Where do they *come from*.

He didn't know what she was talking about; was at a loss. Said, finally: I don't know.

Waking in the middle of the day in the sun-warmed grass of the upper pasture, Della experienced the end of a dream. She looked at the wavering

grass tips above her, framing the washed and distant sky. The grass rustled, the creek perpetually murmured; an insect chorus flared sharply
now, near the crown of her head, and then quieted—and these sounds,
and the heat and brightness, drew her back into the world, oriented her
somewhat. But a moment before, in the dream, she was in Michaelson's
basement, walking up the rotting stairs, in line with the other girls, up
toward the light. The image of Jane squinting beside her. *You are going to
be all right today.* And: *Remember: when he tries to— You should just—*

Being with the men was a thick screen they had to pass through in
order to experience what lay beyond. And what lay beyond? What lay
beyond, Jane? A place to stay, and keep their children. Jane did not ever
tell her, however, what to do if she, Della, was by herself. If Jane was to
suddenly disappear. If Della had no children—if the children too disappeared.

She sat up in the grass now and peered, her head spinning slightly,
toward the cabin. These days she thought she was bored or restless, but
she was neither of these things. She was waiting. But for what, exactly,
she did not know.

S HE CLIMBED INTO the tree.

Clee was the first to swing upon his horse—a graceful buckskin almost seventeen hands high—and took off with a jerk, rode into the horses. They leaped away from him and rolled their eyes. Pressed back their ears like a bunch of scared cows. He rode among them, made the horse upon which he rode pivot as he looked out over the other horses, riding up close to them, reaching out to feel their hides—this they did not like—and soon he chose one. He memorized momentarily the lay of the head—the ears and eyes and length of snout, the architecture of jaw—and the breadth and weight of the horse's shoulders. He lifted an arm to indicate the horse he had chosen, and he gestured again, and the wrangler mounted a horse—he rode with his bottom lifted slightly off the saddle—and drove straight through the other horses, to the horse Clee had indicated, and with a lasso on the pommel of his saddle, swung, and captured the horse in a matter of seconds. Then he dragged the horse back—Clee had ridden back to the clearing by this time and sat his horse, waiting, and the wrangler wore a fanatically grim expression. The horse bucked, and the wrangler's face hardened. He narrowed his eyebrows and smote the horse's flank with the reins, which did not work the first time to suppress and discourage the horse, but after a series more, did. The horse puffed and sidestepped but conceded. The horse upon which the wrangler rode pivoted carefully on its back legs, its chin lifted rigidly.

The wild horse, thus whipped and discouraged for moments, was tacked up with incredible speed by a battery of men. The wrangler, holding the rope taut, sidled up to the horse and, bending over, delivered hot instruction into the furred ear. One man on the opposite side of the horse

charged near and threw a saddle upon its back, and the wrangler tucked
the latigo beneath the horse's belly. In a quick fluid motion the man on
the ground reached forward and caught the strap and fastened it in a tight
cinch under the belly and moved away. In a similar fashion the horse was
fit with a bridle, bit, and reins. Once outfitted, the horse was released by
the wrangler, who pushed it away with his foot, the horse upon which
he rode skipping lightly, and the newly tacked horse spun and bucked
around the central figure, who held it by the rope hanging like a large
necklace around his breast.

Clee, having watched all this preparation, spat on his hands and
rubbed them together, and then bent and scooped up a small handful
of dirt and rubbed his hands together again and stepped forward, all the
time watching the horse as it pivoted and squealed. The man who held
the rope gave it to Clee and stepped back. Clee wound the rope ends
around his fists and worked the horse like an unwieldy kite. He worked
closer and closer to the horse, scrutinizing him, acting as counterweight.
The horse was belligerent, but after twenty minutes or so there came
a lull. Clee waited, rode out two, three more belligerent fits. And then
when the horse subsided Clee came boldly forward, and the horse, surprised, chagrined, jerked back; but Clee had stepped heavily into the stir-
rup and swung his body atop the horse, and the horse leaped like a fish
loping upriver. Clee took this all in stride, and while the horse leaped,
he arranged the reins in his hands, tipped his hat back. Casually. Then
when he decided it was time to begin, he settled his body despite the frantic possession of the horse, and leaned forward and hitched up his heels
sidelong on the horse's flanks and dug them into the meaty horseflesh
and came down alongside the horse's neck, tipping his hat farther up on
his forehead. He pressed his cheek, with utmost concentration, against
the horse's neck. Closed his eyes. The horse resisted, leaped again, and
careened toward the half circle of men; the circle widened.

It took a long time. By the time Clee was finished the horse was shivering, brimming with wildness just contained. Its flesh, and the air around
its flesh, was primed with the energy of corroded nerves, of that which
could not be dominated having miraculously been dominated. When
Clee bent forward and pressed his cheek near the horse's ear and jabbed

the flanks with unforgiving boot heels, the horse widened its eyes in fury and lust and stepped forward, and now backward, whatever Clee willed. Clee touched the cord of wildness and the horse responded, helpless as it was to its own nature. Afterward the horse was stripped of its tack and left to join the others. It trotted back into the herd, nudging its way through the other horses. If they resisted it, it nipped at their ears.

The next morning the horse refused to be caught, and it took three men on horseback to corner it and catch it and drag it back to the pre-scribed area. Again the battery of men, headed by the wrangler on the broodmare, forcibly saddled it.

From her perch in the apricot tree Della watched, and in the silent morning air, under the heavy gray sky, she heard the sound of the iron bit clacking against horse teeth. The curses of the men alternated with soft phrases, almost a croon. Clee stood away as before, wiping his hands with dirt and spit. He mounted the horse and endured the minutes of abuse; he rode out the bucking, the careening, as the horse tried to exor-cise him, in vain. And then the leaning forward, the boots pulled back, the hat tipped back upon his brow. The pressure, the long curious dance. Again, the domination.

D ELLA DIDN'T KNOW what was happening; she felt light.

In her absorption in the horses she was distracted from who her sister was, or continued to be. Because Jane still existed, somewhere, thought Della. It was Jane, after all, and their life together, that Della dreamed about, even if she could not remember all of it, when she slept those long hours in the sun-warmed grass. In unconsciousness Della was remaining available to Jane, faithful to her. Not that she thought that Jane would return, but rather, in that unconscious state, Della might meet her; Jane would communicate herself. Now the horses—somehow, some way—increased the possibility of communication. Della was unclear about how it worked, exactly, but was sure of the impulse: Jane was in the horses, or the horses were in Jane. And Della, by understanding the horses, by being on a horse, might understand the realm in which Jane now moved. It was all but spelled out to her. If she was good enough, if she became powerful enough, Jane might fall around her, in an instant, and Della would feel her again, the old sensation of her.

It was around this time—in April, the apricots were in bloom—that Della accompanied Talmadge to town to sell fruit. As she walked down the main street—he had given her money to buy a soda at the general store—she caught her reflection in the window glass, and started. It was Jane in the window glass, with longer hair, with thicker bangs crowding her eyes. Wearing a scowl the likes of which she never wore in actual life. There was Jane, glowering and swinging her arms like a boy. It was, Della understood, her own reflection; and yet she could not help but believe that it was also Jane's. It was a game she, Jane, was playing. From that point forward Della could never see her reflection without thinking that her sister also looked out at her, was almost on the verge of smiling—with ridicule, with pain.

And then there came a point—sooner, because of this game—when Della could not remember what Jane looked like, exactly, because her memory was now full of her own image. There was actual pain in Della's heart when she realized this. But then there were other things besides the image that she could recall and grasp: the way Jane caught her breath, sometimes, before she spoke; the sound of Jane's voice, deep and sweet, a little husky when she was angry; whole sentences she had spoken—Della woke at night with the sentences suddenly in the room with her—Jane's arms, her armpits, her neck, smelling, faintly, of bread; she had a birthmark the size of a blueberry, black, on her left shoulder. A constellation of moles on her chest. She liked sweet tea, molasses, sour apples.

As Della's preoccupation with the horses increased, her feelings for the child—Angelene—became confused. Even though Angelene was her sister's child, Della was unsure exactly what that meant. What that was supposed to mean. At first Angelene was a leech that needed Della's body, her breast, multiple times a day; and then, over a period of time, Angelene was a chore that needed doing, and a difficult one at that. What was this thing, after all, that had come from her sister? Was it a part of her sister, after all? Was it a part of Della? Della recalled the days, weeks, after Angelene's birth, when Jane fell into a distraction so deep Della had trouble calling her back from it. What was wrong? Was she, Jane, disappointed by what had happened? Their new circumstances? Jane could not locate the source of her ill feeling, but was confused, somewhat, about her feeling for the infant. It—the child—was not what she had thought it would be. The child was interesting in its way, but it did not satisfy all that she expected it would. It did not inspire her. It was not her unspoken ally, but an alien creature. She loved it, and feared it. Once or twice, in her deepest heart, when it would not stop wailing its one constant note, she hated it. At times it was utterly strange to her. What do we call it? said Della, letting the wee thing grab her pinkie as the three of them lay in bed. But Jane was adamant: they would not name the infant before she felt differently about it—before she loved it completely and without reservation. The time would come: but they must wait.

All of this—Jane's ambivalence about the child, and her subsequent death—was too difficult to think about. Della diapered the child quickly, fed her without considering when she had done it last, was slow to come if she heard the wails from the open cabin door in the afternoon, if she came at all.

The man was there, after all, to care for her.

With the coming of the horses again in the summer, Della was intent: she wanted to learn to ride. She was the one, and not Talmadge, who asked Clee to teach her. Clee, after conferring, through the wrangler, with Talmadge, agreed to do it. Of course the girl needed a distraction.

I don't want her riding the wild ones, said Talmadge, as if that needed to be stated. Teach her on one of the tame ones, the tamest one you have, I don't want her scared—

She sat before Clee in the saddle, and they rode slowly around the field and then through the horses.

Listen.

The sun lay on her shoulders; on the top of her head. There was the creaking of the saddle as their bodies pitched with the horse's gait. A pit of sickness in her stomach, from excitement, and the heavy, lackadaisical swaying of the animal. And the sound of the outside herd: breathless, snorting, stomping, crying. The horses, fresh from the mountains, stank under the heat: of sweat and grass, dust; feces. Their coats rippled as they moved under the sun. Some rolled their eyes. At the edges of this, the sound of crows bickering suddenly in the near treetops; and then a cry of a very small bird, far off. As she listened, one horse took the cuff of her pant leg between its teeth and pulled. Clee put his boot on the horse's side and pushed it away, and the horse rolled back, screamed high in the back of its throat. Della, from her new vantage, felt the scream in her spine, and between her legs.

———

We should be grateful, I guess, said Caroline Middey, who had come to visit. She and Talmadge sat on the porch and watched the girl ride in the field below. The baby slept, her mouth open, on Caroline Middey's bosom.

She needed something, didn't she, said Caroline Middey. But her voice was flat; she was unconvinced.

Talmadge said nothing. He had been hopeful about the girl and the horses, but now he did not know what to think. He recalled her toothy grin while walking up the hill to the cabin, after her lesson the day before, when she thought no one was looking. It disturbed him. Her incessant talk of the animals over meals. When the men were there with the horses, she did not sleep the day away, as she had before. She hardly slept at all; had startled him, several times already, dropping out of the barn loft at dawn.

Was it normal, he thought, for someone to change so quickly? If only she would sleep indoors, he thought; if only she would wash herself, and spend more time with the child—

What is it? said Caroline Middey now, sensing his unease.

He hesitated. It was early yet. He should be patient, he should let the childish mania, if that's what it was, spend itself.

Nothing.

She learned to pull herself atop a horse—saddled at first—by the pommel. Pulling her body up by the sheer strength of her arms. She could not do this at first. To gain strength, she hauled rocks, a bucketful in each hand, back and forth across the field—a tedious, body-killing exercise—watching the men ride, in the fall. And then, finally, when the men returned in the spring, she was able to pull herself up. She learned to pull herself atop a bareback horse by holding on to its withers this way. *Up in one clear motion,* Clee showed her, mounting a horse himself, *before he knows what you are doing.* You're not hurting him, said the wrangler, who sometimes joined them, who came when Clee beckoned. The wrangler voiced what she was doing wrong, clarified a point Clee was trying to relate.

Sit up. Look around you. You're riding with your arms. Clee waved his arm to get her attention, then stomped firmly, exaggeratedly, on the ground, stuck his chest out, to show her: *You ride with your legs. You drive the horse by your knees.* Then, watching her: *Why can't he hear you? Are you using your knees? You're not strong enough.*

For the first year she was not even taught how to use the reins. Clee stomped in the dirt, stuck out his chest. *Your knees! Sit up!* After she learned to sit up—her spine ramrod stiff, her shoulders set back, chin lifted, eyes ahead—she learned to lie long upon the horse, put her face against the horse's neck. *The horse knows you now.* She rode different horses constantly. *Now the horse knows you, you can talk to him. Whatever you want to say.* Clee looked over her head, respecting her privacy, while she spoke to the horse. And then, finally, the work with the spurs, and reins. *Still not strong enough.* She had to drive with her knees—she had forgotten—and then she had to lie long: she had to whisper secret words to the horse, but loud enough so the horse would feel it in his brain. She had to hurt the horse: she had to make the horse do what she wanted, but so that the horse wanted it too.

She dreamed of them: the horses in the field. She dreamed of horses in the mountains at dusk. She dreamed from the perspective of a horse: running in a valley of dry grass, searching for yellow mountain daisies to eat. The chevron of the herd. The screaming on the high passes with other mountains in the background.

Della woke from these dreams with her heart beating fast, often in the dank cold of the toolshed. Sometimes after these dreams, she discovered she had wet herself.

I want to go to the mountains, she said to Clee.

He pretended not to hear her.

The gelding paced twenty feet away from them, his dark brown coat shining with sweat. Della stood still in the dirt, watching him. When she was ready, she nodded to Clee. Clee nodded to the wrangler and another man, who captured the horse, brought him forward, then receded. Della came forward, her stomach and head emptying of feeling. Who was she? She was full of air. She was nothing but air with a straw hat on her head, and boots. Just meat and water and a heart. She wanted to tell Clee she couldn't do it: there was the moment when fear passed through her—cleanly, like a knife—but she did not open her mouth, did not turn her face away from what was before her.

She approached the horse, holding up her hands the way Clee had taught her to: attempted to feel the horse—his energy, his intent—through the space that separated them.

But she could not get close to the horse that day. A few times she came very close, but then she or the horse startled, which ballooned into staggering violence: the horse charging her, his head down, or spinning abruptly to show her his hindquarters, to kick out. Out of the way! shouted the wrangler. But Clee raised his hand to him, not taking his eyes off Della: there should be no words now. The girl would have to learn to navigate danger by herself, without help.

Eventually the gelding was recaptured and released into the outer herd, and the handful of men who had drawn in to watch it all retreated to their camps, began their suppers.

But the next day Della was insistent: Again. And again the gelding was captured, and again she approached him, arms held out.

She approached and retreated, approached again. Retreated. One man, and then another, who had drawn from the orchards to watch her, headed to their camps.

Some men remained, thinking that she might do it. But then one man turned away, headed to the camp. Dusk was falling.

Talmadge was walking down the hill.

When he understood what they were all looking at, it was too late for him to call for her to stop. And he had known—how to avoid it, how to ignore it?—this was coming. This was what she wanted. Fear and a kind of disgust rose in his throat as he watched her approach the beast.

But then she rushed the horse—there was no other word for it—and grabbed the withers and wrenched her body upon his back. There was the moment when she wore an expression of surprise; and then she was grinning. The men roused, and cheered; they applauded; some of the men who had gone away came jogging back. She lay now almost horizontally on the horse's back. Her arms almost encircled his neck. She was still grinning. And then the horse bucked—that awful ripple of muscle as he bowed his head—and instead of being thrown, Della slid off the horse while his head was down. Skipped away quickly.

Talmadge was bewildered by what he suspected was not only her luck, but her skill up on the horse. He marveled at the speed with which she had mounted the horse—she had been on his back instantly, almost within a blink of an eye—and when she scanned the crowd and saw him, he raised his arm to her. Waved. But wasn't he angry? He let his arm drop. Was he congratulating her?

But she looked at him only for a moment; and he wasn't even sure she had seen him. She was laughing now, and crying. The men had taken her up on their shoulders.

Clee and Talmadge stood together now, regarding her from a distance. Talmadge did not say, Don't do that again, because he knew it was too late. He was too tired to even reprimand either of them: Clee or the girl. He said, finally, That's enough for tonight, and then, without looking at Clee, trudged back up the hill.

That night, Della ate her supper with the men.

Let her have something that makes her happy, thought Talmadge: it was his refrain at the time. Though frequently he thought it was a mistake to reward her. Her work—in the orchard, and with the household chores—was shoddy. At times she left a mess on the counter after she fixed herself something to eat, or she damaged the scions while she picked even though he had shown her, repeatedly and with exceeding patience, how to do it correctly. She went for weeks without changing her clothes. Her hair was full of knots. He was fairly certain, after seeing her scratching, she had lice from sleeping in the barn. He should not bother her, he thought, he should not pester her. And yet how was he helping her, he thought, if he allowed her rudeness, her standards of squalor, to go unchecked? To put it bluntly, he was unsure of his role in her life. He was unsure if he had a right to tell her what to do. Or, if he did, what tone he should take: one of gentle suggestion, or firmer, one of demand.

In his indecision, he was clumsy, and ultimately let her get away with many things, while at other times speaking roughly to her over matters that seemed trivial. They were both, to certain degrees, confused by each other.

WHEN THE MEN came back into the orchard, Della continued to shadow them. Her skill at riding, but then also wrangling, improved. She wanted to travel with Clee and the men, she said, she wanted to see what they did at auction. And she wanted most of all to go with the men, if they would let her, into the mountains, where they hunted the horses. She told Talmadge this while making a great effort to look at him directly, her gaze peeling away from him.

He listened to her silently. He wanted to encourage her interest in anything other than what lay behind her, but at the same time he did not want to encourage such fantasies with the horses and men. To allow the girl to be taught how to ride was one thing, but to allow her to accompany a group of men to a place where more men gathered, to drink and carouse and observe the beasts they had trained, was another. It was beyond inappropriate that she should go, that he should allow her to go. It was all utter foolishness and danger. He did not understand at first why such a prospect would even be attractive to her. But he did not utter that word—No—that would have, he thought, squelched the hope in her. He did not know then that she did not need words from him, that she would do what she wanted regardless of his opinion.

She began to follow the men after they had left the orchard. She traveled behind them at a distance and joined them, suddenly, at auction. There she appeared, and acted as if she had been among them all the time. The first time this happened a man spotted her a day out of the orchard, and one of them escorted her back. It was amusing to some of the men, since she had been riding one of their own horses that she had stolen at some point and hidden in the woods. And so she was a horse thief too. This first time Talmadge accepted her back and told her, as she ate the food he had prepared for her, that it was wrong to follow the men, they could not be bothered by children in what they did, and it was no place for a child to be, the places they went were very dangerous. She listened impassively. The men returned three weeks later, and when they set out again, this time for Seattle, she followed them and got as far as the river crossing at Icicle, where her horse shied and would not enter the water. Someone noticed her then, and brought her back.

In the winter, the men and horses absent from the orchard, Della helped Talmadge with the chores. Bored, she spoke down at Angelene on a blanket on the floor, made faces at her. Caroline Middey taught Della to knit and can food, but Della did not care for either of these things. When the men returned in the spring, she changed again into her riding clothes, a motley outfit assembled out of Talmadge's old clothes and maybe things that were cast off, or stolen, from the men.

She approached Talmadge one day as he worked in the late afternoon. The men had just climbed out of the trees and made their way across the field to their camp, to eat. They would leave the next day. She said: The only reason they won't let me go with them is because they know you don't like it. If you say so, they'll let me go with them.

At supper that night he told her again that the men could not be bothered with young female company, that she needed to leave them alone. Or at least put it out of her head that she would travel with them. It's not your place, he said, and she looked at him with a gaze that surprised him: it was an adult gaze, calm and slightly amused. He looked away from her, unsettled. Her gaze told him that he did not know what he was talking about; as if he, and not she, was the hardheaded one.

When Talmadge talked to Clee about Della and asked him to forgive her nuisance and to forgive him also for not being able to keep her movements in check, Clee, after waiting to see if he was finished speaking, nodded. Talmadge said: Of course she cannot travel with you. I understand that. And Clee looked at Talmadge in much the same way as Della had, which annoyed him. Is that what you want? said the wrangler, approaching Talmadge the next day. If it is what you want, we will take her with us the next time—

Caroline Middey said that she was only surprised that Della had returned to the orchard at all between her failed excursions to join the men. Why would Della need permission from Talmadge to do anything? Was he her father?

She asked you to speak to the men out of respect, said Caroline Middey, but she does not need your permission.

And so I should let her go because of that? said Talmadge, incredulous.

Caroline Middey shrugged. To her, the girl could no longer be protected. Caroline Middey asked what it was exactly that he had planned for the girl. Was he going to train her in the ways of the orchard? (There was a note of sarcasm to this comment he chose to ignore.) There had been a glimmer, when Della and Jane first entered the orchard, that perhaps he could train them, they could be his apprentices and find a living at it like he had done. And they would have a trade and a way of earning money that would make them independent. Surely that was the most important thing. And they had helped him at first, for a short time, after Angelene's birth. They had all worked together in the orchard. But after Jane died, Della's interest in the orchard ceased. To her the orchard was an empty scene that did not fill until the horses entered it. And now she wanted to be a horsewoman. It was the only thing she wanted.

She was maybe sixteen at this time. If you wait, said Talmadge in the wake of another of the men's departures, if you wait until you are eighteen, if you wait two years from now, I will buy you a riding outfit and I will buy you a gun and I will show you how to use it. I will give you all these things, if you wait. You are too small now, he wanted to say to her. You are stupid and young, he wanted to say, and you still will be two years from now, but I will have less responsibility for you then. Or, he thought, she would have changed her mind. He wished for her to outgrow the desire to ride with the men without ever passing through it. That was what he hoped would happen.

She said nothing to these references—*two years from now*—these gentle bribes. She was puzzled by references to the future, quietly infuriated by them. She attempted twice more to join the men and each time was rebuffed and delivered back to the orchard with increasing grimness on the part of the man who escorted her.

———————

And then one night in May, two months before apricot harvest—her third in the orchard—Della came into his bedroom and stood at the foot of his bed. He had woken a moment before with a start. The air coming through the open window smelled of blossom. The moon lit up a portion of her chest and shoulder. They regarded each other. When she came closer, stepping through the moonlight, he saw she wore a white nightgown and her hair was untied from its braid and loosed down one shoulder. She had bathed. In the nearer darkness he could not make out the features of her face. She pulled up the gown and removed it.

No-no, he said, as one would to a small child, when she attempted to round the bed.

No-no, he said again, but she came around quickly and got into bed beside him. Put her leg over him. She was small, but strong. He laughed out of helplessness and then pushed her off him and she tumbled to the floor with a thump. She grunted and then was on her feet in an instant.

I don't want you, he said when she came at him again. I don't want you!

She stood still, her dark face observing him, both of them breathing hard, and then she turned and left the room.

She did not come to him again. The first few nights after the incident he waited for her, sitting up in bed, his heart beating fast. But she had made her bed in the forest and did not come back for three days. When she returned, coming out of the trees at dusk, smudged and frowning, she did not seem overly bothered or upset. She ate the supper set in front of her with the usual indifference and distraction. It was as if the scene in the bedroom had never happened. But it had happened, he told himself. She had come into his bedroom at night and undressed at the foot of his bed and come toward him—

He would never tell anyone.

THERE WAS A man he saw every year at the plant sale in Malaga, another orchardist, who designed rifles. Ten years ago this man had invited Talmadge to see his work, and Talmadge, standing in the man's workshop, had admired what he had seen. It was this man Talmadge approached now about a rifle for Della. The man was pleased; invited Talmadge again to his workshop.

The rifles were fine, but nothing impressed Talmadge in the way he had hoped. Should he have brought the girl, he thought, to pick one out? The man had a catalog of rifle designs, and he gave it to Talmadge to look at. Talmadge flipped through the catalog but still found nothing. The desire to buy her something special, the certainty that he would find it, had dissipated.

I'll make something for you, said the man, with such quiet confidence that Talmadge was relieved. Who was the gun for? the man wanted to know. Before he realized what he was saying, Talmadge said: My sister.

When she travels with you, said Talmadge to Clee, I want you to take care of her. I don't want her harmed in any way. By which he meant he did not want her harmed in the way of men. He did not say he did not want her harmed in the way of horses, for that was inevitable; he had seen how the men rode, he had seen Della's tutorials down in the field when she was thrown and then rose, holding her elbow or knee or ear, limping momentarily, wiping a bit of blood from her mouth or nose. Grinning that dumb grin. It was not that type of pain Talmadge was worried about. She was not afraid of the horses or of being hurt with the horses. He did not want her to feel scared in the presence of the men, he did not want her to find herself all at once surrounded in a way that she had been surrounded before. He did not want her to feel abandoned or helpless. But the wrangler said they would watch out for her, and the other men would too, they had come to make a space for her among them even if there were those who did not care for her so much. And it was not even her so much they did not care for as the idea of her, a young white woman riding among them. But if it came to it, they would protect her, if not for her sake then for Clee's, who was their leader and whom they respected. They would defer to him.

But most of the men liked her; they liked, were amused by, her fierceness and her earnestness about the horses. They too at different times and in different situations would witness her strange vulnerability and wanted to protect her.

The rifle was a fine specimen of craft proportioned for a young woman, made of cherry and maple and decorated with carvings of roses and vines along the stock. You did not notice the power of the design unless you regarded it closely. The rifle appeared lightweight, and yet it contained the heft of a serious firearm.

He approached Della in the orchard row where she worked and said, This is for you.

She hesitated and then took the rifle and held it away from her body as if she did not know what it was. She was bewildered, which on her face registered as consternation, or disgust. She did not take her eyes from it as he spoke.

You don't know how to use it, do you?

She peered at the gun.

No one has taught you how to properly shoot a rifle, have they? he said, and after another moment she shook her head and he said, No. That's what I thought.

That summer, after her initial lesson from Talmadge, Della practiced shooting in the forest. That fall after apple harvest they left Angelene with Caroline Middey in the orchard and he took Della hunting east of Chelan Falls. As they rode in the endless-seeming scrub, he explained to her that when she traveled with the men she was responsible for securing her own food, she should rely on nobody else. The men could not be expected to make exceptions for her. When Talmadge spotted the first buck, they dismounted at the edge of a wide rock quarry. Lay on their stomachs in the leaves. He repositioned the rifle on her shoulder before leaving her alone and watched the side of her face and then looked at the sky. He covered his ears. Waited while she waited. Finally she pulled the trigger. The gunshot cracked and echoed in the sky.

They hiked down to the area where the animal was struck, and he showed her how to look for blood in the grass. You move in its wake, he told her. He did not know how to tell her about intuition.

It took them a long time to find the buck. The shot had grazed its neck. It was a bad shot. But Talmadge patiently led her in pursuit, and late afternoon they found the animal in a band of aspen twenty yards from a creek. It was the last surge of daylight; the air was golden. Talmadge strung up the deer in one of the trees and then slit its throat. After it was sufficiently bled he handed her his hunting knife and instructed her to make the major incision from the groin to the breast. The knife was old and had belonged to his mother. He reached inside the animal for the innards and spoke to her in a quiet voice about what he was doing. She stood to the side and watched. He asked her to come forward and reach in and detach the liver, and she did so. Peering with concentration. He told her to go wash the liver in the creek, and she set off silently with the organ in her hand.

He continued working. When dusk had fallen and she had not returned, he went down to the water to look for her. At first he did not see her. But then he saw her crouched at the water's edge thirty feet away. When he called to her, she did not move. The creek was too loud, he thought.

She had knelt and put her head to the ground, her arms crossed in front of her. When he reached her and touched her shoulder, she slowly sat up. Her face was ravaged by crying.

What happened? What's wrong?

She would not answer him. She stood with his help, looked out over the water as if searching for something. He helped her wash the blood and dirt from her arms and face and then led her back to the camp. But she could not stand the sight of the buck. She halted and wailed high in the back of her throat when they came out of the trees and saw the bloody form strung up.

What is it? he said.

I lost it, she said, and began to pant with despair. I was washing it, and it went down the river. I tried to get it— And she began to cry, and put her hands over her face.

It's all right, he said, confused. It's all right. Hush, now.

But she would not hush, she would not be consoled.

He packed up everything they had unpacked earlier and rode with her a short distance away and set up another camp. She sat on his jacket on the ground, hugging her knees, rocking slightly on her tailbone. He built a fire. It was nearly dark; the stars had come out. He made some food for her—some oatmeal—and for several moments stood and watched her eating. And then he walked back to the former camp and built another fire and finished butchering the deer. When he was done, it was full black night. Cold. He cooked up a bit of the heart and ate it with some onions and pepper he had packed. His mind—empty, but troubled—was soothed by the flavor of the meat. When he walked back to the other camp, the girl was sleeping huddled on her side. He put more wood on the fire and lay down opposite her and listened a long time to the sounds of the flames and the other distant sounds of night before he too was able to sleep.

You don't have to kill a deer, he told her the next day, thinking it was the size of the animal that had overwhelmed her. You can hunt rabbit, and squirrel—

It wasn't until later that he thought of the deer strung up in the tree, and what it had cost the girl to see something like that. How he had told her to stick her hand into the animal to get its organ so that they could eat it for supper.

He taught her how to clean the rifle. He bought her boys' riding breeches and wool underwear, plaid button-down shirts, and a jacket to replace the strange costumes she wore. He bought her riding boots, and a bedroll. A fine, simple saddle. A pocketknife and a hunting knife with a leather sheath that attached to her belt. He showed her how to clean the knives as well. It was best, he said, that she keep the large knife under her pillow while she slept. So thieves wouldn't get it, he said.

AND SO SHE traveled with the men, at first simply to and from the auctions. It should begin that way, Talmadge reasoned, and then they would determine from there what to do. Perhaps she would tire of it, he thought, perhaps it would not be what she had imagined, and she would abandon her original idea.

But she did not tire of it.

Clee and the men took her into the mountains to the southeast, the ranges there as far as central Idaho, to hunt the horses they would train and sell at auction. When she came back from the first hunt—they had gone into the Sawtooths—she had completed, or nearly completed, the gesture she had begun with learning how to ride: to transform herself from someone powerless to someone powerful. Talmadge could not yet tell if it was a good thing. She still had her child's body—she was short, and shaped like a boy—but her mind had passed into another place. It was not a matter of her being largely a child beforehand, and having passed into adulthood. It had little to do with that: childhood and adulthood. She had passed into a place independent of those two states. Was she happy? He could not say definitively that she was *un*happy. Perhaps she was involved—maybe she had discovered (he hoped for this but did not believe it) a happiness so remote, so calm, and it was this by which she was distracted, that she was so utterly involved with at times, so that when she entered a room where he was, or an orchard row where he worked and looked to greet her, she seemed not to see him.

Caroline Middey watched Talmadge, also, change. Concern about the girl had grown into a stealthy practice, had consumed him, although he did not like to talk about it. His characteristic expression of distant calm was replaced by anxious distraction—his eyes told the world he was thinking not of what was before him but of what was absent from the place. An expression of constant inner speculation: Was the girl, at that moment, safe? Was she afraid? When Caroline Middey spoke to him, as they had been speaking over a lifetime—porch correspondences, meandering but thoughtful conversations—he increasingly failed to contribute: his silence was not that of unspoken agreement, or that which reflected his absorption in their exchange, but was rather that of not having heard her at all. At times he drew himself up while she was talking, as if just realizing it was him she was addressing: that there was another person with him on the porch.

For a time, his anxiety at Della's absence, instead of decreasing, increased. And he was almost impossible to talk to. Like a man in a dream.

She's not yours, said Caroline Middey, finally, one evening.

What?

She doesn't belong to you, Talmadge.

It was a cruel thing to say, she admitted: but was it, really? The girl had come from nowhere to take advantage of him and his kindness, and Caroline Middey, understanding what the girl had suffered, did not blame her, not really—but for Talmadge to pine after her, if that's what he was doing, was ridiculous.

But no, that was not right. She must not rise to the temptation to so easily classify his behavior that way. He was not pining after Della. He was worrying about her. Of course the situation called forth Talmadge's sister: lately, as Caroline Middey observed Talmadge, his sister was never far from her thoughts.

Elsbeth. For a time after her disappearance Talmadge had been all but comatose, and Caroline Middey drove to the orchard often to look in on him. To make sure he had gotten out of bed, and washed and dressed. She'd combed his hair, and cut it when it became too long. Made him meals that would keep. You just have to add water to that and cook it, Talmadge, she would say, and he would nod. During the heavy work times in the orchard she would remain, sometimes for a month at a time. In his grief he might forget to begin work: but when he began, it was difficult to get him to stop.

He had pulled out of that grief, eventually—out from under the suffocating weight of it. Suffering had formed him: made him silent and deliberate, thoughtful: deep. Generous and kind and attentive, although he had been that before. Each thoughtful gesture hoping to extend back, far back, to reach his sister, to locate her somewhere.

Caroline Middey did not know where the girl—Elsbeth—had gone. She had seen, however, when Talmadge did not, that the girl was likely to go. She'd had the look of departure about a year before she disappeared. A watchfulness. Stirrings of restlessness in a creature otherwise inimitably patient. It was no wonder Talmadge had not seen it. The two were uncannily similar, but they were different in that way: Talmadge would remain in the orchard until the day he died, whereas Elsbeth, for whatever reason, wished to go elsewhere. Who knows why the girl had gone like she had, in such a dramatic fashion? That was what unsettled Caroline Middey the most: she did not think the girl capable of such cruelty toward Talmadge, and so believed, reluctantly, that she, Elsbeth, herself had not caused it. Oh, Caroline Middey did not like to think of what might have happened to the girl. The girl setting off, to be caught by something she did not anticipate. What else could have happened, really? The only thing worse, perhaps, than knowing for certain that she was abducted was *not* knowing. That was the sad truth. And Talmadge lived in that uncertainty, he had made his home in it, and there was no possibility of him resting—truly resting—ever again.

And so the fact of Della leaving the orchard upset him, naturally—upset those demons he had slain, carefully and with great strength, in the beginning, and steadily over the years. And now here he sat again—distracted, anxious, afraid. Caroline Middey sought to comfort him by harshly reminding him of their—his and Della's—relationship.

You cared for her for a while, she said. That's all you can do, Talmadge. She wanted to go: and so give her your blessing to go. Now forget her. If she comes to visit, fine. She is a visitor. But she doesn't want to live here, she doesn't belong here—

And, understanding that he needed something to focus on, if not Della:

Think of Angelene now, think of the child—

And always the mention of the child changed him. The change was in his eyes: they focused; the mention of the infant introduced the present again.

And that was the point of children, thought Caroline Middey: to bind us to the earth and to the present, to distract us from death. A distraction dressed as a blessing: but dressed so well, and so truly, that it became a blessing. Or maybe it was the other way around: a blessing first, before a distraction. Caroline Middey scrutinized the point; did not know if the distinction was important. (All distinctions are important.) But she did not think any more about it because at her back, suddenly, the child woke from her nap, and she rose at once to go to her.

If Angelene was within range when Della came to the cabin to rest between bouts of training, Della scooped her up and raised her high overhead, laughing a strange boisterous laugh. Angelene at first was baffled, befuddled—but was soon overcome with the speed of flight up into the air, and squealed, happily, her lopsided grin showing the squares of her new teeth. Up she went, and down she came, the soft featherlike hair suspended and then flattened; and Della embraced her between flights, pleasure on her face, particular satisfaction. But then—if you blinked you would miss it—there came a growing expression of indifference on Della's face. Where did it start? Her cheeks, her mouth, her eyes? When it was in her eyes, it was finished. Della kissed the girl on the neck, absently, before delivering her to the ground. Angelene protested, squirming in Della's arms, before she was left alone, but laughed when she was released, thinking she was going to be captured and thrown up again into the air; and when Della straightened up, Angelene reached out for her reflexively, but Della would not pay her any more attention. It was as if Della had totally forgotten the joy of moments before; she turned and was gone into the distance of grass, absorbed with whatever filled her mind then, whatever came next.

After the trip to the Sawtooths, when Della was gone for two months, when she returned and tried to scoop Angelene from the grass, Angelene screamed, terrified, and struggled within Della's arms, and Della set her on the ground, embarrassed.

Talmadge, perplexed, said: She hasn't seen you in a long time.

Angelene clung to his leg, held her fist to her mouth, looked at Della with wide, glassy eyes.

Jesus, she acts like I'm going to kill her or something, said Della, and laughed, squatted down again, opened her arms, smiled encouragingly, nervously; but Angelene turned her face away into Talmadge's pant leg and would not budge.

Give her a few days, said Talmadge. She just has to get used to you again.

And it was not only Angelene who had to get used to her. Talmadge found himself impressed, and disturbed, by the creature before him. It was the old Della, but definitely changed. Hardened, sun-darkened, stoutly muscular. If he did not know better, he would've mistaken her for a native woman-child riding with the men. She was both more assured and quieter, deeper. It was as if the distances she had traveled had ironed out some of her foolish impulsiveness, her flippancy. She again watched Talmadge over meals but held his eyes longer now before decisively looking away. She was a master, even at that age, of guarding her feelings, her thoughts, and he realized without being aware of it that he had had the possibility to know her, before—had he known her?—but now that had changed. The possibility was gone. Now no one would know her unless she herself willed it. And there was nothing quite like the will he sensed in her now.

Later that week—the men were still in the orchard—Talmadge headed toward the sapling shed for a pair of shears, and found Della leaning in the eave of the side of the cabin, smoking a cigarette. She stood up straight when she saw him, stubbed out the cigarette. As if he had caught her at something, he thought. He looked over his shoulder, to see what she had been looking at. There was Angelene sitting in the grass before the apricot orchard, jabbering to two sticks held in her fists. You couldn't see it, with her sitting like that, but there was a fabric cord tied around her waist. It was something he sometimes did, tying her to a tree, so he could keep an eye on her without fearing she would wander off. He was ready to explain about the cord, which Della had no doubt seen, when she said:

When I left, she was so different. She was a baby.

He noted the sadness, the earnest awe, in her voice. He looked toward the child in the grass.

She's still a baby, he said.

I know, but—she's different.

There was nothing he could say; it was true, she was different. At times when he took her up out of the crate in the morning, the crate she was rapidly outgrowing, it was as if she had grown, changed, overnight; her hair was different, her eyes; the shade and texture of her flesh, her limbs; and, most disconcerting and delightful of all, she was beginning to speak. She increasingly talked back to him when he murmured to her, and he understood that she was becoming what she was destined to become, when he first held her in the open air of the world: her own person, her own independent and particular self. He marveled at it all. And what would she grow up to be like? What was inside her, already formed, that would draw forth with time, and what was it that she most needed him to teach her? Would she be amenable to his help, his advice in worldly matters? And what advice did he have to give? But she already accepted him as her own, wanted him to hold her the first hour of every day, and then, after she climbed down from him, trailed at his side perpetually, looked up often into his face. Trying to determine how he felt about certain things they saw together. She adored him, and he in turn felt himself totally circumscribed by his love for her; the quality of the emotion that bound them chastened him, filled him. And yet the emotion—the severity of it—at times made him afraid.

But he did not know how to communicate this to Della. He did not know the effect those words would have on her. He did not, could not, understand how she saw the child: did not know, exactly, what Angelene meant to her.

Despite Della's absences, and despite Angelene's terror at having her aunt embrace her, there were moments of apparent communion between them. The rest of that summer Della remained with Talmadge and Angelene in the orchard—not so much through a choice of her own, but circumstances having to do with the circulation of the horses;

the whole business was slow that summer—and often in the afternoons the three of them walked to the upper pool. Della walked with Angelene on her shoulders, the child's small fists gripped in Della's own. Talmadge fished for the better part of the afternoon, and then afterward, while he fried the fish over a fire for their supper, the girls swam. Angelene sat naked in the shallows while Della, who had not taken off any of her clothes—just her hat—waded farther out, dove down and then came up again, hair plastered to her skull, water spilling from her eyes, calling to Angelene, who watched her from afar. And what was it Della said to her? What were the words? Talmadge could not remember. Strings of words, phrases, delivered in that singsong she used with the child, which was touching and sad somehow, because her own voice was rough and childish; she who was little more than a baby herself, thought Talmadge; one baby beckoning to another. Della was a little over seventeen years old then. But to Talmadge she was younger than that, a perpetual child.

Another time—this was perhaps a year, two years later, in another season, fall—Talmadge went out onto the porch and saw down in the field Della holding Angelene on her hip. They stood before a horse: a beautiful, muscular sorrel mare. Angelene, who was quite tall for her age, was more than a third of the size of Della now. The child's legs dangled long from where Della's arms were cinched under her bottom. The horse they were looking at was a tame horse: he made sure of that, at once, for he would not have Angelene near any wild horse. It might have been Clee's horse, or Della's own. Yes, that was probably it, it was Della's horse, and she was showing it to Angelene. The field was full of horses, the men moving around purposefully, breaking camp. Maybe Della was telling Angelene good-bye, thought Talmadge, for she, Della, was going that entire season with the men: she was going to winter with them in the south. He thought Della and the child were simply looking at the horse; but when Della turned her face slightly, to look at Angelene, he saw that she was talking to the girl; and the child responded after a moment, lifting her own arm to the horse, pointing something out, before bringing her hand down again.

———

Later these peaceful moments between Della and Angelene were the exception, not the rule. Angelene fussed when Della approached her. At first Della shrugged off the girl's hysterics, laughing: Silly kid. But then it was almost as if she was angry when the girl did not immediately go to her, accept her affection. One time Della arrived with the men and camped below with them as if she had no kinship with neither Talmadge nor Angelene; she did not greet them at all. And when he went down at night and found her among the fires, she looked up at him and said, after a moment: Evening. He asked her if she was going to come up to talk with him on the porch, to see the girl. She did not answer him right away, but stared beyond him, beyond his shoulder. Not as if she was angry; in fact he had a hard time reading her face. No thank you, she said. I'll stay right here. And then, almost as an afterthought, and so softly he would question if he had imagined it: Where I belong—

What do you mean? he said, but she didn't answer him. It was soon too uncomfortable to stand there without an answer, the men around them pretending to ignore them, talking to each other to feign that they weren't listening. Eventually he returned to the cabin.

After that she spent more time with the men while she was in the orchard, not even bothering to divide her time between the men and himself and Angelene; not bothering to come up to the cabin at all. What kinds of things was she telling herself? he wondered. What kind of story had she invented? It was his fault, he thought, one of his many faults, that he was not stricter with her during this time, that he did not insist on knowing what she was thinking, did not demand she explain herself. He did not say to her: This is ridiculous, this is your home, and more important, this is your niece, and she is as good as your daughter, and you are as good as her mother, and it is better that you take her with you on these errands of yours into the mountains than leave her here and have both of you become strangers to each other. This is no good, he should have said; he should have given up Angelene so that Della could ruin her, rather than keep her for himself, so Della could ruin herself, and in doing so ruin them all.

Oh, but he could not have given up Angelene, even if Della had wanted her. He would have done nothing differently. He would have kept Angelene close to him, as he had; but he should have insisted that Della stay too. She was not all cold, and more than that, she was not bad. He was convinced of this. The change with her—this distance, this hardness—did not happen overnight, it was gradual; and since it was gradual, he had taken a part in it. The day she failed to appear for Angelene's sixth birthday party, and then after that, when it seemed that she had actually gone for good, he thought, with gentle surprise: It is done. It is done. And was he, after all, surprised? Had he not been waiting for it? Still he was shaken that she had actually gone and done it, set out on her own.

Is it what he had wanted? Did he want her, finally, to leave?

At times he pitied her greatly; and other times he was moved, watching her, by her unrestrained happiness on the horses. He was awed by, but also wary of, her willingness to go up into the mountains to do these dangerous things, without regard for the fact that she might die, without regard for Angelene.

But there was that fear he had also, when he saw Della go pick up the child. When he saw them standing close to the horse that day, very still, Della talking to the child, he thought: Good; look at them, this is good; but he also thought: Why doesn't she put her down? Why doesn't she just put her down?

He didn't want Angelene to be infected, he thought now. As if Della, and the pain she carried with her, was a disease.

HE DID NOT grasp at first, despite her long absence, that she was gone indefinitely. And then one day—walking down an orchard row, shears in hand, he turned his face to a barren patch of ground—he knew she was gone. Even if she was to come back, the situation between them would be different, in that she would be her own person as she had not been totally, to his mind, before. When she came to the orchard between her other sojourns, she was still a part of the orchard, a part of their lives; and he would still try to protect her from harm, he counted it his responsibility to do so. But no longer. If she came back now, it would be to look at him across the distance of that severed connection. And how had it been severed? It had been severed by her actions, but it was also something that was separate from her, that he could not define: that had to do with himself, and the orchard, and the passage of time. Somewhere along the way he had forgotten to remember her; he had forgotten to constantly call her back from the distances she was always intent on pursuing.

And Angelene, too young at the time to articulate her feelings for Della, regarded her as part of the orchard as the men and the horses were a part of it, interesting and unusual and even phenomenal, but they had nothing to do with, were separate from, what constituted the real orchard life, which was Angelene and Talmadge by themselves. The last few times Angelene saw Della, as a child of four or five, neither made a move to embrace the other. Della was difficult to place for Angelene during that time. She was Angelene's aunt, but Angelene did not understand what that meant exactly. In the grain of Angelene's life Della was the one thing going the opposite direction; she didn't fit. She was always there, the odd detail agitating an otherwise serene existence.

Talmadge did not speak to Angelene about who Della was or where
she came from, and why she was so different from other women. Angelene was too young then anyway to understand. If she voiced any confusion to him, neither of them remembered it. What she did remember was
riding Talmadge's back in the orchard—for pleasure, now, since she had
outgrown the papoose—with grass and honeysuckle stuck in the corner
of her mouth, asking endless questions about the animals, the clouds,
the trees, the fruit. And he answered, beginning: Oh . . . Thoughtful
answers.

They had moved into the time in the orchard when Della came no
more. Angelene always thought she could place the moment exactly, the
beginning of this time. Her birthday was held every year after apricot harvest, with the horses down below in the field, and the men up in the yard,
dressed in their town clothes and sitting in chairs and on the ground, eating food Caroline Middey had prepared. Whether it was a fact or simply
the way she remembered it, this birthday party—her sixth—was the first
that Della did not attend. Talmadge kept drawing to the edge of the yard
to look out at the treeline across the field, expecting Della to ride out of it.

This was the image Angelene had of him at that time, always moving
to the edges of some celebration, assuming a position, looking out for
Della. He was to speak of her less often in the years to come, but he never
lost that air of distraction, of looking out. It made Angelene sad for him,
and resent the one who stayed away.

III

DELLA ENTERED THE picture booth—she had not known what it was beforehand—to satisfy a mild curiosity.

It was a kind of closet, very quiet compared with the outside carnival she had just come from. These carnivals cropped up around the auctions, and she was sometimes let to wander off by herself. *Be back at camp before dusk—*

She sat on a blue velvet-cushioned stool. A man she could not see—he was in the ink-black darkness before her—told her to hold very still. He was taking her picture. Did she know what that meant? Don't move your mouth, he said. Sit still. Try not to blink.

Ultimately, the picture was the size of her thumbprint. She kept taking it out of her pocket, afterward, as she walked the carnival alone among the blinking, lurid lights, and looked at it. This was what she looked like. The girl in the picture was pale (but that was the effect of the film; in life she was rather dark-skinned) and had a startled expression, dark eyes. A mouth almost lost in sternness. The man had made her take off her hat and her hair was raggedy and held together in two braids, one of which lay coiled on her shoulder. A smattering of freckles across her nose. Her shoulders were very narrow. One of her front pockets was torn.

She did not know that you were supposed to give the picture to your sweetheart—how would she know this?—and so she thought she would give the photograph to Angelene, or Talmadge, before she remembered she did not see them anymore. She fit the photograph inside her breast pocket. After a few minutes, when nothing else in the carnival succeeded in catching her eye—and she was hungry, but found no food stalls—she turned campward.

She wondered that evening, watching Clee move around the fire preparing supper, what his image would look like, captured in a photograph.
His frame was tall, heavy; his square head would take up the entire frame,
she thought, not understanding how a camera worked, not understanding that the lens could be adjusted. His hair was brushed up in a pompa-
dour and braids, in the style of many Nez Perce men at the time. His eyes
were heavy lidded; his cheekbones high and set wide apart. He wore a
dark wool shirt and a vest with fringe on the front, and a beaded necklace
with a medallion that he wore inside his shirt. And also a scapular—that
was what it was called, though she did not know it at the time.

She thought about this photograph of him that was not taken. That
night, taking out the photograph as she lay on her bedroll and looking
at it in the firelight—her own small, pale, startled image—she imagined
this invisible counterpart alongside it, giving it substance and weight.

ANGELENE SAT ON Talmadge's shoulders: *I am queen of the orchard!* Singing in the trees while they worked, silly songs he knew, and also hymns. Their voices in the trees. His absentminded whistling. The lilting sound, every once in a while, of Angelene asking a question.

RIDING IN THE herd, the sound like one constant, endless sigh; some horses frantic and others calm, some remembering some wrong done to them while others wanted only to sleep, and each struggling with hunger and thirst; some horses pregnant, others desperate to copulate; and all moved forward as one body amid the heat and the dust. The men and Della spaced out and caught among them like ornaments in a blanket; like disparate thoughts fretting to cohere. The feeling that this would never end, being caught in the herd, heading east or north, west or south, moving for some purpose, though that purpose was for the moment lost; the horses—the herd—carried the men at times more than the men guided them. The men were bound by time—they must reach the auction that evening, or the next day—and yet the riding among the horses through the landscape was endless and timeless, distanceless. It made some men—not the ones who were riding, but others, who lived elsewhere, employed in different occupations—desperate; it made Della sink down under the pressing weight of all that time, all that distance— for it was not deficit but surplus experienced between two destinations— and though she felt at times she could not move, because of the pressing weight, she also felt placed. Ensconced. Safe.

ANGELENE CROUCHED IN Talmadge's closet, among the hanging
flannel shirts. In the corner, atop two boxes of crystal glassware—
Talmadge had found them at a fair and was certain they had value—was
an open-topped box. She reached inside it.

She did not think she was forbidden to be there—she roamed in
and out of his room as if it were her own, and often cleaned there, on
Saturdays—but besides this, she did not even think she would be rep-
rimanded for going into his closet. There were the few times when he
called her for supper and found her there, hidden among his shirts, a
game. But she did not know what he would say about her exploring the
contents of the boxes, disassembling them, without his permission. But
she did it anyway, sensing that he would never be truly angry at her. And
where was he now, as her fingers clutched an object, smooth—glass?—
beneath a gingham wrapping? He was out in the orchard, working, or
sleeping on the porch. Later he would leave her alone in the orchard
while he went to town. But now she was too young—eight years old,
barely that—to be left by herself.

She was used to Talmadge's boxes. There were the boxes of glassware,
but also boxes of old almanacs and newspapers, magazines, other dishes
and knickknacks, in the shed. Things he had picked up over a lifetime of
fair-going and browsing the secondhand shops. People sometimes went
to estate sales in other counties, and brought treasures back for him.
Thought this might interest you, Talmadge. He had a collection of postcards,
tiny porcelain bells, and spoons with emblems of the forty-five states on
the handles. He did not order these from the catalog but kept track of
their production and then looked for them in the secondhand shops. The
storekeeper in town knew his predilections.

Objects too at times, after all, like the landscape, held the potential for meaning—she took out the first object now—and were able to comfort.

These items Angelene had never seen before. Two ambrotypes: one showing a dark-haired woman standing on a hillock with two young children, a boy and a girl, standing in front of her; the woman had her hands resting protectively on the children's chests. The other ambrotype showed the children alone, holding hands in front of a trellis, squinting in the sunlight. There was also a pair of extremely old children's leather boots with a ruffle along the toe; a white christening gown, yellowed with age; and a pair of baby's booties.

Talmadge had not told Angelene about his family, or about his history in the orchard. What, then, must she have made of those images? Did she know that was Talmadge's mother, and the little girl standing beside him was his sister? Did she know that Talmadge was the boy? Did she understand that Talmadge had ever been a boy? It was difficult to know exactly what she made of the images, though she must have been impressed by them, because she returned to them again and again.

One day she was particularly confident and brought in a cup of tea with her to the bedroom. She had already pulled out the box minutes before in anticipation of viewing, and left the room for the tea—and as she returned, coming into the room, she tripped over a slightly raised floorboard, and fell. The cup, like some bad joke, landed in the box, and with horror, as she lifted out the cup and felt the box for moisture, she saw that the boots were relatively unharmed, but the gown was stained and the ambrotypes were ruined. She cleaned the objects to the best of her ability, so shocked and afraid that she was unable even to cry. Her hands shook. She wrapped one of the ambrotypes that had broken in a handkerchief and then put the box back. Maybe, she thought, he wouldn't know that she had done it. Oh no, she would say, when he pulled out the box and asked her if she knew anything about it. What happened?

But at supper that night, unable to contain herself, she burst into tears and told him what she had done. He got up from the table and went into the bedroom and came out a few minutes later. She did not remember what he looked like because she did not look up at him. He did not sit down at the table but remained standing.

Those are not your things, he said, and when she didn't answer, he told her to go to her room. She went, relieved, but also confused. He had never sent her to her room before.

The next day he was what she considered cold to her, and she sulked and grieved. She hid in the grass of the plum orchard and planned to stay there, even when he called her for dinner. But he didn't call her for dinner, or even come look for her. She grew hungry. It was made worse by the fact that she detected—how could it be?—the odor of pancakes coming from the cabin. He had propped the door open. And then, coming on the tail end of the other odor was the odor of bacon. He was in there whistling to himself. Finally she got up and walked around the side of the cabin. When she stood in the doorway, he looked up, as if surprised to see her. Oh, there you are, he said. I thought I was going to have to eat this all by myself.

After they ate, she sat on his lap on the front porch and cried and told him she was sorry. He stroked her head.

You'll ask me next time, he said. I can show them to you.

Yes, she said. I'm sorry.

All right.

And what was he to tell her, about the ambrotypes? That conversation was an invitation to question him about the objects, but he dreaded such a conversation. Why had he left them in the closet that way, why hadn't he put them up? His pointing out—*This is me, my mother, my sister*—would lead to other questions, ones that he felt unprepared to answer. *Where is your sister now, Talmadge?* He would lie about it, with only little qualm— the child was too young to absorb the fact of another girl's disappearance. It would be cruel to introduce a story like that to her imagination. Maybe he would tell her all of it later. Much later, when she was an adult.

But there it was: he did not believe she would ever be an adult. He watched her, thinking: And how does one so small and perfect in her way become an adult? The change would never occur if he kept his eye on her; because how could change happen so quickly? There was only one answer: it could not. But then she had changed so much already—

Also—he did not want to consider this directly—he did not want to excite dormant questions about Angelene's own mother. He and Caroline Middey had decided to tell the girl, when she asked, that her mother had died of sickness. That Jane and Della had come to Talmadge from the forest, and Jane was pregnant; she gave birth, and then died. Della had left the orchard of her own accord; she did not want to stay there, and so had left. Explaining Della's character beyond this—explaining how she could have left, by unspoken agreement, Angelene in Talmadge's care, and did not ever come to visit anymore—was beyond him. Regardless, it was years away before such explanation was required. Or so he hoped.

But the girl, miraculously, had not yet asked about her mother. She was attentive enough to exchanges between certain women and their children in town, but thought, as far as he could tell, that some people have mothers like some have siblings: by chance, and not necessity. He was ashamed to make her wait, to rely upon the great mountain of confusion that would have to amass before she initiated the first, tentative conversation. It pained him to think of it.

But he did not want to disturb her, either. Let her childhood, for as long as possible, remain unblighted—

A week later, while Angelene and Talmadge were in town, they got their photograph taken at the portraitist's studio. It was a surprise for the girl. There was a lilac-colored dress hanging in the back room that Angelene was supposed to change into. Caroline Middey had helped Talmadge pick it out. When Angelene changed into the dress and came out to join him, she could see how pleased he was. He was dressed up too, was wearing a fancy cowboy hat. He reached for her hand.

How lovely, the portraitist kept saying. How lovely.

DELLA LOWERED HERSELF above the horse's back without touching the flesh, holding herself up in the scaffolding above the chute—and both men, one at either elbow, saying Okay? and checking to see that the horse was not caught in the chute, that no impediment would keep the animal from surging with utmost force the moment it was released. As soon as the panel at the opposite end of the chute was wrenched up, Della would drop onto the horse's back. She would be carried forth, crashing through the chute and into the arena in a matter of seconds.

Both Clee and the wrangler disapproved of this spectacle and had tried to keep her from doing it. But at the last moment they had no power over what she did; they just stood by and watched like the rest. Disgusted. Clee's jaw hard.

This entry did not excite the auction-goers so much as make them extremely uncomfortable. Just last year a rodeo man had mounted a bull in the deep chute and been trampled to death before the bull reached the arena. The entrance was unnecessarily dangerous; there was always a moment when the chute seemed too long, and she thought she would be flung underfoot. That dread, that sureness that she was going to fail, to die, was why she did it. She craved, for some reason—she would not look at it directly—that sense of despair.

Now, in the chute, hovering over the horse, her extremities emptied of feeling, and she felt only the steady, increased beating of her heart. She dissolved.

Are you ready? the man on her left whispered to her. Did she respond? She must have, for the panel shot up with a grating noise, and the animal jolted beneath her.

———

She saw despair as one sees a solid object in the distance. And then she was inside it. Through it.

Perhaps it was not the despair she craved, but the moment afterward: the brilliant moment of *not falling.* Success.

But, no. What was recognized as success—the applause, the exclamations, the job well done; she was already off the horse, pumping people's hands in congratulations—did not fill her. Did not even begin to fill her. What she wanted was the despair, or something else that was found there. Something that lived with despair. But the moment she was inside it, she failed to find what it was she wanted so badly.

And so she would ride again.

Aᴄᴛᴇʀ ᴀɴɢᴇʟᴇɴᴇ's ɴɪɴᴛʜ birthday, Talmadge took her to the far apple orchard and showed her a quarter acre that had been sectioned off by small wooden posts in the ground. These posts marked the border of the orchard that was to be entirely hers. She would be responsible for clearing the plot, cultivating the soil, and choosing the trees and planting them. When he explained this to her, she felt buoyant with joy. Her hands began to sweat. In her excitement and confusion, she said: Does Della have a plot like this?

No, he answered, after a moment. At that point they had not seen Della for three years. Angelene would never know why she had asked such a question.

And so she began to tend her own orchard, and think of many things she had not thought of before, such as if she had a choice, which kinds of trees would she plant, and what would thrive there, and how far apart she should plant the trees, and where she would get the trees. Talmadge observed her struggles, answered her questions when she asked him. He bought her a small notebook like his own to fit into her front overall pocket while she worked. She began to be interested in the tools at the hardware store, the prices of different seed. She had a rough understanding, despite her age, of what was expensive, what was overpriced, what was a bargain. She and Talmadge discussed these things on the long wagon rides to and from town.

Mostly she learned from watching him. She watched him in everything he did; she was his shadow in the trees.

———

Clee's men left Della, not at that auction where she mounted the horse in the deep chute but two years later, when she got drunk one evening off corn liquor another man offered her. She came back to camp—she had finally found it in her confusion—and the wrangler helped her to her bedroll and told her to be quiet. When she retched, Clee came out from his tent and sat with her and helped her. In the morning when she woke, the camp was dismantled and the men were gone. They had left her there. When she caught up with them midday, none of the men would look at her. Clee and the wrangler came to her after supper, and the wrangler told her that if she acted that way again, she would not be welcome to ride with them. She said she understood. But she did not apologize.

For some reason—she did not remember why afterward—Angelene wanted to grow, along with four apple trees, a cherry tree, and a peach tree, a pumpkin patch. Talmadge did not even bat an eyelash when she told him this. He was responsible for obtaining the first seeds for her.

It seemed it would last a long time, when Della was traveling with the men. She had a sense, deep inside her, that when she was riding with them, when they were camped on some sage plateau, set to arrive in Spokane the next evening, or perhaps the morning after that, that she would be doing it a long time. For as long as she could envision. And she would never change, she would never be any different from that image of herself in the thumb-sized photograph she carried in her pocket. And yet it had lasted no time at all. She traveled that way, with that ease—but it wasn't ease at all, she just remembered it that way—for two years, perhaps a bit more. And then other things distracted her. Drinking, but that was not all of it. Riding horses wasn't enough, anymore, to access that despair that she needed so badly. Jane had been in the horses, but now she was not. She was elsewhere. What had happened to her? Della could no longer remember the way she smelled, what her voice sounded like. Had she ever had a sister, or was that a dream, like so much else?

Angelene entered one of the pumpkins from her first harvest in the county fair, and won a prize. Afterward, the newspaper wanted to take a picture of her with her pumpkin, and so she sat on a bale of hay with her pumpkin at her feet, her old straw hat on her head, and posed. In the moment after the man took the picture—Angelene was blinded by the flash, and there was the high insect whirr of the box camera—she heard two voices, girls, or they could have been young women. The first said: Who is that? And the other answered, breezily: Oh, she's that whore's girl, she won that prize—

That whore's girl. Angelene did not know what that meant, exactly, but she knew enough to break out into a cold sweat the moment she heard it, and later hesitate, on the ride back home, to ask Talmadge what it meant.

He did not notice anything was amiss. He looked straight ahead in the wagon, on his face an expression of subdued pleasure from her winning the prize.

She let the moment pass, intuiting, even then, what would hurt him.

What's a whore? she asked Caroline Middey two days later, as they peeled potatoes in Caroline Middey's kitchen. They were preparing supper for them all: Talmadge had gone to town but would be back by evening.

Caroline Middey raised her eyebrows but did not take her eyes from the task at hand. She hesitated.

A whore is a woman who lies with men for money, she said.

Angelene, after a minute, said: Oh.

Then, the inevitable: What do you mean, Lies with?

Caroline Middey sighed. She and Talmadge should have talked about this: When was it the right time to talk to the girl about—things? But, she thought, if it was up to Talmadge then the girl would never be told.

Angelene, working slower now, watched Caroline Middey, as if to glean any information—any knowledge—from the other woman's expression.

There is an activity, said Caroline Middey, that grown men and women—married people, but they do not have to be married, do they, no. She hesitated, considering. There is an activity that they do, when they love each other, and they decide they want to be together, where they take off their clothes, and rub—certain parts of their bodies together. This is called intercourse.

The girl drew back her head, puzzled.

No, she said, breaking into laughter. Go on!

Caroline Middey smiled too, despite herself. How strange it all was—the girl was right—and how strange it must be to hear it for the first time.

There is a lot more to it, warned Caroline Middey. And I will explain it all to you one day. But a young girl like yourself does not need to know too much. It doesn't do to know—or be thinking about such things—right away.

There was a silence.

And so a whore does it for money, prompted Angelene. How much money?

Caroline Middey pursed her lips.

Goodness, child!

Angelene pulled back, impressed and surprised that with that question she could have rattled the woman who was so often hard to move.

I don't know, said Caroline Middey. But I will tell you this: it's not something that women, most women, like to speak of, if they're doing it, or they know someone who is. It's not—accepted, mostly. She paused briefly. There are some people who see no shame in it. They treat it like a—business transaction. But then she looked at the girl, carefully.

If Talmadge knew we were talking about this—

But why? said Angelene, her eyes keen with interest. She had stopped working, her hands clutching the rim of the bowl. Would he be mad? But why?

Caroline Middey was helpless.

There are certain subjects that make some people—Talmadge especially—very uncomfortable.

But not you, said Angelene.

Not me, no, conceded Caroline Middey. After a brief silence, both of them working again, she said, I want you to ask *me* questions about this kind of thing—don't go around asking anybody else.

Angelene, apparently satisfied, absorbed in her work again, said without hesitation: All right.

But it did not occur to Caroline Middey until later, after the girl had gone to sleep—in the room with the hanging herbs; Talmadge slept on a cot in the kitchen—that the girl, in order to have asked the question, must have heard the word somewhere. Caroline Middey was going to make inquiries, but upon seeing the girl in the morning, face freshly washed, coming to her with a hairbrush, asking Caroline Middey to braid her hair, she could not bring herself to ask. If the girl was troubled, thought Caroline Middey, then she already knew enough to come to her.

But still Caroline Middey was bothered. What had the girl heard? What was she thinking?

On the way back to the orchard, riding in the back of the wagon, Angelene's mind was washed clean of worry. The girl at the fair had called her a whore's girl—but very clearly she was mistaken, or she was talking about somebody else. For Angelene did not know any whores.

How long had Della been in the wilderness, this time? Had she gone into the forest because she was ill, or had she become ill because she was in the forest? Each succeeding day ate away at her memory, and after a length of time had passed—a week? a month? two months?—she was unsure of the events of her life leading to that moment. One morning she woke and could not remember her name. Dolly? Annie? Annie was the name they gave to girls who would not reveal their true names, at Michaelson's camp . . .

Days transpired. Somehow she was able to sleep outdoors in the cold. She had stolen a buffalo rug. Laughed, not remembering where it came from. Lay whole days under it, feverish. The fever let out some of the old grief. She called Jane's name, or thought she did. Remembered her children, who had not been fully formed, who had died. And how was she still alive? How was that possible?

She dreamed of Talmadge, that he was cooking her food. He told her to pick which closed fist, and she picked one, and he turned his hand and opened his palm: there was an apricot stone. She reached for it, and it disappeared.

In the morning, angry, airy with hunger, she crawled from beneath the blanket and staggered to a road she must have known about, for she went directly to it. Made her way to town.

The fever was over. She would eat, find a horse—her own horse she entered the forest with had disappeared—and then find work.

In the schoolhouse north of Cashmere, along the river, Angelene sat near the window that looked out onto a large cottonwood. She drew courage from that tree, which seemed to have been planted there for the sole purpose of being her friend.

She was very scared in the beginning—the air smelled of chalk and cold, and the voices of the other children were sharp as needles, and intrusive—but that passed.

History was baffling to her. There seemed to be too much of it. She preferred geography, was struck by the idea that there could be different landscapes from the one in which she lived. After a lesson on photosynthesis, she drew diagrams in the small notebook Talmadge had given her, and regarded these drawings often, improving upon them, thinking: And this is how it works: sun, soil, sugar, water . . . She could not wait to tell Talmadge about it.

The other chief love—and how similar it was to science, and how different—was reading. As soon as she realized the figures on the page meant something—could be strung together as words, and then sentences, and then paragraphs—she was covetous of the whole system. It seemed a new universe to her. And it was. Everything opened up. Some stories were meant to inform, and others were meant to entertain. And then other stories were separate from those—this the young teacher did not tell her, it was something Angelene figured out on her own, the first year, when a man visited and read them a *poem* out of a tome of poems— that seemed crafted to relay some secret, and even more than that, some secret about herself. Angelene was mesmerized. What was available for her to know? What secrets did the world hold? Which secrets would be revealed through the soil, and which through words?

IN THE SPRING of 1911 Della traveled with an outfit of men from Pendleton, Oregon, into the Sawtooths. These were not Clee's men—she had found jobs traveling with other men, in other outfits that would accept her. The outfits, like this one, would usually have to be short a few men to agree to take her on; but even so, despite the general wariness to include her, she had been around some all-right types in the last few years. That is to say, she had been with men who more or less left her alone.

This group in the Sawtooths she had been traveling with for a week. They were hunting horses in the high ranges. Some of the men had wanted that morning to return down the mountain, saying they had got enough horses to satisfy the boss, but it had been discussed among them all and finally decided that they would keep at it, go up into some other peaks, another two days, at least, to search for more horses. Otherwise, the hunt, the whole enterprise, would have more or less failed. They had promised the boss more horses than they had captured thus far. But it was hard going; it was May, and yet it had snowed the day before last, in the early morning. These men were among the roughest she had traveled with—loud at night, careless with their words and hands. One or two had touched her, but nobody had outright abused her, and so she stayed. Wanted to stick it out, for the payment, of course, but there were also the horses to think about, the great hunting in the days to come.

After a week of traveling they came into a camp in the late afternoon, just before dusk. Some men began to prepare their evening meals while others went to the river to wash. It was a valley high in the range, and as the sun went down, the snow-covered peaks in the distance glowed. In the valley there was a deep hush, and the noises the men and horses made were tinny in comparison. The entire valley wrapped around them and blanketed them in distance.

Della did not go with the men to wash, and neither did she light a fire right away. She sat on her bedroll and looked out over the valley darkening. And where would she go, what would she do? Ate a loaf-end of bread, incredibly tough, she had found in her saddlebag. Her hands dark with filth. The sweat, as it dried on her body, chilled her. When darkness came the men sat in their camp below—she sat uphill from them, a few yards off—eating and guffawing. Some of the men were still sore about going up into the mountains; any moment that might turn into something else. She was constantly attuned to the noise of the men, the different pitches that would mean that they were talking about women, they were talking about her. The men were tired and lonely, they were angry.

She lit a fire, and heated some beans. As she waited, a form separated from the camp below, and moved uphill. He took only a few steps before he paused and then returned to the camp. That's right, she thought. That's right. Her arm was steady as she transferred the can of beans, which she handled with a mitt, between her knees. Tentatively began to eat them. Watched the camp. She burned her mouth, and cursed. When she'd finished eating, she scoured the empty can with a rag from her kit and then put the can in her saddlebag. Stomped out the fire. Lay down on her bedroll.

Her eyes closed, she listened to the men. They had begun to drink. She listened to them even as she slept. Even though her hand rested on the hilt of the unsheathed hunting knife under her pillow, she was not afraid. She knew what to listen for, and the atmosphere wasn't right for them to come for her. It was close, but still not right. It was not close enough that she would not be able to sleep. Tomorrow she would have to reevaluate the situation. But tonight she could rest.

What did you learn? Talmadge asked Angelene, when she was back in the orchard. She stayed with Caroline Middey three days out of the week now, because it was too far to travel from the orchard to the schoolhouse and back every day. They sat at the table, eating, and Angelene told him all that she could remember. The dates of battles of the Revolutionary

War, some times tables, why there was so much ash in the soil. After supper she studied at the table while Talmadge sat in the chair in the corner,
looking at his almanacs. Sometimes he looked at them only a short time
before getting up and going outside, to do what, perhaps walk in the orchard. He sometimes did that if it was getting close to a heavy work time,
or if he was upset by something, or if his food wasn't digesting properly.
Often when he passed by her he would touch her head, as if to say, Keep
going, I'll be right outside, you keep studying. There was a sort of tender
pride there that made her feel as if she was doing something important,
something that pleased him deeply.

DELLA AND THE men hunted a new peak, and the hunting was good. The men, despite the fact that they had drunk a lot the night before, seemed focused. They were quiet among themselves, and hunting the horses, all as one body, had been a kind of dance. It was one of the best days of hunting by far. And yet when they came into the place where they would bed down for the night, along a creek, the birches bending thick over them, although the men were quieter and more aloof than the previous night, she knew it was not right. She got as far as unrolling her bedroll and getting out her can of beans when she knew she would not even be able to prepare supper. The men weren't even looking at her. As usual, some of them had started their fires, and the others went down to the water to wash. She led her horse a little ways off, under the pretense that she was going to let him wade deep enough to bathe. She just kept walking. Nobody came after her. She walked until she could not hear the men behind her anymore, and the forest mended in silence behind her. They would wonder about her, they would even search for her, and they would hate her for it. But she had no choice. She could feel the old familiar feeling, waiting under the canopy of trees. It had fit her like a glove, and she was certain in her soul she had been there before. She had had to escape her own fate.

She knew, roughly, where she was. She would not be able to travel very far that night, but she would rise before the sun and make her way down the mountain again. She knew where the men were traveling, and she would give them a wide berth. That night, when she bedded down, despite the fact that she knew she had escaped abuse, she was afraid. At times this roving, sharp-edged fear found her. She told herself that she would be all right. She could not see the stars; the trees were too thick overhead. She listened for her horse in the dark, called to it.

The silence and darkness of the forest were extraordinary.

"A ND THE NEXT day, just as it was beginning to get dark," Angelene read aloud, "he went to the tower and called out: Rapunzel, Rapunzel, let down your hair. The hair fell down, and the prince climbed up. At first Rapunzel was—terribly frightened—when a man such as she had never seen before came in to her. However, the prince began talking to her in a very friendly manner, telling her that his heart had been so— touched—by her singing that he could have no peace until he had seen her in person. Then Rapunzel lost her fear, and when he asked her if she would take him as her husband, she thought, 'He would rather have me than would—Frau Gothel.' She said yes and placed her hand into his . . .'"

Angelene stopped reading and looked at Talmadge, who lay sleeping in the horsehair chair, his mouth hanging open, the newspaper collapsed on his lap. He had wanted her to read to him—What's this book you've been toting around? If it's so good, read me a bit of it—but he had become drowsy as soon as she had started reading, and then had fallen asleep.

She read a little further, quietly, to herself, and then after a minute got up from the floor, where she had been cuddled in a nest of cushions and blankets, and went to the small mirror over the basin, and looked at herself. The long face, the dark eyebrows, the careful, pensive mouth. Who was she? she thought. Was she beautiful? Was she strong?

IT TOOK DELLA two days to travel down the mountain. The day after that she reached the town where the boss for the outfit she had
recently abandoned lived. She did not know what she was going to say
to him, but when she reached the building she stood outside the door,
on the platform, with the sun beating down on her head. As she hesitated outside, a man walked out of the office and passed her and then a
moment later he looked at her again and his face changed. She also had
turned to look at him, but then quickly turned forward. It was one of the
men she had been traveling with, but he was washed and clean-shaven
and she had not recognized him right away. His face was twisting itself
in an effort to accuse her.

But she had begun to walk down the street, quickly.

She would not be able to land a job working in an outfit easily after
that, and so she decided to head westward, where she had heard there
was a call for women working in canning factories along the coast.

But she was hungry and could not make it to the coast without money
in her pocket. She debated whether to sell her horse, but decided not to.
What was she, without her horse? She got a job picking cherries instead,
in the Yakima Valley, to tide her over. She was hired easily, along with
other workers and local townspeople, and when one orchard was finished
she was hired on at another. She saw many of the same people among
jobs. She saw, even, some of the men, here and there, who traveled with
Clee, who had worked at times in the orchard up in Peshastin. They did
not say anything to each other, however, but their eyes met once or twice
through the foliage.

———

When Angelene stayed with Caroline Middey, she was expected to help with the chores the same way she was expected to in the orchard. There were chores she performed at Caroline Middey's that were the same as those in the orchard, and there were those that were distinct. Because of the relationship Angelene had with Talmadge, and with Caroline Middey—each relationship was unique and yet at the same time shared many qualities—there was never any chiding involved, or threats, or even raised voices. Angelene did as she was asked, and although at times she was distracted and perhaps sloppy, she did not resent her chores, she was mostly eager to perform them, and had no argument with what was expected of her. That was why it was surprising when one morning, after Caroline Middey had worked several hours outdoors in her garden, waiting for Angelene, who did not arrive, the older woman found the girl indoors, still in bed.

When Caroline Middey opened the door to the bedroom, the girl burrowed under the covers.

What's this? said Caroline Middey. There was a silence, and then the girl said, in a voice high with apology: I think I'll just stay in bed today, if that's all right. I mean—I'll be staying here for a bit, is all. I'm just going to stay here—

What's wrong? Are you sick?

No—

Come out from under there, I can't hear you.

The girl hesitated, and then came out slowly. And burst into tears.

What's wrong?

I don't know. Nothing. I just don't want to do anything today, I just want to lie here for a bit, I have to think—

Caroline Middey stood looking at her.

Angelene soon went back under the covers. She heard Caroline Middey leave the room, and thought that was the end of it. She, Caroline Middey, would go work in the garden, and Angelene would either be pulled out there by guilt, or she would manage to remain in bed for however long she wanted—but how long was that? How was she ever going to think properly, this way, if she was guilty? But one thing was certain:

it was too late for Talmadge not to hear about it. With this, she was filled with dread and shame, and burrowed deeper beneath the covers.

But Caroline Middey did not go out into the garden. She came back into the room several minutes later, hatless and shoeless, changed into her housedress. She carried toast on a plate, and coffee.

Scoot over, she said, and Angelene, who had come out from under the covers again, moved over, and Caroline Middey got into the bed beside her. The mattress creaked.

Angelene accepted the toast and coffee, bashfully. Caroline Middey ate as well, the blankets pulled over her lap. She chewed thoughtfully, glancing out the high window. The ivy out there had to be trimmed.

Now, what's this about?

Angelene's mouth trembled, and she had to replace the toast on the plate. She looked gravely down at her lap.

I don't know what I'm supposed to do.

What's that?

I said I don't know what I'm supposed to do.

About what?

About—my life.

There was silence. Caroline Middey continued to eat.

I don't know why I go to school, said Angelene, doubtful.

Caroline Middey nodded once, to encourage her to keep speaking.

All we do, said Angelene, it seems like—here she became nervous—me and you and Talmadge, all we do is the same thing all the time, and nothing changes, and you have to do it every day, and I just—I mean, why do we do it? I'm not saying I don't like to do it, because I do, but, I mean, why—even the learning, and even doing anything, I mean, I was just thinking about it—

But that's where she stopped. She didn't know how to continue. She was going to cry again. This speech was not at all what she wanted to say, but she hoped that Caroline Middey would see through it, or know what she really meant.

Caroline Middey, after a long pause, so long in fact that Angelene thought she was not going to answer her at all, sighed and patted the quilt under which lay Angelene's hand.

My dear, she said. There is one thing I want to tell you, and I hope you carry it with you to the end of your days.

Angelene felt her body dissolve in anticipation. This is what she wanted, finally: someone to give her *the answer*.

No matter how bad you feel, said Caroline Middey, glancing at the girl now, or how bad you think your situation is, there is always somebody else who is feeling worse than you are, who is in worse shape. And so you should never, ever complain. Never.

And then she sighed again, and patted Angelene's hand over the covers, and wiped some toast crumbs from her chest onto the plate, and got out of bed. She said, without looking at Angelene, You stay in here as long as you want. I'm not going to tell you what to do. You're a growing girl, you're getting big. You get your thinking out of the way, or whatever you like, whatever you have to do. I'll be outside.

After she was gone, Angelene lay on her belly and cried silently and hotly into the pillow and then got up and washed her face in the basin, and dressed. She joined Caroline Middey in the garden and the older woman accepted her without pomp, told her to watch the radishes, they were tough, and she had damaged one already because she did not understand how they were growing. Angelene nodded and listened to her. Very soon the feeling she had woken to—the dread of existence—wore away under the work, and she felt fine. Better than fine—she was relieved, refreshed, although she would have told no one that, not even Caroline Middey, who laid a hand on her shoulder, gently, as she passed to inspect the lettuce farther down the row.

THERE WAS ONE woman during the time of fruit-picking who seemed to seek Della out, a woman roughly the same age as her, but very small and round, with a round, pointed, volelike face. Her dark hair bound up in a red kerchief. She picked alongside Della in the first camp and jabbered at her through the limbs as they worked. She had asked Della's name early on, and Della had told her, and the woman had said that her name was Margaret Peabody but that everybody called her Maggie P. That's the initial, not the vegetable, she had said, and laughed at her own joke, but Della had not known what she was talking about.

Maggie P., for her small hands, worked quickly, and talking a mile a minute did not seem to hamper her work at all. She was propelled by constant speech, and did not flag, even when she commented, Phew, I'm parched, aren't you? Or: Lord, I dragged myself out of bed this morning, what about you? And she was careful but speedy climbing up and down ladders, pausing only briefly in her speech if she encountered a bundle of fruit that needed extra attention. Those times when Maggie P. ceased to speak were golden pockets of silence, and Della reveled in them, knowing that they would be interrupted only moments later by the insistent voice saying, Where was I? What was I telling you about, now?

Though the heat bothered Maggie P., and her mother had told her she was capable of making a better use of her time than working in the trees, Maggie P. said that she enjoyed it. Every year around harvesttime, though she said she was going to enroll down at the stenographer school, like her aunt had arranged for her, every year she was drawn to the fruit on the trees; she saw the people come in, the workers from the south, and she just threw on her old clothes, her denim overalls and her kerchief, and went and worked among them.

There's nothing like it, she said, for how it wears out the body and what you get for it. I'm not talking about money, now, I'm talking about fruit! Twenty pies I made one year, with my mother and aunts and the little ones. Blueberry pies, strawberry pies—you ever pick the berries? It's different work, harder in some ways, but if you get the hang of it, you can make some money—

And on and on she went.

When the cherries were done, they went together to pick a peach orchard that Maggie P. knew about and had picked the previous year. Though she had found Della the job, and they roomed together with two other women in a picker cabin up the hill from where they worked, in the morning Maggie P. found Della's bed empty. After breakfast, she found Della working among others in the trees. But Maggie P. found a place beside her and took up the thread of soliloquy she had left the previous afternoon.

Maggie P. was used to quiet types. Her father was a quiet type. As long as Della did not object to her talking, as others often did, she would just go on doing it.

Maggie P. was not one of those people who talked only about themselves. Early on, she had asked Della where she was from and what she was about. When Maggie P. got monosyllabic answers or none at all, she took the hint and began talking about herself. But that did not lessen her curiosity about her new friend, which was not the rabid inquisitiveness of the gossip, but the true kind.

You say you're from up Wenatchee way? said Maggie P. one day. Well, they have some fruit up there! I haven't picked it, but I've heard stories about some orchards—and hoped the other woman would chime in. And when she didn't, she, Maggie P., hoped she, Della, appreciated, or was at least comforted by, the mention of the place Della was from. She wanted to make her feel at ease.

For the most part Maggie P. bewildered Della in her talkativeness, and annoyed her. Where there was a constant stream of words, Della would have preferred the silence, the minutiae of sound of work in the trees, of movement of bodies and birds, and of faraway sounds the origin of which she could only guess at. Maggie P. brought the world right in front of them; she pointed it out, and then she talked about it. But despite this, despite Della's annoyance with her, there were moments, especially before they went to sleep, when Della, exhausted, tucked into her bed, watched Maggie P. brush her short, thick cap of hair over and over again with equal parts absence and attention, and then, her eyes squeezed shut, apply cold cream to her face, and then also her elbows and chest, talking to Della all the while. Della, during these times, did not feel annoyed, but simply watchful. It reminded her of other times, watching the girls at Michaelson's camp prepare themselves for the evening, when she would forget—but how could she ever forget it?—what came later. Here, watching Maggie P., Della reminded herself the woman was only preparing to sleep: there was no other purpose attached to her self-care.

The other women were asleep, or hadn't come in yet. Maggie P. always liked to read a little bit before she went to bed, did Della mind the light? She didn't. And so Della went to sleep often to the sound of Maggie P. reading, for in reading she was still not silent, but chuckled softly, or sounded out difficult words, grunted, gasped. Turned the page. Sighed.

Della, for some reason, when she slept near Maggie P., slept deeply, and woke refreshed.

IN LATE JULY Talmadge and Angelene packed up the wagon and drove to Malaga, to attend the annual plant sale and carnival. In Cashmere they picked up Caroline Middey, who climbed into the wagon with her shopping baskets and her basket of food, and a large parasol that was not for her—she had a large straw hat—but for Angelene, since the girl sat in the wagon bed, and Caroline Middey worried about her. One could never be too careful about sunstroke, she said.

They always went the same way, south along the Wenatchee River until its confluence with the Columbia. The Wenatchee River was narrow and familiar, clattering and riffling, surrounded by evergreens and then, later, rocky gravel banks, but the Columbia was different. It was kingly. Serious, roiling, wide. It looked as if it was not flowing very quickly, but Talmadge told Angelene that it was. No matter how many times she saw the Columbia, she was always struck by it. She sometimes dreamed about it, about walking along it and staring at its strange opaque quality, or trying to cross it by herself, and drowning.

In Malaga, on the bluff above the river, the merchants had set up their wares, small tents erected to harbor young trees, the saplings anchored in barrels of wet sand. Caroline Middey set off by herself, and Talmadge and Angelene toured the booths along with the other orchardists and homesteaders, and the odd travelers who had come upon the fair by accident and did not know what it was. All of them traveling from booth to booth, taking the wedges of apples and pears handed out, tasting them. It had taken several years for Angelene to realize that the orchardists handed out the fruit for a purpose; they were samples from trees whose saplings were for sale. What you tasted at the fair you could grow yourself, if you liked, if the trees' needs were compatible with the soil and the climate where you lived.

Angelene remembered Talmadge's expression during these trips. He was looking for something, but he did not know what it was. He wanted to be surprised; he wanted one of the orchardists to surprise him. He went from booth to booth with a distracted expression on his face, his brow both soft and furrowed, taking what fruit was offered to him. His lips shone slightly. She followed him closely.

For a long time the highlight of the trip for Angelene was the carnival, appended to the market and lining the bank of the river. Here people milled about, eating food and talking, children darting through the crowd like sparrows. There was an outdoor band, banjos and violas and accordions, and a few couples dancing jerkily before them. Talmadge put Angelene, before she grew too big, on his shoulders to see. A child pushed past, her face decorated with blue and yellow paint. A short man with a mop of greasy curls climbed onto a boulder and shouted that whoever wanted a pony ride should come see him in the next ten minutes. Holding hands now, Talmadge and Angelene moved through the throng. A white-faced clown juggled yellow apples. A fire-eater displayed a mouth large enough to fit a fist into; a dancing dog with a bow tie and tails, a top hat strapped beneath his chin, waltzed with a woman; a troupe of children bent low to the ground and stood on their heads; a man performed card tricks with tremendous flourish; and another man pulled objects—a pocket watch, an egg, a handkerchief—out of his hat by just passing his hand over it, and also coins and small stones from behind children's ears. From behind Angelene's ear he pulled a mountain daisy, the face spanning no more than a centimeter. Ah, he said. A flower! A flower for a flower!

Talmadge, Caroline Middey, and Angelene ate lunch on a blanket at the river's edge, apart from the crowd. They ate food they had prepared that morning, biscuits and venison and apricots, some pickled cucumbers and asparagus in small jars. Afterward Talmadge walked to an old man selling watermelons and purchased one. He brought it back to where they sat and cracked it on a rock and cut chunks out with his pocketknife. They ate bent over and with their elbows held out, so as not to soil their clothes. Angelene laughed. They ate the whole melon, slowly, their hands dripping.

DELLA DID NOT think she was listening much to Maggie P.—hearing her voice but not really listening to what she said—but she found that she knew, somehow, certain details of the other woman's life. That she was born in Ellensburg but her family lived now in Vantage. Her father was a doctor, and she had nine brothers and sisters, of which she was the eldest. Her father came from a large family as well, and Maggie P. had lots and lots of cousins. Among the aunts on her father's side there were working girls—two who had gone into the stenographer business, which had upset the family for a little while, until they—the family— found other things to get excited about. One of the things they loved to get upset about was every year at harvesttime when Maggie P. ran off, as they called it—as if she wasn't ever coming back—to work the trees. They didn't understand it.

Della did not speak to Maggie P. at first, beyond the most basic pleasantries, and it was understood between them that when Maggie P. asked her a question that she, Della, did not want to answer, then Maggie P. shouldn't take it personally. And she didn't. But then in the midst of working, Maggie P. would sometimes pose something so casually, and Della's answer promised to be so safely hemmed into Maggie P.'s quick response, that at times Della found herself speaking, hesitantly, and so quietly that Maggie P., who oftentimes worked below her on the ladder, had to strain to hear her. What was that, love? I didn't quite hear you there— And Della would repeat herself: Well, I have a niece too, and a sister— Oh, they live up Wenatchee way, do they? Yes—

And although it seemed that Maggie P. divulged every detail of her life to Della—it was long hours they worked together in the trees—she did not tell Della everything, because one did not divulge everything.

She did not tell her, for example, that her one great dream in life was to own her own orchard, and live on it with a man from Mexico. She was ashamed to admit she did not have one man picked out, but she saw him in her visions of the future, and he was short and robust and brown, like her, with the lovely square, strong hands of the Mexican laborers. She had learned a few words of Spanish, and had tentatively spoken to a few men as they passed each other in the green aisles, frightening one, amusing another. The one who was amused spoke back to her, but she did not understand what he said. She was haunted by the possibility that she had missed her chance for happiness. But she had not missed her chance, she told herself, for her chance would not let her get away so easily. Each morning she was fortified by hope: the future loomed.

MY STARS, GIRL, said Caroline Middey, pulling a straight pin from between her lips. She knelt beside Angelene, who stood on a stool before the full-length mirror in Caroline Middey's guest bedroom, wearing a gingham dress that Caroline Middey was letting down the hem for.

You've grown two inches, at least, said Caroline Middey.

Angelene said nothing, but when Caroline Middey bent down to work again, Angelene put her shoulders back. Lifted her chin. Gave herself a steely—and by this she meant to be womanly—look. And then saw (but could not be sure): the suggestion of breasts beneath the fabric across her chest.

And then the peaches were done, and Maggie P. was going to pick berries farther south. Did Della want to join her? It was good money, and she would show her just how to do it, there was no better teacher, really—

But Della was going west, to the coast, to the canning factory, as she had planned. Maggie P. kept a straight face upon hearing this news, although she could hardly believe it. Why would any person choose to work in a canning factory if they could pick berries in northern California?

Well, which one are you working at? Which canning factory?

Della said she didn't know, she would find a place when she got there. She didn't ask why Maggie P. wanted to know, but Maggie P. said: I'm going to write to you.

But you don't know where I'm staying, said Della.

I'm not stupid! Maggie P. burst out, and walked away quickly.

It was a common occurrence that whoever met Maggie P. and came up against her immense friendliness thought she was immune to hurt feelings. But she wasn't. She wished people would understand that. It wasn't very nice, really, how most people treated her.

THE FIRST RAILROAD, the Great Northern, came to central Washington in 1893, seven years before Angelene was born. Thousands of men had worked to bore tunnels into the sides of mountains for the trains to pass through, connecting those people and products east of the mountains to those west of them. There was a party in Cashmere when the track was laid. The station was erected soon after, and the first train of passengers rode to Seattle free of charge.

Locomotive travel gave an air of authority and sophistication to the town, at least for a little while. People, even if they couldn't afford a ticket to Seattle, could at least dream about it. If they had enough money, they could step up onto the train—*Watch your step, ma'am, let me help you there*—and travel wherever they liked. And most people did, at one time or another. And then, like all wonderful things—or most of them, anyway—the novelty wore off, and the train—hearing it, seeing it— became normal.

The train also was a boon to the fruit industry. Orchardists and farmers were able now to sell fruit to distributors, who sold the fruit abroad for a greater profit. This was the time the orchardists, some of them, began to think about large-scale fruit distribution, and to bolster these plans, irrigation. Water from the Peshastin Ditch, first begun in 1889, reached the orchard slopes above Cashmere in 1901. In 1902, a box factory opened in Brender Canyon. Three years later, the newly platted town of Cashmere—before, it had been called Old Mission, for the Catholic missionaries who had first settled there to preach to the natives—shipped 135 carloads of fruit down the river to Wenatchee.

The early part of the century was a time of busyness, and pride. "Wenatchee, Washington," the box labels read. "Apple capital of the world."

WHEN DELLA ENTERED a lumber camp and applied for employment, the man said that they did not hire females. But she persisted—she hung around the camp and watched the men, the small tasks they busied themselves with in the off hours, the men unsuccessfully shaking her off—and the lumber boss said that if she wanted, if she absolutely insisted on staying and hanging around, she could have a job in the mess hall, helping with the cooking. She refused this offer, and continued to observe the men, stalking their work. She began to imitate them at chores with which she was unfamiliar—the sharpening of blades, the greasing of ropes and pulleys—and also, as a matter of course, and because she was able, she began to take care of the horses.

And then one day she traveled up the mountain farther than she ever had before, to the site of the felling. She had been rebuffed on earlier occasions—to hang around the base camp where they mended their tools and talked and ate their meals was one thing, but to enter the site where the actual work happened was strictly forbidden—but that day the men who saw her cast her rueful glances, or frowned, but did not order her back to base camp. All attention was given to an argument unfolding among a group of men. A man who was a topper had hurt his shoulder and, at the urging of his friends, refused to go up into the indicated tree. The topper had apparently reached this decision despite himself—he wanted to go up, but upon trying could not even get into his harness, never mind shoulder a saw—and there was the argument among the man's friends and the others who thought the topper should go up regardless of his present condition. What had happened, the latter group argued, that had not happened to other toppers before him, who had ultimately mustered the strength to finish the job? The problem was not that of the body, they implied, but of the will. If he was hurt, he could at least finish the job for that night; tomorrow or the next day they could find another topper. Another topper this late in the season, this far inland? someone cried. It was finally decided that the man would not go up, which meant that one of the others must. But none of them had topped before, and no one wanted to go down to the camp and tell the boss that they weren't going to finish the job because of a lack of a topper—and so they evaluated each other, at first covertly and then outright, impugning each other's courage and character.

In a long pause in the argument, when Della said, in a clear, childlike voice they would not have thought possible to come out of her mouth, that she would do it, some glanced at her, astonished, not realizing she had been standing there. Some looked at her and then pointedly ignored her. But she persisted; and when the argument rekindled, she sidled up to the man's friend, the topper's friend, who held the harness—he was arguing with somebody—and took it and fit it over her body. Hey! said the man, and made a move to reclaim the harness, but she was in the last stages of securing it onto herself. There was a fierce, solemn expression on her face, and some of the men appraised her. I'll do it, she said. I said I'll do it! She's crazy, someone murmured. Damn right she's crazy, said somebody else. It quieted for a moment as they watched to see what she'd do next. Where's the tree? she said. I know what to do, I've done it before. Shit, somebody said. Is that right? said somebody else. Let her do it, said a man at the back of the crowd, and heads turned to see who had spoken. It was a rotund man with black hair and watery eyes. She does it and falls off, we won't have to deal with her anymore. We'll be rid of her. There was gentle guffawing. Della fingered the silver buckle on the strap, which was not unlike a bridle. You send me up there, she said, and I'll get the job done. I just want to do it, is all. You let me be the topper, she said, and I'll work so fast it'll make your head spin. Now the guffawing turned to laughter. Lady, said a man, and then cleared his throat, because calling her that was somehow ridiculous—Lady, you get up there and you just get the job done, is all. You don't have to be good at it. I'll be the best, she said, and now another man said: Send her up! There was no more discussion; and, as it was getting late in the day, a bottle was passed around, and many of the men who had first declined it took a drink on the second round; and they led her to the topper site, and hoisted her aloft, for she was too short to even make the starting point, and as soon as she was set—she had her legs wrapped around the tree—they stepped back, and she began to climb.

A quarter of the way up the tree she began to cry; her pants were not suited to the work, and the insides of her thighs were burned numb from chafing. The men down below passed the bottle around and watched her. When she was halfway up, the sun was setting, and they were shouting encouragement that she could barely hear. When she reached the top, she could no longer hear them. She feared she would be too weak to work the saw. She looked at it and knew at once that she could not do it.

Darkness came. A breeze smelling of duff came from below. She wept, clinging to the trunk. It seemed the air coming up from the ground was warm. There was the sound of innumerable doors opening and closing, and when she stopped crying, she realized it was the other trees creaking in the wind. The first stars came out. She did not know what was real. It was quiet now, the wind had gone. She was in a tree, but it was not the tallest tree in the world; or there were millions of trees in the world, and she had climbed this one because it was the one that she was going to cut; she would cut into the wood with her blade. She had set the saw across the radius but had yet to apply any pressure to it. She looked down at her hands against the saw, very white, childlike but also manlike hands; and before she knew it she had begun to work.

TALMADGE WAS NOT interested in large-scale fruit distribution even when he saw the necessity of it in the changing, increasingly industrialized world. He had made a living since he was a boy tending his own acreage, and even though he accepted the help of the men when they traveled through, the work was never overwhelming to the point where it affected his health. This would soon not be the case—he was getting on in years, and the work the orchards demanded of him was making him tired. Was wearing him out. He did not speak of this, though he and the girl were both aware of it. Angelene becoming more capable with each year, working hard, while also being discreet, to compensate for his tiredness.

He had never had difficulty selling his fruit in town, in front of the feed and supply store or at the weekly market on Saturdays, but with the increased production from the irrigation canals, and the influx of settlers into the area also selling goods, he found he had too much fruit at the end of the day, and did not know what to do with it. The three of them—Talmadge, Caroline Middey, and Angelene—canned and dried what they could, and stored the surplus. Talmadge soon contacted a distributor who agreed to take some of the fruit off his hands. Some of the orchardists sold all their fruit to distributors, but Talmadge did not want to do this if he did not have to. He enjoyed sitting alongside the wagon at market, greeting people, selling fruit, letting the day go by.

He earned more than he anticipated when he began to sell part of the harvest to the distributor, which surprised him. He had never charged too much for his fruit, and now that somebody else had put a different price on it, he was dismayed. It felt, somehow, dishonest.

It's the way of the world, Talmadge, said Caroline Middey. The way the world is heading. You shouldn't feel bad about it, she said, when she saw he was still bothered; you deserve the money, your fruit is by far the best. Why, I bet you could get even more money, if you wanted to! Then: There's nothing wrong with collecting what is rightfully yours, after all these years of hard work—

But Talmadge, disgusted and wearied by such a conversation, did not wish to speak of it anymore.

ONE NIGHT DELLA discovered a group of men playing cards in the mess hall. She stayed in the shadows, and when one of the men noticed her, he said nothing to the others. But the next day, at the fell site, the same man caught her arm—when she looked at him hatefully, he unhanded her—and told her, without looking at her, that she ought to mind her own business and let them alone while they played. I wasn't doing no harm, she said, and he said, It takes one snitch to ruin the one bit of fun we have left out here. It was then she understood that he was afraid she would tell on them. It was illegal to gamble at the camp, a rule that owed more to the owner's wife, who was a devout Baptist, than to the sensibility of the owner himself, who, if the business did not suffer, was willing to overlook much. Della showed up the next night, and when the man saw her, he threw down his cards. The other men saw her too, but they were not bothered in the least. They dealt her in. And though it was not the feeling of the man who had first included her to hope that she was a bad card player, it was the hope of one or two of the others; and they were proved right. At least, that was what Della wanted them to believe. She had been playing these card games, and variations of these card games, from when she was a teenager roaming the country with Clee and his men. She knew when to play straight and when to play badly for a purpose. You paid attention to who you were playing with and took what they were worth from them slowly, if need be (this she taught herself); but you always bled them dry. Because that's what playing cards—gambling—was all about.

She did not care about money; it was not about the money; but she saw that the men brought in a certain amount each week, and she enjoyed the manipulation required to take that money from them, each week, night by night, slowly so they would not become angry and force her out. When one of them began to catch on that though she stumbled and made bad calls like the rest of them, she was overall successful—though she was careful not to brag or to let the money remain long on the table when she won it—when one of the men realized this, she would read it on his face, and the next night she would force herself not to do so well. But she never failed to show up, for fear they would talk about her and come to conclusions between them.

And so she gambled, and began to make money; and she had paper money besides her checks that she had not cashed, and she did not know what to do with it all. In the end she rolled it tightly in bundles and stuck it in a coffee can and buried it in the woods near where she slept.

She could have gone on with the men like that for a long time. It was like any sport, letting them go, pulling them back; letting them think they were in control but really you were in control the entire time, your coffee can bursting with cash and buried in darkness by the riverbank.

FOR ANGELENE'S TWELFTH birthday, in the summer, Talmadge presented her with two train tickets to Dungeness Bay, on the Olympic Peninsula. There was a new rail line going west out of Olympia, and he had gotten a special price.

They left after apricot harvest, and took one suitcase between them. Angelene was flush with excitement as they boarded the train. The air of the car was cold and smelled of new leather and wood polish. There was the sharp chuff of the heating cylinders, and weaving through this the tinkling laugh of a woman Angelene could not see. They took their seats. When the train began to move, Angelene gripped Talmadge's arm—he sat beside her—and looked out the window. When a woman came by and asked if they would like anything to eat, they ordered coffee and sandwiches, and Talmadge paid her cash out of his billfold.

Angelene would remember forever afterward the jostling train, and the passage through the mountains—the thick, dark forests, the occasional waterfall from impossible heights, a herd of deer, once, fading in and out of the treeline, the strange, gloomy shadows as the train was surrounded on all sides by high, steep forest, the utter blackness and cold—she could feel it, clammy, on her face—of the tunnels. On the train platform in Olympia, the multitude of people and noise, and the sudden damp cold that got inside her clothes, unsettled her. There was somebody coughing, somebody laughing, a child crying. Talmadge put his arm around her shoulders. They boarded the other train, which was smaller, more compact, and soon they were traveling again. She slept; and when she woke, there was a golden light inside the car where they were. Talmadge was asleep; the complexion of his flesh was red. Her own hand—she held it up in front of her face—was dark brown. For a moment everything seemed saturated with its own perfect color—deep—and she knew, one day, that both of them would die. (The train rocked gently along the track.) Not soon, perhaps, but one day. He was going to die, and she would never see him again. She was going to die too—

She sat back and looked out the window, at the racing landscape. Hay-fields and strange forests.

She slept.

ONE NIGHT AT the lumber camp—it was the end of winter, Della had been there for almost a year—one of the men took out a bottle, and it was not the regular corn liquor they passed around, but Mexican whiskey. Della, though she did not like the taste—she never had—took a drink. She took one drink and did not like it much but appreciated that it was good whiskey and began to plan her next move. The bottle was passed around, and again she took a drink. And again. A wonderful warmth suffused her, and the markings on the cards took on added significance. One more drink was all it took for her to become confused, and she lost the hand and the pot of money that was as good as hers. The man who won laughed as he embraced his winnings.

After that, the drinking became something she did to assuage a boredom that had taken root in her—boredom with the men, the topping, the gambling—and an unwillingness to do anything about it. It was the old restlessness come back. Drinking became what she did to add challenge to the card game; to become intoxicated but not outwardly impaired. It was, ultimately, another diversion.

After nights of drinking, Della slept badly, and often in the mornings she was sick. Drinking ice water and hot black coffee seemed to remedy her at least until the first shift was over, and she would stumble to her tent in the woods and sleep through the afternoon.

ANGELENE AND TALMADGE stayed in a little boardinghouse on the beach. In between their two beds was a mahogany night table and a small vase with a dusty artificial iris in it. At night mice scuttled in the walls and across the floorboards.

During the day they walked on the beach and in the forest. The forest had the tallest trees Angelene had ever seen—red cedars—beside which a man looked like an insignificant mote. The cedars, she knew from her reading, lived for thousands of years.

In the evenings they ate with the other guests and the landlady and her half-grown son at the boardinghouse, the landlady's cats rubbing against their legs under the table. For supper one night the landlady prepared crab stew. It was served in wide bowls, with fresh, crackling French bread to go with it. You could tell by the way the stew was served, and the quantity of it, that it was a common meal there. But that did not mean it was not delicious. Angelene had eaten nothing like it her entire life. She remembered Talmadge eating a spoonful, carefully, his eyes wide and distant.

There were many memories Angelene had of Talmadge—them working in the orchard, and otherwise deeply ensconced in their normal life; them at the market, selling fruit, buying supplies, eating dinner with Caroline Middey on her front porch; the days upon days of their shared solitude, the long silences and the jokes, the simple but also deep company they kept. But that trip to Dungeness Bay stood apart, it was of a different cloth. Everything about that trip was new, and while excited and stimulated, Angelene was also exhausted by what she realized later was her extreme vulnerability, and what she perceived was Talmadge's too: they were away from home. She kept gazing at him, his visage different now when framed by other trees, other skies, when framed by the ocean, which, before she had seen it—the ocean—had been a myth. Staying the night in the room that was not theirs, she thought they had achieved the impossible: they had gone somewhere together and created an experience totally their own. It felt like trespassing. Where were they? They were outside the orchard. It was an experience not to be repeated. Later she would hear people describe honeymoons this way.

OVERALL DURING THIS time Della made less money from work and gambling, but as the money did not matter so much, she did not care. She began to speak more openly during the card games. The men, at first amazed at her verbosity, became accustomed to it, and amused. Sometimes, when she had had a lot to drink, the men who were able to tell her state of intoxication would ask her a question; and because it was a silly question, she would ignore it; but then she would answer it, an hour later perhaps, and the others who did not ignore her became confused; and, laughing, the one who posed the question would repeat what he had asked an hour before, and everyone would chuckle. Della, when she understood that this was a source of entertainment for them—the first night she caught on—became angry and threw down her cards and stood up and spat on the table. It was a clumsy battery of movement—some men simply ignored her—but the others looked at her, dumbfounded. Hey now! said one man, frowning. Sit down, Little Man—that was what some of them called her, Little Man—nothing to get worked up about! But her heart was beating raucously, and she understood that even in the depths, the intricacies of space and time, the liquor provided, she wanted something else at that moment to bring her a sense of clarity, of justice, of rest. The man beside her was drinking out of a bottle, and as he was lifting it to his mouth she took it and stared at it—the men stared at her staring at it—and then she gripped its neck and brought it crashing onto the table. The noise was incredible, not like she had imagined it at all. She laughed. The men were at once on their feet, some with a look of animal fear on their faces. She did not understand the overlapping insults and demands that were thrown over her like so many nets; just brandished the bottle in front of her, waving it back and forth. When one man lunged forward and tried to take the bottle from her, she turned quickly to him. He had his arms open as if to embrace her. Swiftly, almost without meaning to, she cut his face. She had seen his skin up close and it had frightened and disgusted her. In reality, she had cut his throat. He clapped his hands over the wound, took his hands away, laughed shortly. Sat down abruptly in his chair. Now there was more shouting, and the men who approached her held up their hands to show they were unarmed; but though she was drunk, she knew that they would kill her. She ran out of the mess hall, and it was not until she was halfway to her tent that she realized she no longer carried the broken bottle. She kept running, into the trees. It was difficult to see. She did not know if any of the men followed her—she could not hear them—but when she was almost to her tent she realized that there was no way she was going to stop and pack up her things; she must keep on, she must leave and gain as much distance as she could before the morning, when they would look for her. Would they look for her? It depended on how badly she had injured the man. She had not meant to injure him—had she?—she could not remember all that well. Was it his arm she had cut, or his cheek? Or was it, actually and truly, his throat? She ran pell-mell through the trees.

L ATE FALL THE wrangler came into the orchard alone, without the horses, at a time when he otherwise would not have been there, and told Talmadge he had received word: a young woman who was reported to be Della had been injured in a horse stampede in Idaho. He himself hadn't seen the girl, said the wrangler, but there were reports that it was her. Clee had already gone ahead to the place where the girl was convalescing, in a small hospital outside Coeur d'Alene.

Talmadge made arrangements immediately. Angelene would stay with Caroline Middey. No, said Angelene, I want to go with you. He didn't argue with her, was too distracted. All right, he said.

Angelene didn't know why, exactly, she wanted to go. She did not want to see the woman she barely remembered mangled in some country hospital. But she had seen Talmadge's face when the wrangler gave him this news, and knew she had to go with him. To comfort him, if necessary; to protect him.

They traveled by train to Spokane, and took horses from there. The wrangler went with them. When they arrived at the hospital, the wrangler and Angelene waited in the lobby while Talmadge went in to see the woman. He came out less than a minute later, his face ashen.

It's not her, he said.

AFTER THE LUMBER camp Della avoided entering towns and lived in the forest. For a time she was not ill, but in her right mind. When she finally entered a town for supplies, nobody looked at her twice—or if they did, it was for other reasons—and nobody pursued her. When she ran out of money, it did not matter so much; she found what she needed in the woods.

Trouble in the form of winter was approaching. But still she did not seek the respite of towns. The forest would absorb her, she thought, it would keep her until the future showed itself.

Clee had known before coming to Coeur d'Alene that the girl in question was not Della, because he had seen her—Della—several weeks before, coming out of the forest north of Sultan Creek on the western slopes of the Cascades. He and a small band of men led some horses—what had not sold at a winter auction in Seattle—through the depressed and mostly empty mining town. He had looked over his shoulder once at the road dappled with snow, and saw a figure beyond the horses, fading into the trees twenty yards away. He blinked, and she was gone. But some instinct told him it was her. Had it been her? It could have been anybody, he told himself. And this creature was hatless, and short-haired. Had he imagined the pallor? Her hunched posture?

He was imagining things, he thought. It was some guilt—though he did not believe he was guilty—coming to visit him.

He had left the men, however, and gone into the forest to track the creature. He thought he would find nothing.

But there she was—and it was her—just letting an armload of kindling fall to the ground. He got off his horse and walked, leading the animal, toward her.

But it was as if he was invisible; she did not acknowledge him, after an initial glance. She crouched down, began to prepare a fire. She could not light the tinder, and so he came forward and offered her a matchbook from his vest pocket. She took it from him, wordlessly.

Her hair was short, as if it had been cropped carelessly with shears, and there were sores and scabs on her face and neck. Her eyes were depthless. She was in the throes of some sickness, he thought.

It was early November, and cold. The first snow had fallen a week before, was ankle-deep on the ground.

She wore boots, strips of fabric tied around the soles.

He took off his jacket and put it around her shoulders. She accepted it, pulling it tighter around her, huddling closer to the fire. He hung back and watched her. The sun was beginning to set. He considered taking her arm—or even gathering her whole body up, quickly—and carrying her back to his camp. But he knew suddenly—of course—he could not put his hands on her.

But neither could he leave her. He stayed until darkness fell.

She slept, and he returned to town for food. At a tavern he bought hot sandwiches, and brought them back to the space in the forest. At the odor of the food she rose to eat—and then immediately fell asleep again.

He went to his horse and unstrapped a blanket, put it over her. Covered himself in a saddle blanket and sat at the base of a tree, near the girl, settled against the trunk.

He slept.

In the morning she was gone. She had kicked dirt on the fire. His coat lay in a pile near his feet.

When he heard the rumors about the girl in Idaho, he thought: It could be her. She had seemed witless when he saw her in the forest, but he wanted to believe she could have gotten a job, despite this, working again with the horses. But when he saw the girl in the hospital bed—a large, strapping red-haired girl—he was not surprised.

He would not tell Talmadge about seeing Della in the woods.

Salt in the wound, he thought.

DELLA HEADED EAST, over the mountains.
       She did not realize, in her growing disorientation, that in moving east she was walking toward her past. Was returning to it, unconsciously. Like a dog to its vomit.

There was a man she had traveled with briefly before she found work at the lumber camp. She had met him at the canning factory; he had a job swabbing the floors. He was very tall and lean and had a long face, hazel eyes—one eye was glass, slightly larger and greener, rounder, than the other—and a perpetual thin, hand-rolled cigarette hanging off his lip. He did not try to talk to her at first, but she saw him in the morning when she was getting off her shift and he was coming in. The long, slow movements of him pushing the mop across the floor.

The first conversation they had was about the sickening odor of fish guts. Gets in everything, he said. Your hair, your clothes. Sometimes I think *I* smell like it. He sniffed his arm.

Getting out of here, he said one day. She wasn't even sure he was speaking to her; but they were the only ones in the cloakroom at the time. She nodded. Then, out of simple curiosity, she asked: Where are you going? North, he said. Maybe to Seattle. Inland, anyway.

It was enough for her. She was tired of working at the factory. She knew that once she left she would never see the place again.

Her instinct proved sound: the man was harmless. She would not travel with him far, but for some reason she did not find it repugnant to ride with him—he drove a mule and wagon with his few belongings inside, and she rode a horse—for a little ways.

One night they sat fireside and he told her of his travels in Oklahoma and Texas, of the people and animals he had encountered there. He had not worked with horses but had cared for them, and mostly done cooking for various ranching establishments. He told her about weevils, and sand-storms, and scorpions. Had she ever seen a scorpion? The most satisfying thing he had ever done was to kill a scorpion with a piece of pewter—just stabbed its belly while it slept. I'm not one for killing, he said. But I didn't feel bad killing that scorpion.

That night she dreamed that Michaelson's throat had been cut. He was on his knees; and he wore a necklace of blood. When he upturned his head—to take in some awful visage in the trees, or perhaps gape at the star-filled sky that surrounded him—his head, nearly decapitated, fell too far back, and his neck was a blood-rich stump. In the dream she was moved, awed. Terrified.

IT WAS NOVEMBER, and there was much work to be done. Angelene helped Talmadge in the apple orchard, and in the evenings studied at the kitchen table while he dozed in the chair in the corner. He seemed more tired than usual, she thought.

D ELLA DREAMED OF cold, of snow. And then realized she was awake.
She wasn't hungry anymore. When one accepted the cold, one didn't mind it. Was warm, even.

At times she was walking, and other times she was on her back, staring at the sun, which seemed very close and muted in the overcast, viridescent sky.

It seemed there was laughter everywhere. And then she heard crying—terrible, terrible crying—and was afraid.

Coffee? said Angelene, and rose from the table.

They had eaten Christmas dinner: rabbit dressed in chestnut butter and sage; collard greens and Brussels sprouts; mashed squash with raisins; onion bread. Apples stewed in brandy. Plum cake.

I couldn't eat another morsel, said Caroline Middey. But they would all have coffee, despite the hour. It didn't affect them like other people.

Talmadge, in his chair in the corner, was asleep by the time Angelene had prepared the coffee. Caroline Middey glanced at him, smirked. She sat at the table and beckoned to the girl, who also sat. The coffee steaming before them. Caroline Middey was opening a package—a cross-stitching packet—that she had bought for the girl, but feared might be too advanced. They looked over the materials. Caroline Middey spread the instructions on the table, flattened them with her palms. Cleared her throat. Several minutes passed in silence.

Oh, this doesn't look so bad, said Caroline Middey.

DELLA WOKE STARTLED, lethargic, and hot, in a narrow high-backed bed, her feet near a deep fireplace roaring with flame. She sweated, and when she tried to sit up, her head ached. She eased back again onto a multitude of pillows.

Look who's up, said a woman—a nun, Della saw, by her modest wimple—who pulled up a stool beside her and sat down and took Della's hand, not to hold it, as Della thought, baffled and embarrassed, at first, but to feel her pulse. The nun, after smiling briefly, looked into the middle distance of the room, trying to determine the strength of blood in Della.

You'll live, she said finally, and replaced Della's arm back onto the covers. Patted her hand, and rose. The woman's touch rang on Della's flesh afterward, like the reverberation of a bell.

She lay in the high-backed bed while storms raged and winter spent itself. The cabin was an outpost that functioned also as a hospital—situated high on the pass, meant to cater to cases such as hers: people who had tried to cross the mountains but failed, mostly due to inclement weather.

There were two others who convalesced in the room with her—a hunter who had broken his leg, and a young woman who had tried to cross the pass to reach her husband, who was in Seattle, but got caught in a snowstorm. The woman, who had been pregnant, had spent two days in the snow before the nuns had found her. She had miscarried.

Twins, confided the nun.

They stayed together in a close room, and the nuns slept on either end of it. The walls were made out of a dark wood. The fire roared constantly. The nuns—there were three—fed it as if it was an animal without which they would all perish. And in a sense it was.

They fed the invalids dark broth.

Della knew it would be fruitless to try to leave the place: the windows were white with storm, and besides that, she was not strong enough yet to survive by herself. She drank the broth, she let the nuns prod her and bathe her, she listened to the hunter snoring and the young mother weeping silently in the darkness.

Della would have to wait out this time, she knew, like all the others. The thing was to not fight against it, but let it pass over her; patience was the hardest thing to learn. Eventually, she slept.

She heard the quiet noises of the nuns praying before dawn: voices different from the ones they used with her and the hunter and the mother. Who were they talking to? God, she remembered. And then slept again.

IN FEBRUARY SHE left the hospital, joined a group of mountaineer-salesmen who had stopped at the hospital to deliver supplies. Their route took them north and then east, they told her, over the North Cascade Pass to the mining town of Mazama, west of the Okanogan. Della was welcome to join them if she wished.

She rode with them into the pass. The cold and bitter weather, the merciless days of snow and rain, almost made her regret leaving the hospital. But in the end she was satisfied; she had had to leave that place, that roaring fire, the praying voices of the nuns. She had to fling herself into the openness again, so she could think properly.

At times she and the mountaineers—there were three besides herself—had to pull the mules over the rocks, cajole them, force them up steep boulder-rich valleys. At first these episodes quickly exhausted her, and she feared becoming ill again; but then her strength eventually returned. There was one bad snowstorm during which they could not drive and remained in the covered wagon, drinking condensed milk out of tins, eating corned beef and crackers. But after that—days after that—they reached the high point of the pass, and began to descend into the lower elevations. The temperature rose, and their collective spirit with it. They were on the opposite side of the mountains now; the hardest of the traveling was behind them.

She left the mountaineers at Mazama and rode with others—miners—down to Winthrop. The rains terrible; mud perpetually to her ankles.

Is it always like this? she asked one man.

He laughed at her.

It was too wet to camp in the woods, and so in exchange for doing chores, she slept in the barn loft of a woman whose husband worked up-mountain.

And then the weather warmed, and she was off again.

It was early spring, but before the snow had melted—she was south of Twisp, but still in the Methow Valley—when, coming out of a store in a small, ramshackle, barely there town, she saw Michaelson walking down the street.

He did not see her. She moved down off the platform, into an alleyway between buildings, and looked out. He was handcuffed, and the men he walked with—two in front, one in back—looked like the law, or bounty hunters. One walked with smug superiority, while the other two were modest, slightly embarrassed, even.

She stared at Michaelson. He was familiar to her, and yet altered. She could tell after watching him for a minute that he was in a calm state. He appeared as if he had been in hiding: his skin was yellowish, and his face was grizzled with salt-and-pepper stubble. She remembered his passion for being clean-shaven. (Once, during an excitable phase, he had shaved all the hair from his body; some of the girls had helped him.) As he walked now he squinted and pressed his side with both hands, as if he had a cramp. And then he dropped his hands, grimaced, kept on.

She followed them at a distance. After a few blocks he and the men entered another building—most likely the police headquarters, or a law building. She stepped up onto the platform half a block away and pretended to look at a window display.

Good riddance to old rubbish, said an old man with frog eyes, who sat in a rocker at the end of the platform, and spat. He's been polluting this county for too long, said the man. It's about time the law sat up and paid attention—

What's he done? said Della.

The man laughed shortly. What *hasn't* he done, is more like it—

Della said, after a minute, feigning a lack of interest: What's going to happen to him?

The man removed a tin of snuff from his breast pocket. Sending him to Chelan, last I heard. Hope it's the prison from there—

———

Over the next three days she entered the town. Told herself she was there to run errands, but really she was listening for news. The frog-eyed man delivered the gossip: they were going to send Michaelson to Chelan on the Friday train.

Chelan on the Friday train.

She went fishing, though it was too early in the season to do so; too cold. But she had to do something: she was hungry, and also needed to distract herself.

Her wool gloves with the fingertips cut off were rotten, her fingertips bloated and hard. She baited the hook, stabbing the grub in the belly. *Chelan on the Friday train.* She had been contemplating going south, finding work again in the trees. Maybe heading to the coast after that. And then remembered the nauseating odor of the cannery.

Remembering the lumber camp, what had happened there, she became hollow with dread; stopped what she was doing and simply stood. Stared ahead of her, at the snow-patched opposite bank.

She cast the line, and at the cold *kerplunk* of the bait in the water, her vision narrowed, and all she could see was the dancing water. The light on the water.

Chelan on the Friday train.

She walked into the ice-rimed pond up to her calves—her boots would be ruined—the water numbing her feet, her flesh, her blood. She was panting. But soon she calmed.

She would need a horse to ride to Chelan on.

No! she thought, slogging out of the water. Why would she ever go see him?

Later, walking through the forest, she thought: Maybe.

The next morning she changed her mind: she would not go to Chelan. It was foolish: it did not make sense.

And yet she could not forget him. That strange expression of pain as he walked down the road. If she were to step out and intercept him, would he remember her? What would she say to him? He to her? And how would she respond to him?

She lay on a bedroll in the dark and should have been too cold to think, but in half consciousness she gathered to herself the myriad things she had ever felt for him. Fear—but that was to be expected. He was in charge: and like God, who they sometimes heard about, his reasons for doing what he did were often inscrutable. When Jane and Della first arrived at the camp, they heard stories from the other girls: that at times all Michaelson wanted to do was sleep; to eat special meals prepared for him and lie still in a chair on the front lawn, the sun on his limbs; or stand in the creek a half mile away, sometimes for hours, thinking his thoughts. Or he spent the days in bed alone. He had favorite girls, and sometimes during these calm states he would ask for them. They would be prepared and delivered to him. In his room the favorite girl slept with him, or sang songs, read out of books, if she was able to, or loved him. But most often, when he was like this, he did not want to love, he simply wanted the presence of another person in the room. There were rumors: he made one girl prick another in the center of her palm with a needle; he made a girl burn another on the inside of her elbow with a cigar. But mostly the girl—whichever one he chose—sat beside him on the bed and touched his head, and remained with him while he slept.

The times they—the girls—braced themselves for were the times he had a fire in his blood—when he did not sleep, and paced the house, rushed outdoors as if wild dogs were at his heels. This was a time of his projects and plans, great domestic festivals where the parties of men flooded in, and the girls dressed in their costumes, and there was music and alcohol and dancing. And when the property was not enough to contain him, Michaelson left with a few of his men and they were gone for two, three days, sometimes longer. Most often they were on a quest: to find a girl who had escaped. It did not matter when she had fled: sometimes Michaelson's blood called for him to search for—to turn the countryside upside down for—a girl who had disappeared five years before. There was a girl left in charge when the men went off. Her name was Ellie; she was also the cook, and the keeper of the infirmary. She was not usually mean, but whipped a girl raw once for trying to escape while Michaelson was away. Ellie was fifteen, but to Della she seemed middle-aged.

Michaelson did not ever think Della was special—he never regarded her singularly or treated her any different from the other girls—but Jane was one of his favorites. What does he do? Della wanted to know, when he took Jane privately to his room. He wants me to talk to him, said Jane. That's all. What do you tell him? Della asked. Jane shrugged. I tell him stuff, she said. I make stuff up. Della thought this was funny, and then worried. What if Michaelson found out she was lying? But overall it seemed all right: if Michaelson was keeping her for himself and just wanted her to talk, then that meant she was kept from the other men who would be unsatisfied by just talk. And so Della decided to be grateful for Michaelson's attention.

But then she saw, as Jane undressed one day—she caught a glimpse of—a series of perfect raised circular welts on the inside of Jane's thigh. They were angry, deep purple, puffy. What's that? said Della, though her heart had already begun to pound with knowledge of what they were: she had seen similar marks on other girls. Cigar burns. And then Della could not believe it: Jane lied to her. Bug bites, said Jane, and her eyes obtained a kind of cast. They're not bug bites, said Della. They're burns. From his cigar. But Jane would not answer her, and Della's heart pounded harder.

What did you do tonight? Della asked her, and Jane would say: I sang him a song. Or: I read him a story. She had a burn—blatant—on the back of her hand, on her neck. Her hair was falling out.

And then one day walking down the hallway Della passed by a bedroom where the door was closing, and saw Michaelson, his bare back to her, lying naked on a bed, and Jane, just sitting down behind him, and folding her body—also naked—around his. A shirtless man was closing the door.

Where did Della go after this? Not to the room where she was assigned—and she would be punished for this later—but outdoors, to the barn, where in her rage, she gnawed on saddles hanging on the wall, she ate hay and pulled her own hair, weeping until she was sick.

She hated Michaelson. And what was it to hate? It was not to wish him dead, though she wouldn't have minded that. It was to wish he had never been born. And for similar reasons she also hated Jane, and herself.

She hated the world.

When Michaelson came into the orchard, and Jane had seen him—she and Della and the baby in the basket had stopped in the middle of the field before they knew anything was wrong—Jane told her to go back into the canyon and place the baby in the creek, at a place she had shown Della earlier. Della had never thought it would come to this. Do it, said Jane, not taking her eyes from the man standing before the apricot orchard, waving at her. Michaelson. We will meet in heaven, said Jane, her voice flat. It will be all right. She told Della to do the thing and then meet her near the bend in the path, near the cache of tools.

Della retreated into the canyon and went to the place where they had talked about: where the water was deep enough to drown the infant. She stood creekside, holding the basket with the baby in it, but finally could not do it. She took the child to the upper cabin. Lifted it from the basket. Behind the cabin, in a basin before the hill, she placed the child. Covered it with sticks, but not so many that it would not be able to breathe. The baby cried, and Della shushed it. He'll find you, she said. Be quiet. On the way down the hill, she threw the empty basket into the air; it caught in the low branches of an evergreen.

Jane was already sitting on the limb of the oak when Della reached the spot. What are you doing? said Della, although they had already discussed it. But again, Della thought it would never come to this, or that Jane would not go through with it. She didn't know why she would doubt Jane, who made plans and carried them out always to the fullest degree. Jane had said that if Michaelson ever came to get them, she would kill herself. Della had preferred to think it was an expression only, an exaggeration. We can run away, Della had said, feebly; but Jane did not want to run away. He will find us, she said. I don't want to go back there, ever. She said, not that day but before, in the darkness of the room in the cabin in which they slept: We are cursed for this life. It had the sound of repetition: someone had told it to her, and she was echoing it.

From what she said about their own mother, Della knew Jane held beliefs about another life: about heaven. The details were unclear. But at a certain point Jane was willing to seek entrance to this other life if it meant a swift departure from the one she was in.

Did you— Jane asked, but could not meet Della's eyes. She wanted to know if Della had drowned the infant. She held the rope—the noose—in her hands. Fit it over her neck, then took it off. Adjusted it, put it back over her head. Awkward. Della, who had climbed the tree with the help of the nail system they had devised earlier—there was a series of nails pounded into the back of the trunk—sat beside her now on the branch, sweating and still, gripping her own noose.

Della was going to tell her that she had spared the infant.

There was movement at the canyon mouth. The men were coming.

Like we said, said Jane. Do it now. Della.

Jane—

But Jane fell from the branch before Della could answer her.

S HE STOLE A horse in a neighboring town—it was easy enough, outside a tavern at night—and discovered the next morning, having ridden the better part of the night, a venison sandwich in the saddlebags
and, sewn into a handkerchief and stuffed into a hidden pocket, bills of
money.

In Chelan she left the horse tied outside the general store, where
somebody was sure to notice it that day or the next. She would not return
to it. Bought new clothes at the feed and supply store, a new hat. Went
to the barber's for a haircut. Though they had shorn her at the hospital,
her hair had grown considerably since then, fell almost to her shoulders.

Cut it all off, she told the barber, who regarded her at a loss.

She sat in the café across from the courthouse and contemplated a
course of action. Should she go into the courthouse and ask to see him?
But even if they let her in to see him, what would she say?

After she left the café, she toured the outside of the courthouse. As if
she was looking for something. Around the back side there was a large
fenced yard—for the prisoners, no doubt—and then beyond that, beyond
a stretch of poor, bare field, forest. Foothills rising in the distance.

She came upon a group of boys, in knee-pants and flat caps, all of
them, their backs to her, and as she watched, one of them lobbed some
object—it was a brown soda bottle—over the high fence.

When they noticed her observing them, some flinched, until they saw
she wasn't going to go after them. One boy turned to her and said, Sometimes one of them (by his gesture she understood he was referring to the
prisoners) gets a bottle, and they get into a fight. They use the bottle, they
make it into a—knife. The boy grinned. It happened once. His brother
saw it—he gestured to another boy.

When nothing happened—there weren't even any prisoners in the yard—the boys dispersed.

But she stayed and studied the perimeter of the yard, the fence, for a long time. Before she left, she scanned the ground and tossed whatever she could find—rocks, sticks, other solid refuse—over the fence. And then left at once, not looking back over her shoulder.

Almost since the beginning—or for as long as she could remember, in the life she had lived with Jane—Della had moved according to Jane's direction. Jane was the orchestrator, Della the follower. (Before this time was the time with their mother, and Della knew it should have been black—their mother was ill, and unhappy—but to Della this time was one great brightness.) But after Jane died, Della learned to get by on her own. Mostly her movement was dictated by her will to survive: walk this way; sleep here; eat this, but not that. Watch out for this person or animal; that person or animal is harmless. Today you do not need money; today you must earn money to buy food, because you are starving.

Now, after seeing Michaelson on the road, something inside her—something that had been dormant—woke. Propelled her. She stole a horse, rode to Chelan, drew to the jail, all according to some instinct. She was preparing to do something, but she did not know what it was. She saw its edges, but the thing had yet to reveal itself to her. She had thought she was going to the jail to speak to him, and that was all. But when she saw the boys lobbing objects over the fence, she knew what she was going to do; it was as if a door had been opened, briefly, and she could see what was possible.

The next day she entered the courthouse. Entered an office with a tall ceiling, and a long counter, behind which a young man worked. He looked up at her, all solicitous attention.

May I help you?

She seemed to think for a moment, really consider what she was going to say before she said it. Her coat was folded over her arm; she held her hat in her hand.

I was wanting to speak to somebody. I killed a man last fall, and come to turn myself in—

WHEN IT WAS circulated among the men who frequented the orchard that the girl in Coeur d'Alene had not been Della—and that Talmadge had traveled there, and been disappointed—one of the men approached Talmadge in the spring and told him that the year before last, in the summer, they had seen Della picking cherries in the Yakima Valley. She might go there again, said the man; they would watch for her in the coming harvest.

The Yakima Valley was not too far away, thought Talmadge. Maybe she would return for the work—not to pick cherries, it was too early for that, but maybe she would return to help groom the trees after winter—and come up and see them. But when she did not come, he thought that he would go down and look for her. He would take the mule and search for her in the place where the man had last seen her. Richardson Farms: that was the name of the place. Talmadge wondered where she had learned to pick cherries, and if she liked it. But then he thought: And what if she was not glad to see him? It might embarrass her, even. I thought it was all right for you to go, before, he would tell her, but now I've changed my mind. That was as far into the conversation he got with her, in his mind, before he faltered. He did not know what he would say next.

He talked to Caroline Middey about it. Should he take the mule down there and find her? As usual, she expressed no surprise when he asked her. As if people asked her these sorts of questions every day of her life: serious questions, silly questions. And he supposed that was true, that her life was made up of such questions. What people must ask her, in their most vulnerable states.

She was snapping beans on her porch when he asked her this. Seemed to mull it over.

Might as well just stay put, she said finally. If she wants to come see you, she will.

I know, he said.

Well, if you knew it, you wouldn't have asked me. So why'd you ask?

He didn't answer.

You think she's going to see you and all at once take back her orneriness? You think she's going to see you and remember her responsibility to that child?

I thought she was dead, he said.

Now it was her turn to be silent.

I know, she said. I know what you felt. But running after her isn't going to make it better. She knows where you live. She's got to sow her oats, or whatever they say. Seeing you's just going to complicate things.

But in the end he disregarded what she said, and took the mule to Yakima. It was two years now since she was last seen, picking cherries, and when he got to the farm the trees were busy with workers. The owner hadn't heard of a woman named Della Michaelson, nor seen anyone matching that description. There were a lot of bodies who passed through, he said apologetically. He let Talmadge walk the rows, however, by himself, for as long as wanted, and in the evening invited him to eat supper with his family.

The following afternoon Talmadge, Caroline Middey, and Angelene sat inside Caroline Middey's house, at the table. They had just finished eating supper, and Caroline Middey had cleared the table. They sat with a bowl of walnuts that Talmadge had brought from Richardson Farms between them, depositing the shells in a paper bag.

Where did you get these? said Angelene suddenly.

From town, said Talmadge, before he knew what he was saying, and cracked another walnut. Turned his eyes to the corner of the room.

Angelene, too, looked into the corner of the room, wondering why he was acting so strange.

Caroline Middey stood and asked if they would like any coffee, she was going to make some.

———

Caroline Middey reflected the next day, after Talmadge and Angelene had gone, about how it took everything within Talmadge not to pack up the wagon and go search for Della in earnest. He would have let the orchard go, he would have told the men who passed through that they could work the trees if they wanted, but it would be in vain, for he would not be there to organize and sell the fruit. He would be scouring the countryside, searching for the last place Della worked, the last place she was seen. And when he found her? Maybe he would try to persuade her to come back. And if she didn't, if she wasn't interested in that, then maybe he would continue to follow her, getting work where she was working, to always be there, watching and making sure she came to no trouble.

Of course Caroline Middey had no proof he would have gone to these extremes. He most likely would have given in to more of his whims of tracking her if Angelene hadn't been there living with him. With Angelene there, growing up, watchful, inquisitive, he knew he must remain in the orchard. She was his anchor in the orchard, physically at least.

And there was also the influence of herself, Caroline Middey, to take into account. She told him—almost always when she was asked—when he was acting a fool, and overlooking something more important that was at his feet. Pay attention, she liked to say. You wish she was here? Well, she isn't. She has to come of her own account. Another thing she said often: She knows where you live.

But there was only so much he could take, so many times that he did not go look for her. Even though Caroline Middey told him he was doing the right thing, and there was Angelene, the physical proof of her in the orchard, her working and healthy body, her beauty and intelligence— even though that was in front of him, he always kept a part of himself separate, a space for Della to come and fill. Not only a few times, but every time he did not give in to his urge to go look for her, he resented the moment that came in its place. Even if the moment was beautiful and was something he valued, and made him who he was. He could not help but also long for that other life in which he lived with Della, even if she abused him.

IV

THE LEGAL COUNSEL of Cashmere was a man they called the Judge, though he was not in fact a judge. His name was Emil Marsden, and it was his father who had once been a judge. The father had come from the East with his wife and two children, who were babies at the time, and built a mansion on the outskirts of town. When he was a young man, Emil returned to the East to study law, like his father. When he learned that his father was ill, he traveled back to Cashmere to live in the house with his sister, Meredith, and father until his father died. (His mother had died a decade before, of a bad heart.) The father's illness was protracted, and by the time he died, Emil had already begun to assist the townspeople with their various legal problems, which mostly had to do with the land. He had not yet attained his degree, but this mattered little to the townspeople. He left again for university, returned two years later, having finished what he needed to, and set up a practice. The townspeople accepted him as if he had never left.

He was impressive-looking—tall, dark-haired, with a great bristling mustache—and also soft-spoken, not given to speeches; for this reason Talmadge did not dislike him, was willing to seek out his assistance.

Talmadge and the Judge had been acquainted since the Judge was a boy, when Talmadge sought his father's advice about the occasional land dispute. To call it a dispute was an exaggeration. Talmadge had questions about the land, about the exact perimeter of his property. Once in a while—twice a decade, maybe—a man came around who was interested in knowing just how far Talmadge's claim reached. It was a railroad man, or a surveyor marking new plots. You own this land right here, they said, with your orchards and such, but how far into the woods there? How far up the ridge? Talmadge was unsure of the exact perimeter, since storms and the passage of time destroyed the old markers such as trees and basins, and certain fields shrank or grew haphazardly—and these men were interested in exact measurements, not satisfied with approximations. Talmadge was annoyed with these men, but when they persisted he was forced to go to town and consult the Judge: at first Emil's father, and then, after a time, Emil. The old claim would be pulled from its folder, the boundary markers—or what constituted boundary markers—reviewed, and Talmadge would carry the information back to the orchard, holding the terms carefully in his head, so that if the men were to come back the next day and question him—and they most always came back—he could verify what was legally his land.

The Judge stood up behind his desk when Talmadge was shown in by Meredith, the Judge's sister, who quickly left them alone. The study was wide and spacious, dim and cool. Smelled, faintly, of books. The room was lined with dark shelves. Cherry. The single window looked out onto a flowering plum tree in the yard.

The Judge asked him to sit down, and Talmadge sat in the horsehair chair before the desk. They exchanged formalities: the Judge asked after Angelene and himself, Talmadge. And how was the Judge? The Judge was fine. It was a week of fair weather, was it not? And to think that some folks were predicting rain. Not a cloud in the sky as far as either man could see. But weather was tricky like that. Not that rain would be bad. They could use it, in fact. Rain would be welcome. The Judge asked after Talmadge's trees. They were doing well, said Talmadge, though the winter had been hard. Getting ready for bud break, are you? We are, he said, yes, soon. After a few moments of silence the Judge asked what it was that he could help Talmadge with.

When Talmadge told him that he was interested in composing his will and testament, the Judge nodded. If he was surprised at the request, he did not show it. He drew forward a pad of paper, took a pen from its brass holder. A brief silence followed, and then Talmadge said there wouldn't be much to write, it was simple: he would leave everything to Angelene.

Two weeks before, he had fallen from a tree. Sprained his ankle and wrist. Angelene had trussed the ankle as best she could, and then went off to fetch Caroline Middey. Caroline Middey had inspected his joints, which were, she said, not the real problem. A minute before, she had listened to his heart and lungs with a stethoscope, and asked him about dizziness and vertigo.

You must not overly exert yourself, she said. Do you hear me? If you need the extra help, I'm sure you could ask one of the men to stay out here with you—

He hadn't answered her.

And you best go see the Judge about your will and testament, if you haven't. Go and see him, Talmadge.

He was amazed at the way she told him what to do. After the initial surprise at what she said, he found that it didn't offend him. No one else could talk to him like that without his bristling. In fact, he was relieved at her advice. She would always tell him exactly what she thought, and what she thought, he knew, was sound.

Now, in the Judge's study, the Judge laid down his pen. Of course, he said. Then: There is the matter of your possessions. I have to write it all down, to draw up a formal letter. There's the land, of course. I can get the information from your claim, that won't be difficult. But then there is the cabin and— The Judge hesitated. He saw Talmadge wanted to say something. What is it?

Talmadge was silent for a long time. He was looking out the window.

I'd like to find that girl, he said finally. Della.

The Judge leaned back in his chair. Della, he said. Do you mean—

The girl's kin, said Talmadge. She used to live out there with us.

I remember, said the Judge. Then: How long has she been gone now?

Talmadge was silent.

Going on nine years now.

The Judge nodded again.

And you want me to help you locate her?

Yes—

Talmadge wanted the Judge to know that he didn't want the girl to be located so she could be brought back to him (whether or not this was true was for him to decide later); he didn't want to disturb her now if she had found somewhere else she wanted to be. It wasn't even necessary that Della know that he was looking for her. He, Talmadge, just wanted to know that she was all right, that she had not come to any harm. If any-thing else, it would set his mind at ease; he could not rest—if he thought about it in different terms, he could not "die peacefully"—knowing that she was in trouble somewhere. But then a thought occurred to him: And what if she was? What if she was miserable? What if she was dead? What would he do then?

The Judge asked Della's full name, the last place she was seen, her age, identifying features, any other information that might be useful to him. Talmadge answered the questions to the best of his ability.

I'll see what I can do, said the Judge. He made notes on the pad, and for a moment there was just the sound of the pen scratching the paper. Tal-madge looked out the window, at the plum tree, at the light on the grass.

Then the Judge said, looking up from his notes: Is this in relation to the will? I mean, if you find her, does it make a difference?

Talmadge hesitated—the thought had occurred to him, to include Della in the will—but he said it did not make a difference.

The Judge nodded. Of course, he said. I'll see what I can do. Then, pushing the pad away a few inches: Even if you do decide to change the will, you can always change it back later—

It won't change, said Talmadge.

CAROLINE MIDDEY, THOUGH she held firm in her belief over the years that Talmadge should not go hunting Della, did not like to see the consequences of Talmadge's taking her advice.

Who knows if things would have been worse if he had gone looking for her? There is no one to tell us what would have happened if he tracked her down and persuaded her to come back to the orchard, or, if she refused, if Talmadge, his curiosity satisfied, would have come back to the orchard with a different perspective. He did not go after her himself, but those months after he fell out of the tree, though his physical wounds more or less healed—though he walked with a slight limp afterward—a kind of vacancy, a silence, hung around him, like a mantle on his shoulders.

Am I responsible for that? Did I do that? Caroline Middey wondered at times. But then she always came back to the same answer: Life had done it, not her, Caroline Middey. But wasn't she a part of life? Should she have known better? There were no answers to these questions.

I F DELLA HAD visited Angelene's own plot in the outer orchard at that time, she would have seen what had captured the girl's interest, what had caught her eye, at the Malaga fair the previous year. With each successive trip, the plant sale became more interesting to her. When she knew she was looking for a plant for her very own garden—what would suit the area in the bed between the asparagus and lettuce, for example?—her interest became singular and almost obsessive. What a delicious feeling to walk through the fair with her own bag upon her arm, driven by her own purpose. Here are my pumpkins, Angelene would have said to Della, if Della came through in the fall. Angelene probably would have left at least one on the vine, a particularly large and beautiful one, if she knew Della was going to see it.

Or, in the summer: Here are the strawberries—brushing aside the soft leaves with her hand to reveal the cluster of small red fruit beneath—and of course you may try one, Angelene would tell her, and Della would lean and reach her hand inside, pick one off the stem, put it into her mouth. Please let it not be sour, let it have had enough time in the sun to be sweet on her tongue. Here are the fig trees—not quite ripe, but you can see the general shape of the fruit, quite weird, don't you think?—and the apples—I am working on those, Angelene would say—and the cherries; yes, let's pick some now, and I'll make a cobbler for you, for all of us, to eat with our supper. There is cream in the cold pantry, I was going to churn it into butter, but now I won't, now it will go on the fruit, I will spoon it onto the hot fruit and biscuits—

Though Angelene told herself at the time that she did not care about Della, it was amazing how often she found herself caught in these fantasies, these daydreams: Della coming back to find Angelene alone in the orchard, and falling under Angelene's casual, but powerful, hospitality.

She thought that besides the actual fruit of her labor, she would share with her also—she would give her—those hours spent alone in the quiet, in the resplendent light of the outer orchard, among the half-dug-up plants and roots lying wrapped in wet newspaper, Angelene kneeling, digging in the soil. Angelene would give Della the hours of clement weather, the odors of the earth and sun and pine, and the freedom that comes from knowing you are the only human for miles, and the freedom to sing, to talk to yourself, to laugh, and of course, if need be—but there was hardly ever need for this—to cry.

TALMADGE AND ANGELENE set out from the orchard before dawn, and reached the market by midmorning. The air was cool with pockets of cold, smelled of alfalfa. It was April; the season was changing.

They unpacked fruit—now mostly apples from deep storage—alongside the other vendors, arranged it in bins on tables they kept stored in the warehouse by the river. Afterward they took out their folding chairs, settled within them.

For dinner they ate egg sandwiches Talmadge had packed that morning, and then Angelene went to the man who sold pickles and bought a pickle for each of them. After dinner, when it became slow again, Talmadge dozed upright in his chair, and when the customers came, they spoke to Angelene in a whisper. When Talmadge woke, it was late afternoon.

Angelene retrieved their market mugs and said she was going to the coffee stall. When she returned, she said that Caroline Middey had invited them to supper, and also to spend the night, because it looked like rain.

Talmadge peered at the end of the marketplace, at the sky. Boisterous blue, and cloudless. It did not seem like rain at all.

That's what I said, said Angelene. But she said it would probably rain. She does know things.

She does, he said, and Angelene went off again, to tell Caroline Middey that they would accept her invitation.

When the market was nearly over—it was almost four o'clock—and several of the vendors were already packing up their stalls, Talmadge saw the Judge coming toward them through the crowd. As he neared them he took off his hat, looked down at the fruit with a puzzled expression, from—what was it?—a kind of embarrassment.

What do we have here, said the Judge. Look at this fine fruit.

He had something he wanted to say, Talmadge saw; he had come about something in particular. The Judge glanced at Talmadge and then, frowning, looked down at the fruit again.

Talmadge told Angelene to start packing up the wagon; he would be right back, he was going to talk to the Judge for a moment.

He and the Judge walked out of the market, into the open air. They began to cross the field, in the direction of the river.

What is it? said Talmadge.

It's about Della.

Talmadge wanted to ask what he had found out, but said nothing at first. He understood that he did not want to ask anything because he did not want to know if Della was dead. And yet by the Judge's demeanor it was now a possibility. But he would not ask it; suddenly he did not want to know.

The Judge stopped walking.

Is this something you want to talk about here? I was going to ask you and Angelene to come to supper this evening—

Talmadge asked the Judge to wait for him. He walked back to the market, to Angelene, who was putting away the fruit. She looked at him, amused at first, and then the smile faded from her face. She asked him if everything was all right. He told her that everything was fine, he just needed to talk to the Judge about something. She was unconvinced, he could see; but when he asked her if she would mind loading the wagon by herself and transporting everything to Caroline Middey's—he would meet her there later—he could see that despite her worry she was pleased, satisfied, that he would ask her to do something independently. She said that she would do it.

He returned to the Judge, who waited for him in the field. By unspoken agreement they set off again toward the river.

I got word, said the Judge. She's up in a jail, in Chelan.

Talmadge was so relieved she was not dead that what the Judge said failed at first to touch him. They could see the water now. The colorless grass pressed flat against the sandbank. The odor of the river and the thawing ground reached his face; he inhaled deeply.

I don't know all the details, said the Judge. I just heard from a jail warden up there that a woman by her name is incarcerated there. Talmadge, he said, after a pause. She turned herself in, about a month ago. She said she—killed somebody. A man up around Seattle way. At a lumber camp.

Talmadge stopped walking. The water was loud in his ears, and the sun bright on the field illuminated all the hidden and variegated patterns. No, she could not have killed somebody. That was not right. But the Judge had said it, and the girl had turned herself in. She could have taken a bad turn, she had made bad turns in his imagination these years she was gone, but nothing like this. Nothing short of killing her own self was as bad as this. She had killed somebody. He should not have stopped walking; with a lack of movement his thoughts overwhelmed him. He started forward again; the Judge followed.

Killed somebody? said Talmadge. If it was a man, he thought, and she was just protecting herself—

It's unclear, said the Judge. That's the strange part—she's claiming she killed someone, but there's no proof of it. Or not yet. She might have simply injured the man. The authorities are—investigating it.

You don't know if she killed someone or not? said Talmadge, incredulous. She *might* have injured him? Then: What's all this about? He was surprised to hear anger in his voice.

The Judge shook his head. Seems like she was working out at a lumber camp, and got to roughhousing one night with the men, they were all playing cards, and—they were drinking as well—this man accused her of cheating, apparently, and she got upset and stabbed him with a broken bottle—

Talmadge looked at the river. He did not want to think of the broken bottle. He did not want to think of her playing cards, being near such men. But hadn't he allowed it? What had he done? What had he ever been thinking?

He turned to the Judge.

Is she all right? I mean—

After a silence, the Judge said, I believe she is fine, Talmadge, physically speaking. They say she appears in her right mind—

Her right mind, thought Talmadge. But what did that mean?

He regarded the Judge, who had politely averted his eyes, was watching the river.

You want to come to Caroline Middey's for supper? said Talmadge, after a silence. She wouldn't mind having you, I'm sure. We could—talk more.

The Judge shook his head. My sister's expecting me. Talmadge—

They regarded each other warily.

I'm sorry, said the Judge.

Talmadge, looking away at the ground, his mind full of incoherent, distracted thought, nodded.

As they started back across the field, Talmadge felt the new knowledge inside him: the girl was in jail. He felt as if they walked at an incline, though they did not; there was a dull ache at his sternum that could have been grief. He tugged his hat brim to hide his increasing anxiety.

How long has she been—

At this jail? Only a month or so.

A silence passed.

How much longer does she have?

It depends on what they find out, said the Judge. They're keeping her at the jail for the time being.

If there wasn't proof of any wrongdoing, Talmadge thought, then wasn't that illegal? He said: Can they do that?

The Judge shrugged. It seems she prefers it that way—

Talmadge took off his hat and slapped his thigh with it. She prefers it that way? How could anybody prefer it that way? After a minute, he replaced his hat on his head, said: I appreciate you finding this out for me—

It's not a problem, said the Judge. I just wish I had better news.

THAT NIGHT, AFTER Angelene had gone to bed, Talmadge told Caroline Middey what the Judge had said about Della. They sat on the porch, despite the cold, blankets over their laps. Caroline Middey had brought out her knitting, but as soon as he started telling her about it she left the long needles and heap of yarn in her lap and rocked in the chair, staring out at the dark.

Lord have mercy, she said. Prison? Prison?

Jail, he corrected. Not prison.

Caroline Middey shook her head.

I would never have thought it, she said. Then: What are you going to do?

There had never been a question about what he was going to do.

I'm going to see her, he said.

As he was drifting to sleep he thought of his will and testament. It had only seemed natural, before, to leave everything to Angelene. But now the situation was different. Wasn't it? Logic born of anxiety entered his half-conscious mind: Della was in jail—and would likely go to prison—because *she did not belong anywhere.* His naming her as heir to the land would tie her to a place in the world. Criminals by and large were vagrants, drifters (weren't they?): they certainly did not own land. Della was different from them; he would make her different. As a legal landowner, she would come back to that place that claimed her. Her tie to the land would be official, it would be written down—

And, he thought, she would be responsible for Angelene. Blood and law. That was important, that would be written down too—

———

Angelene sat at the large, ornate dining room table in the Marsden house. Talmadge and the Judge were in the study. The Judge's sister, Meredith, entered the room with a tray of coffee and shortbread, and said, smiling at Angelene, You look very nice, dear. And Angelene said, bowing her head modestly, Thank you. Talmadge had wanted her to wear her nice gingham dress, and her straw hat with the ribbon. Her special shoes. Stockings, even. She did not know why. He would tell her when he was ready. He was thinking about something else all the way to town, and did not speak much to her. What's wrong? she asked him once, and he said that nothing was wrong. He just had to go see the Judge about some business.

Finally the men came out of the study and entered the dining room.

I'll make more coffee, said Meredith, rising from her chair.

Oh, Meredith, that won't be necessary. Will you bring the port?

The port?

Yes.

She left the room and returned with a bottle and a tray of glasses, and the Judge poured the alcohol, and when the glasses were passed around, Angelene was included. She glanced at Talmadge, who nodded at her to tell her it was all right.

To our health, said the Judge, and they all drank.

In the wagon on the way home, she knelt up against the back of his seat, her face pressed against his shoulder.

What was that? she said.

What was what?

What happened back there—with you and the Judge. We drank that—port.

I made my will and testament, he said.

She said, Why?—even though she knew what a will and testament was. But she was suddenly embarrassed, and afraid.

Again he hesitated.

It's so that the land will go to you and to Della, if something happens.

She was as struck by the mention of Della's name as much as anything.

But she forced herself to ask, though she only partly wanted to know: What do you mean, if something happens?

The wagon creaked along in its tracks. She had her arms around his neck. They both stared ahead at the road, the ash and clay mildly glittering.

If I should die, he said.

THEY GAVE HER a cell at the far end of the jail. The twelve cells, and the larger holding cell near the front of the jail, were all empty as she passed them the first day. They're out in the yard, explained the guard who opened the cell door for her and stepped aside as she entered.

They aren't to talk to you, the warden had told her that afternoon, of the other prisoners in the jail. She had spent the better part of the morning and afternoon in his office, after her initial conversation with the young man at the front counter. She confessed her crime to the warden; and then a secretary was let into the room, and she confessed again, and the secretary wrote it all down on a typewriter. Della's throat hurt from talking; she could not remember ever talking so much at one time. Was tired from holding in her mind all the pertinent details she wanted to relate to the warden, so that he would consider her guilty and dangerous enough to warrant incarceration in his jail.

The warden, when he could see Della was tiring, called to the young man at the front desk. When the young man appeared in the doorway, the warden said: Get Miss Michaelson a sandwich from the cafeteria. And—coffee? Do you take coffee, Miss Michaelson?

She said coffee would be welcome.

Knowing what we know, the warden said, we cannot let you room in town. You'll have to stay here. You understand.

She was silent, looked down at her lap.

But, he continued, we can assure you that you will be safe here, quite unmolested by the men, until we figure out—your situation. Do you have any objection? Then, as if he'd just thought of it: Would you like a lawyer?

She pretended to hesitate.

I don't have no—any—objections, she said. And I might get a lawyer— later. But—I know what I did. I killed a man. I deserve to be locked away.

The warden stared at her. When he realized she was finished speaking, he told her he would see her the following morning. The guard had then taken her to the jail, in the basement of the courthouse.

After the guard left her alone, she studied the cell. It was more accommodating than she had thought it would be—a cot along the side wall; a basin on a pedestal; a slop jar behind a canvas partition in the corner. A small rectangular window that overlooked a portion of the front lawn. The jail was not in a proper basement, but was only half submerged in the earth. And the cell was relatively large: approximately ten by eleven feet. Packed dirt floor. Brick walls.

There were seven incarcerated men there at the time, and two in the holding cell. They occupied the cells at the front of the jail. The cell across from her was empty.

She went and looked out the window. There was a great cottonwood on the lawn that the wind was upsetting; it nodded like an encephalitic. She went and sat on the cot, touched absently the wool blanket. She would do all right here, she thought.

The men were let in from the yard soon after, and she went to the bars and observed them as they walked down the hallway past her. They looked in at her, startled. Impressed. One or two chuckled, poked their neighbors in the ribs: *Look, a woman!* They all looked at her but one—Michaelson—who trailed behind the others, shuffling, holding his side. He seemed to be in pain. A guard walked slowly behind him, watching Michaelson's movements carefully.

Neither the guard nor Michaelson looked at her.

That's it, murmured the guard, we're almost there.

Della stepped quietly back from the bars after Michaelson had passed, went to the cot, sat down. Listened to Michaelson's unsteady progress down the hallway.

That's it, said the guard.

The sound of a cell door opening, and then metal on metal: a lock slipping into place.

I'll get the doctor, said the guard.

WHAT'S WRONG WITH that man? Della asked the guard who delivered her breakfast the next morning. It was the same guard—tall, dough-faced—who had followed Michaelson and ushered him into his cell the day before.

The man glanced at her, said: He's sick. His tone neither friendly nor unfriendly.

How sick?

It seemed the guard would not answer her—was ignoring her—he was sliding the tray through the slot, and she took it—but then he shrugged.

Awful sick, as far as I can tell.

She wanted to ask him, What's he done? But she thought it was too soon for that, too quick. And so she accepted the food tray, and that was all.

That evening, when the men were let in from their time in the yard, Michaelson wasn't among them. She came away from the bars again—alert, confused—and sat on the cot. Her heart pounding hard and steadily in her chest.

What happened to that man? The one who was sick?

There was another, younger guard—thin as a stick, nervous, pimply-faced—who served her breakfast. He shot her a startled look.

I just heard he was sick, she said. I saw him. He didn't look well. I was just wondering what happened him—

The boy opened the slot and shoved the tray in; it made a grating sound. Suddenly he muttered, Needs an operation. But he should last for the trial. That's all we care about here—

And he glared at her, as if angry for disclosing so much information. But then she realized he was just excited.

She looked away. Said, flatly: Well, he didn't look well. Glad to hear he's getting help—

TALMADGE HAD THOUGHT, before, that he would just go and see Della directly—he would drive the mule and wagon up there—but the Judge said that since she was incarcerated, there was a procedure to these things. It could be that Talmadge would travel all the way there and not be able to see her, for whatever official or legal reason. And so, with the Judge's help, Talmadge composed a letter to the warden, asking for permission to come see the prisoner Della Michaelson, who, it had just been verified, was incarcerated in his jail.

Two weeks later, the Judge received a reply. Talmadge was welcome to come visit any time between the hours of ten and four o'clock the following Friday.

The next evening, over a supper of trout and creamed spinach on the porch, Talmadge told Angelene that the Judge had found Della. She was living in Chelan, he said.

Angelene, who had been chewing, slowed, stopped.

He did not tell her Della was in jail. That would come later, he decided, after he had learned more about Della's situation.

I'm going to go visit her, he said. I've thought about it, and think I should go by myself this time. I'll take the mule. Then: I just think it's best if I go by myself, this time.

Angelene said nothing at first. She took up her fork again, took a bite of trout. And then said, surprising him: I don't want to go anyway.

Her voice was soft. He studied her profile momentarily before she turned her head away, pointedly, and looked at the trees. Should he ask her what was wrong? Why she didn't want to go? He felt himself rise to ask these questions and then, at the last moment, falter. And then it was too late: the moment had passed.

He would not question her now.

H E SET OUT in the early morning. Angelene came out onto the porch, a blanket around her shoulders, and watched his last preparations.

He asked her again if she was certain she did not want to stay at Caroline Middey's. She shook her head.

You said I didn't have to.

You don't have to. I just don't want you to get scared out here all by yourself.

I'm not scared.

Well. It might get lonely.

She shrugged.

Don't let a bear come and carry you off.

Aren't no bears around here.

I saw one just the other day.

Didn't.

But she had smiled, briefly.

You know where the money is. You know where the gun's at.

Yes, she said. I know where it's all at. And then she looked askance at the trees, half amused, half annoyed. You going to Chelan or what?

All right, he said, and got up into the wagon and waved at her. When he was halfway across the pasture he turned and looked back at the cabin, but she was no longer on the lawn, or on the porch.

The man, Michaelson—but he was going by De Quincey now, she had heard a guard and a prisoner both call him that—was indeed sickly. What she had first observed in town, when he walked, squinting and disheveled, down the street, was not a passing discomfort but a disease. She did not need to know what it was exactly: only that without an operation, at some point soon, he would die.

He was getting progressively worse. She had been at the jail a month now, and passing outside her bars he was a head hulking against a frame of bones. But even so, hunched over, he was still impressively tall. That old rangy frame. He was not able, because of his sickness, to move freely. When he walked down the hall and passed her cell—holding his arms around his stomach as if holding his insides together—he continued not to see her. But then one day the men were led back in from the exercise yard, and she was at the bars, and he passed her, again behind the other men—the guard had not come in yet, he too lagged behind—and she said his name: Michaelson. He looked over at her, confused, a man coming out of a distant dream. His gaze took a moment to recognize her. But then he continued on, was not impressed, or didn't care. But it was him, Della thought, coming away from the bars and sitting on her cot. It was him!

Come on, said the dough-faced guard.

She was let out once a day into the yard, before the men. She, being the only female, was led out there by herself. She walked a circle just shy of the perimeter, strolling but not lingering too much in one place lest she draw attention to herself. Every once in a while she would look over her shoulder and seek the whereabouts of the guard. If he was not looking, or dozing—the dough-faced guard was prone to napping—then she would bend and pick up an object from the ground that might be of use later. If he was looking, she would pretend to be tying her bootlaces. Some stick, wedged into her boot. Rocks, the same. A glass bottle she stuck down the front of her pants.

The guards were lax about patting her down: she amassed a collection of objects in her cell, stuck them in a split in her mattress.

THE DRIVE WAS easy, the roads fine. Although, he noted, even an easy trip now was not as easy as it once was. Discomfort roused in his joints and spread. The first day he drove too far without stopping to rest, and he was overly stiff that night as he prepared his fire. After he ate, he got into the back of the wagon to sleep. The smell of the blankets—the outdoor blankets, his mother used to call them, used for overnight trips—made him remember earlier times, times he could no longer recall clearly.

In the morning—tired, disoriented—he went down to the water and washed his face. His head spun slightly. The day was very bright.

As the wheels creaked along in the wagon tracks, his thoughts turned to what lay ahead. The girl in the jail. And what would she be like now? She was a girl when he had last seen her, but now she was a proper woman. She had turned herself in, he remembered: and so maybe she had had a conversion of sorts. Not a religious conversion, but a change of heart and mind: she had done something wrong, she had committed a crime, but she wanted to take responsibility for it. That was something. And, he thought—the wagon shivering and sighing in the tracks—maybe the girl was guilty about an event, an action, that was not her fault.

He would determine what had happened, and help her. Either way—whether she was guilty or not—he would help her.

A ND THEN ONE day the dough-faced guard led her out into the yard when the men were coming back in. There was a sort of construction project going on in the building that prevented her from going out into the yard earlier, at her usual time. Instead of leading the men indoors and seeing they were locked into their cells and then taking her outdoors, the dough-faced guard led her out and then made her stand and wait as the men filed past her.

The next day, when they passed her again, she had a blade fashioned from a stick hidden inside her jacket sleeve. But when the time came, when Michaelson passed by her, a little more than an arm's length away, she did nothing; she simply watched him. Her heart racing. She wanted him to recognize her, but he did not.

And then she thought, it did not matter if he recognized her or not. The next day, waiting for the men to file inside, when he passed by her, she struck him with the sharpened stick.

But something funny happened. Instead of going for his neck or his face like she should have done and like she meant to, at the last moment she dropped her hand, barely grazed his side. The weapon was short and made for superficial wounding, except if one was going for the neck, where one could press down into the flesh to get at the vein. But at the last moment it was as if she had become bashful, or worse, lost courage. And he grabbed his side and grimaced but did not even so much as look at her. He pushed her aside as if she were a fly. Swatted her away, groaned. And then the other men were on her, trying to get the stick away. Someone hit her in the eye. Her own weapon scraped her knuckles. The guard hurriedly led Michaelson away.

He's already suffering! somebody shouted. What are you doing?

———

In Chelan Talmadge inquired of the first passerby who looked at him about the location of the courthouse. He traveled to it, and sat in the wagon looking at the building in which Della was housed. It was smaller than he thought it would be, though it was properly official-looking, and well made of pale granite and stone. A great lawn spread on either side of the wide staircase leading up from the sidewalk. Automobiles lined up along the street before it. There were only two horse-drawn wagons that he could see.

He found stables nearby, and a boardinghouse. Inside his room on the second floor he washed, using a porcelain basin of water the landlady brought him, and combed his hair. He unrolled the suit he had wrapped in paper and twine, and dressed. Looked at his image in the dented mirrorglass above the basin, but could not quite make out his likeness. Downstairs he inquired of the landlady about a place to eat, and she directed him to a nearby café. He walked outside, taking in the air, which was different; full of the great cold expanse of the lake, which he could not see, and another, sharper odor of pine. And behind it all: dust. On the street the women who passed him were dressed in fine dresses; one who passed him now going the opposite direction wore a straw hat on her head, tied beneath her chin with a blue ribbon. She glanced at him openly with pale green eyes and then looked away.

After a meal of steak and eggs and coffee at the café, where he sat at a booth and looked out at the passersby, he walked down the street in the direction of the courthouse, to where he had seen a barber's. He went in for a haircut and a shave. When the barber was finished, when he was dusting off the back of Talmadge's neck with a large brush, Talmadge looked at himself in the mirror.

Don't you like it? said the barber.

I like it fine, said Talmadge. In fact he was moved by his own image. He did not know the last time his face had been so naked. He was not handsome—he had never been that—but the sharp razor had revealed to him his flesh sagging in folds—around his eyes, mouth, under his chin—and there were the smallpox scars, the pitting, from when he was a child. He was, frankly, uncovered. The only thing he recognized in that face were his eyes, which were the old cornflower blue—that had not changed—and looked out at him like some startled animal.

It occurred to him that he was acting like a boy going to call on his sweetheart, going to the barber's like that. He, who was far too old for such things. He had wondered if he was going too far. But now he saw his reflection and told himself that things were as they should be. He was old, but taking pains. He had been traveling, and she hadn't seen him in a long time. It was only normal that he should take pains.

She had suffered to be in this position, he reminded himself—but did he ever have to remind himself of this?—walking up the courthouse steps.

The inside of the courthouse smelled faintly of gasoline. The sound of his boots echoed down the long corridor. In an office on one side of a wide staircase, he inquired after the jail warden.

A young man with spectacles who worked behind the counter told him the warden was not there, but was expected in the afternoon. Talmadge could either come back later or wait for him. Talmadge asked how long the warden was going to be. The young man shrugged. An hour, maybe two hours, he said. Talmadge was more than welcome to wait outside on the bench, if he would like.

Talmadge settled on the bench outside the door, took off his hat, and put it on his knee. He waited like that for about an hour and then rose and walked the length of the courthouse, looking at the large portraits of the important men—judges?—on the walls. And then he returned to the bench, sat down again. After another half hour had passed, he stepped again into the office. The young man looked up at him, surprised. Talmadge asked if he thought the warden was still coming. The young man hesitated, said he was most likely coming, because he had business there that afternoon. But then the young man faltered, looked away; and Talmadge knew he had forgotten about him waiting outside.

Talmadge returned to the bench. Not long afterward the young man came out and asked him what it was he was there for exactly. Maybe I can help you, he said.

I'm here to see Della Michaelson.

The man's expression changed only slightly, but Talmadge understood

that he knew who he was talking about. The young man excused himself, telling Talmadge he would be right back. He was gone for maybe
ten minutes, and when he returned, Talmadge stood. The young man
said that Della could not receive visitors today. He was not at liberty to
discuss the details, but she had been involved in an altercation earlier that
week and been put in solitary confinement.

The young man, after he said this, stood silently before Talmadge,
trying not to let his embarrassment or awkwardness overcome him.

Talmadge stood still and did not say anything. That word—
"altercation"—alarmed him. He wanted to step forward and place his
hands on the young man's shoulders—how old was he? Twenty? Twenty-
five?—and make him explain. What do you mean, "altercation"? But he
did no such thing. Instead he said:

An altercation, you say? In jail?

Yes, sir.

Can they have altercations in jail?

Oh, yes, sir. The young man, in fact, looked as if he were sorry about
it; winced.

Talmadge hesitated. She's all right, isn't she?

Yes, said the young man, and paused. I believe she's all right—

Talmadge waited for him to continue, to elaborate, for it seemed he
might go on. But the young man blushed, shook his head once to indicate
he was done speaking.

Talmadge said: She's a good girl, I don't know why—

But he didn't continue. His voice even to his ears was unconvincing.
He stared at the wall behind the young man, which was covered with
gray wallpaper.

She's a good girl? said Talmadge. This is the first time something like
this has happened, here?

The young man hesitated.

I can't rightly say, sir. You'll have to speak to the warden about that.
It's all in her file. I'm not at liberty—

Talmadge was nodding, absently.

The young man, though momentarily defensive, was sorry for Talmadge, Talmadge could see that. It was no use pressing him for informa-

tion, or trying to persuade him to let Talmadge in to see Della. This boy didn't have it in him to break the rules—Talmadge could see that clearly—and he, Talmadge, wasn't going to make him feel bad about it.

You can keep waiting, said the young man, or you can come back to-morrow. I'm sorry I can't be any more help.

I can't come tomorrow, said Talmadge. I have to be getting back.

The young man looked pained. I'm sorry, he said.

Talmadge wondered, walking down the street to the boardinghouse, blind now to the novelty of the place, the details that had captured his attention just hours before, what it was, exactly, that Della's file con-tained. Was it everything that they knew about her since the beginning of her incarceration, or did it contain other information as well? Did they know, for instance, anything about her past? Had she told them anything about herself? Talmadge wondered if, alongside all of the information about her, there was a list of names of the people who would be willing to help her in the case that she was released. A list of people who would vouch for her. Surely, he thought, such a list—himself, Caroline Middey, the Judge, Clee, Angelene—would make a difference. He made a note to talk to the warden, and the Judge, about it.

He slept through supper that evening at the boardinghouse, and when he woke, around ten o'clock at night, he dressed and went downstairs. The house was quiet. Several lamps were lit in the sitting room, and un-der one of them, in a chair in the corner, the landlady sat, knitting. She looked up at him as he paused in the doorway.

There's a plate for you in the oven, she said. I didn't want to disturb you. She looked down at her knitting, which she had not interrupted. When he continued to stand there, she stopped all at once, put the knit-ting aside, and stood.

That's all right, said Talmadge. I can help myself to something to eat, if—

It's not a problem—

He followed her down the dark hallway. In the kitchen she lit a lan-tern and told him to sit. He sat at a table near the window from where he

could see the lake. She took a plate from the warming oven and set it before him. It was mashed potatoes and gravy, roast chicken, green beans.

Can I get you something to drink?

Thank you, I can help myself to some water, if you—

Water? It's water you want? Wouldn't you rather have some milk?

Well, I—

She brought him a glass of milk and then left him alone. He ate the
food, looked out at the lake and the trees, listened to the stove ticking.

When he finished eating, he found the landlady again, sitting in her
orb of light, knitting. She looked up at him.

Did you get enough to eat?

Yes, thank you.

Is there something else? You have enough blankets up there to suit
you?

When he didn't answer, she stopped knitting and put the yarn aside
and asked him if he would like to sit.

Again he hesitated.

I have to ask a favor—

She regarded him.

Do you think—would you mind taking dictation for a letter?

There was only the slightest of hesitations, from surprise, before she
answered.

Of course—

And she got up to get a piece of paper.

THE WORST THING about solitary confinement was that she lost the sense of the order of things. What was she doing? Where was she? Was she making a mistake? It had all seemed a bright formula to her, before. But now in the darkness doubt reared its head, rose up before her.

It was very still and Della might sleep and then she woke and there were no men and no horses, there was no orchard and orchardist and child, there was no fruit and no sky, no wet-smelling air; only emptiness. There was no time. There was no wilderness to lose oneself inside. She touched her face in the dark; she had her self. But then, she thought, her self was nothing. She was nothing.

Why are we born? she thought. What does it mean to be born? To die?

TALMADGE WAS HALFWAY back to the orchard—he had woken before dawn in the back of the wagon, in the biting cold, and had prepared a fire and eaten, and taken up the reins in the blue-gray air, before he realized, the sun breaking in the east: he should not have left her there. He should not have been so lenient with the young man. He should have demanded to see the warden, demanded to see Della. It was not impossible, after all, to see her. She was not dead. It was up to the warden whether Della could receive visitors or not. And Talmadge was capable, he knew, somehow—didn't he have the power of speech? Wasn't he, in the least bit, sympathetic?—of changing the man's mind.

But what had he, Talmadge, done? He had written a letter to the girl: *I will come back to see you.* And would it be worse for her to know that he was there, but had not pressed anybody for her sake, had not insisted on seeing her?

He slowed the mule in the road, stopped. Silence of another landscape surrounded him. He considered going back. But there was Angelene, alone, ignorant of all these developments, in the orchard. He did not want to frighten her by his extended absence. After minutes of indecision, he finally urged the mule forward, toward the orchard. Away from Chelan.

A MAN CAME TO see you, said the warden.

Della, who had been in a cell with no windows or light for three days, sat before his desk. She tried to remain indifferent and calm but was unable to hide her discomfort. The light in the office, though weak—the warden had drawn the blinds, sensitive to her condition—seemed to abrade her. The shadows on the wall, the small movement of the warden's face as he spoke now, touched a deep part of her. She was alarmed by the feeling that she was going to cry. But there was no reason to cry, not now.

She eventually came around to recognizing what the warden had just said: that a man had come to see her.

What man?

He left this for you. The warden reached into his front shirt pocket and removed an envelope, handed it across the desk to her. The letter had been opened.

Protocol, he said.

When he had walked with her down the hall after her stint in solitary confinement—gripping her elbow, for she had trouble standing; the darkness had weakened her more than she could have imagined—he had also been gently jovial: Now, I know that was unpleasant, but I'm sure you understand now why we use that as a deterrent—

She took the letter from him. As an object it was completely foreign to her, as if he had handed her a piece of the moon, or a diamond necklace. He was waiting for her to say something.

Hesitating briefly, she handed the letter back to him without opening it.

I can't read it. And by "can't," it was obvious that she meant she was literally unable to read the letter.

The warden let a minute pass in silence. The letter lay before him on the desk, but he did not consult it.

He wants to come see you. I told you before. His name is William Talmadge. Then, watching her face: How do you know him?

And Della remembered: the day before she attacked Michaelson, the warden had come out to join her in the yard. He said he had received a letter from a man, a lawyer, down near Wenatchee, who was asking permission on the part of a client to come and see her.

Do you want to see him? the warden had asked that day in the yard.

He wants to come *here*? said Della. Thinking, after the initial surprise: Of course he couldn't come there. But upon hearing his name she had felt a brightness in her abdomen.

No, she said. I don't want to see him.

That was what she had said that day in the yard. But the man—Talmadge—had come anyway. Della said now, mustering her strength at reason and argument—she was tired and confused, they should have let her rest longer before this meeting—Why did he come, if you said he couldn't see me?

The warden touched a sheaf of papers on his desk. He did not answer right away.

I told him to come, he said.

Della, who had already begun to understand, was silent.

I don't think you realize—I don't think you *understand*—how much trouble you might be in. With the assault you already admitted to, but now, especially, with this most recent action—the warden shook his head. I don't think you're in a position to be denying help. Forgive me. I only have your best interests at heart—

Della said nothing. She was not moved by the warden's words of concern. She had thought he was intelligent, though not beyond manipulation; but after that solitary confinement business, she was not sure he was not like other men she had known: like Michaelson. After that, she did not know what to think of him. These words—*I only have your best interests at heart*—she excused at once without believing them. They were just words, used to further control her.

She let herself think, briefly, of Talmadge. Imagined him coming to

Chelan—did he take the mule? Or would he have taken the steamboat? The train?—and drawing to the courthouse, searching for her. She knew what had happened: he had come at the appointed time, and when he was denied, when he was told what had happened to her—but what would they have told him, exactly?—he had perhaps thought of arguing, but had not. He had accepted the circumstances. He had written her a note. She suddenly knew what the letter said, she did not have to read it: He had come to see her, but had been unable to do so. He hoped she was all right. He would come to see her again.

And when the warden read her the letter—at his insistence, not hers—this is what it said.

Will you see him? asked the warden, folding the letter and inserting it into the envelope.

Do I have a choice? she said: without animosity, without sarcasm. It was simply a statement, reflecting that she understood her powerlessness in the matter.

The warden smiled faintly. It is for the best, he said. Let him—and this lawyer—help you.

I don't need help, she thought, as she was led back to her cell. I need time, and quiet, to think: to figure out how I am going to get through this all, how I am going to complete this task—

THE MULE, WHICH had grown sluggish during the last day and a half, picked up speed in the forest mountainside from Cashmere, feeling the familiar terrain beneath its hooves. Talmadge too felt the closeness to home. His heart beat through him hollow and light; he was dazzled by the sun in the trees. The mule traversed the final hill, wheezing, and Talmadge called to it, and the mule broke out of the trees into the bright pasture and coughed, ambled down the slope, its mouth agape, bridle clinking.

The orchards were blue- and silver-leaved. The regular cries of birds, which the silence of the road had made him forget, rose and crossed in the sky. And there were the mingling odors: of water, of fruit and blossom and dust.

Always dust.

By a trick of light—it was the way the canyon was shaped, the distant canyon rock and upper forest rearing against the sky—some parts of the valley were cast in shadow, and other parts, like the part holding the cabin now, were lit up as if it were morning.

Angelene had come out onto the porch, her hands at her face, shielding her eyes.

She waved. When he came up into the yard, she had gone back into the cabin but soon came out again, went to the wagon, and helped him down onto the grass. How was it she knew he needed help? For he was the one who needed help now, he realized. Had he ever leaned on her like this? (He leaned on her heavily, more heavily than he would have liked. He was shaking; he longed, momentarily, for the old motion of the wagon. He was sick with fatigue.) He said something into her hair as he struggled against her, and she said, What? But she bore his weight and helped him across the grass to the porch, she did it as if she had done it a thousand times. It did not even register on her face that it was something out of the ordinary. They headed up the steps, and then on the porch he lowered his weight into the birchwood chair and she was leaning over him, speaking to him. He saw for the first time that her hair was wet, slicked back, and she wore her market-day shirt, the white shirt with the design in pink thread embroidered on the collar. Had she been to market by herself? She was leaning over him, speaking to him, and then—he did not know what happened next—he was asleep.

When he woke, he was in his bed, and it was dark. Crickets called outside the open window, and over everything wafted the odor of fried onions. She passed by the open door of the bedroom, and when she saw he was awake, she came inside. Sat on the edge of the bed. Helped him sit up. A lantern was bright in the room behind her, and he could not make out her face. After a moment she placed a hand on his hand.

I knew you were coming today, she said. When I woke up this morning, I knew it.

There was a silence. He thought he should tell her about Della. Where should he begin? But before he could speak, she said: Are you hungry?

He nodded.

She rose, and returned with a plate of food. Eggs scrambled with bacon and onions, bread and tomatoes thinly sliced, coffee. She sat on the edge of the bed while he ate.

Aren't you going to eat? he asked her.

I already ate.

How long have I been asleep?

Three hours or so.

After she took his plate away, she came and sat beside him again, but this time in a different position, and he could see her face. The dark, generous eyes, the puzzled brow. They regarded each other.

He began to speak.

You don't have to tell me now, she said, and averted her eyes, picked a piece of lint off the quilt. Smoothed the fabric with her hand. You don't have to tell me now. You rest—

Was she still angry? At him? There was that hardening of her mouth—anger, but also sadness.

It would all become clear, he thought, it would all come to the surface, when he talked to her, when he told her what had happened—recently, on his trip to Chelan, but also in the past. It would all become clear—

Did you go to market? he asked her the next day.

Yes—

How did you get there?

The horse, she said. And then, when it failed to register on his face that he knew what she was talking about, she said, The horse Clee left the last time. I took a small load and set up where we usually do—

The horse? he said, and at his tone, she looked at him, silent now. He knew which horse she meant. Clee would at times leave a horse behind so that Talmadge could use it in his work, if he needed a creature stronger than the mule.

Yes, she said, and looked away from him now, soberly. It's all right, Talmadge, it was fine—

He was amazed that she had sensed, before he realized it in himself, that he was upset with her. But why, he thought, should he be upset with her?

It was the old reaction, him and the horses—but this girl, Angelene, was fine. She was *fine*, he admonished himself, and reached out, touched her shoulder, pretended to brush something off that was there, a bit of leaf, a strand of hair. She smiled faintly. The smile meant: I forgive you.

Della, alone in her cell, took the letter out from the envelope and looked at it, the words on the page.

He hadn't written it, she was certain of that; it was a woman's hand. She wondered, briefly, if it was Angelene's hand, but then dismissed that. It was too mature-looking.

She went to the window, looked out.

So he had been to see her, and would come see her again. She supposed there was no harm in it, not really; she supposed seeing him would not disturb her plans too much. It was nothing for her to see him—she would see him and get it over with—but it was imperative that he, Tal-madge, not find out that Michaelson was there in the jail as well. That might change things.

But he did not necessarily have to find out about Michaelson. Even if the warden discussed what had happened—her attack on Michael-son—he, Michaelson, was going by a different name now. Talmadge would not, unless he investigated further, come to any easy conclusions by himself.

But still, she worried.

But there was nothing to do but to see him. She must not raise a fuss, not about this; she must be patient, she must bide her time.

H E WOULD LEAVE the orchard again in two weeks. He had talked
to the Judge about it. He would tell Angelene—what exactly he did
not know, but he would tell her *something*—and also try to fit as much
work as he could into the weeks before he left. He could feel her wondering at his renewed energy, his bustle, which he knew was agitated: but
she said nothing, perhaps thinking he still suffered from his recent over-
exertion from the trip to Chelan.

They worked in the apple orchard outside the canyon mouth when,
suddenly, Angelene pulled her arms out of the limbs in which she worked
and turned her head to the forest. Expression like an animal sensing
weather. It's too early, he told her. He knew she was waiting for the
men; he was waiting for them too. But it was too early. They came the
first week of July, and it was barely June. She went back to working, reluctantly. A minute later she stopped again, pulled her head out of the
limbs, turned to the forest. She began to say something, and the forest
line shook, began to produce horses; first two or three abreast and then a
great surge of them, the bulk moving from the trees into the field.

Well, he said, and he and Angelene began to disengage from the trees.
Headed down the hill to the creek, toward the horses.

He was struck, as he was always struck, by the horses' simultaneous
ugliness and beauty. Different shapes, heights, colors: cream-colored,
black, brown, yellow horses, horses with dappled rumps, with stockings;
some white horses with pink snouts and blue eyes; tall horses, with muscular necks; others short, stunted, dwarfed-looking. All weighing around
a quarter ton, some just over. He had seen these herds for years, and yet
when they came through the trees he was always surprised by them. They

were dirty, unkempt, stinking; overall unpredictable. Perhaps what made them so impressive was their *unhandledness*. They had encountered no human up there in the mountains where they were captured. The men had gone up there, to the places where the horses lived, and dragged them— the horses—down to the plateaus and lowlands, and as a result the horses held the deepest grudge; they tore this way and that, tossing their heads, breathing rancid horse breath out of their rancid horse lungs. This is how he imagined it, as a boy lying awake at night, unable to sleep because of their presence in the field. He did not understand what they were. What do you mean, what are they? his mother had said. They are horses, Talmadge. But they were unknowable, both singly and as a herd. Even now it was difficult to look away from them.

The men on horseback came out of the trees, one after another, and lifted their arms in greeting. Clee's horse, a dark palomino with yellow-stained mane and tail, a silver medallion on its breast strap, came stepping out of the forest. Clee too lifted his hand, but seriously, unsmiling. Something had happened, Talmadge thought; something had happened on their journey to make them early, this was why Clee looked so grim now. He and Angelene had by this time made their way into the field; the men simultaneously rode through the horses toward them.

When Talmadge and Clee and the wrangler settled on the porch and removed their hats, and Angelene had gone inside to get coffee, the wrangler told Talmadge that one of the men had spotted a scout—the law— two days before, and they, the men, decided to go another way—to go north, and loop around, which they usually avoided because the terrain was rougher and more difficult to navigate. But the possibility of danger was less threatening than certain danger seen at a distance; and so they had risked it, this other route, and passed unscathed. That's why they were early. While the wrangler talked, Clee wiped the sweat from his face with a large handkerchief, his eyes closed, and then replaced the handkerchief in his pocket.

Talmadge nodded. He said that he and Angelene were more or less ready for them. What they needed to do in order to prepare for them, the last work, could be absorbed by all of them in the next couple of days.

In fact he was relieved to have the men come early, because he had not yet told Angelene about Della. Angelene seemed to not want to talk about it. Now they could work, all of them, and he could put aside the task of discussing Della for at least a little while longer. But he must tell her soon, he thought, because the situation involved her. He would tell her after the men had gone, when by that time the excitement of the men would have diluted the fact of his trip to Chelan; the trip would have waned, become unimportant; would have less potential to hurt her.

The men had hunted deer that morning, and the carcasses were thrown over the backs of several of the horses. Soon after they arrived, some of the men, Clee included, took the deer to the opposite side of the field, downwind from the horses, and butchered them. They erected a camp and cooked the venison over large fires.

Clee, having overseen the food preparation, sat beside a fire and packed a pipe full of tobacco. Talmadge sat beside him, in a collapsible chair made of wooden poles and canvas. He watched the other man's movements dully, but thought about all the years he had watched Clee do this. Pack a pipe full of tobacco. Clee's movements, his face, were as familiar to Talmadge as his own, and yet there existed a chasm between them that they never regarded directly. Different lives. He had seen this action—this habitual movement—since he was a teenager, sitting beside Clee, the odor of the horses and woodsmoke in the air, but the movements at the same time seemed singular, new—the deft hands, the long fingers, working. It was the casualness, but also the ceremony, the severe quietness, that Talmadge appreciated.

Clee's hands were stained red from the butchering. Blood smudged on his cuffs. He pulled on the pipe a few times and then there was the odor of tobacco smoke mixing with the odor of fires and venison. The sky overhead was darkening, and when Talmadge pulled his face away from the fire—the smoke was in his eyes—the outer air was cold. Evening had set in. The fires sent their flames high. The men talked and laughed, and behind and beyond them was the sound of the horses, which never died. The sound was loud and soft at the same time, like the sound upon which other sound was built. You didn't hear the horses until you listened for them; and then they were very loud. Already Talmadge was becoming used to them. How that presence equated with silence until it was gone, and then you understood what silence really was.

Clee was regarding him; held up his pipe: Where was Talmadge's pipe?

Talmadge held up his pipe, which he had gripped in his palm, lying in his lap.

Clee passed him the pouch of tobacco, and after a moment—what had he been thinking about?—Talmadge began to pack the pipe. His hands shook slightly. Clee watched him for a moment, then looked away.

They sat smoking in silence, and then Talmadge said:

The Judge found the girl—

Clee looked up. He pulled on the pipe, blew smoke rapidly out the corner of his mouth.

She's in Chelan, in a jail there—

Clee remained still; and then, after a moment, he leaned forward, removed the pipe from his mouth. Spat. Paused for a long time, his eyes downcast and unmoving.

She tried to kill a man, said Talmadge. Stabbed him with a broken bottle, something like that. Well—I don't know the half of it. It was the Judge that found her—

Clee put the pipe in his mouth, slowly.

Angelene doesn't know about it. I haven't told her yet. I mean, she knows I went to go see her, but I didn't tell her about the jail—

Clee nodded, understanding. Then he looked at Talmadge. He made a slow, deliberate, heavy movement with his head, staring hard at Talmadge, which meant: You went to see her?

Talmadge brought the pipe to his lips, found the fire had gone out in it. Clee, after a moment, dropped his eyes, fished for matches in his vest pocket.

I didn't see her, said Talmadge, and leaned so that Clee could light his pipe. She was—in a cell where they wouldn't let her see anyone. She was—misbehaving. She did something wrong. They wouldn't tell me about it. He put the pipe in his mouth.

Clee, after a minute, nodded.

They're going to keep her in there—I don't know how long. She might have killed the man she stabbed, they don't even know. It's like she—well, like she wants to be there. She turned herself in—

Clee glanced at Talmadge. They were silent for several minutes.

When Talmadge looked out, he caught sight of Angelene as she loitered between the fires and the men. She passed among them meekly, letting them know by her insistent presence that she was available to help them, if they needed it. But, like always, they largely ignored her. It had always been that way. It had been that way too, in the beginning, with Della, he remembered. At times, after a long day of working in the trees, they might acknowledge Angelene; they might even joke with her or tease her; but for the most part they simply let her be among them, they did not bother to pay her any special attention. This was not in anger or resentment; it was, Talmadge thought, a sign of respect: toward Angelene, toward himself. Not to be coddled, not to be made an exception. She understood this, he thought, though she was puzzled at times at their seeming rejection of her.

Just now, a man whistled softly out the corner of his mouth and nodded to the nearby low table beside Angelene, meaning, Bring me that plate, and she hurried to the plate and brought it to him, and he put some meat on it. He spoke to her briefly, not looking at her, and she nodded and took the plate to a group of sitting men, one of whom took the plate from her and said something to her, smiling. Angelene said something back, and the group of men laughed. When Angelene turned, Talmadge saw that she was smiling, also blushing.

Later he remembered Angelene moving through the darkness of the camp. By the firelight she looked as if she wanted something; there was a kind of sorrow there. But if he were to call to her, she would turn and come to him, and by that time her face would be closed; or, if not closed, then there would be another expression there. The plain, the normal gentleness with which she always regarded him.

But what was that expression before she came to him? What did it mean? Was she unhappy? Did she too, or some part of her at least, wish to leave?

This look of sorrow as she walked among the fires—it was familiar to him, he had felt that way too, when he was younger. How to talk about it, how to talk about such things. When he was a boy he was happy when the men arrived, and in a way wanted them to remain forever—but he was also anxious that they had arrived, that he was no longer alone. The sorrow came from those two feelings—the happiness of company, the anxiety of interrupted solitude. That was what he had felt, he thought, and what to some extent he still felt. But never to the extent he had then, when he was young, when he did not know what to make of his feelings. When one is young, he thought, one thinks that one will never know oneself. But the knowledge comes later; if not all, then some. An important amount.

Angelene: he could only guess her mind. Did she herself know the root of her sorrowful expression? If she were to know it, if he were to tell her, Your face is full of sorrow, would she understand even a little the feeling that gave rise to it? Maybe she was truly sorrowful; maybe she was unhappy. Of course she loved the land; but maybe she did not know what else was inside her. Maybe she wanted to leave the orchard but did not know it. She was still young. She still had much to discover about herself. He had not told her yet—how could he have this conversation with her?—that it was all right to think of leaving; one should not expect to be constant one's entire life. He certainly did not expect her to stay: or this is what he would tell her. If she ever wanted to go, she could leave. He would not try to stop her. But then he wanted her, in a way, to remain constant in her childish dream of becoming an orchardist alongside him; because she was good at it, and—this was the main reason, he knew—because he loved her and wanted her to remain close to him.

But he would try to tell her eventually that it was all right to leave. There was the possibility, he reminded himself, that her future did involve the orchard, and that her choice to remain there was made not out of fear of the outside world but rather a knowledge and willful rejection of it. There was the possibility that her becoming an adult did not necessarily mean that she would move away from him. She could change, he told himself, and still remain in the orchard. But despite her apparent love of the trees, despite her intelligence and skill and aptitude in caring for the entire homestead, he remained doubtful. It was too much to wish, much less assume, that she would remain by his side.

Angelene walked over to him, leaned against him, put her hand on his shoulder. She smelled, faintly, of licorice.

The wrangler, who had come and sat beside Clee, addressed her, his eyes smiling: Are you coming to the auction, then? Talmadge was just telling me how much you wanted to go— There was an edge of laughter to his voice, although he was not laughing; he was teasing her, because he knew she was a homebody, and even though she was awed by the horses, she wanted little to do with them.

But Talmadge waited to hear what Angelene would say.

She squeezed his shoulder.

I don't want to go, she said, shyly, glancing down at Talmadge. Not really. Or, I would go, if Talmadge comes too—

Well, go if you want to go, said Talmadge, and his voice, surprising them all, was gruff. There was a moment of silence, and then Angelene took her hand away.

He shifted in his seat. Incredibly, he heard his voice again:

Those places are no places for girls. I should have known that a long time ago, but like a fool—

Clee peered out toward the forest. He puffed on his pipe. Angelene was still. He knew that if he were to look at her, there would be a look of confusion on her face. But underneath, he knew, she understood. She understood exactly what he was talking about.

AㅤNOTHER GUARD REPLACED the angry, pimply-faced guard who had told Della that Michaelson needed an operation. This new guard was also young—maybe just twenty years old—and was what others would call handsome. His name was Frederick. He stuck his arm through the bars the first day, to shake her hand. She stood away and observed the gesture, surprised.

Frederick smiled at her—he had a complexion the color of newly washed buckskin, and dark ash-blue eyes. Dimples one could fit a knuckle into. When she didn't come forward, he pulled his hand back through the bars. But kept his smile.

That's all right, he said. Then: I heard about you. Only woman they've had in here for quite some time. Then: You turned yourself in, didn't you? Isn't that what I heard?

I have no idea what you heard, she said, and he laughed. Not a mocking laugh. She glanced at him, despite herself, thinking: And maybe this one was different. Maybe.

For his second trip to see Della, Talmadge would bring gifts. Some green apples, and candy—lemon drops, she had always like those—and magazines. He stood before the magazine rack at the feed and supply store, deciding what she might like. The clerk, when he saw how long Talmadge stood before the rack, asked if he could help. Talmadge said he was looking for something to give a young woman. The clerk said, Angelene? and Talmadge immediately regarded him. He was younger than Talmadge would have thought—he had in fact hardly taken note of the young man when he entered the store, barely saw he was a copy of the owner, and assumed he was the owner's son; or could it be his grandson? In any case Talmadge did not recall ever having seen him before. The boy was no older than seventeen, had hair the color of a newly hatched chick. No, said Talmadge, after a moment, and turned his attention back to the rack. Someone else. The clerk pointed out the domestic magazines and the fashion magazines. Talmadge picked these up, looked at them. They were all wrong, of course. He put all back but one, and then withdrew two horse magazines, and a Wild West magazine. He didn't know what she would like, but there was something there for her, anyhow, out of the ones he had chosen.

He told Caroline Middey, later that day when he went to see her, that Angelene hadn't wanted to come to town that morning; she had told him at the last minute, after he had prepared the wagon, that she had chores in the orchard she wanted to tend to.

Caroline Middey didn't say anything to this at first. They settled on the porch and ate some sliced bread and cheese, some cherry tomatoes. She was going to say something but then checked herself and rose, went inside for coffee. She returned, and sat. They poured their coffee. Caroline Middey asked again why the girl hadn't come.

Chores, you said? But shouldn't you be out there helping her?

Talmadge brought his mug to his lips. Of course they could both see through the girl's excuse; but Talmadge did not particularly want to discuss it. He said: She wanted to get a head start on things. I told her we could wait, but she didn't want to—

Caroline Middey picked some bread crumbs off her dress front. Without looking at him, she said: She's not jealous, is she?

Jealous? Even as he said it, an idea was blooming in his mind.

Caroline Middey looked at him.

You going around all over town collecting gifts—I don't know, a girl might get jealous of something like that. Then: You better have a superior gift for her, is all I'm saying. For her birthday, she said, when her statement failed to garner any reaction from him.

Talmadge looked to the road across the field. In fact he had forgotten the girl's birthday, that it was coming in a month's time.

Oh, Talmadge!

He cleared his throat.

I'll think of something.

You'd better, said Caroline Middey. And then, a minute later, hesitantly: You're going to tell her? About her mother? You always said you would tell her when she got to this age—didn't you? In my opinion she is ready, she was ready a year ago at this time, she is a proper young woman now, it's right to tell her—

Heavy clouds had moved in since he had arrived. The landscape darkened; a cold wind moved over the porch. And then the clouds moved over the sun and all was mellow gold, and a fine rain fell.

Caroline Middey peered out at it.

You going home in this? You want to stay the night?

This? I'll be all right.

How you planning on getting to Chelan? You're not taking the wagon again, are you?

He shook his head.

Taking the train, he said. In fact it was the Judge who had recommended it. Talmadge had gone to see him the week before, to tell him about the trip, and the Judge asked him how he had gotten to Chelan the previous time, and suggested the train might be more convenient, more comfortable for a man in his situation. He too thought Talmadge was getting old, thought Talmadge.

The girl going with you?

Talmadge shook his head again.

She doesn't want to go on the train? Incredulous. Does she know about the train? You told her you weren't taking the wagon—

I told her about it. She's taking me to the station.

He had not told Angelene about his plans to visit Della again, but she had guessed them. The day before, as he took out his suit from the closet, he turned to see Angelene in the doorway of his bedroom, regarding him.

You going to see her again?

He folded the suit over his arm.

Yes—

She nodded, shortly. Then, as if trying to hide her interest: You're not taking the mule again, are you?

I was thinking about the train this time.

They both stood in silence.

Is the Judge coming out to—

No.

I'll take you, then, she said.

Caroline Middey sighed and got up from her chair, went inside. When she came back a minute later, she wore a shawl and had two packages wrapped in butcher paper in her hands. She held up the package in her right hand.

This here's what you asked for. I was able to mend them all right. It would help if we knew how big she was now. Probably hasn't gained in height, but in other ways—well, she's still a growing girl, I suppose. But I guessed, I did my best. If they're way off, bring them back, and I'll work on them.

Talmadge nodded.

And this—Caroline Middey held up the other package—this is for our girl Angelene. Tell her it's an early birthday present. She smiled to herself as she handed it over. Oh, she'll like it, she said.

He held both packages, one in each hand. The one for Della was bulkier, heavier than the one for Angelene.

When you get back, said Caroline Middey, come see me and we'll talk about Angelene's birthday. And, she said, regarding him frankly, of course I'll want to hear about your trip.

He arrived in the orchard at dusk. When he entered the cabin, packages in hand, Angelene was sitting at the table in the front room, a notebook open in front of her. At her elbow sat the lantern and inkwell, blotting paper, flannel scraps. She was practicing her penmanship exercises. When he came in she looked up at him, frowned; touched distractedly the old cigar box in which she kept her supplies. There was an ink smudge on her cheek. He came up behind her and touched her shoulder and looked down at her work. After a moment he said: Have you eaten?

She shook her head.

Are you hungry?

No.

Well. I could make us something to eat—

She leaned over the page.

I want to finish this—

He went into the bedroom and set the packages on the bed alongside the suit he had put out that morning. He found his shaving kit in the top bureau drawer, placed that on the bed as well. All this would have to be assembled and packed.

Angelene stood now in the doorway. She looked at the items on the bed.

All that stuff for her?

Talmadge thought of what Caroline Middey had said, about the girl being jealous.

Before he could say anything, Angelene turned from the doorway and was gone.

He didn't know whether to go after her. He sat down on the bed.

She came back a moment later, leaned in the doorway. When she spoke, he knew that she had been preparing to say it—her voice, at the last moment, quavered.

Seems like she could get all that stuff on her own. Then: What's wrong with her? Is she sick?

He understood: these were things you would take to someone who was ill.

She's not sick. She's in jail.

Angelene was silent.

Jail?

Yes.

She was looking at the things on the bed.

What do you mean? You mean she works there?

He looked into the corner of the room. No—

Oh, she said, after several moments. Then: You didn't tell me that.

No, he said. I was waiting to tell you. I should've told you sooner. But I didn't know—

She was still staring at the bed.

He took up the package from Caroline Middey.

This is for you. It's from Caroline Middey.

She took the package, but continued to stand there.

Are you going to open it?

Now?

She hugged the package to her chest. Across her face drifted a crimped expression of confusion.

Is she coming to live with us? When she gets out of there?

Talmadge surveyed the items on the bed, as if an answer lay there. He saw the magazines. It occurred to him for the first time that Della might not be able to read. She could look at the pictures, anyway, he thought.

I don't know. I haven't asked her yet. When I went there, to the jail—he forced himself to look at Angelene now, to speak to her as an adult—I didn't see her.

Angelene stared at him.

What?

I went there, but they wouldn't let me see her. They had her locked away.

In the jail? But you couldn't see her?

Talmadge shook his head.

But—you're going to see her this time?

I hope so.

Again she hugged the package to her chest. She looked at the things on the bed, on her face a confused, faraway expression. Then, as if she had just discovered something—there was the same helpless expression: Is it her birthday?

I don't believe so, he said. No. And then he realized that he did not know when Della's birthday was.

Angelene was looking at the items on the bed.

It's my birthday soon, she said.

He hesitated.

I know, he said.

The next day they set out from the orchard in the early morning, and by the time they arrived at the station it was early afternoon. People were filing onto the train as Talmadge stepped out of the wagon. He gripped the top of the canvas sack in his fist and looked up at Angelene where she sat in the wagon seat.

You going straight to Caroline Middey's?

She nodded.

I don't want you to go back to the orchard today. Too much driving in one day.

She nodded, then hesitated.

But you drove all the way here. If I drove back, it would be like I was driving just once—

He looked at her.

She looked down the road.

All right, she said.

Caroline Middey's expecting you.

All right.

He continued to stand there. He glanced at the people getting onto the train.

You better hurry up, she said.

He looked up at her. He wanted to tell her something but had forgotten what it was. For a long and untethered moment—how frightening it was—he forgot her name.

Talmadge, she said.

What.

You're going to miss it.

But he didn't miss it. He got on and found a seat and sat down and looked out at the girl sitting slightly hunched in the wagon, looking straight ahead of her. She did it—she remained there—for his sake, he thought; she would much rather have made her way immediately to Caroline Middey's house, or back to the orchard.

What are you going to do today? he had asked her, and she had said, after some contemplation, hesitating, glancing at him: I might go fishing.

In the river? In that place by—

Yes.

He nodded. That should be nice, he said.

The train pulled away and she was gone; soon there was new country out before him, rolling by.

H E HAD SAID to Caroline Middey two days before, when they were discussing Della: She will come stay with us, later—not soon, but later—

Caroline Middey looked at him sharply.

Maybe after I'm gone, he said. She's the one—she's going to stay with the girl.

Caroline Middey was silent. But then eventually she said: And you've spoken to Della about this? Angelene? They've agreed to it?

Talmadge turned his head slightly as if hearing a sound across the field. He sniffed, was silent.

Talmadge.

He did not answer at first. Finally he said: They're kin.

Caroline Middey stirred. Said: I knew the girl only a short time, of course. Lord knows I have sympathy for her, for her situation. And then she was silent for a minute, reflecting, remembering. But if she remembered too much, if she called too much forth, she would be unable to say what she was going to say. We each of us decide for ourselves. You can't force her into coming back.

Talmadge was silent.

You are Angelene's family. I am her family, if you want to think of it that way. Leave the girl alone. Della, I'm talking about. Let her go. She wants to wreak havoc, get into trouble, why hold on to her? Is that who you want to come back to take care of Angelene?

Talmadge lifted his chin as if he was going to speak, but he did not speak. He was waiting for her, perhaps, to spend herself. To convince him.

Have the two ever even spoken? I mean, since you found Della? Do they want each other? Does Angelene even want her, Talmadge?

It doesn't matter what we want, he said. It's blood—

Oh, Talmadge, said Caroline Middey, surprised. The chair squeaked suddenly as she shifted again. Blood! Blood, you speak of! Blood means nothing—

WITH TALMADGE GONE from the orchard and Angelene working alone, the place took on a delicious strangeness, and she often felt as if she was looking at things for the first time.

There was the creek, endlessly clattering, and the main room of the cabin, smelling, no matter how much it was aired out, of beeswax and old paper. There was the smell of the shed, of damp wood and sun. The smell of earth and grass, the leagues of forest, after a rain. The smell of cornbread in the oven. The crows in the yard, the glossy midnight of their backs. The interminable chores, both large and small, that constantly, rightly, occupied her. The bright and silent stars at night, so close you felt you could walk into them. The cacophony of birds at dawn.

There was a certain uncanniness Angelene felt opening her closet in the morning, her oatmeal-colored dress hanging in the space on its hanger, her workboots leaning against each other on the porch. (You turned them over and shook them, knocked them on the post, for mice.) The narrow bed with its purple, red, and green quilt, the bedside table with its jar of rocks, piled books. The porcelain basin near the window where she washed her face, the pitcher with the brown rose painted on it, the large crack like a vein in the bottom of the basin. The apricot orchard, the buzzing bees like a haze in spring. The barn—the smell of hay and manure, grease, old leather. The sun streaming through the slats. The mule's nose in her palm.

All of these things she kept inside herself, constantly rearranged them, to create her happiness. Being alone, she was able to see each thing more clearly. Although there was fear in solitude, somehow this only made things sharper. It could not be sustained, this solitude, this level of sensitivity, but for the short time that Talmadge was away it was glorious, it was a great gift to herself.

Let him visit her, she thought, going down to the creek for water. What was it to her, Angelene, anyhow?

It was not the presents laid out on the bed, or the airing of, the constant fussing over, his suit. Not the slow, deliberate polishing of his good shoes, and wrapping them, for safety, in a paper bag. She was only a little wary of these things. Suspicious. But what she feared most were his silences. The times when she felt him prepare to speak, but ultimately falter. Turn away. The leagues, which his eyes revealed at times, of what he did not say.

At the boardinghouse in Chelan, Talmadge unpacked his canvas sack: his suit, his shoes, his shaving kit, Della's gifts. There, at the bottom of his pack, he spied something foreign: a small flat box the size of his palm, tied multiple times with twine. A note stuck within the twine—he carefully disengaged it—read "For Della." The deliberate script, the hand, he knew immediately. He replaced the card and held the box for a moment, considering it, and then put it on the bed beside the others. He shaved, and then combed his hair, put on the suit, looked at himself in the dented mirror. But as before, he could not adequately see himself.

A young woman stood behind the desk at the courthouse. She had red hair piled on top of her head, and a small nose, eyes the color of ice. When he told her he was there to see the warden, he had an appointment for three o'clock, she slit her eyes and then opened them very wide and said in a quiet voice: Oh! You must be Mr. Talmadge! and then she turned and went immediately to the back of the room, exited through a doorway.

Talmadge remained standing there.

When the woman returned a minute later, she was followed by a slight, bespectacled man of middle age. The warden introduced himself. He was soft-voiced, hoarse. He and Talmadge shook hands.

The warden's office was small. There was just enough room for a desk, two chairs, and a drab green filing cabinet. At the warden's back were two large panes of beveled window glass. In the corner was a small potted ivy that the warden fussed with momentarily—he bent over it, gently pinched its leaves—before motioning for Talmadge to sit in one of the chairs before the desk.

Talmadge sat, and removed his hat. Cleared his throat. Said, surprising

the warden, who was preparing to speak: I wanted to talk to you about—
Della. About her situation here.

He cleared his throat again, touched his hat on his knee. He had practiced saying those words, was relieved to have executed the sentiment
without blunder. He wanted, as he and the Judge had discussed, to show
the warden that he, Talmadge, was a serious, dependable sort: he wanted
to make a good impression.

The warden nodded. He aimed his frown over Talmadge's shoulder
and said, as if just remembering: I was called away on important business
that day, or else I would have been here to meet with you personally. And
I recognize you came quite a ways. Down near Wenatchee, isn't it? If I
remember correctly, when we determined you would be unable to see
her, we sent you a telegram—

Talmadge nodded, vaguely. He had never received a telegram. Where
would it have gone to? The post office?

—but I fear it reached you too late. You came—cross country, I suppose? By horse?

Wagon, said Talmadge. Mule. But—the train, this time.

The warden nodded again. His eyes traveled to the sack leaning
against Talmadge's knee.

Gifts, said Talmadge. For her.

The warden nodded absently and then briefly met Talmadge's eyes.
There followed an uncomfortable silence.

Forgive me, said the warden. It is perhaps—none of my business. But
who are you? What relation do you have to Miss Michaelson, if you don't
mind me asking?

Talmadge stirred. He had anticipated this question, of course, but was
still unsettled by it.

I looked after her for a while, when she was younger, he said. Before
she—set out on her own. I took care of her. Her and her sister. And I'm
here to help her now, if she needs it.

The warden was watching him closely. I see, he said. Then, after several moments passed: I assume Mr. Marsden has updated you on all that's
happened? About—

The man at the lumber camp, yes, said Talmadge, and cleared his throat again. I heard about that. And, he said—his voice rising, as if he were trying to convince the warden of something—she turned herself in . . . and, well, that's a good thing, I'd say.

Yes, of course, said the warden. He was thinking about something else, testing something, Talmadge thought. He was looking over Talmadge's shoulder, scrutinizing different sections of the wall.

They are investigating her claims, said the warden. It might be a while until we hear anything. We haven't heard anything yet, and it's been a month and a half—

I want to know why—Talmadge interrupted—why she was locked up the last time I was here. Why I couldn't see her.

The warden raised his eyebrows at Talmadge's interjection but otherwise did not move. I apologize for not being here the last time to explain it, he said, and then fell silent. Again he considered the wall over Talmadge's shoulder. He doesn't know whether he should trust me, thought Talmadge suddenly, and was both impressed by the man's discrimination, and bothered.

She misbehaved, said the warden, frowning. She—acted out.

Talmadge waited for him to continue. He imagined Della throwing a temper tantrum, like a child. Throwing her food tray against the bars, throwing her boot at a guard. But surely that would not warrant locking her away.

How?

The warden pursed his lips. Hesitated. Said, finally: She—attacked somebody.

Attacked somebody? Talmadge's voice reflected that he did not believe it, that it was an impossibility. Almost scoffing.

Yes, Mr. Talmadge.

But—how? Who did she attack?

The warden clenched his jaw. It seems, he said, she procured—or, more likely made—a weapon, and when she was passing one of the male prisoners, she attempted to stab him with it.

Stabbing again, thought Talmadge, and tried to imagine it; but despite what he knew of the girl, he could not imagine it.

And what happened? asked Talmadge impatiently. Was he hurt?

The warden shrugged. The injuries sustained were negligible, he said.

What was *not* negligible were her intentions. To stab another prisoner? In my jail? The warden laughed shortly. That is why I insisted she be put in solitary confinement—

Talmadge could not bring himself to nod, to agree with the other man, and so kept still.

What did he do, this man? said Talmadge, after a silence, after he had again tried to imagine it. Obviously she would not attack him, he implicitly argued, had he not done something first to provoke her.

The warden shrugged. What could the other man have possibly ever done to her? As far as the warden knew, the two had never even exchanged words. She hadn't spoken to any of the other prisoners; they were kept away from each other, except, he admitted, lately, when this—embarrassment—happened. The guards were lazy, he said, and had been bringing in the men from the yard while Della was being led into it; their paths had crossed.

We have recognized our fault in the situation, said the warden. A man has been let go. But as far as this being a personal attack— The warden paused, and shook his head, and then his words came slowly, as if he had thought carefully about them, and wanted to deliver them with the same care: I think it is more that she wanted to act out, show her superiority somehow. He paused, thinking. Maybe it is a message to me. I don't know.

Talmadge did not know what to make of this speculation. They were both silent for a minute.

What does she say about it? said Talmadge.

The warden shrugged again, and sighed. She doesn't. She was a fount of information when she wanted to get in here, and now she's shut up. I don't know what she's got up her sleeve. Or if she's just crazy. I can't decide. He appraised Talmadge. Maybe *you* can tell *me*.

Talmadge did not respond for a moment. He had not liked the warden calling Della crazy. He did not like the other man's tone at all now. He said, looking away: I haven't seen her for a while. I don't know—I would have to talk to her first.

The warden nodded. Said, after some thought: Has she always been this—violent?

Talmadge didn't answer at first.

No, he said, but his answer was too late. He could feel the warden's skepticism.

Talmadge followed the warden out of the outer office and down the tall-ceilinged, boot-echoing hallway to the eastern end of the building. Down a flight of whitewashed stairs. A very grave and portly guard stood on duty outside the jail. The warden spoke to the guard, and the latter unlocked the door; and the warden turned to Talmadge and said he would return shortly.

The guard patted down Talmadge.

Do you have any gun on you? Any knife?

No, said Talmadge, and then remembered his pocketknife, took it from his pocket, and handed it to the guard, who placed it on a shelf beneath the counter.

Pick it up on your way out.

The guard asked Talmadge to disassemble the canvas sack and laid the contents on the counter. Talmadge pulled out the magazines, the packages from Caroline Middey—I'll have to unwrap these, sir—and then the loose apples, the sleeve of lemon drops tied with twine. Candy, said Talmadge, and the guard eyed him warily, and then turned to weigh the apples on a scale at his back. As he did so, Talmadge felt within the bag at the last item in there, Angelene's gift. He did not want to hand it over to the man, did not want him to cut into the carefully tied twine. Did not want that small tag "For Della" in the impressive script to be damaged or, for that case, seen by another person. He wanted to give Della one gift untouched by the guard, and unseen even by him, Talmadge. And so before the man turned around again, Talmadge slipped the box into his jacket pocket without even so much as a tremor of his hand or of his voice when he answered the guard when asked if that was all.

You have to leave some of these apples, said the guard. You're over limit here.

Can you save them for her? Talmadge said, just as the warden came out of the open door and beckoned to him. Talmadge repacked the sack, only taking two apples—I'll get the others when I come out—and the guard placed the apples on the shelf under the counter without comment.

Talmadge followed the warden into the jail. His ears felt immediately stuffed with cotton wool. It was dim, quiet. The air smelled of cigarette smoke and humidity.

He coughed.

We usually have you go to another room—we have a room for when visitors come—but unfortunately it was flooded last week. . . . Did you get rains down there? No? And we have men still in there working on it. Damaged some of the floor, which is a shame. It's the original floor, pine boards— The warden paused. But she's the only one here right now, and it doesn't hurt, I suppose, to leave you here. Twenty minutes, no more. And I'm keeping the door open. You call the guard if you need anything—

But Talmadge did not hear these last words, or witness the warden leave, because he had seen Della.

She sat on the edge of the bed. Only after a minute did she turn her head to him. It was a brief glance, not scared so much as alert and disbelieving—as one looks at a ghost—and then she looked ahead of her again. All this while hardly moving her body.

Several minutes passed in silence.

Hello, he said. Then, in a voice that belied its message: You look well.

Again she turned her face to him, briefly.

He removed his hat.

Was she scared? Was that it? He did not anticipate this, that she would not speak to him.

He stood there awkwardly.

We found out where you were. I came the last time. You got my letter? I was here before—

Down the hallway, outside the door, the guard cleared his throat. Somewhere in the jail a faucet dripped.

Then Della wiped her nose with her forearm. When she cleared her throat, he strained to listen, to hear what her voice might sound like now. But she did not speak.

They told me what happened—

But he should not speak of that. Her features tightened. It was a very slight change, and he could sense it more than see it. She put her hands on the mattress, moved slightly.

I've been talking to the Judge about when you get out. When you get out, we'll—

It was not the time to speak of it. Why was he speaking of it?

He lifted the canvas sack after a moment.

These are for you. From—all of us. From me, and Caroline Middey, and Angelene.

She glanced at him.

He reached inside the bag.

Come over here, I'll hand these things to you. I have to take the sack back with me.

It seemed she would not move, but then she got up and came over to the bars. He had the impression when she rose from the bed that she was larger—she had grown—but as she came closer he thought she had shrunken. It wasn't a normal shrunkenness. What was left of her body was her eyes, and her torso—muscular but also tough-poor in the mean way of those without a home, who live in the weather. Her face—her expression—was faraway and strange. It lied that she knew nobody on the earth. There was the hardness to her mouth: he wanted to touch it, suddenly, wanted to change it, to when she was a child and was characterized by dumb passion. He had not liked that expression then, but it was preferable to this distance, this resignation. He wanted to bring back her former pain. But this mouth was beyond pain. If he were to slap it, it would not change. Her eyes were both beautiful—black-dark as always— and empty. He wanted to touch her through the bars, he wanted to reach inside and grab hold of her arms, not so much as to shake her but to squeeze her. As she reached toward him—he was offering her a maga- zine now—he glimpsed a tattoo on the inside of her small, hard wrist.

One by one he handed her the gifts, her arms becoming uncomfort- ably full. At his prompting, she deposited the magazines and candy, the fruit, on the bed and stood in the center of the room and unwrapped the packages from Caroline Middey—he had rewrapped and tied them messily after the guard inspected them; held up, awkwardly, the leather pants and the lilac-colored shirt. On her face utter blankness. The pants might be all right, she might wear those, he thought; but the shirt was something else. It was ridiculous, he thought—she would never wear it—but it was something she would have worn when she was younger, it was something she would have worn to supper, once in a great while, after washing her face in the creek and brushing her hair and letting it fall thick over her shoulders. That was the other thing; her hair was cut short, curved close to her skull. It made her eyes look large, owlish.

This is from Angelene, he said, and reached inside his pocket and withdrew the box. After a moment she came forward and took it from him through the bars. She did not open it, but stood holding it.

He looked into the corner of the cell.

If there's anything you need, you should tell the warden. Tell the warden and—

I don't need anything from you.

He looked at her.

She went to the bed and sat down in the position he had first observed her, and stared ahead. The gifts were scattered around her, some of the butcher paper on the floor.

He would remember how she had looked at him then—once, slowly, with blankness—before he moved down the hallway, toward the opening of the jail. And also he would remember those words, that phrase—*I don't need anything from you*—the only phrase she had said to him that day, in her measured voice that was without emotion, without animosity even. It played in his mind, and he checked for emotion but constantly found none—*I don't need anything from you*—and it was not her, he thought, but it was her, he had gone to see her and this is what she had said to him, and he thought about this as he made his way down the hallway and then out past the guard, on the way to the boardinghouse, and then as he was sleeping and failed to sleep—she turned her face to him, slowly, with hatred now—and the next day, on the train. *I don't need anything from you.* But you do, he wanted to tell her—you do need something from me. But he did not know what it was. Like her, he did not know what it was.

Della recalled the day she had first seen him, that day in town when she and Jane stood on the street platform, waiting for him to fall asleep so they could steal his fruit. She had been amazed that day, through her hunger, at how slowly he had moved, how alone he seemed. Or maybe this was something she thought later. He was quite large, and tall, but he did not scare them in the least. And in the beginning, when they were all together, Jane kept aloof from him, and Della knew that she should too, but there were those weeks in the orchard when she followed him, and he was kind to her. His kindness was there—it had not changed—as he reached through the bars, his hands clutching the top of the bag.

He was speaking, but she had not been paying attention. He reached forward and gripped one of the bars. She stared at his knuckles. She realized, when she stole a glance at his face under the brim of his hat—the world of his face—that he was utterly familiar to her.

What did she say to him? *I don't need anything from you.* But that wasn't important. What one said wasn't important.

When he was gone, she went to the window and looked out, but couldn't see him.

H E SLEPT LITTLE on the train to Cashmere. The motion and the constantly changing landscape outside the window gnawed at him and kept him awake. He was dismayed by the thought—his mind kept coming back to it—that he could board a train in Chelan and be delivered to Cashmere the same day. This was the reason for the confusion that kept welling in him, that his mind would not fully accept. And each time he had to reassure himself that such a thing was possible, that he lived in a time when it was possible; and wasn't that grand? His body did not understand; he had been upset the other time as well, taking Angelene to the ocean. His stomach gripped, he was distracted, kept drawing his face to the window to verify that it was true: he was in Chelan before, but he had left that place, and soon he would be in Cashmere; but that morning he had been at the boardinghouse in the city in which he had seen her. It seemed impossible that he could hold those two places—Chelan, where she was imprisoned, and the orchard, where she was not—in his body at once, that his body could access both places in the realm of one day. It did not seem right. It was the rapidity that overwhelmed him and bothered his sensibility. He had moved slowly all of his life. He was used to seeing things drawn out of themselves by temperature and light, not by harsh action.

But this was something different. This was how people lived, now.

B UT WHAT DID she *do*? said Angelene. She and Caroline Middey sat on
the porch, peeling potatoes. What had preceded this question—this
outburst—was a timid line of inquiry, begun by the girl, and paced out
slowly so as not to jar Caroline Middey, not to upset her. But when Angelene received vague answers—She's led a different life than you or I, poor
dear; or, She just came to her senses, bless her, she's taking responsibility for her actions; and that from someone who had always been honest
with her and avoided simple answers, told her straight what she thought,
what the facts were—finally she lost patience and asked the question, the
answer to which Caroline Middey kept stepping around—

What did she *do*?

Caroline Middey paused in her work, and then wiped her brow with
the back of her hand. It was as if she hadn't heard Angelene, but Angelene
knew she was thinking, and would speak when she was ready.

Well, I'm going to tell you, said Caroline Middey. And it's going to
be something to take in, all right, but I'm warning you—she lifted her
eyes from her work—you will want to judge her, and you are allowed
that, I suppose, but it is also your responsibility as . . . part of her—
family—to know the whole story about her. Well, she stabbed a man.
Yes. And that's terrible. Just terrible. But—we do not know the whole
story, not even me, not even Talmadge. He and the Judge are sorting
it out. She stabbed a man—we don't know why, not really, or who he
was—and then she turned herself in. That's what's happening. But I
doubt we know the half of it.

Angelene listened carefully. She did not know if she was unimpressed
by such news—if she had been expecting it to be something like that,

violent—or if she was numb from the shock of it. She hardly felt anything at all. What impressed her most was that Talmadge was visiting *somebody who had stabbed someone.*

Did he die? said Angelene. The man?

We don't even know that, said Caroline Middey.

Two guards and the warden came into Della's cell before breakfast, and the warden told her to step into the corner and remain there: they were going to search her cell for weapons.

There aren't any, she said.

Kindly step back, Della.

She did as she was told. What shocked her was that he had called her Della. He had always called her Miss Michaelson before. She did not know why it bothered her so much.

She stood with her back to them so she wouldn't have to watch what they were doing. They found another stick in the middle stages of being sharpened, and her collection of stones. A bottle.

This is very bad, said the warden quietly, as he passed her. The guards shuffled behind him. The door was closed, locked behind them; and she was left alone.

TALMADGE IMMEDIATELY FORGOT about, but was revisited, days later, by the warden's phrase: how Della had been "a fount of information when she wanted to get in there," meaning the jail. Talmadge had been surprised, at the time, that the warden had put it that way. Why on earth would anybody *want* to be incarcerated? Or—he forced himself to ask the question—why would Della?

Maybe the answer was simple. It was the end of winter—or was it early spring?—when she had turned herself in. Maybe she was cold, and hungry. Warmer weather was coming; but maybe she could not wait any longer. He assumed, at the time of her confession, she was itinerant. Maybe—because of her physical state—she was not in her right mind. He was able to imagine that much: in such a situation, he would concede the possibility of certain mental weakness.

And maybe, after turning herself in, she realized what she had done—confessed to something terrible, and untrue—and was ashamed to retract her story.

As for her attacking this other man at the jail—Talmadge did not believe the man totally innocent. He had most likely called to Della, teased her. Provoked her. Talmadge did not believe the warden's claim that Della and the men had no contact—of course they did. He did not see how the warden could be so naive. Della and the men lived in the same environs. Physical contact was only part of the potential harm.

Della had her reasons, he believed, for everything. He just needed to talk to her, to understand what had happened—the *truth*, if you will—so that he would know how best to help her. He had been overwhelmed upon seeing her the first time; but the next time he would gather all the information and not accept silence or any evasion; he

would have to be prepared, he would have to be stern. Even intimidat-
ing, he thought; though he did not know exactly what that meant, or
how it would manifest—

Now the warden made the guards sweep the yard for objects that
could be made into weapons.

But the yard was large.

On her tour around the perimeter, in a depression at one end of the
yard, near the fence, was a sort of quarry—the smaller stones had been
collected by the guards, and only the larger, half-submerged stones remained. There, shining for a moment in the sagebrush—but was it a
mirage?—was a flat green bottle, most of the surface coated in dust. A
long-legged spider crawled out of the mouth as she took it up.

Her back was to the courthouse, where the guard might or might
not have been watching. She fit the bottle into her waistband and pulled
her shirt over it. Smoothed her shirt and glanced over her shoulder. But
nobody was watching, nobody was paying attention. She continued on-
ward, toward the other end of the yard.

ANGELENE PREFERRED USUALLY to dress in dull, unassuming frocks, complete with her signature straw hat when she went out into the sun or on wagon rides to town, but for her birthday she wore dresses the shades of pale flowers. Also she washed her hair and braided it over her shoulder, as she had when she was very young. It was he who had braided her hair then, securing the ends with bits of twine tied very tight. He had never questioned her about this birthday ritual where she dressed remarkably different from her usual self; thought, somehow, his drawing attention to it would embarrass her.

The day she turned fourteen, a week after he came back from his second trip to Chelan, he came out of his bedroom in the early morning to see her preparing breakfast. The last year or so she had been waking before him—at dawn, or just after—and spent the mornings alone, outdoors, walking, looking at the fruit. Thinking her thoughts, some of which she told him and others not. This morning she glanced at him, brought him coffee as he sat at the table. She wore the pale purple dress Caroline Middey had sent with him two weeks before, as an early present. It was, he thought, made of the same material as Della's new shirt, the one Caroline Middey had sent with him as a gift. The morning was cold; the door stood open, and the girl had wrapped a shawl around her shoulders. The way she gathered the shawl across her front, he thought, was distinctly womanly. She glanced at him again, and said: What?

You look nice today.

Well— She turned back to the stove and stirred the eggs. Blushing.

Caroline Middey arrived late morning. She looked out at the men and horses below as if she had seen them every day of her life, and told Angelene to help her unload the sacks of groceries from the wagon.

There was a ritual to this day: the men would have arrived two or three days beforehand and begun their work in the trees, and then on the day itself, Caroline Middey would arrive, with the groceries necessary to feed twenty people. Bread and corn stew and pickled vegetables this year, with strawberry cake. It was her contribution, said Caroline Middey, when Talmadge tried to give her money for it. He tried to give her money every year, and every year she refused him. Besides this, she would have another gift for the girl; the dress that she had sent with Talmadge before did not count. Spreading out the gift-giving like this was her way of reassuring herself that she was not spoiling the child. But she had another gift for the girl, stowed up with her in the wagon; she would present it after they had eaten, when Talmadge would give her his gift as well, and Clee.

The men this year had arrived two days before. In the morning the wrangler reminded them of the girl's birthday, the day they would all take off work early and participate in a feast up on the lawn before the cabin. They worked until noon and then hiked to the upper pool to wash. Afterward they dressed in their fine town clothes if they had them, or at least made an effort to look polished. There was a lot of goofiness with flowers and grass; flowers in their buttonholes, crowns made of grass and cattails. (Some of these were given as gifts to Angelene, who took them and donned them all, or as many as she could, some unspringing from their knots; she crouched down to fetch them up again, tried to reassemble them, on her face her usual look of intense concentration.) Waiting for the call, some men milled about talking and watching the horses, others napped, and others, because they could not help themselves, drew again to the trees, began to do light work there. But all were waiting to be called at the particular time when they would be invited up to eat before the apricot orchard. Finally the time came; the girl went to the ledge above the creek and beckoned them with uncharacteristic boldness, and they traveled to the upper lawn, some settling in chairs or on the grass, some standing. Wordlessly, they took the food offered by Caroline Middey or the girl. They ate second and even third helpings if they were offered, but did not ever ask. Talmadge sat in one of the birchwood chairs on the grass, near the porch. Clee sat beside him, in the other chair; the wrangler beside him, perched on one of the walnut chairs that had been brought out; and Caroline Middey and the girl on the porch steps. They sat with plates of food in their laps.

How does it feel to be—what is it now—fourteen? said Caroline Middey.

Angelene looked at her, smiling.

What? said Caroline Middey.

It doesn't feel any different, said Angelene. Or none that I can tell, anyway.

Fourteen, mused Caroline Middey. That is an important age.

Is it? Angelene regarded her, half smiling, guessing the woman was teasing her.

Certainly, said Caroline Middey, but did not explain right away. She took a bite of her bread, chewed it.

You are almost a young woman. Almost. Some girls are still children at this age. Playing with their dolls and such, talking in their baby voices. Some girls at this age can still be forgiven for doing and saying such things. But we think you are a young lady, we have thought so for quite a while. You are beyond your years, my dear, in many ways. I've talked to you about that before, haven't I?

Angelene nodded absently, wiped up some soup from her bowl with a piece of bread. Talmadge did not know what Caroline Middey was talking about. Talking about the girl's womanhood seemed premature. He looked out at the orchard.

Do you feel like a young woman? persisted Caroline Middey.

I— said Angelene, chewing. She swallowed, peered out at the trees.

Oh, now, said Caroline Middey. What I mean is, are you ready to put away childish things? Are you ready to embrace your responsibilities as a young woman, and especially a young woman on a homestead?

Angelene looked to Talmadge suddenly, thoughtfully.

He had the impression Caroline Middey was leading up to something, but he didn't know what it was. She hadn't informed him of what was about to happen, if anything. It had to do with the gift-giving, most likely.

Caroline Middey smiled wryly down into her lap.

I'm just saying, she said, last year I got you that set of whistles—

Angelene laughed. The woman had bought a set of bird whistles for the girl, who had delightfully confused the local bird population for two weeks after her birthday last year, whistling up into the trees the different calls of their kind. It had amused her for a short time, but the calls had gone unheeded since then. It was, he thought, a child's gift, and by then, even last year, Angelene was not so much of a child. She was already something different.

Well, I brought you something different this year, and I wanted to let you know that this is a gift for a young woman, for a serious young woman with a homestead to run. And she put down her bowl and plate to the side of her, on the porch steps, and lumbered up; Talmadge and Clee both rose to assist her, but she waved them away and went inside the cabin. Angelene looked again at the trees. When Caroline Middey returned, she had a package under her arm, and she sat down, gave it to the girl.

Is it time? said Talmadge. Usually they waited until after the cake and coffee was served for the presents, to draw out the anticipation. Now it was Caroline Middey's face that turned red.

I just couldn't wait, could I? she said.

Well, I have to get mine, said Talmadge, and stood. Clee and the wrangler stood as well.

I'll start the coffee, said Caroline Middey, and the girl rose also to help.

Clee touched Talmadge's elbow, and the wrangler said that Clee had something to show him. The three of them traveled across the lawn, where the other men lounged, sated from the meal; smoking, some talking, some napping. Others had gone down to the camp on the edge of the field to sleep in earnest, and this is where the three of them walked now. Clee went into a small tent, and then came out a moment later, carrying a rifle. He handed it to Talmadge.

For the girl, said the wrangler.

It was Della's rifle. Talmadge glanced at Clee, who was watching him, attentive, almost smirking with pleasure. Talmadge held the rifle in his hands, motionless, for a minute, looking at the different shades of wood that he had almost forgotten, and the intricate carving along the butt and forestock. He gripped the rifle tightly in his hands, rubbed his finger across the carving: brambles, ivy. It was, he thought—as he had first thought, holding it those many years ago—unusual and beautiful. He felt for a moment a welling of jealousy that Clee had found the firearm. But the jealousy dissolved as soon as it arose; he gave the rifle back to Clee, who watched him expectantly.

It's beautiful, said Talmadge. And then, understanding Clee would give the rifle to the girl now, said: She will like it very much.

But Clee shook his head, and glanced at the wrangler, who said: He would like you to give it to her. It is an important gift—

Yes, said Talmadge, after a moment. He was going to say that Clee should give her the gun himself, because he had found it, and there was no reason why Clee should not give her the gun, and not himself. But then he thought about the book of clothing patterns wrapped in butcher paper waiting in the top drawer of his bureau, and gravely doubted himself. Why had he not thought of something as grand as this for the girl— and she had been wanting her own rifle for two years now—something important, with weight?

The wrangler was speaking:

He would prefer you give it to her. He found it for you to give to her. If you do not want it, he will take it back, he will trade it when we go to auction—

No, I will take it, said Talmadge. How much?

They settled on a price.

When they walked up the hill, they saw that the men were drawing to the porch for their cake and coffee. Talmadge put the rifle in the lower branches of an apricot tree, and they continued to the porch.

The girl opened the gift from Caroline Middey first. It was a set of hide curing and flint knapping tools. It did not come from the catalog, she told Angelene, but was an amalgamation of different tools she, Caroline Middey, had used over the years, and also those identical to the ones she still used, and swore by. If you are going to be an expert knapper, she said—in a way that made Talmadge understand that they had discussed this before, the girl's eyes bright with satisfaction and pleasure—then this is where you start, and I shall show you how to do it all, after a bit here. The girl rose and embraced the older woman, and Talmadge wondered: Since when had the girl wanted to learn how to knap? And then Angelene came away from Caroline Middey and turned an expectant look at Tal-madge, so open that she blushed and turned her face away.

Young lady, he said, I believe your gift is over there in the orchard somewhere.

She smiled at him, took a tentative step in that direction, confused.

You mean—

I mean, he said, you should go over to the trees, the one on the end there—and look for it.

She traveled across the grass, some of the men looking at her curiously—perhaps they had seen the gun too and known what it was she was getting even before he, Talmadge, did—and she went into the trees and then hesitated and then came out a minute later, holding the rifle.

Oh! said Caroline Middey.

Angelene came across the grass, holding the rifle awkwardly, turning it in her hands, looking at it. She paused before them.

It's so—nice, she said. It has—flowers on it.

Let me see, dear, said Caroline Middey, and the girl went to her, handed her the gun. She seemed relieved to not be holding it. She looked at Talmadge, confusion drifting across her features.

Thank you, she said. I thought— She hesitated. It's very nice. She would not look at him. When she did look at him, it was as if she had mistaken something about him; he had surprised her. She was looking at him as if she had just understood who he was. He was surprised at such an expression. What had she been thinking, before? Why was she so confused? Again he thought of the book of clothing patterns, which he had seen on display in a window in Chelan. He had thought the women on the package seemed sophisticated, cosmopolitan, and strong; and like a fool he had gone in there and inquired of the lady clerk about a gift for his young friend—that was what he had called her, his *young friend*—and she had suggested the book of patterns.

Where did you find this? said Caroline Middey now. It is a piece of art— Then, a minute later: It reminds me of something—

She handed the gun to Clee, who admired it. He nodded at it and smiled at the girl, and then handed the gun to the wrangler, who studied it briefly before handing it to Talmadge.

You-all haven't had any coffee, said Angelene, moving suddenly toward the cabin door.

Clee stirred, and the wrangler said, Clee has something for you.

Oh, yes, said Angelene, drawing toward them again, blushing.

Clee took something out of the inside of his jacket pocket. It was a narrow wooden box that opened on a hinge along its spine. Angelene took it, looked at it. Oh, she said, opening it. It's a cedar box. Smell that— She handed it to Caroline Middey.

Talmadge, when it was his turn to admire it, turned it over in his hands. The cover was carved with roses.

I've always wanted a pencil box, said Angelene, and, surprising them all, went to Clee, awkwardly embraced him. Clee looked askance, patted her back.

We find all kinds of things, said the wrangler, at the fairs and auctions—

When Angelene pulled her face away, she was crying. She smiled at them all. I don't know why I'm crying, she said. My presents are very nice. And the food—the food—the cake—it is all very good. I just—it's my birthday—and then she covered her face with her hands.

Now, now, said Talmadge, after a moment. We haven't sung the song yet.

No, Talmadge, don't sing it, please, she said.

But he began it. *For she's a jolly good fellow.* Caroline Middey sang, and so did some of the men who knew the song, who still remained in the yard.

When she was younger, when she was four, five, even six years old, he would put her on his shoulders and they would walk through the apricot orchard, she grasping at the ripe fruit, he veering jerkily this way and that, and by her knees she would steer him, and she would shriek with laughter as he skipped and then slowed to a walk. Into the field! she would yell, and he would obey, hurry on his legs (already old then) down across the creek and into the waist-high grass. Why had they begun that ritual? The birthday walk, they had called it. They had begun it to wait for Della, he remembered, those years when she was tardy on the day of the girl's celebration; to entertain the girl, distract her from the fact of her aunt's absence, they would take a long walk, sometimes roam the field, pretending Talmadge was a horse and Angelene an explorer, and other times venturing as far as the outer orchard, waiting for a sign, waiting for the other's appearance. They no longer went on the walk, he thought, because they knew she was not coming; and besides, he could no longer carry her on his shoulders. Standing, now—she had come over to him as they sang—her head rested against his sternum. Difficult to think that he had ever bore that substantial body on his shoulders. Even thinking about it now made him tired. To think of walking to the outer orchard and back after a day like this, of activity and the men's faces in the yard, the unusual sight of them dressed in town clothes, of their like weariness, made him want to sit in the birchwood chair and give himself over to sweet unconsciousness.

The girl pulled her face away. Talmadge, she said. She was serious now. Talking about how this year she wanted to try a new apple in the outer orchard, she had been reading about it, she wanted to talk to him about it—

The girl was fourteen, he thought—fourteen!—and was immediately elated, and sad.

THE HANDSOME GUARD—Frederick—patted down Della before leading her back into the jail, and found the bottle. He told her to remove it from her waistband. Get it yourself, she said, and when he reached for it—after pausing momentarily—she grabbed it first and then brandished it in front of her. He stepped back—but unhurriedly, and with a strangely amused expression. But there was also concern there. He watched her warily.

Della, he said, and pushed his cap far back on his head. What are you doing, love.

Don't call me that, she said. Then: You let me see him.

Frederick raised his eyebrows, feigning ignorance.

I want you to set up something so we can talk.

You must be dreaming, Miss Michaelson. Prisoner Michaelson.

I'm not dreaming. I need to speak to him. Wanted to say, but did not: You all harp on about civilized behavior. Well, that's what I'm trying to do. Talking before killing. Letting him know—reminding him—why I'm killing him.

Seriously, said Frederick, giving her a frank smile—but still teasing her, she felt—you best throw that away, or give it to me—

No. You—you set it up so I can talk to him, and—

Me?

Yes. You do that, or else—she stopped to think for a moment—I'll tell them you tried something with me. The warden won't like that, will he? A young man forcing himself on a prisoner. A female prisoner! Paused. Then, quietly: I just want to talk to him, is all. For a minute.

Who?

You know who.

He turned his head, looked out over the yard. Squinted in the late sun. Chewed something in his back teeth. She felt, suddenly, that he might help her; and what a miracle it was. After a minute, still not looking at her—she had tucked the bottle again into her waistband—he said, quietly: Are you ready to go in, Prisoner Michaelson?

He did not take the bottle from her.

CAROLINE MIDDEY WAS not the only one who remembered the rifle. When Angelene first saw it, held within the low boughs of the apricot tree, she caught her breath. But why? Because she had discovered her birthday present? She put her hands on it and disengaged it from the branches and thought—or some part of her *registered*, for memory still worked hard within her to locate where she had seen the rifle before— that it was simply uncannily familiar to her. She must have seen one like it in town, she thought, or in a catalog: but those two possibilities failed to ring true to her. She carried the rifle out of the orchard, across the grass.

And that was when she knew, when she saw how Talmadge looked at it, and how the other men—Clee, the wrangler—feigned surprise, and how it caused Caroline Middey's sudden, alert confusion; all of this, but mostly by Talmadge's face, which was a touchstone for her, she remembered, she *knew*, the gun had belonged to Della.

It's her gun, isn't it? she said to Talmadge, two days after her birthday, when they were alone again in the orchard.

He sat at the table, the lantern lit—it was after supper—polishing his boots. He was planning to leave for Chelan again in two days.

Yes, he said, and put his fist, which held a flannel scrap, on the tabletop, held still.

She stood before him.

Are you angry? he said.

No—

They remained still, each one waiting for the other to condemn, to burst out with anger or apology, explanation.

Angelene, for a moment, could not remember if she was angry or not.

She was—had been—impressed by the gun, by the majesty of it, and also by the fact—and this is where most other girls her age would disagree with her—that the rifle was not brand-new, but used. The wood had a fine patina that made Angelene appreciate it, its worn beauty. About who had used it—Della, in the beginning—she harbored feelings of helpless anger, but also—she hated to admit this—a certain tender fascination: young Della, the Della she remembered, toting this weapon on her early excursions into the mountains. She appreciated this too, despite herself.

But Talmadge had not explained any of this to her. This, the accompanying story, seemed like part of the gift, but instead he had marred it by more silence.

But this desire—to have it all, the object and the history—was unconceived in her mind, and she knew only that she was unsettled, unsatisfied.

I'm sorry, he said. You don't like it?

I like it—

Then, a minute later: It is very beautiful. I love it. But—I wish—

And what did she wish?

I wish—you would tell me about her.

She was alarmed she had said such a thing, for she did not think she meant it. She did not want to know about Della, did not want to hear about her. Had said it, perhaps, to hear how it would sound. That was all.

Talmadge was looking into the corner of the room. He too looked alarmed.

Oh, I don't know! she cried. You are so—quiet!—about it! You won't tell me anything! And Caroline Middey won't either! Or—not all of it. There's something you're not telling me, and I don't know what it is—

She held out her arms in front of her, as if trying to shape in the air all that she could not say, all that she did not understand.

He looked at her, and she regretted everything. Her arms returned to her sides. She regretted stepping out of her room—it had been a whim, after all—to speak to him.

His face was full of immense sadness.

FREDERICK CAME CLOSE to the bars and said that Michaelson would speak to her, if she still wanted him to. He would come and stand outside her bars after lights-out that evening, and she could say what she had to say to him then.

Let me go see him, she said. Let me go see *him* in *his* cell.

Frederick was incredulous. He tipped his hat back on his forehead, then pulled it down. Laughed shortly. You're crazy, he said.

ANGELENE ENTERED THE canyon. Entered the orchard. It would be there, he said, at the bend in the path. It was afternoon, the road was lit up. The rest of the orchard was shadowed by the overhanging canyon wall, but this part was still illuminated. And then the road bent, up ahead, and she could see the tree he was talking about. She saw it and then looked away from it. And then looked again.

How many times had she looked at this tree? Not once like this. She stood now at the base of it. She had thought in some indirect way, throughout her life, about how large the tree was, how it stood there like a sentry, marking the bend in the road. After the bend the road leads— where? She had never followed that road, never. That amazed her, suddenly. At what point did the road end? She would ask Talmadge about it. No, better yet—she would see for herself.

But now she looked at the tree. How did one get up into a tree like that? She went to the trunk and looked at the bark. A galaxy of cracks, rivulets. Shining, porous, fibrous skin. She looked up. The nearest branch was maybe fifteen feet up. She scouted the ground as if she would see some sign of how her mother had gotten up into the tree; as if some clue would have waited all these years for her to find it. Of course she found nothing. She rounded the tree slowly, looking at it from different angles.

Jane would have been there, higher up on the limb. And Della would have been there, a little farther down. It was not hard to imagine two girls sitting on the branch, their legs dangling, fitted with their own nooses. Like a game. And the one on the left—her mother, Jane—saying to the other: The men are coming. I'm going to do it. Come on—and then she jumped. The moments before, that conversation leading up to the moment of jumping, were not hard to imagine. But the moment itself—a girl leaping from a tree, the rope suspended in midair between them, the girl and the tree—that was difficult to imagine. How does a girl get up into a tree such as this and at the same time fix her own circumstances of death? Where did the rope come from? How did she tie the noose? How did she know it would work?

But an element even more difficult to imagine—even more so than the body of Angelene's mother hanging in the air—was that what was coming had been more terrifying to the girl than the actual experience of hanging. This was what Angelene could not comprehend.

She thought of Della. Who, in order to have survived, in all likelihood must have hesitated; she must have watched her sister jump first, and paused on the branch. Why was this other one not as afraid as Angelene's mother? What was it about the life they had shared that made her, Della, want to remain in the world, when the other one did not? And Jane, Angelene reminded herself, had a child. She had just given birth to an infant who had lived. But the one who hesitated, who somehow found life worth living, had just suffered enormously, had lost two children who had lived inside her. But she, and not the other one with the living child, had hesitated.

But, thought Angelene, looking up into the tree, Della *had* jumped, in the end. Something had persuaded her at last to jump. It could have been her sister struggling. It could have been the despair and the realization of what was happening. It could have been that.

Angelene could not find a way to climb the tree. And so she returned to the cabin for a ladder.

Michaelson stood before the bars now. In the dimness Della could barely make out his facial features. From his outline she could tell he held his stomach as before. She had heard him come shuffling down the hallway ten minutes after the lights turned off; Frederick had escorted him, but now he left them alone. You best not try anything, Frederick had said, dead serious now, to Della before leaving. This is a favor, now. You best behave.

She said nothing.

Michaelson stood in the dimness, unmoving as a statue.

What do you want? he finally said. And his voice was low, gravelly, almost slurred.

Despite herself she came closer to the bars. Hung on to them and pulled herself up so she could get as close to him as she could. She tried to pick up his odor but could not; he smelled of nothing.

Come closer, she said. But he did not move.

What do you want, he said again.

You know who I am?

Again he was silent. But then he sighed.

There are so many of you.

And then it was silent.

I'm Della, she said. Della Michaelson. Then, when he didn't say anything: I'm named after you. You gave me your name! I can't even remember my other name!

He shifted slightly. That is what I did, he said. Sighed again. That was the way I used to do it, it made things easier. But—that is over now. I am not that person anymore. I have changed. Do you not know it is possible to change?

She had been waiting for it without even being aware that she was waiting for it: the old familiar note of self-righteousness. He had hit it perfectly. She gripped the bars and pulled herself up, almost off the ground. Her hands were sweating. Liar, she said, quietly.

Hush, said Michaelson.

Hush, she said.

That was before. I am a new man now. I have—changed my ways. And he coughed quietly while holding his stomach.

She whispered again: Liar!

He ignored her, said: It's true. While I have always been sensitive to the Lord's instruction, I have now learned to—reinterpret—some of His teachings—

I'm going to kill you, she said.

No, he said sadly. I believe this sickness will do it first. This sickness is doing things to me that you are not capable of. You should be thanking the sickness, if anything.

She tried to shake the bars, but of course they did not move.

I'm going to kill you! said Della. You killed my sister!

In the silence she could tell that he did not know who she was talking about. Before she could stop herself, she said: Jane! You killed Jane!

And then the air between them changed. Michaelson did not speak for several minutes.

Jane, he said. Ah, yes.

You remember her—

There was another silence, and then he said, Yes. And then, several moments later, And you must be that pesky sister of hers—

Della, she said. Della!

And she felt him study her anew in the dark.

Look what you've become, he said. In prison, and threatening to kill a man of God!

A man of God! she bleated. A man of God!

Mock me if you want to—

You're a liar! You are not a man of God! And if you are—then I do not believe in God!

Blasphemer!

She was crying and shaking the bars. She hit her head on the bars. She reached through the bars and tried to catch him, but he stood too far back from her.

Look at you, he said. Ah, now I remember! Now I remember you well!

She screamed, and in between her screaming—living in her scream—she could hear him laugh. But she did not know if he was laughing now, or if it was her own scream that contained his laughter that she was hearing.

ANGELENE SAT ON the limb from which her mother had hanged herself. From there she could see out over the orchard and beyond a
portion of the field. It was the best vantage, she decided, from which
to observe people entering the canyon mouth. It must have been this
factor—the ability to witness the shaking trees, the hides of the men's
horses and the flesh of the men themselves glimpsed through the foliage below—that spurred Della at last to jump. Jane could imagine what
was coming, and that was enough for her to act, but Della needed the
rawness of the calamity opening right in front of her to urge her off the
branch.

Angelene waited for the trees to shake, but no trees shook for her. All
was still.

All at once the birds set up a clamor in the deep forest. The sun was
setting.

She climbed down out of the tree, her heart pounding. What if Talmadge had found her there? Somehow it had been necessary to climb
the tree; but she would not do it—there was no reason to ever do it—
again.

The night Michaelson came to see Della, they put her afterward in
solitary confinement. Although she had not touched him. She could
not stop screaming. She screamed to cover the sound of her own
screaming. Frederick rushed Michaelson back into his own cell, and
by the time the head guard on duty came inside and fixed the lights,
Della had bloodied her mouth on the bars. What is she doing? the head
guard asked Frederick. What happened? Frederick shrugged, his face

red. They opened Della's cell and put their hands on her and took her away.

The warden will come see you tomorrow, said the head guard, who had blood now on his shirt. He released her into the new cell and pulled the door shut behind him. Bent and spoke through the small window: Try to get ahold of yourself, for Christ's sake—

TALMADGE ARRIVED AGAIN at the courthouse. The warden, when he came out to meet him, told him that he would like to speak to him privately. He led Talmadge through the hallway, to his office.

Talmadge knew, without the warden saying anything, that Della had gotten into trouble again.

The warden motioned to the chair before his desk, and Talmadge, after a moment, sat down.

It's inexcusable, really, said the warden, also sitting. She's had—a fit, of sorts.

Talmadge experienced a twinge of panic. He waited for the warden to continue.

A fit?

The warden made a face of disgust. It happened after lights-out, two days ago. She threw a tantrum. The head guard on duty judged it necessary to put her in solitary confinement, for her own safety—

For her own safety? said Talmadge, bewildered. What do you mean?

The warden pursed his lips, would not meet Talmadge's eye. It was a full—raging—mad—fit. The walls of the solitary cell are padded, there was less likelihood of her hurting herself—

Talmadge was speechless. Imagined her now, in a cage. He gripped the arms of the chair in which he sat.

The warden seemed embarrassed. She's calmed down, he said. She's—contained now.

Contained? said Talmadge. She's still in there?

Yes, said the warden, and for a moment seemed embarrassed again—or was it shame? But the moment passed, and his expression was hard. Like I said, it's for her own good. She doesn't even seem to want to come out—

Talmadge grunted in dismay, and the warden looked at him sharply.

There was a silence.

Well, something must have set her off, said Talmadge. A person just doesn't fly into a fit. What happened?

The warden frowned.

Somebody must have said something to her, said Talmadge. Then, after a moment: The man she attacked a while back, maybe. Where was he during all of this?

The warden was staring stonily into the corner of the room, distracted. As if a new line of speculation had just been introduced to him, and he was busy following it now.

This man, said Talmadge—what was his name?

De Quincey.

De Quincey. Where was he when she had her fit?

In his cell, of course.

Could he have—called to her?

The warden, after a moment, shook his head. Someone would have heard them. Someone would have reported it, if he was abusing her. Or the guard would have heard something. The warden looked uncertainly at Talmadge. No matter what has happened thus far concerning Della, we actually run quite a tight ship here, and we pride ourselves on our humane treatment of the prisoners—

Talmadge was silent.

And besides, said the warden. This man—De Quincey—he's sick.

Sick?

The warden nodded, looked again into the corner of the room. He has cancer of the stomach. He can barely walk to the yard, let alone call down the hallway. He's quite weak.

Silence passed.

Who is he? said Talmadge, thinking: There must be more to the situation than this. Della would not harass or hurt a man just to do it. There was something here that neither man was seeing.

The warden looked at him quickly, annoyed. I told you, Robert De Quincey—

No, said Talmadge, and cleared his throat. I mean—what is he like? What does he look like? What is his—profession?

The warden sat back in his chair.

Large fellow. Sick, like I said. He paused. He was brought in around the same time as Della, as a matter of fact. Again he paused. We found him up on the highlands, he was wanted for running a still up there, he had some sort of outfit there in the woods, gambling and whatnot. Strange man. The warden shrugged, as if to say that it made no difference if he was strange or not. Quiet fellow, he continued. Intense. Then, as an afterthought: People up around Ruby City say he was into all kinds of things—gambling, girls, gunrunning—

Talmadge sat forward.

What did you say his name was?

The warden looked at him blankly, surprised that he, Talmadge, would ask the question again.

De Quincey, he said. He regarded Talmadge a moment later, sharply, with curiosity. Why? Do you know him?

But Talmadge didn't answer. If it was true, what he was thinking— the man was Michaelson—then surely there was no mercy in the world.

What is it? said the warden. Do they know each other?

Why hadn't Della told him, thought Talmadge, when he was there to see her before? Didn't she know that if she told him, he would be able to help her?

He stood.

The warden, also, stood.

They stared at each other.

I want to see her now, said Talmadge.

The warden looked over Talmadge's shoulder, at the wall. As if considering the request.

Was it possible, thought Talmadge, that after all this, the warden would not let him see the girl?

I'm not going anywhere until I see her, said Talmadge quietly.

The warden, after a moment, glanced at him. He moved toward the doorway.

Follow me.

The cell where Della was kept—in solitary confinement—was separate from the other cells. They entered the jail, the warden leading Talmadge, and instead of heading straight down the hallway, they took a
sharp right, and walked with the holding cell on their left—which at that
moment held two men, both of them on bare cots, apparently asleep.
Through the bars Talmadge could smell the alcohol. The warden, before him, cleared his throat: and the sound was absorbed immediately by
the walls, the air. They turned right, quickly, again; the warden quietly
cursed his lack of a lantern, and they continued down the hallway. Near
the very end, on the left, was a door, with one small rectangular window
at waist height. It was incredibly dark, and Talmadge could not understand why the hallway was unlit. The warden rapped three times on the
door, then took a ring of keys clutched in his fist—he had carried them
from his office—and unlocked the door, opened it.

The darkness was almost beautiful. It was wet-black and rich, smelled
of soil.

Della? the warden called.

There was no answer.

Someone is here to see you. Mr. Talmadge is here to see you.

Still no answer.

Again he called into the darkness: You are allowed to see him if you
wish. You can go outside, if you like. Wouldn't you like to go outside?

And then a sound from within, a croak:

No.

Talmadge touched the warden's shoulder, said: It's all right. I'll go inside, if you'll let us be for a few minutes—

The warden, hesitating, finally stepped aside.

This is highly unorthodox. I can't be responsible for—her actions—if
you go in there. I don't know what she's capable of doing—

It will be all right, said Talmadge. Then: I take responsibility for whatever happens. I just want to talk to her. It will be all right.

Della, called the warden again, after a moment, into the dark. Della,
I'm going to leave Mr. Talmadge here with you. He's going to talk to you.
This is a favor to—both of you. Then, when there was no response, the

warden turned to Talmadge: I'll be waiting down the hall. Please don't be too long.

Talmadge entered the darkness.

Della?

I'm here. Don't touch me.

I won't touch you.

And indeed he couldn't even see her. He felt as if he had lost his bearings, was beginning to lose sense of his physical boundaries, his body. He raised his hand in front of his face but could not see it. There was a suggestion—a ghost—of a lesser darkness near where he guessed the door was at. But still he could not locate her form.

He became aware, suddenly, of the sound of his own breathing. And it was creaking, somewhat labored.

Oh— he said.

There was the sound of her movement—a shifting—in the space below him.

What do you want. What are you doing here.

Are you sick? he said, confused. Are you all right? They say you had a fit. Is that true?

A fit, she said. I suppose so. A fit. She laughed, but ceased abruptly.

I know who it is, he said after a moment, deciding to address the problem directly and at once. I know what's going on.

Silence again. He felt, for a moment, that she was not there. There was a startling lack of attention.

Della? Are you there?

Listen, she said, and her voice was so quiet it was almost inaudible. He strained to hear her. Don't tell the warden. Don't tell anyone about this, or I'll—

Don't threaten me, young lady, he said, his voice loud; and again he heard his own terrible breathing. He could not hear Della's breath at all. I'm here to help you, and you'd better listen to me. I'm going to tell the warden and the Judge about Michaelson, and I aim to get you out of this place. Or transferred, at least. This is no place for you. I don't care what you did. And—he said suddenly—I want to know: Did you kill that man in the first place, or was that a lie to get you in here? The possibility—the likelihood—of what she had done, her strategy, was forming rapidly in his mind now, took shape before him in the darkness.

I probably killed somebody, she said after a long silence. Even if it wasn't the one I thought I did—

Hush, said Talmadge, startled. You just hush. Don't go saying those sorts of things in here. We got to get the Judge's help, we got to know what he would do—

Please, said Della, and he could feel her now in the dark rise, there was a subtle breeze. Please don't say anything to the warden. It's—important to me. Please. I'll—tell him myself.

Talmadge grunted.

Please, Talmadge, she said, and it was this—the sound, unselfconscious, of his name in her mouth—that instigated his relenting. He was silent.

It's my trouble, she said. Let me tell him.

You tell him, he said finally. All right. But you better do it.

I'll tell him.

All right.

He moved toward the lighter darkness. His body ached. It seemed he would never reach the door.

Are you coming? Della? They said you don't have to stay in here anymore. Come on out, now.

There was a brief silence.

I'll come out, she said.

I'll get the warden—

No, she said. You go first. I'll come out later.

He hesitated in the threshold.

Della, he said. Come on, now.

I don't want you to see me, she said.

CAROLINE MIDDEY AND Angelene stood in the wet heat of the main room of the cabin, immersed in the project of canning vegetables. Water roiled in the large cast-iron basin on the woodstove and the girl, on a stool, eyed the water level over the tops of the jars, touching their tops with a wooden spoon.

Caroline Middey had arrived that morning unexpectedly. Angelene, when she heard the far-off noise of the bells on the mule's breastplate and the creaking of the wagon, realized she had been waiting for her to come. The wagon was full of bushels of vegetables and fruit and Caroline Middey's own tools, although there were tools there, Angelene's and Talmadge's, she could use. But depending on what she was canning, Caroline Middey preferred to use her own things.

They had sat on the porch and shucked the corn and shelled the peas in silence. It had taken a long time, and every once in a while one rose to get water or iced tea for them both. Now in the cabin, with the windows shut and the door closed to keep in the heat, it was too hot to talk. Angelene had stripped to her underclothes and wore her hair up in a kerchief. Caroline Middey had rolled up the sleeves of her dress. Both were barefoot. The fine hair at Angelene's temples was dark with sweat, and both were deeply flushed.

Caroline Middey was pouring more boiling water into the basin, careful so the cloud of steam did not rush into her face, when she heard a sound of pain behind her. She set the kettle down and turned. Angelene, at the table, had cut her hand on a jar top, and stood clutching her arm to her stomach, forcing herself to look ahead at the wall. She did not want to look at her hand, did not like the sight of blood.

Let me see.

Angelene showed her without looking at it herself. The cut was in the center of her palm. It was not deep enough to fret about—it did not need stitching up—but Caroline Middey made her sit down while she fetched the iodine and bandage.

The vegetables, said Angelene.

We're watching them.

Caroline Middey, leaning close to her, began to clean the wound. Holding the girl's hand open in her own, she said quietly and suddenly, as if just remembering it: I had a girl, once, who lived with me. You knew that. (Angelene didn't.) They sat silently, and then when Caroline Middey began to wrap the hand, she said: She was learning about the herbs, the midwifery. She was what they called my apprentice. When there was another long pause, Angelene looked at Caroline Middey, who was concentrating on the bandage, lost in thought.

What happened to her?

Oh— Caroline Middey pinned the end of the soft bandage, and stood. The consumption, when it came through. She died. It was a long time ago.

When they were finished canning, they opened the door and the windows and went out onto the porch. Then, when that wasn't enough, they went and crossed the grass, went down to the creek. Waded into the water.

Oh, Lord, said Caroline Middey, her skirts gathered up around her hips. The water coursed around her knees. She closed her eyes. Oh, that feels nice.

Angelene sat down carefully so that she was waist-high in the rushing water. After a moment she lay back, holding her bandaged hand up into the air.

After they cleaned up after the canning, and properly washed and dressed, they ate a meal out on the porch. Caroline Middey had packed a meat pie for them to share, and for dessert she had brought the little cinnamon cookies that Angelene liked so much. Caroline Middey made coffee and they sat in the birch chairs, sated and barefoot, stuffed, tired, content.

Angelene had closed her eyes, and although she had been distracted from thinking about Talmadge and Della since Caroline Middey arrived that morning, she said: Do you think she'll come back with him?

Caroline Middey, after a minute, sighed. I think it's gone beyond that, she said. Maybe, before—but not now— And for a moment, confused, Caroline Middey realized she did not know how much Talmadge had told the girl. She looked at the girl's face, but could read nothing there. The girl's mind worked—she could see the emotion moving there—but at the same time her face was closed. She had seen that before—but where?—and then she remembered it: in Della.

I don't pretend to know anything anymore, said Caroline Middey finally. And that was all they spoke of it.

DELLA DID NOT leave solitary confinement after Talmadge visited her, but stayed another day. The warden withheld food until she came out. They let her immediately, after she had eaten a little, into the yard.

The sun assaulted her; she did not know what to do with herself. She could not see properly, but walked in the direction of the fence. It was nearly twenty yards away. She would not make it there, she would turn before she reached it. But this was the only way, to walk in this direction, to reach the exact center of the yard, the place at which she was equally far from every point: the jail and the surrounding fence. In this way, being equidistant from all points, it was almost like being free.

Before she reached this point she smelled woodsmoke. The odor was coming from the direction of the lake. She stopped walking and tilted her head up at the trees and sky. She couldn't see the smoke. She couldn't see the lake. There was a sound coming out of her that frightened her. It was a quiet sound. She touched her face, as if to verify she was still there.

H E SLEPT MOST of the train ride back to Cashmere. He had barely made the train, had run to the platform, wheezing. He held up his hand. A porter leaned down to help him up. Took his bag from him.

That's fine, I've got it, Talmadge said, and coughed loudly.

Are you all right, sir?

Talmadge walked down the carpeted aisle, gripping the backs of the seats for support, and sat down at the far end of the car, in a seat by the window. Closed his eyes, and willed his body to calm. It hardly felt like his body at all, it was like a wild animal. He removed his hat, his forehead clammy with sweat. Suddenly he was cold. His heart beat raucously within him, and blood thudded in his ears; the world before him tilted. He feared, for a moment, he would faint.

But he calmed, eventually, and was able to sleep. Woke, and opened his eyes to the dun-colored hills under late afternoon light. He felt extraordinarily empty. The sun a great honey-colored orb he could not look at directly. Caroline Middey would meet him at the station, or the girl. He knew, suddenly, with a sort of detached dread, that once he stepped down off the train, he would be sick.

The train slowed, switched tracks with a slight jerk, and then slowly and steadily gained speed. He thought of Della—of her voice in the darkness. *I don't want you to see me.* But why? he thought. Had she hurt herself so badly? Was she so unclean? Surely she knew he would not mind. But was that really true? he thought. If he had seen her face contorted by injury, or seen the filth on her flesh, would he have been unable to leave her? He felt contempt, suddenly, for the warden, for his brand of gentleness. Must he put her in that godforsaken cell? *Solitary confinement.*

Any punishment seemed better than that. The warden spoke of being humane.

Talmadge looked out at the hills.

She would not tell the warden about Michaelson, he decided. But he felt he, Talmadge, had no choice in the matter, to believe her when she said she would tell him herself. Caring for someone meant trusting them. She would not tell the warden the truth: but Talmadge had to give her the choice, at least.

He continued to gaze out the window. He would wait until the end of the week, he decided, and then visit her again. He hoped his body would recover in the meantime. He could not wait any longer than that. He would go there and tell the warden the truth. Surely the man would agree that one of them—Della or Michaelson—must be moved. Talmadge would get recommendations from the Judge. If the authorities had not found any body in Seattle, or complaints, any warrants out against her, then maybe she would be let go—into his, Talmadge's, care. He would take her home, to the orchard.

But the girl—Della—must remain calm, he thought. She must stay out of trouble. And trust him to figure out the details of her release.

Outside the train, light raced through a line of birches planted at the edge of a massive field. Tessellation of light through branches and between leaves; an exodus of light, repeating interminably. But it was not the light, he thought, but himself—the train—that moved.

A week was too long, he thought.

What happened to you, said Frederick.

He and Della stood in the yard, near the entrance to the jail. Frederick stood in the shadow of the overhanging roof; Della stood in the sunlight, squinting. Hatless.

I don't know, she said. Then: You don't know what he's like. When he talks to me, I get so mad—

Well, said Frederick, after a silence. It's a shame something like that had to happen.

It didn't have to happen, she said. It was my fault. I forgot what he's like. But—it won't happen again. I remember what he's like now. I'm ready, now.

Frederick appraised her.

You'll help me again?

Frederick said nothing. After a moment he leaned, spat.

I heard what he done, said Frederick. I heard what kind of place he had up there in the woods. He glanced again at Della, to see if he wanted to question her; he did not.

She had turned and stared ahead, out across the yard. Her thumbs in her belt loops; a stiff, artificial pose.

I might help you, said Frederick. Or I might not. You got to have some plan. He shook his head. I'm not taking any part in something like what happened the other night. Forget that you almost killed yourself. I almost lost my job.

Della said nothing to this. She continued staring out at the yard, the dust baking in the heat.

I'll think of something, she said.

I don't know if it makes much difference, Talmadge, said the Judge. I don't see—

But Talmadge did not understand how the Judge could *not* see. To Talmadge it was as clear as glass: Della should not be kept in the same place as James Michaelson.

It's not only for her sake— Talmadge began.

He can't hurt her, can he? said the Judge. They don't have access to each other? And Talmadge, she was the one who attacked *him*—

Talmadge did not know what to say: the Judge was right. How to express—he had almost said it, before the Judge interrupted him—that he suspected Della was up to something, was possibly planning another attack. It did not matter that she seemed to be without resources: it had seemed that way before, and look how much damage had already been done. He was about to share his suspicions with the Judge, but now he thought it was best to keep such thoughts to himself, lest it cast Della in a more negative light.

Once the warden knows— said Talmadge.

He doesn't know? You didn't tell him? The Judge regarded him, shocked.

Talmadge looked away. The girl wanted to tell him herself, and I thought it was best—

The Judge was quiet, considering. He looked down at his desk, touched some papers before him.

I'll draft a petition, asking for one of them to be moved. You can take it with you when you go. Give it to the warden after he finds out about their relationship. He paused. We're not standing on solid ground here. But I guess it doesn't hurt to try.

We have to do something, said Talmadge.

When Talmadge failed to exit the train, the day before, Angelene and Caroline Middey sat waiting for him in the wagon. They discussed between them if one of them should approach a train official, ask after Talmadge. Or maybe he had decided to take a later train. It was possible. And then Angelene, while they sat in silence, pondering their next action, was suddenly moved with anxious fear and rose, stepped down from the wagon. Told Caroline Middey over her shoulder that she would return in a minute.

She boarded the train with the help of a surprised-looking porter. Explained, briefly, what she was doing. Who she was looking for.

The porter led her down the length of the car and then opened a narrow door; helped her across the grated platform, and then into another car. And another.

I asked him if he needed assistance, said the porter, but he seemed to prefer to be left alone—I thought I would let him rest awhile, there's no harm, really, this train isn't set to leave for another two hours—

She saw Talmadge immediately upon entering the third car. Several rows down on the left, facing her, sitting beside the window, asleep.

She touched his shoulder. Talmadge.

He stirred. For a moment after he opened his eyes he was still, gazing out the window, and then he sighed, deeply, stirred again. Are we here already?

Angelene spoke to the porter: There is an older woman in a wagon just outside, wearing—a straw hat with a green ribbon. Please fetch her, and tell her to come help.

The porter offered to assist Talmadge off the train.

That's all right, said Angelene, shaking her head. We can manage ourselves.

The porter obeyed.

Caroline Middey heaved up into the train car, clapping her hat on top of her head to keep it in place, and held still for a moment, gazing down the aisle.

There you are—

Together, she and Angelene helped Talmadge from the train.

Angelene and Talmadge stayed that night, and the following, at Caroline Middey's house. Talmadge spent most of that time sitting in one of the chairs on the front porch, a quilt over his legs. (A quilt over his legs, though it was July. Angelene's own scalp perspired; sweat ran down her spine as she walked slowly through the town, her shopping basket on her arm. That was what bothered her most: not his being too weak to dismount the train by himself, but the image of him on the porch, in July, with a blanket over his legs.)

Angelene went to town the morning of the second day, and when she returned, crossing the field before the house, and approached the porch, where Talmadge and Caroline Middey both sat, they abruptly ceased speaking: she had interrupted an argument.

What is it? said Angelene. Then, when neither of them answered her: Would you like me to go?

Caroline Middey gazed sharply at Talmadge, who refused to look at her.

You might as well tell her, said Caroline Middey. Tell her all of it.

Talmadge's jaw worked beneath his flesh; he was swallowing hard—in anger, Angelene thought.

Talmadge, said Caroline Middey. You can't tell her only half of it. It's worse—for everybody—if you tell her only half of it. You'd see that, if you weren't so doggone stubborn—

What, said Angelene. What's going on?

Neither of them looked at her.

Talmadge, she said.

He looked at her then. His face was livid, but closed.

Get your things, he said. We're going now.

He was silent nearly all the way back to the orchard. But finally, as they left the road between wheatfields and entered the forest, he said that Della had been getting into trouble at the jail. She had been getting into fights. (With a *man*? she asked.) Talmadge hadn't known who the man was, before, but this last trip he had discovered it was somebody from Della's and Jane's past, someone whom Della had reason to hate. The man was, he turned out to be—

Michaelson, said Angelene. She was driving the wagon, and at this utterance was careful to keep her posture stiff. But fear—or maybe it was a kind of excitement—had landed on her shoulders, substantial and terrible, like a bird of prey. She was chilled, and broke into a sweat.

Talmadge was silent, but she could feel his surprise. He had forgotten, perhaps, that he had told her the other man's name.

What's going to happen? said Angelene.

Talmadge was silent for a minute. I talked to the Judge. He's writing up a petition, to get one of them transferred. He paused. When I go back to Chelan, I'm going to give it to the warden. He was quiet for several minutes. I want her to come home, he said. I'm going to try—with the Judge's help—to bring her back here.

Angelene stared ahead. She did not know if she was angry. She wanted to be angry. She was dismayed, and irritated, by the tenderness in his voice. He was a fool, she thought suddenly.

What did Caroline Middey say? said Angelene. Back at the house. Was she angry?

Talmadge didn't answer right away.

I didn't want to tell you about him. And she thought you should know.

Does she want Della to come back? said Angelene, carefully, after a pause, and it was that question—she could feel it in the air between them—that Talmadge did not want to address: the real reason why he and Caroline Middey had been arguing.

Again he waited to answer.

Of course, he said.

THERE WAS NOTHING but time for her in the jail, and yet she could not come up with a plan to get close to Michaelson. In order to kill him, she must be close to him; and in order to be close to him, she would either have to find a way—by herself, or with Frederick's help—to overcome her cell. She could not fit through the bars, even if she starved herself; she had tried it already. (Her body, miraculously, almost fit; but her head was too large.) Frederick would not lead Michaelson back to her cell. And there was no way to access him by simply passing him in the corridor, as they had done in the beginning (her perfect chance! she realized now). Now she was led out separately from the men to the yard, with a margin of several hours between them, for safety.

The other prisoners, as they passed by her cell, did not look at her anymore. They thought she was insane.

And so how to go through with it? She thought of poisoning Michaelson's food, but ultimately rejected that idea because she could see no way to execute it, and besides that she wanted him to die by her own hand—and in a more direct way than poisoning him. She thought to stab him, and then strangle him, would be the best way. Weaken him just enough, and then place her hands around his neck—

Envisioning this, she slept poorly, and woke sweating in the sheets. At times the fetid odor of the jail seemed new to her, and she longed for the open air. She was suffocating. Became superaware of the bars, their immovability. And began to feel, during certain dark, boundless moments, the possibility of an existing chaos; that she was moving in a chaos so complete she could not fathom it, much less navigate it.

But she was in control, she told herself, waking suddenly. She rose with difficulty from the cot—at times her body ached now, from what? a unique tiredness—and shuffled to the window. A band of tepid darkness. If she bent low and craned her neck, she could just see the moon. Sometimes it was a bright island on the floor of her cell and she watched it, sitting on her cot, her legs drawn up. Suspicious, and then eventually calm. Sad. Finally, empty. When the moon disappeared, she felt an awful grief in the back of her throat, in her mouth; and she held it there for as long as she was able. She swallowed it. Eventually she lay on her side, and slept.

W HEN TALMADGE ASKED Angelene to accompany him to see Della, she said yes.

She sat creekside, in a ladder-back chair, doing the washing, the basin at her feet and the washboard between her knees. She wore her washing dress, which was large and shapeless but nevertheless was draped high over one thigh. As she worked, some of her hair had come undone from its bun. In her concentration she poised on the balls of her feet, flexing her calf muscles.

It was a womanly pose, he decided; and as he regarded her, walking down the hill, he was surprised again at how she was changing, how youth seemed to fall away rapidly now, like a snake shedding its skin. Youth dropping away from her like veils, revealing: What?

He left his bedroom now in the mornings expecting to see Angelene the girl, but now there was this girl-woman moving about, making coffee and mending his clothes, who sometimes smiled like Angelene but who also donned another face that was gaining steel. Her smiles tended to be absent now, she was distracted; the great wheel of thought had begun to turn. She was off now, and he had to guess more than ever before, these last few weeks, the meaning of her expressions.

There was something about her appearance now, about her bare leg and the undone hair, that seemed uncouth to him. He was almost angry—but about what? he thought to himself—striding across the grass. She grimaced down at the ground in concentration, plunged her arms again and again into the grayish water. When he approached her, he did not know what to say. But then she glanced up at him, and a moment later sat up straight, ran her arm across her forehead. She was pausing for him, waiting for him to speak. And then he asked her if she wanted to come with him to Chelan, to see Della. Which was not what he had meant to say at all. But he continued: He didn't know when he would go, but it would be soon. Maybe before the end of the week. She breathed heavily from the exertion of the washing, ran her arm across her brow again, and this time there was a slight change in her eyes—she was not looking at him, but farther down the creek—and she nodded, said, Yes. All right. She curled her lips slightly in anticipation of working again, and then bent to her task.

Lately she had been taking on more physically demanding chores, the kind that wear out the body completely, or those menial tasks that exhaust just by their mere repetitiveness. He did not ask her to do any of these tasks, and in truth some of them were unnecessary; but he woke in the mornings and she was pulling weeds in the plum orchard, or emptying the pantry, stuffing the cracks in the wall with newspaper. Repainting the shelves. (Where did you get that? he asked her, of the paint. In the shed, she said. For the life of him, he could not recall ever purchasing that paint, but she had it there in her hands, there it was: and so it must be true, he had purchased the paint.) Yesterday she combed the apricot trees for pests, lightly brushing the bark with her fingers, feeling the underside of limbs, pinching off the larvae, squelching them under her bootsole. And today it was washing the linen, even, he saw with astonishment when later it was hung to dry in a tree, the mule's blanket.

He turned and headed up to the cabin, unsure of what had just happened. He had gone to tell her to cover herself, to remember her age and sex and where she was, but he had invited her instead to go to Chelan. He did not know what was more strange, that he had asked her such a thing, or that she had said yes.

That night she asked him, over supper on the porch, when he was planning to go. He said that he hadn't decided yet. She nodded, but there was an expression on her face: disappointment, or anger, something. After a minute he asked her if there was a time she would prefer over another. She hesitated, then shook her head.

It's just, she said.

He waited.

It's just—I need a hat.

He paused. A hat?

She nodded. I just have to make sure that before we go, I have time to go to town and get a hat.

He nodded, as if he understood. But then he asked:

At the feed and supply store? You mean a work hat? He wondered what was wrong with the hat she had, the good sturdy straw hat they had bought the year before, at the Malaga fair.

She shook her head. No; the hat I want is at—the lady apparel store.

He had to remember a moment where it was, the lady apparel store. He did not think he had ever had occasion to go there before. He wondered if Angelene had set foot in there; and if she had, when, and what for. He was mildly curious.

The lady apparel store?

Angelene nodded. We are going on the train, aren't we? If we are going on the train, then I shall—I shall require a hat.

He had never heard her talk like that before. He didn't know what to make of it. Ultimately, however, if it was a hat she wanted, then a hat she would have. She would be nervous; perhaps the hat would comfort her. And she never had been a child to ask for things: when they went to town she never begged him for sweets or trinkets like he had heard other children whine for; no, she had always been a spectacle of goodness and obedience. Or obedience was perhaps not the right word, for he never set out rules for her to obey; but she obeyed him nonetheless; she obeyed his unspoken will. He had been lucky, he thought. If she wanted a hat, then she would have a hat.

If she wanted two hats, she could have two hats.

IN TOWN THE next day, with the Judge's help, Talmadge wrote to the warden, stating that in three days' time he would be coming again to visit Della; was that all right, and was that a good time, and to please send word immediately if it wasn't. He posted the letter, and then went to the café to wait for Angelene, whom he had left at the lady apparel store that morning. He had not offered to accompany her inside, and she had not asked. She seemed to know beforehand exactly what she wanted; but as soon as she opened the door to the store, as soon as she let go of his hand on the platform, a lost look came over her face and she moved disoriented through the doorframe. A lady would be there, he thought to himself, to help her. A woman who would know exactly how to help her, who would be much better suited to help her.

At the café, he ordered a cup of coffee. He sat at the counter. In the corner, a group of men held an anxious discussion. A man called out to him: You're not set to take the train today, are you? And Talmadge shook his head, asked what the problem was. The man said that a portion of track just up into the mountain pass had been damaged by a rockslide early that morning, and they had shut down the whole system for maybe as long as the rest of the summer. The man shook his head, incredulous, disgusted, but also delighted in the way that people are often delighted by bad news, or the opportunity to discuss bad news that does not immediately affect them. Another man said that they would most likely get things up and running before then, they just had to tell people that it would be much longer than it would, so people would be surprised and satisfied when things were up and running sooner than expected. The men all agreed that this was what was most likely going to happen.

Talmadge wondered, as he left the café, why they would close down the whole line if only a portion of the track was affected; why not run the line up until the station before the portion that was ruined? But he wasn't an engineer; those men had their reasons, no doubt.

When he met Angelene on the street—she had come out of the lady apparel store bearing a hatbox awkwardly beneath one arm—as they walked to the wagon, he told her about the train. There was an alarmed look on her face that softened into blandness a moment later, then resoluteness.

We'll take the wagon, she said. Was it a question, he wondered, or a statement?

He considered. With both of them driving, he might be able to do it. If she was with him, he knew, he would be able to stand it; he wasn't even afraid of the bone-weariness that had possessed him the last time.

I can drive, she said. I can drive the whole way.

No, he said, and cleared his throat. We'll take turns. He paused. It'll be cold at night, we'll have to—

I washed all the travel blankets.

It was true. She had. He said, after a minute: And you can wear your hat.

Her mouth curled up a little at one corner, but she said nothing.

There was a different way she walked now, he noticed. She walked with her head high, almost haughty. Proud.

THEY ARRIVED IN Chelan three days later, in the late morning. They deposited the mule at the stables, and then made their way to the boardinghouse. The landlady was not there, but a young man—friendly, with a head of thick brown hair combed back from his brow—was stationed behind the front counter.

He introduced himself as the landlady's son.

We thought you might be arriving today, he said, and showed them to their rooms on the second floor.

They washed and dressed separately, and afterward Talmadge went to Angelene's room and knocked on her door. She opened it.

He said nothing at first. She wore a pale sky blue silk dress with a dark green sash tied around her waist. Button-up black boots. And there on the bed, in an open-topped box, just unsheathed of tissue paper—Angelene lifted it now—was the hat. It was white and gigantic, a behemoth. Decked out in snippets of blue and green ribbon. She fit it carefully onto her head. It looked like a cake, he thought. Carefully, again, her eyes wide with concentration, she tied ribbons beneath her chin. When she finished, she stood still, and then turned her body slightly toward him.

She was waiting for praise.

Oh, he said finally. Well, I've never seen one quite like it. That's a hat, all right. This is the one you got in town?

She nodded.

Well—it's a dandy. A dandy.

They walked down the stairs, and past the startled expression of the young man, who arrested his arm as he lifted it in farewell.

Outdoors, the air was incredibly fresh. Cool. Piney. She took his arm.

What is that? she asked after a minute, and he knew she was referring to the clean, wet, rich odor of the air. It smells like—

The lake, he said. We'll go see it later. Then, because it had just occurred to him: We've never been here before, together, have we?

She shook her head.

Talmadge, she said a minute later.

What?

She hesitated. Nothing. Never mind.

There was the courthouse, and the great lawn before it. Men sat on benches set up from the sidewalk, reading newspapers.

They began to climb the steps. When they were almost to the top, she slowed. Halted.

It's just in here, he said, and continued to attempt to guide her upward.

She pulled her arm from his. When he looked at her, he saw her expression. Of indecision. Fear.

Talmadge, she said again.

He looked away from her, at the steps they had climbed, at the lawn.

All right, he said.

I can't.

He hesitated.

I'm sorry—

It's all right.

She bowed her head; and despite his disappointment—the girl would not go in after all to see Della—he feared that the girl's hat would overbalance her.

She had lifted her head again. Began to untie the ribbons at her chin. Removed the hat. Her head now—her skull—looked unnaturally small.

You wait out here, he said. I'll be—no more than an hour. He paused. You're sure, now?

She hesitated, then nodded.

He watched her descend the steps and then cut away across the lawn. Head to a tree in the near distance.

Angelene walked across the grass. She was a coward, she thought calmly: she must accept it.

She had thought herself brave, when Talmadge that day had approached her as she did the washing and asked her to go to Chelan. She had not wanted to go, had not felt herself rise to the invitation: but she said yes. Because she had been told—she now knew—what had happened to Della and Jane, and the structure for sympathy had been laid: Della was worthy of her pity, and so she, Angelene, would pity her. She would comfort and help her, because that's what Talmadge was doing. And though he did not say this, this is what he expected of her too.

To go along with this new benevolence she did not feel but was prepared to feel, she sought to alter her outward appearance accordingly. She changed her posture; she bought a hat. Any day now she would be flush with the clarity and confidence of adulthood.

But she did not know where the doubt, the fear, began. It had always been there, but she had sought to rearrange it within herself; and in the constant rearrangement was transformation. This is what she told herself; what she hoped. And then when she decided that it was in fact doubt and fear that she felt, she told herself such feelings didn't matter, ultimately. What mattered was that she was trying to feel otherwise. But the walk to the courthouse proved her undoing: her hand felt cold in Talmadge's hot one. She could not do it, she decided as they ascended the steps. She was not an adult; she was not benevolent, she was not brave. If she were made to stand before the bars and confront that person—that hero and monster out of her youth—then she would throw a tantrum. She would pull her own hair, she would kick the bars. She would howl. Della knew something about her, Angelene, that Angelene did not yet know about herself; and that knowledge infuriated her.

She was not yet ready to see her. And so Talmadge continued up the courthouse stairs alone.

Angelene sat now on a bench affixed to a giant tree—a pine—overlooking the lawn gently sloping to the street below. A band of lake showed between the storefronts on the opposite side of the street.

Her hat sat beside her on the bench, a failed friend. The wind rose and got into the collar of her dress, and bathed her head. She breathed deeply, not feeling so ashamed anymore. She waited.

DELLA SENSED TALMADGE coming before she saw him; and then, before the guard appeared leading him, she smelled his pine-scented hair dressing. And then heard the telltale clearing of his throat. A nervous tic she remembered from her adolescence. She avoided looking at him for as long as possible.

Eventually she lifted her eyes to him.

The guard left them alone. Talmadge stood close to the bars, gripping the top of a canvas sack in his fist.

He saw her looking at the bag.

Not from me, he said. They're from the girl. When we left— But then he hesitated, and looked away from her, briefly. Said: She thought you might like some apricots.

Della told herself she would not go to him, but she felt herself drawing toward the bars. She took the sack from him, looked inside. There were nine apricots—she counted them—glowing at the bottom of the sack, some still with leaves on them.

Have you talked to the warden? said Talmadge.

Della turned and walked to the window, looked out. She had caught that slip of his—*When* we *left*—that made her think the girl—Angelene—was close by.

She looked out the window.

Is she here with you?

He didn't answer right away.

She didn't want to come inside, this time, he said.

Della peered out at the courthouse lawn. Far away, near the street, stood a tall pine with three benches built around its trunk. On the bench on the opposite side of the tree from her sat a girl or woman, turned so she could just make out her profile. But then the girl-woman moved, and was gone from view. Della could just see a portion of her shoulder. And then the girl turned again, and there was the side of her face.

Is she outside?

Talmadge was silent.

The girl-woman shifted back and forth by the smallest degrees. What was she doing? Reading? Speaking to somebody? Feeding squirrels or birds? The wind came and pressed the tree boughs down over the benches, and the girl was obscured from view.

Della wanted, suddenly, to see her in her fullness. She wanted the girl to get up and walk across the lawn, toward the window, so that she could see her.

Is she outside? Is she wearing a—white dress? Or—blue?

Pause.

Yes.

The evergreen bough had risen, and the girl, revealed momentarily, scratched her shoulder. Angelene.

You behave, said Talmadge. You keep to yourself. I have the Judge working on this. We're trying to get you out of here. But you have to be good. You have to leave him alone. Della?

If only Angelene were sitting on the bench facing the courthouse. Then Della could see all of her. But who would want to sit facing the courthouse, when you had the other view? Della didn't blame her at all.

Why won't she come in? Are they—won't they let her?

When Talmadge was silent, Della understood. Of course the girl didn't want to come inside. Why would she?

Della went to the cot and stood beside it. Feeling like she had missed an important point. Someone had once told her what to remember, and she had forgotten it. She forgot it a long time ago but had now just missed it. She had been paying attention to other things. She had made a mistake, somewhere. For a moment she was untethered. Weak.

Della—

But she put up her hand to silence him.

After several moments, she said: How old is she? She must be nine, or ten by now—

He was silent, but she could feel his incredulity.

She is fourteen, he said.

Long moments passed while she absorbed this.

Della, he said. I'm going to talk to the warden—

No, she said, moving toward the bars now. With great effort. No, please, don't—

I have to—

No, please, not yet, give me—another week, at least—

His eyes became hooded. Why? Why another week?

I just need another week.

A S TALMADGE EXITED the courthouse, Angelene drew to him from across the grass. When she reached him, gazing at him—shy, expectant—he could not bring himself to greet her. Silently they descended the stone steps, turned onto the street.

The air was clear and bright. The sky overhead a brilliant blue.

There were many people out. She again—but hesitantly this time—clasped his arm. The afternoon was expansive, the air was golden: it felt as if evening would never come. The women wore wraps around their shoulders or head, and some glanced at Talmadge and Angelene, curiously, as they passed. They passed a woman and her two children going the opposite direction, a boy and a girl, the woman putting her hand on the back of the boy's skull to drive him toward the curb of the platform to avoid the pedestrians. The boy wore breeches that came down below his knees, and his hair was plastered around his brow and ears with pomade. They were headed somewhere important: a church service, perhaps, or a funeral. And sure enough, by the time Talmadge and Angelene reached the end of the street—the street continued down the hill in a series of steps and platforms to the lake—church bells pealed. A great gale of swallows erupted over the scaffolding over which they looked; a few crows flew silently; and there was the lake out before them, green-blue and sparkling under the sun. They stood at the south end; the northern end was away into the canyon fifty-five miles. They began to make their way down the steps to the lake. His legs shook, which embarrassed him. Angelene held on to his arm.

When they reached the bottom of the platform, there was a whole culture at the level of the lake. Couples promenaded under the afternoon sun—Chelan, besides being a business capital of the region, was also a popular spot for honeymooners, for sweethearts—and again, despite the cold that swept over them now, despite the air smelling of smoke and glacier, children played in the water, their guardians hunched under coats and watching them from the shore.

They walked toward a large warehouse in the distance. The building was placed where the lake curved, was seemingly built on the water, backed by forest. Perhaps there was a café or a food stall there, he thought; he and Angelene had neglected to eat since that morning, and he was hungry.

Inside the warehouse was a great boat. It was a steamboat, painted white, with green and blue trim. People were boarding the steamboat by way of a wide gangplank bordered by heavy ropes; men and women together, the honeymooners, and other, older couples, and families. One or two others boarded singly. A man at the entrance to the platform sold tickets. Talmadge, after observing the boat for several minutes, went to the man and asked what it was for; where did the boat go? The man— short, mustachioed, wearing a derby cap—looked at Talmadge as if he was stupid. A cigar, which had gone out, was stuck between his lips. Angelene regarded him with barely concealed distaste. When the man spoke, it was in the manner of a drawl, and Talmadge could tell it was a rehearsed speech (he didn't even look at Talmadge): Haven't you heard of the Lady of the Lake? The steamboat that goes all the way to the tippety-top of Lake Chelan? You are in luck, my friend, because she only goes twice a day, and you are catching her for her second trip. If you don't go right now, you will have to come back early, early tomorrow morning, and if you miss that— Here he made a face, as if smelling a bad odor. Well, you might as well go right now, it's the same trip, different day— And he shrugged, as if he didn't care. But then he chewed on his cigar for a moment and said, still not looking at Talmadge, What'll it be, friend? For you and the young lady? Today or tomorrow? Tomorrow or today?

They bought ice cream cones at a stand on the opposite side of the warehouse and returned to the beach, sat on a pile of old railroad ties that dampened the back of their clothes. He looked out at the water and the children splashing in the shallows, their guardians on the shore. It was too cold for swimming, too cold for ice cream. And yet it was the height of summer. Or just beyond. There were still very hot days to come. The girl ate her ice cream, squinted in the sun reflecting off the water. He did not ask if she wanted to take the boat trip. They had to get back to the orchard. Suddenly it seemed they would never arrive there again. He sat holding the ice cream cone, confused.

Talmadge, said Angelene: look. The boat was setting out over the water. It moved very slowly, it seemed, but in fact it moved quite quickly.

By the time they reached the top of the platform, the sun had set. He was upset and shaking, and the ice cream had made him sick.

She held him lightly by his elbow, but he shook her off and said, gruffly: I'm fine.

TALMADGE WOULD TELL the warden about Michaelson: and so now Della had only a very small window in which to act.

She was not even angry at Talmadge for declaring that he was going to tell the warden about her past. Understood that that was what he thought he had to do. She was tired, and confused. If she had her wits about her, perhaps she would be angry. But she was not angry.

Please don't do it, she had said. Please don't.

He had been perplexed at her tone—helpless, tired, beseeching—but was resolved. She could see the emotion move like weather across his face.

I'm going to tell him, he said. He needs to know, Della. We have to—get you out of this place. This will help. Don't—be afraid.

She had been silent, and gone with the sack of apricots to the cot, sat down. Wished he would go away. She needed time to lie down and perhaps cry, and sleep: to invent a plan. A plan had eluded her the previous handful of days, but now, tonight, it might visit her. She had to prepare for it.

Please go.

Her voice was not angry, but conveyed that she *needed* him to go, because she was incapable of composing herself any longer for polite company. She had allowed him to remain there speaking to her for a short time, but her patience—her tolerance—for such an exchange had spent itself. She was withering.

She had closed her eyes, and remained that way for several minutes. When she opened her eyes again, he was gone.

———

They have read the petition, said the Judge. They have heard our request. They want to send her to Walla Walla—

A man's prison? said Talmadge, rising swiftly as he was able from his chair. That's their bright answer—

Talmadge, after a minute, sat down again. The Judge stared at the corner of his desk with a slightly embarrassed expression.

The Judge explained to Talmadge that Walla Walla accepted female prisoners too; but it was as if Talmadge was incapable of hearing it.

I don't think there's anything we can do, Talmadge.

Tell them I want to see her.

I'll do that, but—

I want to see her, and I want to take her out for a day before they send her away. They can at least give us that.

Talmadge, said the Judge, carefully, they don't owe you—or her—anything. He paused. She tried to kill a man, Talmadge. More than one. What do you want them to do?

Talmadge stood again.

I want someone to take her out of there! I want someone to take her out of that place!

After a minute, the Judge drew a piece of paper toward him on the desk. He cleared his throat.

I'll see what I can do, he said.

IT WAS NEARING harvesttime, but Talmadge, Angelene noticed, did not prepare as he usually did. He was often in the trees, walking the rows, but he had a harried expression on his face, and he actually did little work. In the weeks before the men came into the orchard, the time Talmadge and Angelene usually devoted to grooming the trees and do-ing some early picking—the routine was different every year, depending on the state of the trees, and the weather—Talmadge, this year, did not tell her what he was thinking in terms of picking and preparing; he did not share his plans with her at all. She did not even think that he had a plan. Even a year ago such a prospect would have been impossible, in her mind. But now she was not surprised. When had that change, that specific change, occurred?

She woke at night and heard him moving in the cabin, making coffee, coming in and out from the porch. He could not sleep. He was also losing his appetite.

THE SECOND WEEK in September the men came into the orchard, and despite the state of the trees—it seemed not to matter, suddenly, that they had been neglected—fell to work immediately. Talmadge and Clee did not work with the other men or with Angelene but walked up into the canyon, into the far apple orchard, and then beyond that, to the upper cabin, and the pool.

I don't know any other way around it, said Talmadge. I need your help—

He had leaned down and with great effort overturned a large rock half submerged in the earth. Was searching for—grubs?—beneath it. A distracted expression on his face. Strands of black hair escaped from the pomade slick and fell into his eyes. He pressed his lips together.

Clee, beside him, had been listening to it all: the waning health of the girl in the jail, her delirium; her insistence on needing more time. Talmadge's conviction that she wanted to kill this man, Michaelson.

But she would not kill Michaelson, he wanted to tell Talmadge. She might have indicated her desire to do otherwise, but she would not do it. He recalled the time she had traveled with the men, her wariness at killing any animal for food. Talmadge had taught her how to shoot, and she had successfully—though perhaps not skillfully—hunted and killed animals during her tenure riding the countryside with the men. But Clee watched her closely and saw she would rather not eat meat at all, if it meant she had to kill it herself. Soon after she had joined the men, Clee saw she hardly used her rifle, of which she had been so proud at first, at all. But, he thought, she was proud of it as an object that signified her independence, and not necessarily of its destructive use as a weapon.

To shoot a creature from a distance was perhaps enjoyable at first, as a game, but to see the effects close up—the bloody corpse, or the suffering animal pulling its mangled appendage across the forest floor—was not only distasteful to her, but appalling. She would, even if often she could not be found to do the chore, help butcher a deer. But a shade would come down over her eyes, and she would perform the task perfunctorily, her attention divorced from the job at hand.

She had stabbed this man Michaelson so superficially and embarrassingly in the jail, he thought, because she had not the stomach for close physical violence. That was the simplest answer—or one answer—to why she would not kill him. She might think she wanted to kill him; but finally, she was incapable of it.

Clee stirred from where he had been holding still, watching Talmadge, who had given up his quest for the grubs and now watched the soil, scanned it, disinterestedly. What was he looking for?

If there's another way, I don't see it, said Talmadge, as if talking to himself.

Let her be, Clee wanted to say. Let her—finally, finally—alone. She will kill him, or she will not. If she does not, something else will come in its place. It's not for us to decide.

I have to do it, said Talmadge, staring, defeated, at the soil.

THEY STAY UP there, said Angelene—I don't know where they go—but while the rest of us work, they go up there into the canyon, and don't come down until the sun has set. I don't know what they do up there, or how they eat. They don't even bring any food with them, she said, flustered.

Caroline Middey had arrived in her wagon in the afternoon, and Angelene had gone to her, drawn to her from the trees, and when she reached the older woman, Angelene embraced her, placed her head on the other woman's breast, unabashedly, like a child. What is it? said Caroline Middey. What's happened? And Angelene, after shedding preliminary tears—these quickly ceased after a flood, and she was embarrassed—led Caroline Middey to the cabin, where Angelene removed the older woman's boots, and then made her tea. They sat in the birchwood chairs in the new darkness, and Angelene told her what was happening: that Talmadge and Clee held deep conferences in the canyon, leaving the rest of them to work. And lately he hardly spoke to Angelene at all.

It's like he's sick, said Angelene. It's like he can't help himself.

Caroline Middey was nodding. She was silent for several minutes, lost in thought. Eventually she said: He has got it into his mind that he is to be the savior of that girl, and it won't let him alone. He is going to die of it—

Don't say that, said Angelene, sitting up.

I'm sorry, child, said Caroline Middey. But I have not seen the likes of it before.

She was silent then, because she had just remembered an exception: his feverish existence after the disappearance of his sister: him refusing food, combing the forest, pocketing different objects—rocks, sticks, flowers—which, he claimed, bore some sort of sign within them. Some sort of map that would show him the way.

I'll talk to him, said Caroline Middey. We'll get this sorted out between us.

Angelene was silent. Didn't want to say what she was thinking: that she—Angelene—and Caroline Middey had receded in importance to Talmadge; they had become insubstantial to him. Della was the only one who mattered to him now.

A ND THEN FREDERICK appeared outside the bars, in the darkness. Della sensed him more than she saw him, and rose from the cot. Nearing the bars, she observed with surprise that he held the posture of one who had been waiting a long time. What had he been doing? Watching her sleep? He was looking at her almost as if he disapproved of her—as if she had done something to deliberately betray him, and he had come to have it out with her. A grimness plagued his mouth.

What, she said. Then: How long have you been standing there?

He still peered at her. It was hard to see him in the darkness, which seemed, with every passing moment, to increase. What time was it?

And then Frederick spoke. At the end of the week, he said, they were taking Michaelson to the hospital ward in Seattle.

Della waited, alarmed. Why was he telling her this? She asked him if this news was supposed to make her happy. He hesitated and then said it didn't seem right that a man like Michaelson should die in the comfort of a hospital, while someone like her, Della, for example, was locked up for a crime she committed when she was probably just protecting herself.

Isn't that right, he said, looking at her. And that was when she understood what was happening. She told him he was right. He's going to die anyway, said Frederick, looking away. Probably doing the son of a bitch a favor. And he snorted quietly, gathered phlegm to spit; but he did not.

Somebody had hurt him, she thought suddenly, without wanting to know it. But she knew it. Big, strapping Frederick. Or not him, but his mother, perhaps. A sister.

Della asked if he was really telling her what she thought he was telling her.

He said he was working the morning of the transfer, and would come open her cell. He would come and do that, and then be on his way, he said. What you do outside of that is up to you. I won't have no more part of it.

But then he looked at her again.

They'll catch you more likely than not, he said. Even if they don't catch you in the act—and they probably will—they'll know who did it. This isn't good for you. He winced with frustration. I mean, you're going to do it, but—you have to know they're going to catch you. You have to—decide if it's worth it. If it is, fine. But if not—

But Della could not absorb this, she could not listen. Her body had become cold and her fingertips beat. I am a bird, she thought. I am as light as air.

Harvest was not over yet, but the men had done their preliminary picking and were packing up to leave. Talmadge was preparing to go with them. He and Clee would ride with the men for part of the way and then split off to go to Chelan.

He did not tell Angelene what they were doing, what was happening. We're going to go see Della, he said, but would not look at her.

Is she coming back with you? she asked him, baffled. Were there developments he had failed to tell her about? Correspondence from the Judge? The warden? Della herself? And if so, why hadn't he told her? Why wouldn't he look at her now? He wouldn't even answer her questions.

I can help, she said. Whatever it is, I can help—

You'll help by staying here and not asking questions.

Hurt, she withdrew, went deep into the orchard with her picking bag. He would regret the way he had talked to her, she thought, and come find her, penitent. But he did not. When she went back to the cabin, hungry, after dusk, he had already gone to bed.

Clee had picked out a horse for Talmadge to ride, and in the morning, at dawn, when the other men were decamping, Talmadge packed his saddlebags. Angelene sat wrapped in a blanket on the porch and watched him. After he was done packing, he went inside the cabin and saw that she had prepared breakfast enough for the both of them. The meal laid out on the table. He hesitated, then retreated to the porch. Stood in front of her.

Thank you, he said.

After a moment she rose, and they went inside to eat. They did not speak during the meal.

He did not want to hurt her. He thought, after he had set off with Clee and the other men, that he would make it up to her when he returned to the orchard. When this whole situation was resolved. He knew he had been absentminded, he had neglected his duties in the orchard and toward her. He had not cared for her as he should have. But it was only because the other one in Chelan needed him so much. He had neglected Angelene for a few weeks, but the other one he had neglected for years— since the beginning, almost. It was time to make up for that now.

He should have taken Della in hand much sooner, instead of fooling himself into believing he was giving her her independence and freedom. He should have said: No, you may not travel with the men—excusing all his reasons why he had decided otherwise. He had learned, these last few months, the extent of how much he had been responsible for her, and how he had failed her. Where had it begun? He was not fool enough to believe it had begun with him not taking up arms against Michaelson—or not taking up arms to the extent she might have expected, or wanted, him to. It was not as simple as that. The beginning of his failure was unclear. He was not even sure that it was something that he could have prevented. And that, finally, was the hardest part, the hardest thing to accept. His only excuse was that he never knew that it would go this far. He did not know Jane would kill herself from fear. He realized the girl, Della, might have blamed him all this time for not standing up to the other man—she thought he, Talmadge, was weak—but this was only what she felt superficially. Her anger at him was deep, but finally had little to nothing to do with him. The anger was the mask of an emotion that would not show its true face. She fought against the same force against which he fought. Fate, inevitability, luck. God. He would fly in the face of this force now, for her. If she could be freed from it, he would free her. He would make it all up to her, now.

Della half turned toward the bars, squinting in the sun coming through the small window. There was something she had just remembered or wanted to remember; she did not want to forget it, and at the time of remembering it, it had seemed impossible that she would ever forget it, but now she had forgotten it. She stood and looked at the sun-covered wall. Her mind struggled, but she could not grasp it, that thing.

A moment before, she had gotten up from the cot on which she lay looking at the window because someone down the hallway was trying to get her attention. Someone had not called her name but something close to it. It was the call and then something after it like a cough and a moan. And then silence. She had risen and gone to the bars, strained to look down the hallway. But it was silent and nobody was there. She had thought for a moment that it was Michaelson trying to get her attention. Trying to communicate a message to her, trying to persuade her not to kill him.

She had waited and then turned to the wall. Saw the sunlight. There was something she had been thinking about, before, when she lay on the cot. She went to the cot and lay down again. But she could not remember it, that thing. It would not come to her.

THE SOUND OF water roiling in the kettle drew Angelene from the bedroom. Alone in the cabin—in the orchard—she took the towel and lifted the kettle and poured water into the mug with coffee powder and then replaced the kettle onto the stove. Wiped her hands on her apron front and returned to the bedroom, where a white dress was laid out on the bed.

MIDMORNING OF THE second day there was a rainstorm, and Talmadge and Clee hid in a stand of evergreens. It seemed the rain would go on and on. Clee managed to light a cigarette and sat smoking, and by his posture he seemed ready to wait a long time. Talmadge, despite himself, dozed. Woke to Clee stirring. The rain had stopped. They urged the horses out of the trees. Water from the branches poured onto their hats and shoulders. Clee grunted. Up ahead was a railroad track, and they approached it. As they crossed it, the sun came out.

Della took the box wrapped in twine—had she been saving it for this moment?—from the slit in the mattress where she had hidden it along with the fruit—the apricots that she had not eaten had begun to rot—and untied it. Unlidded the box.

Inside was a square of cotton batting. She stared at it and then took out the cotton, and something—she barely sensed it—fell out of the box. She bent and inspected the floor and found, a minute later, what had escaped: an apple seed. She picked it up and went to the window, held it in her open palm in the light. Studied it.

I T TOOK TALMADGE and Clee three days to reach Chelan. They separated once they reached town, and Talmadge deposited his horse at the
stables. As he was checking into the boardinghouse, the landlady smiled
tentatively at him and told him that his daughter was already there.

Pardon?

But then he looked up to where the lady was smiling and saw Angelene, in a white dress, standing on the staircase. On her face an expression
of excitement, fear.

Out of the landlady's gaze, in the upper hallway, Talmadge took Angelene's arm and steered her into his room. She sat on the bed as he shut
the door. She bowed her head.

She had taken the train, she said, her head still bowed, and had arrived
the day before. She had gone straight to the boardinghouse, and had not
gone out at all. Only the landlady knew she was there. She hesitated before continuing. She didn't know what was going on, she said, but she
knew Talmadge wasn't there just to visit Della; she knew it was more
than that, and that what they were planning, he and Clee, was maybe
illegal, or else they wouldn't be so secretive about it.

Talmadge held still. He looked over her shoulder into the corner of
the room. While traveling to Chelan, he had gone over and over the plan
in his head—if one step succeeded, then it opened the possibility of exe-
cuting the next step, and the next—and the more he thought about it, the
more hopeful—though hesitantly so—he became. There were moments
of grave doubt; but those were just moments, and they passed. There was
dread, but that was also to be expected. Now, with the entrance of the
girl, the foundation of the plan shifted, groaned with the effort to sustain
the feasibility of succeeding in these new circumstances.

I don't know what you're doing, she said. But I want to help you.

He didn't speak for a long time. He didn't want her involved in any way, but did not know what to tell her now. If he asked her to stay out of it—and what tone would he use for this? What would be most success-ful? Would she listen to him? Or would his protestation finally work to encourage her? She was no longer a child, but neither was she an adult. He had shielded her from so much already. Whatever speech he directed at her, whatever he asked her to do or not to do, could bring a myriad of consequences. Oh, he was tired of thinking about it all. How his words and deeds affected Della and her trajectory; and now Angelene too.

Finally he said: I thought maybe, in the beginning— He faltered. I thought maybe, once she got out, she could come and take care of you. But now—

She watched him.

What was he saying? The girl, as ever, had this particular effect on him. He spoke things to her, when she solicited them, that he was un-aware of even in himself. Opinions. Long-held beliefs and judgments. What was he saying? That he had given up on Della being a guardian for Angelene? That is what he had said. And then, suddenly, he was con-fused: Della would never return to the orchard. (But that was too much, he thought, that was too far—) He turned his face away, exhausted.

I can take care of myself, said Angelene, her voice shaking. You don't need to worry about me.

Several minutes passed in silence. Talmadge did not know what to say anymore.

Even if she doesn't come back to us, he said. We just have to get her out of there. He paused, searching for the right words. She's sick, he said finally.

Sick?

Yes.

It was quiet for a minute.

Then we should help her, said Angelene.

He looked at her.

No, he said.

She looked at him, startled.

Why?

Because I said so.

That's no answer.

Because—it doesn't have anything to do with you, he said. I'm the one who got her into this fix. It was me. And now I'm going to help her. But you got to stay out of it. It has nothing to do with you, now.

She wanted to talk back to him, he saw, but after she met his eyes, she fell silent.

I have an appointment, he said, finally, and as soon as he said this, and saw her face looking at him, expectant, full of compassion, he experienced vertigo. He put one hand on the bed frame and the other over his eyes.

Talmadge? Her voice was frightened. Sit down.

I'm all right. He sat.

She left the room and returned a minute later with a glass of water. He took it from her and drank. Afterward, hesitating, he reached for her, and she came and sat beside him, laid her head on his chest. He put his arm around her.

You shouldn't have come, he said.

When she woke him from his nap, an hour later, he saw that she had laid out his suit and polished his shoes. After he dressed, she brought him up a plate of roast chicken and mashed potatoes. Placed it near the basin.

It was four o'clock. He told Angelene that he would be back in an hour or so, and that she shouldn't leave the boardinghouse. She nodded.

I'm serious, now.

I know.

He walked down the stairs and touched his hat to the landlady, who spoke to another lodger at the counter. He exited the boardinghouse into the expansive, sweet-smelling late afternoon.

In the warden's office, the warden sat in strange dimness. It was the time of day when the sun illuminated the opposite side of the building; Talmadge had never visited the warden this late in the afternoon. The warden could have turned on the overhead electric light, but he did not. He sat in the soft darkness and watched Talmadge warily. He had risen to shake Talmadge's hand when he arrived, and then asked him to sit. Now the warden regarded him with a neutral expression.

You received our letter, I take it? About the transfer?

Talmadge nodded.

The warden gazed down at this desk. A grim, sad smile on his lips.

Talmadge cleared his throat.

It's strange, said the warden suddenly, and raised his eyes to Talmadge. We told her about the transfer, but it's like she doesn't care. Or she doesn't hear us. Sad, he said in the ensuing silence. She seemed so—bright— before, when she first arrived here. Maybe that's not the right word for it. But she has deteriorated mentally. Physically as well. He sighed. It is a shame—

Talmadge lifted his chin, as if to speak. He didn't care for the warden's words anymore—they didn't matter—but neither did he want to seem rude. He needed to maintain the warden's sympathy.

About your request to take her out, said the warden, leaning back in his chair. It is highly unusual. But, seeing she's going to be sent away anyway, and there are no laws against such visits, or—he smiled an un- characteristic, mischievous smile—at least no laws that cannot be cir- cumvented, I've decided to allow it. As long as you're supervised, he said. He continued: he had always been sympathetic toward Della, he said, until a certain point, but when it came to Talmadge—here he looked at Talmadge, unsmiling, serious—he had no qualms.

Talmadge walked back to the boardinghouse in the waning light. It was done. The first step was completed, it had cleared the way for the rest of it.

There was a chill in the air.

Inside the boardinghouse they were having supper. He stood at the base of the stairs and listened briefly to the voices in the dining room, and knew Angelene was not among them. He climbed the stairs, carefully so that he would not make any noise, and made his way down the hallway. Paused outside her door. He should go straight to bed, he thought. He knocked. She answered immediately for him to come in.

She was in bed, in her nightgown. Her hair loose around her shoulders. She looked frightened. He sat on the edge of the bed. After a moment he took her hand. He told her all of it. That he was going to meet Della tomorrow and take her down to the beach; that Clee was going to create a diversion, which would distract the guard; and that Talmadge was going to lead Della onto the boat, where she would hide, and then the boat would set sail, and she would be free when she reached Stehekin, the small community at the top of the lake. In the silence that followed, he said there were people waiting in Stehekin for her, there was a horse.

Angelene's face flushed as he spoke.

I'll help you, she said.

He shook his head.

Please, Talmadge.

No.

Her mouth was hard; her eyes filled with tears.

He squeezed her hand. You'll stay here, out of it, he said. It's the best way.

But in the morning he returned to her door, and knocked quietly.

Come in.

He opened the door. She sat fully dressed on the edge of the made-up bed. As if waiting for him.

Come with me, he said.

It had occurred to him, when he had gone to bed the previous night, that he had wanted to keep Della safe, but had failed. He was trying to keep Angelene safe, but might very well be in the process of failing her too. Perhaps the better decision was to include her, after all.

But in nothing truly dangerous, of course. He was not a monster.

They walked to the boat together. It was set to depart in one hour, the first of two times that day. Talmadge bought them both tickets, and as they walked up the gangplank, he explained: an hour before the second departure, she, Angelene, was to board the boat and go to the cupboard— they had reached it now—and store a jar of water there, and some food. The supplies were in his saddlebags back at the boardinghouse. All she would have to do would be to open the cupboard, place the items inside, close the cupboard, and then exit the boat. And then go straight to the boardinghouse and wait until he came for her.

Let's go, he said. He did not want to linger too long on the boat. As they passed by the ticket collector, Angelene said, What about him? And Talmadge said, after a long pause, You don't have to worry about him.

CLEE STOOD AT the side of the arena and watched the horses. There were about twenty-five of them, and some of them were from the mountains. As he stood watching, a man came over to him from inside the arena and touched his hat in greeting.

Morning.

Clee nodded.

They looked out at the horses.

You doing some buying?

Clee nodded again.

The man nodded too, amiably. Seems like you wouldn't be needing any horses with all them you got.

Clee did not respond.

Anything look good to you?

Clee was watching a white and black and ocher horse near the center of the herd, and also a gray horse with a spotted rump, near the outside. But he pointed to a pair of roans instead.

Which?

Clee pointed again, more emphatically.

The man looked at the ones Clee pointed at. The roans, there? Those look like fine enough horses. He cast a mild puzzled glance at Clee. But like I said, what's a man like you doing buying horses? You don't have enough to suit you? And then, seeing Clee's hesitation, he laughed.

The owner on the other side of the arena came over to them and greeted them. The other man moved away. Clee, with a gentle but authoritative flourish, again indicated the roans.

You want to see them first? You want to ride them?

Clee shook his head. He took out his wallet. After he had paid the man, he pointed at the man's shoulder to get his attention—the man looked at him, surprised—and then pointed emphatically to the horses and then gestured to the sky, and then drew a small hill in the air with his finger.

The man stared at him.

Clee repeated these movements, patiently.

I don't—

Again.

The man hesitated. Tomorrow? he said. You'll pick up the horses to-morrow?

Clee nodded.

Suit yourself, said the man.

The wrangler told the boy—young, Cayuse, with large, beautiful black eyes—what to do. To wait until night and then take at least ten horses, and include the roans and the white and black and ocher horse and the spotted gray horse. He told the boy to go look at the horses be-forehand, in the daylight, and to come back and tell him if he had any questions about which horses he meant. The boy said he understood. The wrangler said that he and Clee would be watching, in case anything went wrong. But nothing should go wrong. Did the boy understand what they wanted him to do?

I understand, said the boy, and wanted to say but did not, We have stolen horses before, this is nothing new, I know what I'm doing—

Clee went to see the owner of the horses in the morning, but when he arrived, the owner was abashed, pale.

Somebody stole the horses, he said.

O N THE BENCH in the garden where she had fallen asleep, Caroline Middey woke. It was late afternoon and she had been dreaming, but about what she could not remember exactly.

She had been troubled since she dropped the girl off at the train station the day before.

Around her the garden was in verdant bloom; the smell of the air was almost sickening with odor, and although it was late in the day the last bees were industrious in the crocus, the birds had started their racket in the trees. There was a shadow over most of the grass, and for a moment Caroline Middey did not remember what month it was, or her age; and then she remembered, and knew that she was nearer to death than any of her young enterprises—and why should this surprise her? But the knowledge seemed new—she was going to die, like all the others, and the knowledge was absorbed by the garden, which simultaneously cradled her and drew her out of herself, into the perfume, into the noise.

Why had she said those words to Talmadge, about Della—that she was beyond help? She heard her own words in her mind as if they issued from another person. She wept now, silently, for herself and for the girl. Her hands rested on either side of her on the soft boards of the bench.

We do not belong to ourselves alone, she wanted to say, but there was no one to speak to.

The next day, at one o'clock, Talmadge went to fetch Della. He was allowed to take her for the afternoon; she was to be back by dusk.

She came up into the courthouse hallway, flanked by two guards. She looked very small between them. She wore a soiled cowboy hat and a man's shirt. She didn't look at Talmadge until she stood before him, and then she glanced at him. There was a trace of curiosity there, in her face, before she looked away.

The warden explained to them both: he was assigning them a guard, a young red-haired man named Officer Wallach, who would shadow them, who would make sure Della didn't try to run away. Talmadge watched Della's face as the warden said this, but there was no change. There was to be no leaving the city limits, said the warden; there was to be no consumption of alcohol. Did they understand? Yes, they understood.

Released, they walked in the direction of the lake. The young man followed behind them, at a distance. As they passed by the storefronts, Talmadge asked Della if she was hungry.

They went into the café where Talmadge had first dined several months before. They sat at the counter—the young guard took a nearby booth—and Della ordered eggs and sausage and toast, orange juice and coffee. They were silent until the food arrived, and then Della removed her hat and began to eat.

Talmadge, strangely, did not feel the need to speak to her. He simply watched her. She ate deftly, her eyes downcast. Her hair had grown a little, and she wore it tucked behind her ears. It made her appear even more like an adolescent.

When she was done eating, she wiped her mouth with her shirtsleeve. She asked if he had any tobacco. He said he did not. She wiped her mouth again, this time with her fingers, and then slid off the stool and went to the guard, who paused in his own eating—he had ordered food as well—and took out a pack of cigarettes and gave one to her. She stood before him a moment longer—her back was to Talmadge, but he could hear her speaking quietly to the guard—and after a moment the man frowned, gave her another cigarette, and then another, and then put the pack away. She bent slightly, and the guard lit her cigarette with a match.

She returned, sat beside Talmadge.

The waitress brought her an ashtray.

Talmadge watched her smoke. What ease. She glanced at him again. Her eyes had taken on some of their sharpness again, after their blandness—detachment—while eating.

Where are we going?

I thought we'd go down to the lake.

She didn't answer at first.

Why?

He looked at her. What do you mean, Why? He thought, but did not say: Is there somewhere else you would rather go?

She frowned; was going to say something, but stopped herself. All right, she said.

He watched her smoke.

What kind of tobacco is that?

She held the cigarette before her, regarded it. Why?

What is it?

She shrugged. Pall Mall.

You like those?

She shrugged again, turned and looked out the window to the street.

What are your regulars?

What?

I asked: What are your regulars?

She glanced at him. Lucky Strikes.

When he paid the bill, he bought three packs of Lucky Strikes and two matchbooks, and gave them to her. She held them in her hand for a moment, as if testing their weight, and then put them in her pocket.

Thank you, she said, frowning.

Going down the platform took a long time, since his legs were still shaky. She did not say anything about this; did not offer to help him. She waited for him at intervals, smoking. Wallach, respectful, stayed far behind. When they reached the bottom, they strolled along the shoreline until they reached the pilings that Talmadge had sat on with Angelene. He sat down, relieved at the opportunity to rest. Della stood near the lapping water, her hair blowing in the wind—she had taken off her hat and slapped her thigh with it—before joining him.

They looked out over the water.

Pretty, ain't it, she said.

He looked at her. She withdrew the cigarette pack from her pocket.

It was the time of day when the light on the water winked and sparkled.

A few children played again in the shallows. As they watched, the great steamboat came toward them out of the distance, a spot of white gaining shape. It trudged through the water, its whistle groaning.

It took a long time for it to reach the warehouse. It maneuvered slowly into the building.

I want to do right by you, he said. Won't you let me help you?

She replaced the cigarette pack in her pocket, looked over the water. Did not answer him.

After a while, he said: He's dying, you know. He's going to die without you helping him do it.

She frowned.

Some people just can't die fast enough, she said.

Talmadge leaned, and spat. Well. He's on his way. You ought to leave him alone.

When she turned to him, he could read, in the sudden openness of her face, some of her old self, her old meanness and innocence, there.

You don't know nothing about it, she said. You ought to stay out of it.

He wanted to take her by the front of her shirt.

Didn't I near kill the man myself? Didn't I about stab him to death on my own property?

Well. Not near enough happened to him.

A breeze came up off the water, smelling cold. He stood suddenly.

Take my coat.

She would not take it at first. But he did not relent, and so she took it. It hung heavy from her shoulders.

I'm not cold, she muttered, and took out another cigarette from the pack, attempted to light it. But there was too much wind. She tried for several minutes but then ceased.

He turned toward the platform. He could not be sure, but he thought he saw Clee among a group of people watching out over the lake. A tall man wearing a black hat. And then the man—Clee—raised his arm. It was him.

Talmadge, too, raised his arm.

What are you doing?

Nothing, he said, and lowered his arm. Listen, he said, and stepped toward her. When he took her by the shoulders she startled, and tried to pull away.

Hey—

You're a young girl, and he's at the end of his life. He's going to die as sure as anything. You can see that, if he's as sick as the warden says he is. Why can't you let him be? You hurt him, and you only hurt yourself. You hear me? He's going to die. But if you get at him again, they're going to put you away for longer—

So?

He shook her. He was ashamed, but he did it. And don't you care? He spoke louder now, into her face. A young person like yourself? And you got your family—Angelene—to think about? What's she going to do, if you get locked up for longer? I'm not going to be around forever, and you're going to be all she's got—

She ain't my responsibility, I ain't got nothing to do with her—

But her voice shook.

He shook her again. Bullshit, he said, his voice quavering, and let her go.

From way off down the beach, a shot rang out. All the people on the beach, the children in the water, the parents, the strolling couples, turned their heads in the same direction.

Della, who had stepped back, was rubbing her arms where he had gripped them, and looked in the direction of the shot. Vaguely curious.

Wallach was walking toward them, turning his head to look over his shoulder at the people beginning to move in the opposite direction down the beach. He jogged the last part of the way toward them. He was frowning.

You got to come with me, he said.

No, said Talmadge, and both young people looked at him, surprised.

The warden promised me my day, said Talmadge. We'll sit right here for you, we won't go nowhere. We might go up into town, to get something to eat—

Old man, said Wallach—almost laughing with surprise—you're going to follow me. He took a pair of handcuffs off his belt beneath his jacket and put them on Della, who looked down at them disinterestedly.

Every time I look over my shoulder, I better see you two, said Wallach, wholly serious now, and turned and set off across the beach.

They followed him. They moved in the direction of the warehouse. As they neared it, more and more people joined them; and the young man in uniform before them appeared and disappeared among the crowd. Wallach looked back a few times, but then he was gone; there was something happening up ahead; a large crowd—

Talmadge stopped.

Della stopped too. What?

They were near the warehouse. Come on, he said. She didn't move at first, but when he looked over his shoulder, she was following him, moving against the current of people, a blank expression on her face.

Before they reached the ticket man, Talmadge took off his outer flannel shirt and wrapped it around Della's bound wrists, to hide the cuffs. Della said nothing. He bought two tickets and then they went together up the gangplank and then onto the boat. Talmadge led her to the cupboard. He slid open the door, and saw the jar of water the girl had put in there. A brown bag of food. A wool blanket. He slid the door back closed, testing its resistance. It was a shallow space, he thought, but she would just fit.

You want me to get in there?

Hurry up, he said, and looked around them. Now he sweated. The world, for a moment, seemed ready to burst at its seams.

When she didn't move, he said, unable to keep the impatience from his voice: What is it?

Her mind was chewing on something. She stood there, unmoving.

He turned and looked around them again. There were not many people on the boat; some had unboarded to see about the commotion on the beach. But they would all be back, and soon.

You want me to—

Get in there. Yes. There's room. And—Angelene left some food in there for you, and water—what is it? You'll fit, he said again, thinking that was what daunted her.

But she continued to gaze at the space, as if it were some foreign beast.

You don't get caught, you don't go back, he said. You stay in there for an hour or so, and you can come out. Just keep your cuffs hidden. You get up into Stehekin, you have some time, but not much. Get those cuffs taken care of. There's a place—

I know, she said. How did she know? he thought. But then, he thought, she probably did know. This girl had lived many lives. But still she hesitated.

What is it?

She would not look at him. She looked down into the cupboard once more—he had slid open the door—and then straightened up, gazed around at the deck. It was as if she was coming out of a dream.

No.

Talmadge stood there. It occurred to him at once that if she wouldn't get into the cupboard, and the young man, Wallach, found them arguing on board, Talmadge would go to jail too, and Angelene would be left alone. Why was it that the most terrible possibilities reveal themselves only at the last moment, when it is too late to change course?

What do you mean, no? he said, and he heard the anger in his voice. He had to resist the urge to take her arm and throw her, in one violent motion, down into the cupboard. She was not very big, he thought suddenly; he could easily overpower her. And the way she stood there— almost nonchalant, as if they had all the time in the world—made him seethe with incredulity.

Della, he said, his voice shaking. I'm not going to argue with you, now. You get into that cupboard—

She looked at him, but as if seeing him from a great distance. She stirred slightly.

I can't go, she said. And then, enunciating: *I don't want to go*—

How can you not want to go? he said. His voice was quiet with astonishment. How was it possible that she was refusing him? The extreme obviousness of the mistake she was in the process of making robbed him of sense. He stood there, silent. Helpless.

It seemed a long time before she turned her body, as if to leave the boat. She hesitated. The guards will be coming soon, she said, without inflection.

He was staring above the cupboard door, at the white painted boards, a slant of light revealing the cracks and bubbles, curls of peeling paint.

I wanted you out of that place, he said. I wanted to help. But I also—
wanted you to check on her. When she's older. I wanted you to—

But he did not finish his sentence.

Wind came off the water and moved into his hair, got into his clothes.
She would not be entering the cupboard. Neither was there a rush to get
back to the crowd on the beach, to save themselves. When Talmadge
thought, finally, that's what they should have done—that's where he
should have led her, at once, after she refused him—three officers rushed
onto the boat, and seized them.

V

W HEN TALMADGE CAME to take Della down to the lake, she thought
it was a gesture meant to inspire her to be good. They were going to send her to Walla Walla—or that is what they told her—but she
only half believed they were prepared to do it. She could imagine the
conversation between Talmadge and the warden: if Della improved her
behavior, if she showed a drastic change in attitude—if she apologized,
and perhaps explained her motives, which included divulging her past—
then the warden would be that much more likely to consider transferring
her elsewhere. Or maybe nowhere at all, if Michaelson was in fact being
moved. Chelan did not seem so bad, or so far away, when compared with
Walla Walla. This outing to the lake, Della knew, was an opportunity for
Talmadge to persuade her to be good: to tell the warden her story, and
ask for leniency.

The officer assigned to them—Wallach—she had never seen before. A
new group of officers had arrived lately at the jail for training. Puzzled,
earnest, curious faces peered at her now at mealtimes, sometimes offering a tentative greeting through the bars. They all knew who she was,
what she had done, but she was indifferent to them. Did not bother to
learn their names, or determine in which ways they could be useful to
her. She would most likely never see them again, she reasoned, beyond
next week and only valued her alliance with Frederick, which was indis-
pensable to her now.

She had to remind herself that it was real, it was actually going to
happen: at the end of the week Frederick would unlock her cell, and she
would go to Michaelson, and kill him.

But that was five days away.

Now it was nice to be on the beach, it was nice to be out of the cell.

And Talmadge had bought her a meal at the café, and cigarettes. She thought it would be all right: and then he began to act funny, trying to talk to her about Michaelson. And he also kept looking over at the platform as if he were waiting for somebody; he even waved at someone. But when she asked him what he was doing, he didn't answer her. And then the gunshot; and everybody moved down the beach at the same time, to see what was going on. Wallach handcuffed her, and she and Talmadge went down the beach behind him. It was difficult to see; there were many people. Talmadge spoke up, told her to follow him. Reluctantly she obeyed, followed him to the steamboat warehouse. Then he wanted her to get onto the boat. She hesitated, confused. He bought them tickets. On the boat, he led her to a cupboard, and told her to get inside.

She had not anticipated this. He wanted her to escape! Through her confusion—and utter surprise—she of course recognized the blinding opportunity he was offering her. She hesitated, despite herself. She did not want to leave Michaelson, but—what was this other way?

What was this other way? And then she thought, looking out over the water, there was no other way. This seeming escape would only lead her farther away from Michaelson, and therefore she could not accept it. She dimly appreciated what the old man was trying to do—and the girl had helped, he said, which piqued her interest—but ultimately what Talmadge wanted did not matter. She had made up her mind. She knew what *she*—Della, herself—wanted to do.

The guard who approached her on the boat could have been rough with her, but he was not. He was distant, and even respectful, as he drew her across the deck. When they neared the gangplank, he called to another officer—I've got her!—and Della saw Frederick standing near the bow, looking out over the water. Their eyes met, and then she looked away. He would think the escape was her idea, and judge her a coward for it.

The officers led them off the boat. The man beside her was nervous, excited: he had caught a prisoner. He had been calm enough in the beginning, but the reality of what he had just accomplished had begun to sink in. He was going to be recognized, his name was going to be in the papers. He would be a hero.

As they approached the crowd—what had happened? Had somebody been shot?—Della saw at once, when he moved only slightly: Clee.

In her sudden uprising of emotion—and what was this emotion?—she raised her hand to him, and he widened his eyes, shook his head, and the young officer at her side yanked her arm. Hey! barked Talmadge, and Della, startled, turned to him and said, It's all right, but Talmadge lumbered into the man. He didn't know what he was doing, thought Della. The man embraced Talmadge in a rough bear hug, trying to calm him, but Talmadge, in one sudden movement, pushed away from him. The officer stumbled back and Talmadge was several feet away from him now, hatless, his hair mussed. Why was he wearing only an undershirt? she thought, before she remembered that *she* wore his jacket; and he had removed his shirt to wrap around her handcuffs as well. As he stood, now, breathing heavily, there was an unreadable expression in his eyes. People yelled and moved around them. He was like a child, she thought. A child who suddenly did not know where he was at.

She felt herself moving toward him.

Della! Frederick called, somewhere behind her. But she did not turn around.

Della!

And a gunshot. She felt a bite just above her right elbow—which soon spread to coldness. She twisted her posture to look at the back of her arm: blood-soaked canvas. But she was all right, she thought, her heart pounding furiously. The bullet had just grazed her.

And then—how could she have not noticed this before?—Talmadge had fallen in the space before her. Two guards—one was Frederick—ran to him. Leaned over him.

She stepped forward; but someone caught her from behind, pulled her sharply backward.

Talmadge! she yelled, and tried to get out of the grip. Talmadge!

And then a person—a young woman—hurried from the crowd, drew to Talmadge and the guards. Frederick held out his arm to keep her away. When the woman came forward again, Frederick shook her off—she had gripped his arm—and touched her chest with the back of his hand, pushed her. Rebuffed, she tried once more to reach Talmadge, ducking under Frederick's arm. But Frederick snatched her back with one arm, flung her to the side. Get back! he yelled generally, to them all. Get back! The girl held her hands in front of her—gripped, beseeching—as if she were praying. And then she let her hands drop.

The girl—it was Angelene—turned her head left and right, slow but frantic, searching for help; Della saw she was sobbing.

She is mine, Jane had said. But she is also yours. We are the same. Our children are the same.

Let me go! shouted Della. She realized she was screaming. Let me go!

Clee was shouldering toward Talmadge and Angelene now, grim-mouthed, alarmed—but was caught by the elbow before he reached them, pulled toward the platform.

Do something! Della screamed. Do something! Angelene!

The girl turned in her direction, puzzled; their eyes met briefly, before Della was hauled, twisting and kicking, up the platform steps.

TALMADGE HAD TOLD Angelene to stay at the boardinghouse, and she had told him with a straight face, and not a glint of hesitation in her voice, that she would do it. It would not make a difference if she argued with him—she determined that was useless after the first night, when he had been so angry and shaken by her arrival. And so she stayed out of his way, even assisted him, as much as she was able without leaving the boardinghouse, the day of Della's escape. Anything so that he, Talmadge, would ignore her, Angelene, and not lend thought at all to the possibility that she might betray his wish that she remain indoors.

But how could she stay at the boardinghouse with all that was going to happen on the beach? Of course she would not stay there.

She dressed in a cream muslin dress, her good boots, a small straw hat—she must have been suffering fever when she bought that other one, she thought again—and moved with the calm of one who has invested fully in disobedience, down the staircase.

Going out, are we? the landlady asked politely—but also a bit chidingly, Angelene thought—when Angelene reached the front entrance.

Yes, said Angelene, and exited without another word.

She had waited that afternoon, sitting on her bed, and then drawing to the window—pacing—for forty minutes or so after Talmadge left to fetch Della. She had been sharply anxious before, in the confines of the boardinghouse, but now she was filled with a strange, airy exaltation as she moved down the street. There was little to no chance—unless something had gone wrong—that she would cross paths with Talmadge and Della. As she neared the platform above the lake, her body hummed with excitement; her heartbeat filled her.

She stood on the platform and looked out at the water. The beautiful, massive, sparkling body. The wind rose and pulled at her hat. She placed one hand on top of her head, reflexively, to keep it in place.

What was it, she asked herself, she wanted to see?

She wanted to see the plan executed successfully. And she wanted most of all to witness Talmadge come out of it all unharmed.

A crack of gunfire startled her. A group of three women standing near her turned their heads in the same direction—away from Angelene—down the beach. And then one of the women looked back at Angelene, a conspiratorial grin on her face. What on earth was *that*? said the woman. Angelene, in response, tried to smile. Her mouth was dry. She was not able to hold the expression for long; the corners of her mouth drooped. She thought, even, she was going to be sick. The other woman turned politely away, embarrassed. Angelene walked to the platform railing—it was wood, and wet, almost spongy beneath her palm—and gripped it. Closed her eyes and breathed deeply. Tried to calm herself.

When she opened her eyes, she saw a tide of people moving down the beach.

She studied the crowd, but could not pick out Talmadge or Della. And then she saw, very far down the beach—in the opposite direction everyone was heading—three figures: a guard, she guessed from the khaki uniform he wore, and then Talmadge and Della moving slightly behind him. And then, as they continued down the beach, the distance between them—the guard, and Talmadge and Della—increased. That was part of the plan, thought Angelene. That was part of it.

She walked, too, kept pace with them along the platform, trying to hold them in her gaze. And then, when she looked away for a moment, to navigate an uneven section of the platform, she lost them; they had melded into the crowd.

She stopped, and watched everything below. She still could not find them. It must be happening, she thought. Talmadge was leading Della onto the boat.

Now down below her—she had resumed walking for a moment, and then halted—a great knot of people had formed on the beach. Was this what Talmadge wanted? Was everything still going according to plan? She hesitated. Should she watch from above? Should she try to pick out

Clee? Maybe, she thought, she had seen enough. But still she stood, rooted. Waited for something to happen.

How much time passed? A new wave of fear seized her, rendered time meaningless.

And then the crowd began to part—rather dramatically, when seen from above—and Angelene realized, without believing it—without *feeling* it—what it meant: that Talmadge and Della were being escorted—led—by officers roughly in the direction of the knot of spectators on the beach. She started. Of course something had gone wrong. Almost without realizing what she was doing, she began to descend the platform steps. Soon she was level with the crowd: moved into it.

When the next gunshot came, she jumped. Covered her ears with her hands. When people ducked around her, she saw, not fifteen feet in front of her, Della's back. Della twisting to see something on her shoulder. She lifted her arm, twisted again to inspect it. Was she shot? Angelene wondered. Her body became weightless with fear. She pushed forward. And then there was a quietness—those rare moments of deficit that sometimes pass through loud crowds—and she could hear individual voices now, waving like loose threads, murmuring women: Is he shot? And then, louder: I think he's shot!

And then all at once people scattered—including Della, who was wrenched to the side by a guard—and Angelene saw Talmadge in a surplus of space, by himself, on his knees. His hand over his heart as if he were pledging something. His lips moving.

She moved toward him. For a moment he was obscured by the crowd, and she could not see him. She fought her way through bodies. And then saw him again, facedown on the ground.

Talmadge! she screamed.

She pressed forward again, but a guard moved and blocked her way. She clung to his arm.

Please—

He shook her off. Get back! he yelled, over her head. Everybody get back!

She moved stiffly beneath the guard's arm. She was almost kneeling, to put her face down close to Talmadge—she saw her hands flutter toward him—and then she was pulled back by her waist so sharply that she lost her breath: her teeth snapped shut. She had bit her tongue. She was crying, tasting blood.

What did I say? said the guard. What did I say?

She looked right, and left, for help.

And then she heard someone call her name. It was an oddly familiar voice. But who did she know, besides Talmadge and Caroline Middey, who was able to strike that chord in her? Maybe it was a person from Peshastin, she thought, who had recognized her. Someone who would help her now. As she frantically searched for the owner of the voice, she saw Della being half carried up the platform steps. Della struggled; and when she turned her head to find Angelene again, her jaw was set; her eyes sparkled. For a moment Della's face—her anguish, but also her resolve—was all Angelene could see. And then—all at once—she was gone.

THERE WERE NO witnesses but the officer who took the action, who said that Della had reached for her weapon. Never mind that she was unarmed. The officer had reason to believe, said his lawyer, that Miss Michaelson could have been provided with a firearm during the time she was outside police custody. The officers in training, of which this officer was one, had heard about Della's predilection for violence, and thought the likelihood of her being armed was *very great*, said the lawyer. The officer, breathless from running down the platform stairs, shot a bullet that grazed Della's elbow and lodged ultimately in Talmadge's shoulder. The officer had forgotten, the lawyer admitted, the rule he had recently learned in training, about firing into crowds; and he was sorry for that lapse in judgment. But, the lawyer said afterward, quickly, wasn't it better to be safe than sorry?

The warden explained to the courtroom that to the best of their knowledge, Clee and the other native man had been meant as a diversion for Della Michaelson's escape. The man on the ground, or perhaps Clee, had fired a gun into the air, and then Clee had hovered over the other man, attracting attention. Meanwhile, Della had attempted to hide herself on the boat, which was set to leave for Stehekin minutes after she boarded it.

Della was reincarcerated, and Clee was taken into custody. Talmadge, who was recovering at the hospital, was also under arrest. The police were searching for the man who had feigned unconsciousness and who had disappeared in the confusion and noise after Talmadge was shot, who so far had not been found.

After the trial Talmadge was sentenced to three years in prison. But he was examined afterward, and after much argument on his behalf by legal counsel, he was deemed in too poor health to undergo the sentence. They should not overlook the fact also, his counsel argued, that he was sole guardian of a minor. Finally, after being in the jail for two weeks, his prison sentence was shortened to fourteen months.

Clee's sentence was two years. He had been the only one of the conspiracy who was armed, and he would not tell who his partner—the man feigning unconsciousness—had been, and so he was uncooperative as well.

Della, on the other hand, was finally brought to trial for her other crimes. The initial man she had stabbed—had claimed to have killed— had not died, and did not at first wish to press charges. But then his family and the other workers persuaded him otherwise.

No one believed that Della had not been a part of the conspiracy of her own escape, and so she was given an even harsher sentence. She was to be transferred to the prison in Walla Walla, and serve a ten-year sentence for assault—the stabbing—and attempted escape from a penal institution.

Some of the newspapers noted that the minor in question, mentioned at times during the trials, was a Miss Angelene Michaelson (in some instances Talmadge), aged fourteen years, of Peshastin, Washington. The *Leavenworth Echo* described her as "tall, slight of build, with strong likeness to her aunt, long dark hair not done up in the style of the young ladies of the day but kept in twin braids down her back, like a schoolgirl." In some accounts, Angelene was crying in the second row of the courthouse gallery while Talmadge was questioned; in others she simply stared ahead. In all cases she was accompanied by Miss Caroline Middey, a family friend from Peshastin, who was also acquainted with Mr. Talmadge and the older Miss Michaelson.

There was an effort on the part of the jail administration to keep certain details of the case confidential, mainly those details pertaining to James Michaelson, or Robert De Quincey. These details had no bearing on the case, the warden insisted, but weakly. Perhaps it was even him, frustrated by the whole debacle, who had first set the reporters on that particular trail. Who would ever know? Once the salacious details of Michaelson's business—or former business, since he was reformed, or so he stated—and his relationship to Della were disclosed, the press exploded. Talmadge, who had been seen by some as a reckless, selfish parent hellbent on loosing his dangerous criminal daughter to the world, no matter the cost or consequences, was now viewed as heroic; a gentle, unassuming orchardist from the mountains who had risked everything, even his own freedom and life, to save a woman who was not in fact his daughter but whom he loved regardless, and was attempting, after all, to give her a chance at life that she had never been given, that her fate and society had firmly denied her over and over again. Did he have a choice? some journalists asked, incredulous. What would you have done, dear reader? It was an argument that no doubt affected the court's decision to amend Talmadge's original sentence, to let him return eventually to the orchard.

The newspapers contradicted each other. When, for instance, Talmadge was formally questioned after being taken into custody. For some newspapers, it was Tuesday afternoon. Others, Wednesday morning. A reporter wrote that Talmadge was stone-faced during the interview, though there were no reporters let into the room where it took place. It had to be, then, one of the guards who described him that way. But why was the guard, who was most likely young and flattered to be asked, to be believed? If another account was to claim that Talmadge was crying, or complained of chest pain, would that be any more believable? Angelene would not, after this time, when she saw blatant falsities published without a second thought, put her trust in what others called the record, the truth. She would learn to trust only what she saw with her own eyes, what she experienced firsthand. And even then this was problematic, for the tricks memory played. But that was another lesson a long time in coming. For now she was simply shocked and dismayed by what she read; her faith in the outside world diminished rapidly in a matter of weeks.

It was Caroline Middey and not Talmadge who finally told the Judge, Emil Marsden, about Jane's suicide in the orchard. The Judge had, incredibly enough, not known about it before the trial. No one knew about it, except of course Talmadge and Caroline Middey and, only recently at that point, Angelene—though not as many details as she would soon learn. Caroline Middey wanted to tell the Judge about Jane because, she argued, it would help them all in their cases. If the jurors knew that Della's sister had killed herself out of fear of the same man with whom Della had been so recently incarcerated, they might better understand Della's fear of him. Or they might better understand her impulse to hurt him, and thus understand also Talmadge's desire to free her, his desire to liberate her from such an impulse. He wanted to free her so that she wouldn't murder a man who, if she was forced to live with, she would be compelled to murder. Because she could not help herself.

But when Caroline Middey explained to Talmadge how disclosing the story of Jane's suicide would help both his and Della's cases, he refused to tell the Judge about it. With more reflection, he most likely would have changed his mind. Because Caroline Middey, in theory, was correct. But before he could change his mind, Caroline Middey, acting on her own, told the Judge what had happened in the apple orchard those fourteen years before; she told him the whole story.

After this, the reporters and journalists took a different interest altogether in the case. It grew into what it did in fact resemble, a sordid saga of sex, murder, and mayhem. And the focus was not only on Della and this new character, Jane, and their tormentor, James Michaelson; the *Wenatchee World* also picked up on a cue from the *Leavenworth Echo*, where somebody in town reminded the writer about Talmadge's past, primarily the fact that as a young man, just seventeen years old, he had lost his sister in the forest beyond the homestead. She had gone out with her basket to pick herbs in the afternoon, and simply disappeared.

It was astounding how one fact can blossom, with the nourishment of speculation, into myriad stories. Talmadge, who was orphaned utterly (*utterly* because his sister was taken away too) at a young age, lived in the orchard alone for more than forty years before Della and Jane came to live with him. In all that time, some said, he had not stopped grieving for his sister, whom he had loved dearly. One old-timer was tracked down in Peshastin and quoted as remembering the two siblings, Talmadge and his sister, both of them dark-haired and very quiet—"mute-quiet"—walking down the main street of town, holding hands, looking into storefront windows. She was his everything, his alpha and omega, gushed one writer, and then pointed out that it was not surprising that later in life— but did time really matter in affairs of the heart?—he would cling to and act so protectively toward other females. Just as Della Michaelson could not be blamed for wanting to punish her abuser, Talmadge could not help attempting to rescue her. It was as simple as that.

The stories were traded at a fever pitch among reporters and then, of course, among strangers, those who came to watch the trials in Chelan but also the townspeople of Cashmere, Leavenworth, and Peshastin who were acquainted in different ways with Talmadge, with Angelene, and even with Caroline Middey. All of Angelene's classmates and their parents reading the newspaper, openmouthed, shaking their heads. It was impossible to say how many people thought they deserved it—You take up with trash, you get what you pay for, one Leavenworth citizen was quoted as saying, bizarrely—or how many people were shocked with them, grieved for them. It was only too bad that to gossip and support mean ideas was easier and more enjoyable, really, than to keep quiet and know in silence that the true story can never be told, articulated in a way that will tell the whole truth. Even if it is better to be quiet, quietness will never reign. People talked, even the best of them.

Talmadge sat defeated at Della's trial, a look of incomprehension on his face. The most closely held stories of his life had been plundered and spelled out in the newspapers, his business there for all the world to see. It seemed nothing was kept private, nothing sacred.

Because of the grand portraits that were drawn of Talmadge and Della, of their pasts and their emotional landscapes, many people sympathized with them. What they had done might not seem right, exactly—the law was the law—but it could certainly be understood why they had done what they had done.

There were others who were able to keep their distance, who looked at the situation objectively, kept their cool while reading the feverish emotional accounts in the newspapers, and finally decided that the law had been broken, and the reasons why the players had done what they had done didn't matter, ultimately. If Talmadge had cared too much for the girl, then he should not have adopted her. And what ridiculous logic, they said, a lie really, that Della didn't have a choice in punishing Michaelson. Of course she had a choice. We all have a choice. She just did not practice self-restraint. These people were amazed by how much print was devoted to, and ultimately wasted on, the feelings of the people involved. As if feelings finally made any difference at all.

CAROLINE MIDDEY AND Angelene were allowed to see Talmadge after his surgery. Caroline Middey stood by while a nurse bathed him; Angelene excused herself beforehand, waited in the hallway.

Talmadge, who was overcome perhaps with embarrassment, perhaps by it all, wept silently. Caroline Middey pursed her lips in frustration. It's all *right*, she said, after the nurse had gone and she, Caroline Middey, buttoned his pajama shirt and eased him back into the bed, covered him up. He had shut his eyes but was still crying. Caroline Middey sat beside him. Held his hand.

It's my fault, he said.

No, said Caroline Middey. *No.*

Soon he was asleep.

THE DAY DELLA was to be transferred, two weeks after her sentencing—almost a month after the attempted escape—Caroline Middey and Angelene made their way to the courthouse. There was already a crowd forming. Suddenly it became obvious that there would be newspapermen there, and those men would want to talk to them—Della's people. And so Caroline Middey led Angelene across the street to the café, where they had a view of the front of the courthouse.

Vermin, said Caroline Middey.

When a guard came outdoors and stood on the step and spoke to the people waiting on the lawn, Caroline Middey and Angelene went out.

When people saw them coming, they let them go to the front. There was a hush as Della was let out. For some reason Angelene thought there would be shouting, or jeering, but there was not, it was very quiet.

Della came out flanked by two guards. She was squinting, as if it was too bright outdoors. She and the guards reached the bottom of the stairs and began to head toward the prisoner wagon, which was a short distance away.

Della! Caroline Middey shouted, and raised her hand.

She looked over at them, confused. Blinked.

Caroline Middey waved to her.

There was the sound of someone taking a photograph, a mechanical expulsion of air. It was that quiet in the crowd.

And then the guards ushered her onto the wagon, and they couldn't see her anymore.

VI

ON THE WAY back to Cashmere, on the train, it began to snow. Caroline Middey, who sat across from Angelene, dozed. Angelene looked out the window, at the flakes floating silently in space. It was late afternoon, and the sky was neither light nor dim.

She recalled the time on the train, only two years before, when she and Talmadge went to Dungeness Bay. Do you remember? she wanted to ask him now, and was startled again—the core of her startled—at his absence. Where was he? But even before this thought was completed, she knew: he was gone. Elsewhere. Another space held him.

She watched the snow.

That trip to Dungeness Bay, that whole time, seemed very far away now.

T HEY ARRIVED TO find the orchard in a state of squalor. The late apricots had gone unpicked, and the fruit, having rotted on the limb and in the avenues, lately frozen, had thawed under the sun. A quiet, gleaming excrescence. The rodents and other animals had begun their work. The apples below in the field and in the canyon hung heavy on the limbs, expectant. Some wore hats of snow. They would be useless if a frost had already got them. They glanced at it all. It was pointless to perform an inspection now, this late in the day, said Caroline Middey, wearily. They entered the cabin.

I'll make coffee, said Angelene.

The men arrived two weeks after Angelene and Caroline Middey returned to the orchard. They came into the field as they usually did, thronged by horses, but this time was different because neither Clee nor the wrangler was with them. No one came to greet Angelene right away, though she stood at the lip of the apricot orchard and watched them. Finally a man detached from the herd and came to her. Caroline Middey came from the cabin and stood behind Angelene, her hands on Angelene's shoulders. Protective. The man was young, broad-shouldered, handsome. Angelene faintly recognized him. A distant cousin of Clee's. Caroline Middey had never seen him before. He gazed beyond the women, at the cabin, and then looked at Angelene.

We have something for you, he said.

The women followed him down into the field. The other men, as soon as Angelene entered the field, drew to attention. Whoever had been sitting, stood. The man who had come up to Angelene and Caroline Middey went into the herd, and appeared at the far edge a minute later, coming toward them now. He was leading a gray horse with a spotted rump.

What's this? said Angelene.

It was the horse that Talmadge had paid for and Clee had arranged to be waiting for Della in Stehekin.

He paid for him, he's yours, said the man. We brought him for you.

Angelene took the rope from him. The horse was enormous, beautiful.

Thank you, said Angelene.

You couldn't have sold it? said Caroline Middey.

The man said nothing. He turned, and joined the others.

By dawn the next day, the men were gone.

Caroline Middey stayed for a month, helping with the fruit. She was also, Angelene knew, worried about leaving Angelene alone. But that was what Angelene wanted. She didn't want to go back with Caroline Middey, stay in her house.

Are you sure? Caroline Middey had asked her. I don't think— But then she faltered. Had trouble sorting out if she wanted the girl to come live with her, Caroline Middey, for the girl's sake, or for her own. Whose loneliness were they discussing? Did she, deep down, think the girl capable of caring for herself?

I'll come see you, said Caroline Middey. Every other week or so I'll drive out. And you can come see me when you're in town.

Yes, said Angelene.

Talmadge did not want her to visit him in prison. But if she must contact him, a letter was permissible. Caroline Middey—who was allowed to visit him—would give him reports on the girl's health and well-being, as well as on the state of the orchard. Likewise, the girl could expect to learn how Talmadge was faring through Caroline Middey.

That's not fair, said Angelene, barely able to contain her anger—and sadness, and despair—when this request was presented to her. I want to see him—

But in the end she finally decided to obey him. She had come to understand that the specificity of the request spoke volumes about his state of mind there, or one he was trying to cultivate. Seeing her might disturb him in a way she was unprepared to take responsibility for, ultimately; and sensing this, she stayed away.

But she wrote him letters.

Dear Talmadge, Caroline Middey and I have cleared the apricot orchard and near apple orchard but the far one is a wash this year. Ground froze over before we could help it. It will be easy to recover in the spring, I am not worried. . . . Made you some raisin buns, which I hope keep. I wish you would tell Caroline Middey what you want to eat, so I can know what to pack for you. . . .

But he never told her things he wanted, just thanked her through Caroline Middey.

One day Caroline Middey told her that Talmadge had asked if Angelene had been to see Della. Angelene looked at Caroline Middey quickly. The older woman was darning a sock heel in her lap and did not look up. What do you want me to tell him? said Caroline Middey, and from her tone Angelene knew the woman was prepared to lie for her.

Don't tell him anything, said Angelene, softly. He can ask me himself.

Fourteen months translated into nine months. They let him out early for good behavior.

Angelene and Caroline Middey met him at the train station in Wenatchee. They met him there so they could ride the wagon north, and Talmadge could see the country, the orchards in the height of summer.

Caroline Middey drove. Talmadge sat on the wagon seat beside her; and Angelene knelt behind him in the wagon bed, her arms encircling his neck. He held her hands with both of his. At times brought her hands up to his cheek, to his lips, kissed them.

Talmadge approved of the orchard, of all the work that had been undertaken in his absence.

The men still come? he asked, and she nodded. Although they came less, and more sporadically, now. It was difficult to depend on them; finally, unwise. And so she did not depend on them.

He absorbed, during the first month, how much work she had actually done.

Caroline Middey helped too, she said.

He asked her one day, grabbing her wrist, startling her—it was meant to be playful, but it also contained some anger, she thought—when was the last time she had gone to school.

She did not answer. But inexplicable to her, tears welled in her eyes. Why should she be ashamed?

I couldn't go, she said. I had all of this, here—

And then he released her, and accepted her as she drew forward to be embraced. She wept against him.

I'm sorry, he said. I didn't mean to hurt you. I'm sorry.

THE FIRST TWO months he woke in his bed, in the orchard, and did not know where he was. Was he still in the prison, on the low-slung cot? He waited a moment for the odor of piss and standing water to reach him. For a moment he imagined it did, and his soul shrank. And then a sound in the outer room—the stove ticking, a wind bracing the window frame, the girl clearing her throat—familiarized the darkness. This was not a darkness to fear, but his home.

Only then did he relax and was able to sleep.

There was this confusion, in the beginning, at night. And then—he did not know why—it left him.

After that he could recall almost nothing about the prison, about his time there. What he had thought about, how he had passed the hours. What he had eaten, whom he had spoken to. When he thought of prison he imagined Della's jail cell, and her drawing to him from the other side of the bars. I was in prison, he told himself, had to remind himself. But some odd mercy had found him, and covered, like a cool hand, his memory. He did not know if he should be grateful for this or not.

I T SEEMED AT first that the townspeople did not know how to regard Talmadge and Angelene. When they began to sell fruit again at market, people approached them cautiously. The townspeople did not make small talk like before, and if they smiled, the quality of the smile was peculiar: it either contained fear or a kind of excitement, as if the person was on the verge of asking them outright about what had happened on the beach. *Have you been to see her? Have you heard from her? Where is Jane buried? Does the girl* (meaning Angelene) *know who her father is?* Other people stayed away completely, as if Talmadge and Angelene had done something wrong. And Angelene supposed they had, but for people to hold a personal grudge was puzzling to her.

Talmadge looked through people now. He did not comment about the quantity of the fruit he and Angelene sold, which was about normal, in the end, because while there were those who had bought from them before who now stayed away, others began to buy their fruit for the novelty of it, to say that they had. To show others a nickel Talmadge had handed back to them as change—*He touched it*—to put it in a ring box, perhaps, to pass down to their children. The worst times were when a lady would approach with a casserole or a cake, determinedly walking toward their booth, and state her condolences outright, or say something about the Lord or about their souls, or Della's. Talmadge and Angelene did not know what to do with the food. They could not bring themselves to eat it. They would take it home, where it would remain in the icebox, or tucked away on the counter, and go bad. Eventually they dumped it in the scrap heap behind the outhouse.

It was wonderful when they came into contact with a person who acted as if nothing had ever happened, as if he had not read the newspaper for the last year. Angelene didn't know if it was reasonable to believe that people were ignorant of her and Talmadge's personal lives at that point, but she supposed it was possible that some of their acquaintances simply refused to read, after a certain point, about things that they deemed none of their business. One such person was the man at the Malaga plant sale, the orchardist who also made rifles, whom Talmadge had known for many years. After the plant sale in late July, the man invited Talmadge and Angelene to his home south of Wenatchee, and they sat on his porch and drank lemonade, and he showed them his workshop where he was working on guns. In his presence Talmadge seemed to relax, and the entire time the man's face remained neutral, there was no trace of anxiety or pity. Was it possible he did not know what had happened to them? But then once, while Talmadge was talking, Angelene looked at the man and he was staring at her almost as if he was angry. But it was not anger. He was trying not to let the pity through. They looked away from each other. The entire exchange transpired in a matter of seconds.

And of course Talmadge and Angelene regularly visited Caroline Middey while they were in town, and also, at times, they stopped by the Marsdens'. Talmadge would be driving the wagon north on the road out of town, toward the foothills, when suddenly he would urge the mule across the field and onto the lower road that led to the Marsden mansion. There were no more long talks in the study between the two men; now all four of them—Talmadge, Angelene, the Judge, and his sister, Meredith— sat in the dining room with the curtains pulled back on a view of the river, and ate pie and drank coffee. The talk was light, of weather mostly, and of the orchard. There were awkward moments when it was apparent one of them was thinking of Della, or a detail of what had happened the previous year, but no one ever spoke of it. It was awkward enough that Angelene was incredulous every time Talmadge urged the mule to the lower road; as if he could not, for some reason, help himself.

He had always enjoyed, Angelene thought, being acquainted with people; he liked the long hours of simply sitting over a cup of coffee with a person whose company he enjoyed. Clee. Caroline Middey. The man from Malaga. A stranger, perhaps, at the café in town. But after what happened in Chelan, he could no longer relax into effortless camaraderie. He was always somewhat restless and distracted. Angelene thought those times when he turned the mule to the Marsdens' was an attempt to prove to himself that he could be happy in friendly company, he could relax, he could be like he had been before. But he couldn't. Things had changed.

She did not ask him about his time in prison. Could not bring herself to begin the conversation that she knew he would abhor.

He would often walk by himself, in the evenings, after supper. Even in winter. He would walk up into the outer orchard and be gone for hours. Angelene did not know where he went. She knew that when she looked at her orchard, her garden, later (this was the following spring), it was untouched—he kept his word and did not fuss with that area that was portioned off as her own—but it had the feeling of having been looked at. He said one evening after supper that he had heard somewhere that if you shook lime over the strawberry bed a week before bud break, the fruit would be larger and heartier. Angelene thanked him; said she would consider it.

She often sat on the porch and waited for him to come out of the canyon mouth. He walked incredibly slowly across the lower field toward the cabin, so slowly that he seemed at times to be losing distance. It seemed like he was perpetually reaching the middle of the field, perpetually walking, coming forward, yet never arriving. His pale shirt glowing in the dusk.

Talmadge wanted, after apple harvest, to tear down some portions of the orchard. It was too difficult, he said, without the men coming through for assistance—they did not come regularly anymore—especially for harvest, to do all the work themselves. They would be able to manage, briefly, perhaps, but to maintain such a level of labor, especially when Talmadge's health was declining—this he did not like to talk about, but it was increasingly apparent—was unrealistic. We could get outside help, said Angelene; we could hire workers, get people from town to come and help. He made a face when she said this, as if to ask for help was like a bad

taste in his mouth. Surely it would be better, she pointed out, than destroying perfectly good trees. She thought about what they would have
to do to tear out the trees, what specifically they would have to do, and
her mind balked with sorrow. She could not imagine tearing out trees on
the scale he was proposing.

He began to tear down the apple trees in the outer field early one
morning before she had risen, in November. A week before there had
been snow, but there was only a light dusting on the ground. Perhaps he
could not bear to wait until spring because he thought he would change
his mind, or the sight of the newly blossoming trees would prevent him
from carrying out the task.

He did not ask for Angelene's help, but that morning she went to the
shed and found a pair of work gloves and went to help him. He was cutting the trees at their bases and then tying a rope to them and dragging
them, with the help of the mule, to a large pile roughly in the middle
of the field. He wanted to burn them. Angelene agreed, reluctantly, it
was the best way, though he had not asked her opinion. She helped him,
wordlessly. After about an hour she went into the cabin and made coffee
and something to eat. She called him from the porch, but he kept working. Angelene sat inside and ate her breakfast. She could have gone out
onto the porch, but she did not want to see what he was doing down in
the field.

Talmadge had an appointment the next week to go see the distributor
in Wenatchee. Two days before, as he and Angelene sat after supper in
the lamplight, trying to stave off sleep—they were both exhausted from
working all day cutting down trees, dragging them to the field, throwing
them onto the heap—Talmadge said that he was not going to be able to
make the meeting. There was a pause before he said that he needed to
stay in the orchard to finish the work. But Angelene knew that what he
was really saying was that he was not physically able to travel as far as
Wenatchee, that after this week of working as he had been, he was too
worn out. She thought that he would ask her to compose a letter to the
distributor and deliver it in town the next day, and she was prepared to

do that, of course, but then he asked if she would travel to Wenatchee and speak to the distributor herself. They would not be doing business with him anymore, said Talmadge. It was something that needed to be communicated personally and not through a letter.

Angelene rode to Wenatchee the next day on the spotted horse that was meant for Della. The distributor's offices were in an enormous warehouse down by the river. She walked through the large open floor that in the height of harvest would be filled with workers packing apples into boxes. The foreman himself was younger than she was expecting. He was surprised to see her. Seated in his office, she stated her purpose, and he simply nodded. She felt that he wasn't really listening. She stood up to go. He glanced at her, surprised. How old are you? he said. For some reason she lied, said: Seventeen. He nodded again. We need people for the late apples coming in next week. You know how to pack? Yes, said Angelene. And then: No. But I'm a quick learner. He nodded again, and told her to come Tuesday of the next week and be ready to work.

She told Talmadge that the distributor had offered her a job and she had taken it. He didn't say anything to this at first, but then he asked later that night, standing in the doorway of her bedroom, if she had everything she needed for the work. Did she have the right clothes, did she need money for anything? She couldn't see his face because the lantern was lit in the other room, at his back. She said she would be fine. It's hard work, he said, and Angelene said she expected it would be.

ANGELENE WAS TAUGHT how to pack apples by a rotund woman named LaVerne. LaVerne had light blue eyes and wore her hair up in a blue kerchief she no doubt starched every night. She watched Angelene work and then told her in a straightforward manner what she was doing wrong, showed her again how to do it properly. The other workers, mostly women, watched LaVerne and Angelene while they worked, their eyes flitting over to the strange pair. Some of them snickered, smirked. LaVerne told Angelene not to pay attention to them and to concentrate on the task at hand. All these women started in the same place, said LaVerne. And then, later: It's not that difficult, child! Buck up!

The job lasted only two weeks. Angelene was not particularly astute at packing apples, it turned out, but she felt that with more practice she would not be quite as terrible. Despite the humiliation of stumbling through the job with all those eyes watching, she felt good having money in her pocket that she had earned herself.

Somehow the job at the warehouse eased her transition back into high school. She had taken a year off to work in the orchard, and so was a year behind her former class. Angelene knew that if school was unbearable for whatever reason, she would be able to go back to the warehouse and work. She would be able to get by. Among the students there were whispers, stunned gazes cast in her direction. Laughter. And of course the old pity. Later she was certain there must have been people who were kind to her, but she did not remember them.

Talmadge did not speak of Della that first year, and neither did Angelene. Angelene had learned, through Caroline Middey, that Talmadge was not allowed to visit either Della or Clee in prison. He could not even send them letters. It was part of his punishment—their collective punishment.

One morning—this was almost a year since Talmadge returned to the orchard—Talmadge asked Angelene to bring him an apricot. He sat on the porch, an afghan covering his legs. Angelene had just taken away his breakfast dishes and brought him coffee.

She had stepped off the porch, squinted in the sunlight. They're not ready—

Bring me one anyway.

She went and picked an apricot from the nearest tree—hesitating, finding the best one—and then brought it to him. He brushed it against his upper lip, bit into it, chewed.

You pick a half peck of these first thing tomorrow morning, he said. Then you go and see her.

Angelene was confused. Then, a moment later: Go see—

Get on the train and go see her.

She looked away from him, wiped her hands on her dress front.

They'll be ripe enough by then, he said. They'll ripen in the bag.

I probably can't see her, she said, after a silence. I'm probably not allowed to—

You are, he said. I checked into it. You'll see her, he said.

Let the girl bear it, he thought, as she turned and walked across the grass. His original plan—to get Della onto the boat—had failed, but Della was still Angelene's family. Della's loneliness—whether she admitted this or not—was still real. As was Angelene's.

Perhaps it was awkwardness, embarrassment, that kept Angelene from Walla Walla. She did not know what to say to Della; perhaps that was it. But how little that mattered. She would have to learn that awkwardness must be overcome if she wanted any kind of exchange. He would force her, now, for her own good. He had hoped, while he was in prison, that she would take the initiative and go see Della on her own. She had not; but that was all right. It was a disappointment, but it was all right. The girl was still young; she still had to be pushed.

We all have to be pushed, he thought. It doesn't end.

WHEN ANGELENE THOUGHT of the penitentiary in Walla Walla, she imagined a cement institution somewhat drab but also like a castle, with mountains not unlike the mountains around Peshastin towering on all sides. The prisoners all wearing navy uniforms, and when they came out into the bare yard they might raise their faces to the mountains and breathe the cold air.

She did not know why she imagined the penitentiary that way, where this image came from. Walla Walla was surrounded not by mountains— she knew this—but by desert.

In Walla Walla she rented a room from a gray-faced woman with a voice deep from smoking, and asked her if the penitentiary was within walking distance. Without batting an eyelid, the woman told Angelene how to get there.

The building was made of yellow clay brick and surrounded by a twelve-foot-high chain-link fence with barbed wire along the top. Angelene told the guard at the entrance who she was there to see, and he waved her inside even before she was finished speaking, told her to go directly to the office. Do you have an appointment? he asked, and she said, No, although she was aware that Talmadge had probably made an appointment for her.

But they let her in to see Della anyway. A guard led Angelene into a large room, the far wall lined with whitewashed booths. She sat down at one of them and waited before a mesh screen, her hands in her lap. When they led Della in, on the other side of the screen, at the far end of the room, she met Angelene's eyes immediately and then looked away. She shuffled slowly, accompanied by the guard, to the chair. Sat down. When the guard left, Della brought her hands to her face. After a moment, Angelene realized she, Della, was crying.

Eventually, Della put her hands down.

I didn't know you were coming, said Della, in a voice that Angelene still faintly recognized: husky, like a boy's. But also thin. Perhaps she had recently been sick, Angelene thought. Now Della aimed her gaze over Angelene's shoulder, awkwardly, but took darting looks into Angelene's face, as if she could not help herself. Shy, thought Angelene, and remembered that about her: Della had always been shy.

Angelene gripped her straw hat in her lap, suddenly nervous. Said: Talmadge wanted to come too—

And then she regretted speaking at all, for it drew attention to the fact that Talmadge was unable to come see her.

But Della did not seem upset; she looked over Angelene's shoulder, nodded absently. They sat in silence for several minutes.

And so he's back, said Della. They let him out.

Yes, said Angelene. They let him out early for good behavior. And then regretted speaking again: Was that an all right thing to say to her? To someone who was still incarcerated? Was that even an option for Della—getting released early for good behavior? Angelene felt stupid; looked down into her lap.

But Della seemed to be only half listening.

The silence grew, and with it Angelene's awkwardness. She looked to the corner of the room, hoping she appeared calm. She felt Della's eyes on her. Let her look, thought Angelene. And strangely, the woman's eyes on her did not bother her; even relaxed her somewhat, though Angelene did not know why. When she looked back at Della, Della looked away.

They brought your horse, said Angelene, and Della looked at her, raised her eyebrows.

The horse they kept for you, in Stehekin—

Again Angelene experienced a pang of stupidity. Why talk, why bring attention to what had not happened? She looked quickly away, felt herself blush.

But Della didn't seem to notice Angelene's discomfort. What kind was it?

It was gray—with a spotted rump.

Appaloosa.

Yes. Angelene added: It's quite large. I have to use a stool to get up on it. I'm—riding it now.

He let you do that.

Yes.

Della was nodding, but absently.

What do you think? Della said. You think I should've gotten on that boat?

Angelene was startled.

What do you mean?

You would have gotten down into that cupboard? On that boat? You would have done it?

I can't say, said Angelene, after several moments. I'm not you. Then, softly: I don't know what I would have done.

Della considered this briefly.

But you would have done it, if he had asked you to.

Angelene didn't answer at first. I can't say, she repeated. I didn't have your—reasons—for doing what you did. If I wouldn't have gotten on the boat, it would have been for my own reasons. Everyone has to decide for themselves, she said, and knew she was echoing some other saying, some other person.

Della listened to this, was nodding. But, still—you think I made the wrong choice?

Do *you*? The question was posed more out of despair than anything else. Angelene did not like to be the center of this interrogation.

The question did not surprise Della. She looked into the corner of the room. It was a long time before she spoke.

Yes. Even if I didn't want to go along with it, I should have done it. She paused. Because he had gone to all that trouble. And, she said after a brief silence, it was the only way that I could have come back to see you, isn't it. So I should have done it, for that.

They sat for several minutes and did not speak. Angelene tried to re-call her feelings after the botched escape. Some memories of that day were so clear: the mass of people on the beach, seen from above, moving as one body; the feel of the cold, spongy wood beneath her palm when she gripped the platform railing for support; the grin—the lurid grin, she would think later—of the woman in the group of three who had turned to her and said, What on earth was that?; Talmadge on his knees, murmuring unintelligible pledges; her hands, very white, reaching out to him; Della being wrenched away up the staircase— But for the most part it was a blur. The weeks between the event itself and when Talmadge was sent to Walla Walla, the trials and the sentencing, she could hardly remember. Was she angry at Della? All those months Talmadge visited Della in Chelan, Angelene experienced different levels of resentment. If she experienced anger, it was aimed toward Talmadge himself: frustration at his insistence at fighting what seemed to her—and this opinion too was informed by Caroline Middey's feelings—a losing battle.

But when Talmadge told her about Jane and Della as children, coming pregnant into the orchard, and Della's own suffering, which was distinct from Jane's, that portrait of Della alone in the world after Jane hanged herself rendered her singularly pitiable. At the time, those weeks after Talmadge had told her the truth about Della's past, Angelene was so shocked that she felt nothing. She was numb. Was she angry at Della? No: but she was angry at the silence surrounding Della; she was angry at the deficit of information that always attached itself to her. Angry most of all at the reason why there was so much silence: because what had happened to her—and to Angelene's mother—was too terrible to be uttered. They had suffered; and Angelene did not know how to help it.

But then there was that day on the beach, when Angelene, despairing, had heard someone call her name, and turned and found it was Della. Angelene, seeing her, had not pitied her then, though Della was in a state to be pitied: shot in the arm, caught in a crime of which she wanted no part, and now being physically forced up the platform steps, fighting against a swarm of young men. But when Angelene saw her—that adult, piercing gaze that held real tenderness, real intelligence—Angelene was in awe of her. Was captivated, suddenly. This was the one who had lifted her to see the horses in the field; who had thrown her into the air with joy, and caught her. The most powerful person in the world.

And here she sat.

What happened to— said Angelene, but stopped herself.

What?

Nothing.

Ask it.

Angelene took a deep breath. I was going to ask, Whatever happened to Michaelson? Do you know?

Della scratched her neck.

He died.

Oh, said Angelene.

You didn't know? It wasn't in the papers?

Angelene shook her head. Didn't tell Della that she didn't read the newspapers anymore.

But Della seemed unmoved, unimpressed at the mention of his death. She crossed her hands in her lap.

You hated him, said Angelene, softly. You should be glad about that, at least: he's dead.

Della, after a moment, shrugged. Stared again into the corner of the room.

Thought I'd feel glad about it. Or sad, maybe. She shrugged again. Maybe that sounds strange. I don't know. Thought I'd feel something. She paused. But I don't.

DELLA OFTEN THOUGHT she saw the girl, Angelene, on the prison grounds, but it was always somebody else. Reason told her that there was no way the girl could be incarcerated there, but during those moments when she thought she saw the girl, she believed it was her with her whole heart. Reason had nothing to do with it.

The other prisoners were not unkind to her, and among the other women there was the possibility of friendship, but she kept herself separate from them. She was already thin, but she lost more weight; she looked at herself in the mirror and hardly recognized her face. She developed eczema on her scalp so badly that the prison barber had to cut her hair off for it to be properly medicated. She looked more like a boy than ever, but she didn't care.

She worked in the laundry, spending the afternoons sorting and washing sheets and prison uniforms. The filth and the stains disgusted some of the workers, but she was immune to it all. Such things did not disgust her.

The days went by. One day was very much like another. She enjoyed her job at the laundry, which was the easiest job she had ever had. And then she reminded herself that it wasn't actually a job.

And then in the summer—she had been in prison for almost two years—the guard came to her cell where she lay on her cot and told her she had a visitor. She did not even ask who it was, thinking it was Caroline Middey, who visited her every few months. She got up and waited while the guard unlocked the door and then led her down the hallway, showed her into the room where she would see the visitor through the screen. She saw, a moment later, the figure standing, the girl.

She wanted to speak to the girl, but could not. She felt as if someone had punched her in the stomach. She made it to the chair before
the screen, and sat down, and the girl sat as well, and then soon after that Della started crying. She was sick. There was too much she
wanted to say.

But eventually she calmed, and they had a conversation. For some reason Della heard herself asking if the girl had thought she, Della, had made
the right decision not getting into the cupboard. The girl was ambivalent;
would not answer definitively either way. And so that was something,
finally, she, Della, could grasp: the girl did not blame her for doing what
she had done. Indicated she understood Della had had her reasons for not
getting onto the boat.

Mostly it was fine just having her there—a young woman to be certain, and so refined and polite, Jane's daughter—sitting there before
her. How similar to Jane she looked; but when she spoke, Jane disappeared. That's how it was, Della thought. That's how it was supposed
to be from the beginning. Jane had warned her: children come to dis-
place. They live on the earth after you are gone, and forget you. It's not
their fault.

Your mother used to say— said Della, suddenly, after she and the girl
had already said their good-byes; the girl had half risen from her chair.
Now the girl looked at her wide-eyed. Surprised.

Your mother— continued Della, despite herself, knowing she should
stop, but then found she could not go on. How to describe a dream? A
feeling?

What did she used to say? said Angelene, after a silence.

Della, staring into the corner of the room, had forgotten what she was
going to say.

She said—that you would be wonderful. That you would be better
than all of us put together. And she was right. She paused. Nothing
bad has happened to you. You have a good life. You have a good life,
don't you?

There was silence before the girl answered.

Yes.

Della wanted to tell the girl many things. She wished she could embrace her.

The girl stood awkwardly in front of the screen.

Della forced herself to meet her eyes, if only for a moment.

The girl was shy.

Thank you for coming to see me, said Della.

WHEN CLEE WAS let out of prison, no one was waiting to meet him: he had arranged it that way. He had asked the wrangler to leave him a horse at the stables; and that was the only favor he asked.

The horse was a sorrel gelding: muscular, tall, with a white star on his forehead, white stockings. He saddled the horse and led him outdoors, and drank in the color of the day. The sky; the sheen of the horse's coat. The odor of horseflesh and dust, sun. Clee placed his hand on the horse's side. The wrangler had chosen well; had known what Clee would have liked. Hesitating—the anticipation was great, but the joy was in the anticipation—he mounted the horse. Settled himself within the saddle, situated the reins in his fists. The horse stepped back, and forward. Snorted. Pawed the ground. Clee grabbed the withers with one hand and simultaneously drew up on the reins. Walked the horse in a tight circle. By the way the horse moved, Clee knew it was the wrangler who had trained him. Clee spurred him, and set off at a rocking lope toward the road. Away from the stables, away from town.

Clee left Walla Walla forever.

He rode alone for two weeks. East, and then north, then east again, and then south into the mountains. It was late summer: in the early morning, in the Sawtooths, hoarfrost glistened for miles. He rode. Finally entered the Wallowas, and then knew where he was going.

The wrangler was in the outlying field when Clee rode up onto the Wallowa homestead, and lifted his arm. A child ran out to greet him, the sex undecipherable until the child—a boy—was at Clee's knee, and then the child tore away again, shouting Father! Father! in Nez Perce.

He stayed for supper. The main house—narrow, smoke-filled, two-story—held the wrangler and his wife, their children. Those who could not fit in the house slept outdoors, in tents and tepees and outbuildings.

Children in all states of dress ran around, coming straight up to Clee or peering at him from around trees and shacks. Other families—or just single men—lived and camped here too.

They ate venison and summer squash the first night. He sat and listened to all of them speak. He did not get tired of it. Babies were passed to him, and he held them. Looked into their new, unblemished faces. One he held—his eyes dark and ancient—reached out and grabbed his nose.

There was one child, a girl—nine, ten years old—who kept bothering the wrangler, tugging his sleeve, sidling up to him and speaking to him with her hands cupped around her mouth—a secret—and glancing intermittently at Clee. The wrangler kept brushing her away. But finally, in agitation, the wrangler conceded to the girl's request, said, Yes, yes, shooed her way. The girl came over to Clee, hesitant but smiling. Her hands held carefully behind her back.

She wants you to watch her ride, said the wrangler. She's been waiting for you—

Clee looked at the girl. He did not recognize her. But then, there were many children over the years, and he could not remember them all—

Don't bother him, he's eating! said one of the women, in Nez Perce.

But Clee rose. The girl grinned, and took his hand.

She led him only a few feet away, outside the light of the multiple fires. She attempted to mount a gray mare much too large for her, but could not. Clee, when he saw she was becoming frustrated, boosted her up onto the horse's back. And then stepped away.

The girl walked the mare in the outlying field, never going very far. Every time she circled past him, she beamed. He nodded at her.

The stars shone bright above them, and the intermittent heat from the fires reached his back. The sound of the people talking was constant, rising and falling, rising and then falling. The girl was heading back to him, out of the greater darkness, the horse's movement making no sound. A gentle wind, a kind of sighing, moved over the earth; and for a moment he felt as if his body had evaporated.

Watch me, watch me! pleaded the girl, and he nodded, his heart beating through his body, which felt hollow with fear and joy.

ANGELENE WAS PACKING up at market one day when a boy came up behind her and touched her shoulder.

She was alone. It was late summer; she had been coming regularly since the spring to sell fruit. Talmadge was too weak to travel now, stayed perpetually in the orchard.

What? she said to the boy, who was standing still and staring at her. She continued to place the fruit in bins, packing it all into the back of the wagon.

The postmistress wants to see you. She said to come by before you go home.

All right.

She said to come right away.

Angelene looked at the boy, who, she noticed now, appeared frightened. She finished packing up the wagon, and then afterward drove to the post office. A telegram had been sent from the prison.

She rode to Caroline Middey's house and showed her the telegram. They sat in the chairs on the front porch, and then after a long time Caroline Middey went inside to make tea.

What do we tell him? said Angelene, wiping her face.

Tell him the truth, said Caroline Middey. What else is there to say?

But still they sat there and did not move. Their tea grew cold. Angelene spent the night there, and then they left together in the morning for the orchard.

Della had volunteered in a work project that involved, among other things, scaling buildings under construction—she was allowed to do this, they learned, because she had worked once as a topper in a lumber camp. The day before, she had fallen from a scaffolding and broken her neck. She had died immediately. There were harnesses and other safety devices she was supposed to be wearing, but she wasn't wearing them.

THE TRAIN BEARING her body came from Walla Walla, and Talmadge, Angelene, and Caroline Middey were at the station in Wenatchee to meet it, dressed in their finest clothes. Talmadge wore a new hat, leaned on a cane. They watched the box that contained Della's body be loaded onto a wagon, and then they all got up into the wagon and with the driver and another man headed north, in the direction of the orchard. They arrived in the afternoon. The driver and the other man hiked with the casket down the hillside and across the creek, through the field. Talmadge, Angelene, and Caroline Middey followed behind them.

She would be buried on the upland ridge next to Jane.

On the plateau the yellow grass waved in the wind and the air smelled of honeysuckle and duff. The hole had already been dug in the ground. Talmadge had hired other men to do that as well, because he was too weak to do it himself. But still he had insisted on helping. The men lowered the casket now into the ground, and then they walked away, to give the family their privacy.

Talmadge had refused to believe, at first, that she was dead. And then he refused to accept the circumstances of her death: someone had killed her, he insisted. Michaelson, or one of his associates, a guard. She had been murdered. He was sure of this; and after Angelene and Caroline Middey had arrived in the orchard and told him what had happened, he walked alone into the trees in the dusk, leaning heavily on his cane. It wasn't until he had reached the outer orchard, the tree at the bend in the path standing still in the darkness—the tree, the inimitable trunk darker than the outer darkness—that he began to weep.

He had not seen Della or communicated with her these last few years. But the girl—Angelene—had gone to see her, and though he did not know the specifics of what had passed between them, he did know that the girl was planning to see her again, and so he liked to think that she, Della, had begun to accept her life, and calmed. He did not expect her to be happy—how that word lost meaning as the years progressed—but he only wished her to be unafraid, and able to experience small joys. He wished that she would get out of that place—prison—and find her home again in the orchard. Or wherever else she thought would welcome her.

He leaned down and grasped a handful of dirt, threw it into the grave. Caroline Middey did the same. Angelene broke away and returned with a shovel, staved the head into a pile of dirt. Began to move the earth in earnest. She was inexpert but steady. One of the men wandered back over, to say that she needn't do his job; but he watched her and then turned away, left them alone again. When he reached the other man, he shrugged slightly.

Talmadge and Caroline Middey stood away and observed the girl work. When it was finished, none of them were able to speak. Angelene was shaking, her face mussed with sweat. As they turned and headed away—they had to, for the sun was setting, and they had neglected to bring lanterns—Angelene leaned against Talmadge. He put his arm around her. Caroline Middey placed her hand on the girl's shoulder. They walked thus across the grass, incredibly slowly. Angelene cried tonelessly all the way back to the orchard.

Where are her *things*? cried Angelene, coming into his bedroom in the middle of the night. Her *clothes*—her *things*. Where are they? Who has them?

He had sat up in the bed, trying to orient himself. What had happened? Where was he? The girl, Della, had died—

Angelene came around the side of the bed and got in beside him. He lifted the quilt, and drew her inside. She huddled against him, her head on his chest, weeping.

We'll send for them, he said, putting his hand on her head. Don't cry now. We'll find them. We'll bring them back. Hush. Hush.

VII

THERE CAME AGAIN, during that following spring and summer, the feeling that Angelene had almost forgotten, of being alone in the orchard, of being utterly herself. She was not really alone—Talmadge was always somewhere around, in the cabin or working elsewhere in the orchard—but she had begun, through working again on her own plot, the feeling of sinking into that solitude as she had before, when Talmadge was away in Chelan. The sun hovering in its zenith, the birds squawking in the high canopy, the earth giving off its tremendous deep odor. The sapling roots frail in her hands.

She did not know if she reflected at all upon the relationship between what she was feeling—the depth of her own privacy—and what Talmadge might have felt all those years living alone. She knew that there was a difference between their situations: where she had his company to steep herself in at intervals—she had that possibility of companionship—he had not. He might have had friends or acquaintances in town—Caroline Middey, for example—he could visit with every other week or so, or they could come visit him, but it was not the same as having somebody who lived with you. It was not the same as having family. Even if that family was very quiet, as Talmadge and Angelene were, at times, with each other.

When she was alone, when she was working, it was as if she forgot about herself. It seemed strange to state it this way, but it was as if she had no outline, no body, even though the work was very physical. Where did her mind go? Her mind was steeped in the task at hand. At such times she felt a depth of kinship with the earth, and also felt very grown up, unshakable, rife with compassion.

The knowledge was cultivated in her also that while Talmadge was her family, her deepest friend, his health was in a state of decline. And Caroline Middey, too, who was like her mother, was nearly eighty years old. The one who might have accompanied her through adulthood—maybe, maybe—was buried now. (And she admitted to herself that in light of this, Talmadge's plan to free Della, that incredibly ill-advised plan, did not look so foolish to her now as it had before, when it was first presented to her. Talmadge had known what he was doing. She appreciated this now, she appreciated what he had attempted to do for her.)

She revered solitude, but only because there was the possibility of breaking it. Of communing at last with another. What would happen when Talmadge died? Caroline Middey? Their particular sensibilities would be gone; and with them they would take their knowledge of her. Then she would be truly alone. This was another solitude. It terrified her.

As he lay inert on his bed, which the girl had pulled out near the woodstove—the girl leaning over him, fixing his bedclothes—the past receded, diminished to a point.

He had never been a boy, afraid and hoping perpetually for his sister. He had never been seventeen years old, or twenty-five, thirty, dying of lust after supper. Never the happy man working alone, laughing to himself at some joke he had heard others tell in town. Never wanted to lay his head on Caroline Middey's breast. Never sung hymns to himself, out of absence or loneliness. Never admitted to any person the fact of how his own image pleased him, though he knew he was considered ugly, even without the smallpox scars. Never was he kind, or cruel. Never fed the two girls who came to him, never pitied them. Never regretted not laying hands on Michaelson—the day on the Okanogan, or later, when he came into the orchard. He had never been awed by Della, puzzled by her—never was relieved when she left. Never missed her severe quirk, her tendernesses that cut him to the quick. Her strange hair, her eyes, her glances. Her *way*. Never witnessed her, a girl barely reaching his shoulder, on a horse as mean as any snake. Never sat with Clee in silence, smoking pipes on a summer evening. Never roamed with Clee as a boy through the tall grass, running after his sister: a game. Never was in prison. Never cried for his mother. Never sought to conjure his father's face. Never tasted an apricot, or trout, or soil. Never slept under the slow-wheeling constellations, or bathed in a winter creek.

The wonderful as well as the terrible impressions receded, and the world when he opened his eyes each morning was altered; and then in the afternoon, and after that, every time he slept and woke. The same four cabin walls holding different shapes of light and shadows. The woodstove. The girl moving in the domestic sphere. He knew her name, and then it was no longer necessary, somehow, that he remember it. It was not his fault; he did not feel that it was his fault. She sat beside him and spoke to him and it wasn't even necessary anymore that he understand what she was saying. She touched his head and wiped his brow with a wet cloth, and that was pleasant. He might have spoken too, but what he spoke did not matter. She came and went; he called her by different names.

Angelene, he said. I was here when you were born.

I know, she said.

I N THE FAR apple orchard Angelene climbed each tree expertly and
picked the apples in the coming darkness—they glowed, the Rhode
Island Greenings glowed; the Pippins were more difficult, she felt the
scions with her fingertips. She had always been a slow picker, and this did
not change according to circumstance—she was the one left to harvest
the acres of trees—and so after a day of picking she rested only a short
time, to eat and to nap, and then worked again until it became too dark
to see. If the moon was not out, then she would have difficulty and would
retire early to the cabin, where she slept badly and dreamed of picking
and of following bodiless voices through the avenues; and in the morning again she rose raw-eyed and grasped her canvas sack and headed out
into the cold. She must redouble her efforts that day, for as usual, she had
failed to pick the requisite amount of fruit the day before. Even so, she
did not rush. Talmadge said: Do not rush. Only a fool rushes. (But his toil
was constant; his toil was normal. When she was a child he used to walk
the orchards—slowly—from dawn until dusk; and then sometimes after
supper, until the stars turned over in the sky.)

The days she picked well, she slept deeply. She prepared food and
spoke to Talmadge, on his bed by the woodstove, who lay with eyes
open. He was increasingly mute. Sometimes his eyes followed her as she
moved around the cabin, but mostly they did not. She experienced an
urge she did not understand: to surround his bed with boxes of apples she
had picked, to see him lying there in the midst of them. Of course she did
not do this or tell him about this. But the image haunted her, made her
clench her fists in longing.

———

What do the seasons mean to a dying man? Talmadge opened his eyes midmorning and watched the air in the room. The air had something to do with the light and the quality of light—piercingly golden—and also the lives of the trees, exuding oxygen, the air that silently racked the cabin. The air he drew into his lungs still had something of the trees' inner life about it, the saturated dreams of chlorophyll and sunshine and water, gravity and roots and the roots' design. Fruit. This was autumn light. Somehow he had always known this would be the season into which he would disappear. He anticipated the girl, her moonish face fastening to the space above his face, listening. Listening for breath. She stood at the stove, preparing food. When she spoke to him, she still had her child's voice that had not dropped. Time would fix that. Mildly he was sorry that he would not be there to witness that change, that drop into the lower register. Her hair gathered at her neck, its color in the lantern light like young oak. How like the orchard she was. Because of her slowness and the attitude in which she held herself—seemingly deferent, quiet—it appeared even a harsh word would smite her. But it would not. She was like an egg encased in iron. She was the dream of the place that bore her, and she did not even know it.

He felt an ambiguous desire rise in him when she left the cabin, and he knew she was out there among the trees, working in her slow way that he hesitated to remedy because the slowness denoted something deeper within her that he did not want to penetrate or to steal. The slowness had to do with the deliberation that would always be with her, that gravid, searching countenance. She would never say that she loved, because they did not use that type of language; they did not say "love," for instance, or "beautiful," or any descriptive language at all. At times, commenting upon the sky at dusk, he would call it "pretty," and she would nod her head, once, in agreement. When she entered a room that he occupied, or he entered an orchard row in which she worked, they did not greet each other with words but touched an appendage of the other with their eyes, and could tell by the other's expression or posture if they were pleased or discomfited or bothered, or if they were sated by the day's weather or by the other's presence. They intuited these things about each other as one decides about one's own body: thoughtlessly, organically.

Recently in his sickness she took his hand in hers when she sat on the edge of the bed, and leaned and kissed his eyebrows, separately, like unsentimentally massaging a leg that is cramping.

He woke to the empty cabin, to the wall spangled with afternoon light. Behind everything was the sound of the creek—the creek that came from the mountain and flowed into the river north of Wenatchee—and above the sound of the creek was the sound of the ash trees shaking in the wind. The trees bordered the pasture, which was filled with long grass, uncut and uneaten by any horses. The sound of water and the sound of the wind in the trees, which were fed by the creek and so were partial to the creek, occupied Talmadge as he slept and woke. It was a sound highly expressive, highly communicable. He listened and thought, Yes, Yes.

Talmadge, said Angelene. It had taken all evening to come up with what she was going to say. She sat on the edge of the bed. She said: Tonight the sky is the color of new plums. . . .

In the morning she left the cabin to pick walnuts, and as she had been doing for the last three mornings before leaving, she went to the bed by the woodstove and leaned down and watched carefully for his breath. He did not seem to be breathing, but then he sighed. She stood.

Outside was quiet. Light clear as water created shadows of leaves curled and minuscule on the ground. She looked at the sky as she walked, a passionate blue. Cloudless.

In the grove by the far apple orchard the apple trees were in shadow. The sun postured along the curvature of canyon and illuminated the walnut trees starkly. She climbed the bank on which the trees were lodged and picked walnuts and noticed that her hands were beginning to change. They were raw. She flexed her fingers in the cold. She would make plum conserve with walnuts and raisins for her and Talmadge to eat through the winter. They would eat it smeared on toast and by the spoonful when they got cravings.

She felt a nauseous pulse in her body when she reflected on Talmadge ever having a craving again. The last two days he had not eaten.

And then she reached for a walnut on the stem and entered a silence within the overarching silence, and thought she could hear insects percolating in the grass; she heard them in all their privacy and intimate murmurings. The sun on the porous bank near where she stood was lit up, incandescent, the minerals glittering and the dull mud peculiar and particular even in its dullness. Each pore and streak and detail was washed and brought forth as is a person's face by the light.

When she returned to the cabin, she discovered Talmadge had died.

VIII

ANGELENE REMEMBERED THOSE quiet orchard nights when she was alone, when Talmadge spent the night in town, or in Chelan, when she opened the cabin door and saw the sky just off the porch. The stars so thick and close you could walk right into them. Those times she thought that if she could just remember the stars, she would be all right. Things might get very bad, things might be worse than she ever imagined, but the stars existed, and that was something.

When she was twenty-five she sold the land to a man who wanted to make a go at growing apples. He had a wife, and a young child. Three years later, she came back to Cashmere for Caroline Middey's funeral, and traveled to the old homestead to see how the family was faring, and to see the orchard. She found the place empty. The front door of the cabin was unhinged, and there was no furniture in the room but the woodstove, the old table, and the horsehair chair in the corner. For some reason, on that particular trip, she did not look into the bedrooms. It would have been too much. She learned later that the land had been sold to a man out east, who had bought up several lots in the area and was preparing to move west, but had yet to do so.

When she came back five years later the place was only a little better taken care of than when she had seen it last. There was a man living in the cabin, an older black man who told Angelene that he was the caretaker, he worked for the man who had moved from out east. The man, his boss, lived in Spokane and didn't visit the orchard very often. Angelene told the man that she used to live there, and asked if she could look around. The man told her to take all the time she wanted. And then he studied her carefully, said that she must have been very young when she lived there.

I was born here, she said.

She did not go inside the cabin. The man did not invite her, and she did not want to make him uncomfortable by asking. And, ultimately, she wouldn't have wanted to see the rooms filled with his furniture, to see him move so confidently in that space, leading her under eaves through which she had passed so many times before.

The biggest difference, and the one she noticed right away, even before the man came around the side of the cabin to greet her, was that the apricot orchard was gone. Not just diminished; it was gone. All the trees had been pulled up and the land cleared. Now in its place was a vegetable garden. Lettuce, mostly, said the man. They were also going to try corn.

What happened to the apricots? said Angelene. The man said that they had pulled up the trees three—or was it four?—years ago. Shrugged, blankly, as if to say the apricots hadn't meant anything to him.

The front of the barn had been removed, and there was an old Model T up on blocks, which the man had evidently been working on when Angelene arrived. After they spoke, he went back to work, and Angelene walked to the far apple orchard.

This orchard was the same, though overgrown. She wanted to find her old garden, but after searching for a half hour, she could not find it. She walked to the place where she thought it was, but only found more orchard. She kept walking, losing her perspective, and just when she was about to give up, she found it. It likewise was overgrown and was not producing anything but weeds, but there were the posts Talmadge had put in when she was nine years old, and a twist of wire left over from the fence. She stood looking at it for a long time.

She thought it would be better if she found the man and told him she was going to hike up to the plateau to see the graves, so he wouldn't wonder at her long absence, but then she thought that he was the kind of man who wouldn't worry, he would give her her privacy. He knew she knew the place well, after all, and wouldn't worry about her. And so she hiked up there. And was surprised that it was neither very long nor very difficult, as she had always imagined it was. It took twenty minutes, at most, to reach the plateau. She had expected to be winded and exhausted, but she hardly had time to let her thoughts wander. She saw the cottonwood under which the graves were kept—no longer towering, as she had remembered it—and walked toward it with a sense of unreality. Surely this was not the tree. But the graves were there, under crosshatched shade, among the yellow grass. The matching pale stones, and Talmadge's stone, which Angelene had picked out. Three graves side by side. She stood there and looked at them all. Another person would have picked the grass covering the stones, but she left it all untouched. It didn't matter.

Afterward, when she thought about the orchard after that visit, she thought about it in terms of the black caretaker living there, with the apricot orchard gone, and the open-faced barn with the Model T up on blocks. The old beagle the man had for a pet coming around the side of the cabin, sniffing her ankles.

But when she dreamed about that place, it was the orchard out of her childhood, the apricot orchard looming in the sunlight, the horses roiling in the field, woodsmoke and coffee in the air, Talmadge knocking his boots against the porch railing, speaking to Clee—

Some nights she dreamed only of the apricot orchard. She is walking along the outside of it, looking down one row and then another, and another, searching for Talmadge. It is suppertime. She is in a hurry, she is tired of looking, and so she walks faster, and then begins to run, but not too quickly, gazing down one row, and then another. Seeing slight variations of one visage: grass and trees as far as she can see, one row and then another. One row, and then the next. And then his denim form slides into view, way down a row, he leans against a ladder, the top half of him eaten by the understory, and she is moving toward him, hearing nothing but her own breath.

How full of light these dreams are, the multitude of grass soft and green.

There was another dream she had, but rarely. She is in the outer orchard, in the canyon, and somewhere far back there, farther back than she has ever traveled, there is a huge white house on a hill, and before it, an enormous sloping lawn. There is a long gravel drive for the cars and carriages, and Angelene knows that in the house her mother is there— her anonymous, beautiful face—and Della. Talmadge is in the front yard, coming down the long slope to reach her. There is a dog bounding before him, and the dog reaches her first, and she stumbles over him and falls to the ground, and lies for a moment in the dirt. Somehow she knows there is a piano in the house, and so much good food. All the food in the pantry, in the cupboards. Her mother is putting on an apron that suits her. Della is making a bed in the upstairs bedroom. Caroline Middey is walking down the carpeted stairs, quietly. Angelene is on her feet, running now. Talmadge is walking toward her, patiently, not even thinking of her yet, and he is wearing not his overalls but a fine gray jacket like a gentleman, and he is wearing loafers like he never did in life.

He will stop, and look out; will watch her, she knows, until she reaches him.

ACKNOWLEDGMENTS

Thank you to the following people for inspiration, help, and support:

Beverly Coplin, Terry Coplin, Matthew Coplin, Beverly Sanders Perry, Donna O'Brien, Lindsey Dart, Ted Salk, Julie Johnson, Cheri Johnson, Mike McGriff, Carl Adamshick, Matthew Dickman, Michael Dickman, Dorianne Laux, Joseph Millar, Micha Patiniott, Robert Yates, Cathy Falk, Susan Mabry, Louise Westling, Debra Gwartney, Cindy Heidemann, Joni Tevis, David Bernardy, Laura Flynn, Rachel Moritz, Sari Fordham, Josh Wallaert, Jack Baur, Charlie Conley, Jennine Capó Crucet, David Treuer, and Joseph Laizure.

Special thanks to Charles Baxter, Salvatore Scibona, Bill Clegg, and Terry Karten.

Also: the Omi International Writers' Residency Program at Ledig House, the Fine Arts Work Center in Provincetown, the Minnesota State Arts Board, the University of Minnesota's Program in Creative Writing, the English and creative writing departments at the University of Oregon, and *Third Coast* magazine.

W&N blog

For exclusive short stories, poems, extracts, essays, articles, interviews, trailers, competitions and much more visit the Weidenfeld & Nicolson blog at:

www.wnblog.co.uk

Follow us on

facebook and twitter

Or scan the code to access the website*

*Requires a compatible smartphone with QR reader. Mobile network and/or wi-fi charges apply. Contact your network provider for details.